THE LION
WOMEN
OF
TEHRAN

ALSO BY MARJAN KAMALI

The Stationery Shop

Together Tea

THE LION WOMEN OF TEHRAN

Marjan Kamali

G

GALLERY BOOKS

NEW YORK   LONDON   TORONTO   SYDNEY   NEW DELHI

G

Gallery Books
An Imprint of Simon & Schuster, LLC
1230 Avenue of the Americas
New York, NY 10020

First Gallery Books hardcover edition July 2024

GALLERY BOOKS and colophon are registered trademarks of Simon & Schuster, LLC

Simon & Schuster: Celebrating 100 Years of Publishing in 2024

Interior design by Kathryn A. Kenney-Peterson

Manufactured in the United States of America

ISBN 978-1-6680-3658-7

Dedicated to the brave women of Iran

When my life was no longer anything,
Nothing but the tick-tock of a wall clock,
I discovered that I must,
That I absolutely had to
Love madly.

Forugh Farrokhzad, *The Window*

Ocean waves begin their journey thousands of miles out at sea. Their form, size, and shape come from the speed of prevailing winds in the atmosphere, the power of currents hidden beneath the sea, and their "long fetch"——the distance between a wave's point of origin and its point of arrival . . . Events that seem to appear in the present from out of nowhere in actuality have a long history behind them.

George Lipsitz, *Footsteps in the Dark*

Part One

ONE

December 1981

I stood on the lacquered floor—a small woman in black with a rectangular name badge on my chest. My coiffed, contented look was calculated so I'd appear not just satisfied but quietly superior. In America, I'd learned the secret to being a successful salesperson was to act like one of the elite, as if spritzing perfume on customers' blue-veined wrists were doing them a favor.

A sea of haughty New Yorkers swerved to avoid my spray. Thank God for the more down-to-earth women—the cooks and bakers coming up to the first floor from the basement home goods section—they were too polite to reject the fragrant droplets I offered. Orange, lily, jasmine, and rose notes nestled in the lines of my palms and the fibers of my clothes.

"Look at you, Ellie! Soon you'll take over this whole brand. I better watch my back!" My friend and coworker Angela, returning from her cigarette break, sidled up and whispered in my ear. The scent of her Hubba Bubba gum couldn't hide the smoke on her breath.

I shivered at the reek of tobacco. The bitter, sour notes would forever remind me of one long-ago night in Iran. The night when an act of betrayal changed the entire course of my friendship with Homa and both of our lives.

From the moment I'd read Homa's letter last night, I'd been a wreck.

I batted away Angela's compliments, said I wasn't doing all that well, really, and that I had a headache because I hadn't eaten all day.

"*I just might faint,*" I added with a touch of melodrama.

It was a relief when Angela was whisked away by a needy customer.

My mother always said the envy of others invites the evil eye to cast doom on us. She'd often told me that being perceived as too competent, happy, or successful could summon misfortune. I knew belief in the powers of other people's jealousy and the jinxing of an evil eye needed to be cast off. But at the age of thirty-eight, in the middle of that massive Manhattan department store, I was still unwittingly beholden to superstition.

The truth of who I was could not be escaped. Nor could the flaw I had spent years trying to quash and erase.

The guilty one had always been me.

Earlier that morning, in our apartment on the Upper East Side of Manhattan, my husband, Mehrdad, had tried to comfort me with breakfast. He prepared toast with feta cheese and cherry jam. He brewed bergamot tea. But I couldn't eat or drink. The jam was made from Homa's recipe. The bergamot tea in the white teapot adorned with two pink roses reminded me of her. With the arrival of her letter, her absence dominated my life all over again.

When I had first seen the red-and-blue-bordered airmail envelope, I'd assumed it was from Mother and would contain the usual mix of laments and updates about the dangerous political situation in Iran. I knew those letters were probably opened and read by regime forces, but my mother often didn't care and wrote bluntly: *Aren't you lucky, Ellie? You left and escaped the violent demonstrations and deafening riots. You skipped our country's slide back into medieval times. Women have lost decades, no, centuries, of rights in this country. I'm glad you're sitting comfortably with your professor husband in America. Thank goodness you got out!*

But when I pulled the onionskin paper from the envelope and unfolded it, my heart almost stopped. For there on the page was the unmistakable curlicue handwriting of my old friend, Homa.

As girls, we'd sat on the same elementary school bench in downtown Tehran. Together we scratched out hopscotch grids in our neighborhood alley and raced to school with satchels bouncing against our hips. With Homa, I had zigzagged through the mazes of the Grand Bazaar and shared ice cream sandwiches and dreams for the kind of women we'd become. In her stone kitchen, I learned to cook. With her hand in mine, I jumped over the largest bonfires. When we'd hiked up Alborz Mountain and seen Tehran laid out beneath us, it felt like the world could be entirely ours.

Until one moment of striking carelessness ruined it all.

For the past seventeen years, we had been *ghaar*—purposefully estranged—with no contact save one unplanned encounter. Now her letter was in my hands. How did she know where to find me? She must have gotten my address from Mother.

One page of Homa's letter was filled with questions about my life in America. And another was about her situation in Iran. Her health was good (*pressure in the sinuses but nothing more*), the weather (*cold and yet delicious in the mountains—remember the teahouse we went to?*) was fitting for the season, her job as a teacher kept her busy. But her mind was not at ease (*You wouldn't recognize this country, Ellie. I don't know where we went wrong*). At the bottom was a sentence about Bahar, her daughter, and how she loved to sing. She closed the letter with *Can you call me, Ellie? Please. My number is 272963. I need to speak to you. It's urgent.*

After I told Mehrdad about the letter, he held me close and said gently, "It's good she's reached out. You were the best of friends. Time to air it all out, Ellie. Speak to her."

How I wish it were so simple.

I couldn't blame Homa for cutting contact. But now she had flown back into my life all innocence and zest, creating a crater of questions with her sign-off. *It's urgent.*

At the end of my shift, I removed my name pin, put it in the counter drawer, then pulled on my warm camel coat and striped leg warmers.

As I rushed outside toward the subway station, the cold December air carried the scent of roasted nuts from food carts and diesel fumes from hiss-ing city buses. Large-bellied, tired-looking men dressed as Santa Claus rang bells, pointing to their kettle buckets and shouting, "Merry Christmas!" Gold and silver tinsel framed the insides of shop windows and trees with shiny ornaments winked behind glass displays. There was a chill in the air that made my breath float in visible rings.

The words in Homa's letter ran through my head. Suddenly a taxi swerved far too close to me and honked loudly. My heart fell as I remem-bered another time a car had almost hit me. But this time, the only damage done was sludgy puddle water soaking through my leg warmers.

A neon pizza sign flashed red and yellow close to the subway entrance. I got giddy at the thought of a slice.

Since arriving in New York almost four and a half years ago, I'd strolled through Central Park, visited museums filled with global art, and dined in a few fancy restaurants. But no cultural experience topped eating a salty, cheesy, hot slice of New York pizza. Every pizzeria seemed to be in on the secret recipe for tangy tomato sauce and a perfectly foldable crust.

I looked at my wristwatch. No point in getting into the train hungry and drained of energy. I slipped into the pizza place and waited in line to order. After paying my seventy-five cents, I walked out with a cheese slice snug in a triangular cardboard box. I opened the box to take my first bite.

I heard her before I saw her. She moaned rhythmically as though in pain. Under the dim light of the streetlamp near the subway station, I made her out: an old woman huddled against the lamppost, two plastic bags on her feet, a flowered headscarf barely covering her hair. In between moans she asked unresponsive passersby in a weak voice on mechanical repeat: "Madam, can you spare a dime? Mister, can you spare a nickel?"

I wanted to get to my train. Get home. I needed to think, to decide whether I would call my old friend. But how could I ignore this woman? I went to her and stooped down. She smiled, and I was surprised to see straight and perfect teeth. The old woman held my gaze. Her eyes were watery and opaque-looking. She shrugged slightly. In that small movement, I detected a silent acknowledgment of the randomness of the wheel of fortune.

I handed her my triangular cardboard box—the pizza in it still hot and untouched. From my bag, I found the kiss-lock purse Mother had given me as a child in Iran, opened it, and took out all the coins and a few scrunched-up bills. American money still appeared strange to me: so green and thick compared to our bills back home. The lady took the pizza, coins, and bills I offered with a look of bewilderment.

I got up and walked away. As I descended the subway station steps, I turned around only once.

She was eating the pizza quickly—her face an expression of complete relief.

When the train rushed into the tunnel and screeched to a stop, we all jostled and hustled to get inside. The crowded subway car smelled of urine and damp wool. Thankfully, I got a seat. Wedged between strangers, I was grateful for the anonymity. Not one person in that dirty, busy, fascinating, energetic, depressing, alluring city knew about my past or the guilt and regret that swallowed me whole.

The train lurched and blasted forward. Someone by the door sneezed and a gentleman in a baseball cap hummed a tune that was strangely cheerful.

I closed my eyes. I remembered all of it—every single bit. Those days of connection and chaos that had shaped our friendship could never be forgotten.

TWO

Spring and Summer 1950

"You can't expect me to work, Ellie," my mother said, using my nickname. "The descendant of royalty should not touch a thing to make a wage."

Mother's biggest source of pride was that she was descended from kings and queens. She constantly told me how her grandmother was the daughter of a Qajar king. That she had named me Elaheh because it meant "goddess," because we were royals, and she was desperate to ensure our superiority did not go ignored.

Of our life in the big house uptown, I have only a few memories. I remember falling asleep to the sound of my parents' arguing in the next room. I remember my father's thick-browed, good-natured face and his musky scent and the deep timbre of his voice as he recited ancient poetry. He called me "Elaheh Jaaan," drawing out the term of endearment "Jan" after my first name, and sometimes "Elaheh Joon," using the more informal version of the word for "dear."

He passed away on a spring day in 1950, just after my seventh birthday.

There were no other siblings to mourn him. As I got older, I assumed one or two may have come before or after me and perhaps been lost to the many ills and vices that back then frequently swallowed up newborns and infants. But before my parents could try again to bring another child into the world—one who'd survive like I had—tuberculosis infested my father's body. He was laid to rest shrouded in white, buried nearby, hallowed in name.

To this day, sometimes when a man walks by, a musk-like scent jolts a memory of my *baba*. At his burial, I held his black lamb's-wool hat and ran my fingers across the velvety, textured fur. Later that evening, my mother gave the hat away to a beggar on the street.

Growing up, I always wanted to know more about him, but Mother clamped down whenever his name came up and said it saddened her too much to remember his fate and the power of the evil eye.

Baba—dead so young—had only two brothers. One rode a horse to the Russian border, secured a bride there, then settled in the Baku region. The other brother, Uncle Massoud, took charge of our affairs and became our financial guardian, responsible for paying our rent and expenses.

After the funeral, Uncle Massoud came to see us with his own black lamb's-wool hat in his hands. He said—very apologetically—that Mother and I would have to leave our big house, her home since she'd married at sixteen. My father hadn't left much money behind, he explained gently. We'd have to move south to a small place he'd secured for the two of us in *payeen-e shahr*, the "bottom of the city."

"Don't give me that nonsense, Haji Massoud," my mother said. "You just want me to . . ." She pulled me toward her protectively. Then she whispered to him, "How sad that you would punish me like this."

Later, when I was alone (the servants were all asleep for the last hours before they would be sent packing), my mother came to say good night. For an Iranian family of that time, my mother's was a small one. Her parents left no inheritance and her only sister passed away shortly before my father, adding to her grief and sense of being cursed by the evil eye.

Mother stroked my hair and promised me that our move downtown would be only temporary. She spoke about morals and decency and respect for widows and how Uncle Massoud had none of those qualities. Then she abruptly stopped stroking my hair and said Uncle Massoud wanted only one thing, but that she wouldn't give it to him. I didn't know what the one thing was, but I didn't dare ask because Mother looked furious as she said it. The last thing I wanted was to trigger her mercurial temper.

The next morning, walking one last time through the house, Mother screamed about not wanting to leave her paintings behind, nor her lace, china, and French-style Louis IX chairs upholstered in damask. In the bedroom, I pulled on her legs as she hugged the fancy dresser. We entered the *andarun* inner rooms, and Mother cried for the children she said she could have birthed had my father's destiny been different. In the *birooni* courtyard, where the garden was lush with shrubs of pink and red and white flowers, she cursed my uncle. I was surprised at how our garden could be so beautiful despite my father's absence.

My last glimpse of that life was a blurry, hazy image of the mansion, accompanied by the sound of my mother's sobs as we walked away.

The first night in our new place downtown, Mother and I rolled out the mattress on which we would now sleep together. She stared at the floor. "Ellie, did you ever think you'd live to see the day when your own mother, descendant of Naser al-Din Shah, would live in the slums?"

I was still trying to comprehend my father's death. "It was just a cold at first, wasn't it? The turmeric I dissolved in sweet tea for him should have warded off his fever. Why didn't it?"

"We were *cheshmed* and given the evil eye, Ellie Joon. We were cursed. That's all."

"I wish he was still here."

"Never underestimate the power of jealousy, Elaheh," Mother said, addressing me by my full name. "The eye of the Jealous can destroy happiness. All those who were envious of your father and me when we first married jinxed us with their evil, resentful thoughts."

Mother's words seemed deemed for a friend, or the sister she'd lost, not for me, a barely seven-year-old confidante.

"Madar, he was sick. I think it was the disease that killed him."

"Jealousy has powerful energy. It can swirl in the air and destruct true happiness. I know you don't believe me, Elaheh. But you will see."

I imagined clouds of evil envy energy circulating in the atmosphere. There was something wholly peculiar and frightening in accepting that others could have this power over us simply through their emotions. I had to rescue my mother from sinking even further into despair. "At least we have Uncle Massoud," I ventured.

As soon as I said it, I regretted it.

"Oh, please, don't talk to me about Uncle Massoud!" she said. "He could have let us remain uptown in our home. But I refused his conditions. Because I have standards. Because I won't . . . oh, never mind, Ellie. Never you mind. It's just that we are stuck. My parents—God rest their souls—all their funds went dry during their lifetime thanks to others giving *them* the evil eye too! And your father's other brother galloped off to Russia. Now this one—your beloved uncle Massoud!—thinks he's doing us a favor by paying our rent in the slums. But it's his duty to provide for the widow and child of his dead brother." She looked around the bare room. "He won't even send for our old furniture."

I tried to think of something positive to say. "It's good Uncle Massoud won't send for our old furniture because it wouldn't fit here anyway."

My mother stared at me and burst into tears.

Uncle Massoud checked in on us and brought us meat and chicken and sweet *gaz* nougat. Even at age seven, I knew it was not unusual for a man to marry his dead brother's widow. Uncle Massoud was single—no one would have batted an eye if he'd married my mother, as a duty to his dead sibling, if nothing else. But Mother said it was beneath her to marry her husband's brother just for the sake of security. *I will not let that man so much as put a finger on me. I am not property to be passed on.*

Mother never forgave life for my father's fate.

Our private orb of grief was broken those first few weeks only by regular visits from Uncle Massoud and a few stubborn relatives. Mother had never been lighthearted, but after my father's "going," she told me it was too painful to be seen in the slum by family members who had once known our riches. Eventually, they stopped subjecting themselves to her rude and distant treatment.

Even as Uncle Massoud continued his visits, I began to think it was out of spite and anger at her refusal of him that he had us move from a high-walled mansion to a brick house in the slums. Then I began to notice the simple advantages of our tiny new place. We had two clean rooms and a street view. I could easily look out the window and see boys and girls playing right outside.

On the rare occasions we went out, Mother hissed at the neighborhood kids as she walked past. She lifted her long skirt and made her way around their gangling limbs as if to ward off risk of infection. "It's unbecoming," Mother said. "Children in the streets. Look at them, throwing rocks and hopping like fools."

I loved that our home was in an alley teeming with kids. I loved that in this part of town boys included girls in their games. That girls could even play outside.

But Mother said she would not have the descendant of the descendant of Naser al-Din Shah running around with *dahati*, "peasant-like" kids and screaming like a street urchin.

So, most afternoons, I stayed inside. I turned away from the window to sit with Mother and play with a cloth doll I had named Turnip.

At night, I lay on the mattress I shared with my mother and drew in my mind the perfect friend. She'd have dark brown hair. Kind eyes and a calm demeanor.

Months passed and our first summer downtown was ending. One afternoon, Mother asked for her tea as usual. I brought it to her with a chunk of sugar. She put the sugar between her teeth and sipped the amber brew, her face damp from the steam.

"Ellie," she said, "I have registered you for school."

As she spoke, telling me how hard it had been to register my name knowing it was a slum school in a slum neighborhood, but what could you expect when your father's greedy brother wouldn't pay for us to be in better straits, my body buzzed with a strange mixture of anticipation and excitement.

My fortunes had changed.

School. Real school. A whole building separate from Mother. A yard. Schools—I was pretty sure—had to have yards. Teachers. And—my heart beat faster at just the prospect—girls my own age!

I was petrified and electrified at the thought of this otherworldly portal. A world where I'd find—perhaps, perhaps—my dreamed-of, kind-eyed friend.

We'd meet on the very first day of school. Maybe outside in the yard. We might be shy at first, hesitating to introduce ourselves. But after the initial caution, we'd become fast friends. We'd do everything together. Play at recess and do homework (I was supremely excited about both prospects).

Mother had told Uncle Massoud to buy me notebooks and even two pencils. I would learn to write! In a real notebook with a sharp pencil. I had seen my mother write—it was a constant heartbreak, she said, to be surrounded by illiterates in her new life when she was educated and had completed ninth grade.

Few things thrilled me more than the prospect of learning and finding a friend. I wanted to learn everything. I would become the best student the school had ever known. And we'd go everywhere together—my new friend and me. We'd play the five-stones game I'd seen the neighborhood girls play. Maybe Uncle Massoud would give me money for ice cream. If he knew I was doing well in school, if he knew I had a friend, he might treat me to that. As I lay next to Mother, I imagined bringing this imaginary friend to our house. My friend would make my mother laugh. We could eat together sometimes. I let my imagination soar with the delicious dishes we'd share.

I could not wait for the new universe that awaited when summer ended and autumn arrived.

THREE

September 1950

A jumble of butterflies fluttered inside me as I walked to school. I gripped the satchel Uncle Massoud had shown me how to clasp shut and felt the weight of the notebook and two pencils inside it.

I was nervous but also grateful. The beginning of everything seemed possible. Uncle Massoud had not protested my going to school. He believed girls should be educated too. Even at age seven, I recognized that was not an opinion all men or women held. But my mother and uncle did. I knew the route to school and which building to go to—not because my mother had led me by the hand showing the way, but because Uncle Massoud had recited directions in his deep voice when he'd dropped off my uniform and school supplies. And I had practiced going there twice already.

The air had lost most of its oppressive, end-of-summer heat. A fresh, crisp breeze helped ease my nerves—until I reached my destination and stared into a large, commotion-filled courtyard.

At the school gates, I placed my satchel between my knees so I could free my hands to work a personal superstition. In the middle of summer as I suffocated in the heat, I had created a ritual for myself. I practiced it whenever I wanted something good to happen. I tightened first one braid (left), then the other (right). Must squeeze the braids tight—first left, then right.

I had done my braid good-luck motions and just weeks later my mother had announced she'd registered me for school, hadn't she? And I had done it the previous week, right before I practiced walking to the school gates. And then again the day we went to the *hammams*. I'd been assigned the nicest washer in the baths, hadn't I? It worked. It had to work today.

After I tightened my braids, I took in a deep breath, removed my satchel from between my knees, put the strap back on my shoulder, and walked through the gates into the schoolyard.

Girls as far as the eye could see. The butterflies inside me flapped and I imagined them colliding into one another. Girls in uniforms just like mine. Endless gray *ormak* dresses with white collars. Everyone looked spiffed up. I moved farther into the courtyard, looking for our alley girls. If any of them were lucky enough to be here, I probably wouldn't even know. We all looked like scholars!

A piercing, unfamiliar sound hurt my ears. So high and trill. I turned and saw an older woman with a small object in her mouth (I would later learn it was a whistle). She swung both arms in the air. *Line up, line up!* Groups of girls organized themselves into lines as if by magic.

"*Kellas-e aval!*" a woman in a navy skirt yelled out. *Grade one.* My grade. I followed the woman, made my way to the line, and stood stiffly in place. The teachers were demanding quiet.

A poke.

I ignored it.

A jab.

I didn't want to get into trouble, but I turned around.

Her grin showed two missing front teeth. Her hair was black, curly, and messy. One curl bobbed right above her forehead like a renegade hook. There was mischief in her eyes.

I was instantly jealous of her looks, mainly because I hadn't yet lost my front teeth. "*Nakon!* Don't!" I said in a whisper.

The girl who had poked me leaned in until her face was close to mine. Her breath smelled like radishes. Who had radishes for breakfast? Her skin was dark and there was a mole below her left eye. "*Midooni chi?* Guess what?" she said.

I wanted desperately to turn around and be a good student facing the teacher. But her gaze was addictive. "What?" I murmured. She'd better hurry up and tell me.

"*Hichi!* Nothing!" Her hand flew to her mouth. She shook silently at her own ridiculous joke, her eyes squeezing shut.

I turned back around, unimpressed. I looked to my left and to my right, desperately. I wondered if she was here. The friend I had imagined. The kind one. The one with the dark brown hair and quiet demeanor, the one with whom I would get ice cream. Even as we marched into the building behind our teacher, I scoured the schoolyard for her.

In the classroom, we lined up against the wall and waited to be given our assigned seats. I looked around the room for the perfect friend. When my seat was called out, it was right next to the poking girl from line. Panic rose in me. Had my braid-tightening good-luck routine not worked?

I sat at the two-seat bench and placed my satchel carefully down.

The rude girl turned to me. "My name is Homa," she said. "What's yours?"

I gave her a side eye. "Elaheh," I mumbled.

She smiled her gap-toothed smile and laughed for no reason.

I ignored her.

Those first few days of school, I held on to the hope that the friend I'd conjured in my fantasy would still show up. Maybe I'd bump into her at recess (was she in another class?) or maybe our teacher would look up and announce that a new student had joined our grade.

I ignored Homa as best I could, though she was always next to me with her silly grin.

In the fifth week of school, on a Wednesday, an encounter changed my mind about Homa.

In those days we had a two-hour lunch break. Students would go home and eat with their families. I was sure the other girls arrived to find the *sofreh* cloth laid out, plates set, tin cups filled with cool water.

On that fifth Wednesday, I walked home quickly. Mother said her tired eyes couldn't catch the little stones and dirt in the rice the way my young ones could. Her eyes were "broken" from crying about my father.

She had set the rice on a tray and waited for me to remove the grit. I poured the remaining good grains into a bowl and rinsed them under water several times. We were lucky in this part of town to have access to water. We were lucky to have a jug and a sink with a pump. But Mother missed her old kitchen and hated the new pump.

I handed the bowl of wet grains to Mother and she poured the rice into a pot on the stove. She wouldn't let me cook the rice, though, because she worried I'd burn the house down and then what would she do? She said she was tired and didn't have the energy to cook anything to go with the rice, so when it was ready, we ate it with yogurt. Then I helped wash the dishes. By the time I put my shoes back on to return to school for the afternoon session, I was worried I'd be late.

Outside, out of breath and perspiring, I walked in as large strides as possible without running because Mother said running didn't befit a girl. My satchel drummed against my hip as if my body were a carpet being cleaned of dirt.

"Hey! *Sabr Kon.* Wait up!"

I turned around. It was Homa. She ran toward me, her curly hair flying. "I want to tell you something!"

I said nothing and kept walking.

"Why are you always so afraid to be late?"

At that moment, I saw Homa the way my mother would have: *a lower-class girl below your dignity with whom you are stuck in a dinky school.* I continued to walk fast.

"If you just wait for me one minute, you donkey, I could talk to you!"

I stopped. "Did you just call me a donkey?"

She caught up to me, panting. "You heard me, Donkey."

We faced one another, both of us out of breath from rushing.

"Did you know," I said, my mother's cadence and tone infusing my speech, "that the daughter of Naser al-Din Shah was my great-grandmother?"

"*Chi?*" She used the least formal form of asking why.

"You heard me, Donkey," I parroted her. Smaller and definitely physically weaker, I felt at a disadvantage because the sun blared in my eyes.

"*Khodeti Khar!* You're a donkey!"

"Royalty," I mumbled. But the word lost its fizz as it came out of my mouth. I shifted on my feet. The sun continued to blare as I looked at this bold brat who had dared call me a donkey thrice. I didn't lift my hand to shade my eyes. I had to stand my ground and show her who she was dealing with.

Homa slapped a hand to her cheek dramatically. "O-ho! You're a *Shaz-deh* princess!"

Mother had told me repeatedly how the boys and girls in this "slum" part of town were *vahshi* savages. Prone to outbursts of violence. At that moment, I felt suddenly scared.

Homa pulled the strap of my satchel away from my shoulder. I flinched and backed away.

"I don't care if your great-great-grandmother was the Queen of all of Persia." She smoothed out the strap of my satchel. "All I want to know is do you want to play with me?"

"What?"

"Hopscotch?"

I couldn't believe it. She was asking me to play? And hopscotch at that? She was so earnest. And seemed to truly want me to join her. "I don't know," I said, stalling for time. "I have to get my mother's permission."

"Ask her, then! And guess what? We can play five stones too." She jumped up and down. "Well, whatcha waiting for, Turtle? Let's race!"

Homa placed one foot in front of the other and bounced in a lunge. "Ready?"

The gap-toothed smile. The curls in the sun. That silly, crazy look of hers. It was impossible to be near her energy and not want to jump or run or act like a fool as well. I wasn't ready, but almost reflexively I imitated her position.

She counted to three. "*Yek, Do, Se!*"

As if launched by an unknown power, I took off at the exact moment she said three.

We ran, satchels clutched to our chests so they wouldn't hurl against us. My braids flying, wind whooshing in my ears, I sprinted with a speed I had no idea I possessed. We were in sync. It felt like we moved in a vacuum sealed off from the rest of the world in a funnel all its own.

When the school came into view, Homa yelled a huge *hooooooraaaah* and a sound rose from within me—a yelp that would have wounded my mother's high-minded sensibilities—an enormous, delicious release.

We arrived at the school gates out of breath but in time. We practically propelled ourselves into the wrought-iron bars. I clutched the bars and rested my head against the gate, huffing and puffing. Homa did the same and then straightened up. She took my hand. "Let's call it a tie, Princess."

We marched in together.

FOUR

October 1950

"What's her name?" Mother asked as she sat cross-legged on her floor seat cushion with its carpeted bottom under her and the back of the cushion against the wall.

"Homa."

"Oh." She closed her eyes. "I've always loved that name. A bird from the fables. A bird from our ancient Persian Zoroastrian mythology. The homa bird never rests on the ground. They say this bird lives its entire life invisible above us all."

Was this a hopeful sign? My new friend had a name my mother loved. Maybe the "homa" bird she had in mind was a beautiful and graceful creature. Of course, my Homa, the toughest girl in our class, was hardly graceful. But she seemed to have a spirit set apart. She seemed to float on a different plane.

My mother opened her eyes and studied me. For a second, she softened at whatever she must have seen in my expression. "Fine," she sighed. "But not here. I don't want her in my house."

"I can go there," I said quickly, my heart racing at her acceptance. I didn't want her to change her mind. "Homa said she doesn't live far from here. Can I please go next week? After school?"

"Oh, dear God, you'll be one of those children in the alleys after all."

I looked at her, afraid to say anything.

"See what happens when you're all alone in the world? I had parents, a sister, a husband. But they left me and now this aloneness means being at the mercy of your uncle. *Tanhayi* loneliness is the worst of all afflictions. Did you know that?"

I nodded. My mother always claimed to be so alone in the world. But didn't I have my mother and she have me? I couldn't help but think that if my father had lived, it would all have been enough.

"Do you think Baba would have been able to recover from the illness if only we had caught it sooner?" I asked, unable to stop myself. "Do you think he would have been proud of me going to school?"

"Enough with the questions!"

"But Baba was a scholar, yes? He liked reading?"

"I don't want to talk about him, Ellie. I've told you that numerous times." Mother rubbed her temples. "It can't be stopped, I suppose," she said. "Sooner or later, you'll meld with these children. Unless . . ." She looked past me. "I've refused." She put her head in her hands.

"Unless what?"

"Go do your homework," she said.

I retrieved my satchel from near the door and got out my notebook. I did not want to upset this newfound balance. I was pretty sure Mother had surrendered to acceptance of my first playdate!

As we walked to her house the following Wednesday after school, Homa did not stop talking. Mother had warned me to wash my hands as soon as I got inside. *IF they have running water, that is.*

"You have to be careful around the big boys in my alley," Homa said. "Especially around stinky Saman. We call him Sammy. But don't worry— I slapped him last week and now they've *all* been less annoying. I mean, Sammy's still a bully. He had a fistfight with the other boys on Friday and his nose bled! I'm working on having the boys let me play the game with the sticks. They think I can't play because I'm a girl. Don't you think it's absurd to not let me play because I'm a girl?"

"What's the game with the sticks?" I envisioned humongous fourth- and fifth-grade boys brandishing thick branches. *Lat o loot* hooligans, my mother would have said. I wasn't so sure I wanted to be around them.

"Oh, their stick game is fantastic. If they just let me join in, they'd see I can play just as well as them," Homa said dreamily.

She and I clearly had different goals regarding the stick game. "Do you have a *baba*?" I asked, because I associated big boys with men and men with fathers.

"Of course, silly."

"Mine's dead," I said.

Homa stopped walking. "Did he die when you were a baby?"

"No, he died a few months ago. Before we moved here."

She grabbed me and squeezed me in a tight hug. "*Tasliat, tasliat,*" she said. Then she paused. "I think that's what I'm supposed to say, right?"

"Yes," I sighed. "Condolences are always what people say."

We started walking again. As if to change the uncomfortable subject, she blurted, "Do you want to know a secret?"

"Of course."

"My father's a communist!"

"What?"

Homa looked at me with widened eyes. "He's against the king!"

I had heard from Mother about what happened to people who were against our king. She'd told me how the current king's father, Reza Shah, had taken over the throne from the different Qajar king from whom Mother was descended. Despite never having gotten over how Reza Shah dethroned her great-grandfather, Mother always warned me that speaking out against his son, our current king, whom we just called "Shah," was dangerous. "I don't think it's safe to be against the king," I whispered to Homa. "You can go to prison."

Homa looked around furtively. "I just remembered I wasn't supposed to tell anyone that. Oh, dear. I don't want my *baba* to go to prison." She grabbed my hand. "Promise you won't tell anyone. Promise me right now!"

"I promise, I promise!"

She let go. "Though the main reason you go to prison isn't because you've been against the king."

"Why do people go to prison, then?"

"They go if they drink blood," she said with a confidence that was unsettling.

"Oh." For the rest of our walk to her house, I felt mild anxiety about how she knew that.

In Homa's alley, the big boys—about seven or eight of them—stood in a huddle. I couldn't see any sticks, but they could have been concealing them in the middle of their circle. Three girls sat cross-legged on the ground, sorting out stones. In a corner, two smaller boys and a little girl sucked on dried sour cherries and ejected the pits from their mouths in what appeared to be an elaborate spitting contest. Homa's alley was already more exciting than mine. Homa waved hello to the big boys. Most of them ignored her, but one whipped around.

"Hello, hello," he said almost breathlessly. "And who's this?"

"None of your business, Sammy."

She led me away quickly.

"I can't believe he was nice to you after you slapped him and everything," I said.

"Don't pay attention to him," she said. "He is nothing but trouble."

We arrived at a white gate between low cement walls. Homa went straight up to the gate and opened it. At first, I thought she was going into someone else's property. But I followed her into a well-kept courtyard with a *hoz* koi pond in the middle. The bright blue water shimmered in the sunlight, which created kaleidoscoped geometric shapes across the shallow pond's surface. A few fat orange fish swam there. I looked up at the house. It was made of brick just like ours but was larger.

"*Khosh omadi!*" Homa welcomed me.

So this was her house. I had not expected it to be this big.

A baby's wail rang out. We walked to the front door, took off our shoes in the little foyer, and went inside.

After the sunlight of the courtyard, it took a minute for my eyes to adjust. We were in a sparsely furnished main room. A baby cried on a threadbare kilim rug in the center of the floor. The crying was loud but also strangely sweet. The scent of something yeasty baking surprised me. My mother only baked for the Persian New Year.

A woman rushed in with a white house chador on loosely. From the part of the chador that was slightly open, I saw she had on a patterned blouse. One long black braid wound from her neck down the front of her body.

"Who's this, then?" she asked. I didn't know if she was asking about the baby or me. But then she scooped the baby up and balanced it on her hip in one effortless motion that proved she'd done it countless times. She bounced the baby and it stopped crying. The baby stared at me and Homa with accusatory tearful eyes, sweaty dark curls matted to its head.

"Maman Joon, remember I told you Ellie is coming to play with me?"

The woman didn't seem to remember, but her smile was welcoming. When she came close, I saw the pattern on her blouse in more detail: tiny blue flowers grew out of curlicue miniature green stems on the white fabric. The cloth of her chador seemed like it would feel supremely soft. She smelled like yeast and milk. "I'm Monir Khanom," she said. "Would you like some cherry *sharbat*? You must be thirsty."

"In a bit, Maman Joon," Homa said. "After we play."

I would have loved some cherry *sharbat*, but I wasn't about to look impolite and greedy.

"*Bereen, bacheha.* Go on, children. I'll have a snack for you here if you get hungry." She smiled again and turned around. The baby stared at us from the top of her shoulder.

"*Merci, Khanom.*" I called her by the respected term for lady, hoping the snack was related to the delicious baking smell.

"Isn't she pretty?" Homa asked after we went back outside.

I wasn't sure how to respond. "Your mother is beautiful," I said.

"No, silly! I mean, yes, she is. But I was talking about my baby sister, Sara. Don't you just want to eat her?"

I hadn't considered eating the baby, but she was chubby and adorable.

"She's almost thirteen months!" Homa said with pride. "Thirteen!"

We were in first grade. Sara had just finished her first year of life. I had hoped to have a sister or a brother, but I knew my father being dead meant it wasn't part of my fate. How lucky Homa was to have that *topoli* baby sister!

Homa grabbed my hand and pulled me out into the courtyard and then the alley. There she looked at the ground as though hunting for a lost coin. She finally picked up a sharp stone. "Perfect!"

She dragged the stone across the ground, scratching out lines. As she drew, the lines connected into big squares. She looked up at me. "Don't just stand there. Find a good stone. We have to number them."

I selected a jagged small rock and proceeded to scratch out numbers inside the squares. In class, we had practiced writing numbers from one to ten. I was proud to use my newfound knowledge to create the grid for the game. I couldn't believe I was lucky enough to actually be playing hopscotch. For weeks, I had watched other schoolgirls play. Lying on the mattress next to my mother, I had nighttime fantasies about hopping perfectly into a square with my imaginary friend.

After we marked all the squares, Homa found two small pebbles and gave one to me. "Want to go first?" she asked. But it was clear she was itching to go.

"No, you," I said.

Homa tossed her pebble and it landed on the four square. She balanced carefully on one foot. "*Yek Do Se!*" she shouted, and then hopped her way to the square with the pebble in it. With one leg in the air, she bent and retrieved her pebble from where it had landed, closed her fingers over it, held it up, and looked back at me with an expression of absolute triumph.

I couldn't help but clap and cheer as she hopped back.

After hopscotch, we jumped with a frayed yellow rope tucked in an upside-down bucket. Homa said this was the secret hiding place for the rope so Sammy wouldn't steal it. She said Sammy was a thief and a liar. We spied on Sammy and the boys until Sammy turned around. Homa pulled me away and we ran back to her house, giggling.

Homa's mother, Monir Khanom, sat on the floor now on a seat cushion much like my mother's, with its carpeted bottom under her and the back of the cushion against the wall. Her legs were stretched out in front as Sara loudly and enthusiastically sucked at her breast. Monir Khanom covered part of her breast with her chador when she saw us.

"There's *ghotab* for you in the kitchen," she said. "Make sure you wash your hands first."

"Thank you, Maman Joon," Homa said.

I knew I should *tarof* and engage in the ritual of denying what a host offers until they insist again. I knew the first refusal was not just polite but expected. But the house smelled so good and I felt comfortable here somehow. "*Kheyli mamnoon, Khanom,*" I thanked her.

"*Nooshe Jan.*"

Homa led me to the back of the main room and down a stone staircase. Beneath my socked feet, the steps were smooth and cool, and I could feel where they dipped in the middle as though years of walking had softened each center. After descending seven steps (I counted), we entered a cool, cave-like kitchen. It should have been damp down there, but the air was warm and dry and infused with the delicious baking smell I had detected when we first walked into the house. Copper pots hung on the wall above the huge stove. On the burner was a samovar, on top of which sat a white teapot etched with two pink roses. Various dishes were stacked on shelves. Every surface was clean and shining.

A plate covered with a white cloth sat on the counter. Homa tiptoed to it dramatically and whisked off the cloth to reveal a bundle of small half-circle pastries.

"My mother's *ghotab*," Homa said with reverence. "The best thing you'll probably ever eat."

We poured water from an earthenware jug near the deep ceramic sink and used a sliver of soap as though engaging in ablutions for prayer. We carefully dried our hands with a towel that hung on a hook near the basin. When we stood in front of the main counter again, Homa lifted the plate up to me. "*Befarmayeed*," she said, using the formal verb tense to invite me to partake.

Again, I did not *tarof*, did not engage in the back-and-forth dance of refusing an offer so my hostess would have to insist and beg me to eat. I grabbed the semicircle of pastry—it was still warm. I bit into it. Crispy on the outside and then surprisingly tart inside. A tangy explosion of sweet and sour took over my mouth.

"What's in here?" I asked, my mouth full, aware of how horrified Mother would be at my bad manners.

"Pomegranate!" Homa said, her eyes shining as though sharing the code to the vault where the Shah kept his crown jewels.

"I thought *ghotab* was filled with almonds and walnuts and dusted with sugar." I remembered the box of *ghotab* pastries Uncle Massoud had brought for Mother's birthday. The light sugar had powdered our mouths as the three of us shared them. I knew Mother missed the fancy parties she used to throw for her birthday when we lived uptown.

"That's the other kind. This one is from my grandmother's recipe. It's her specialty."

I chewed and, in my heart, thanked Homa's grandmother. Together we ate several more and stopped only because it would be impolite to finish them all, though I was pretty sure Monir Khanom would insist. From the way she welcomed me when I first came into the house, from how she handled the baby, Sara, I had a feeling she wasn't the kind of mother who complained to her children about her woes.

My lucky, lucky friend.

A small tug in my chest, almost an ache, overwhelmed me. It was accompanied by a strange new hollowness.

I couldn't define it at the time. But in retrospect, even from that very first visit, I wanted what Homa had. I wanted her family. Her living father, her kind mother. I wanted her fat, edible baby sister. I wanted the warmth and safety of her home. I wanted the coolness of that kitchen, its cavernous magic, its ability to transform pomegranate seeds and dough into a dish divine and delectable. To my great shame, as I stood there, I had a flash of something awful happening to my mother so I could become an orphan and be taken in by Homa's family. Folding into her clan would make me one of them. Part of them.

I adored her.

I was already jealous of her.

FIVE

November 1950

From then on, we fled to one another naturally. It was with Homa that I mastered jump-rope games, her back that I massaged by stomping my feet on it as she lay facedown, from her that I learned how to spit cherry pits out far (and far away from the eyes of my disapproving mother).

It was in Homa's kitchen where I first learned to use a knife. Under the guidance of Monir Khanom, we placed an onion on the counter. Together, we peeled away the thin, crackly skin, the membranes underneath surprisingly slippery and slick against our fingers. Monir Khanom opened a drawer and took out a giant knife with a multicolored abalone handle. She brought the knife right to Homa and me, placed our hands on the sparkling handle, covered them with her own, and guided us into halving the onion, slicing each half facedown, rotating it and slicing the other way in rows. When Homa's mother slowly pulled back the knife to reveal a heap of perfect tiny onion cubes, I felt we had performed magic. I couldn't believe the control we had over changing the shape of things.

At home, Mother sat on her floor-cushion seat, seeming to disappear more and more into the wall. She continued to complain about my "cavorting with riffraff" and mixing with "the lower types." But she did not stop me from going to Homa's house. Perhaps part of her—the motherly part—wanted to preserve my newfound happiness. That's what I wanted to believe. Desperately.

The skills I learned in Homa's cool stone kitchen were skills I brought home to Mother. She let me take on more and more of the meal preparation, though I still wasn't allowed to use the stove.

I made for my mother the *shirazi* salad of chopped onions, cucumbers, and tomatoes and served it with fresh mint. I increased the lemon juice and lessened the salt and dared to drizzle some of the olive oil Uncle Massoud had brought. Mother couldn't resist the taste.

And I couldn't stay away from the magic of that stone kitchen.

The process of cooking captivated me from the instant I first stood by Monir Khanom's side. How a simple onion could transform from the peeled orb to the thin white slices to the petite cubes and then the sauteed brown translucence from heat and fat in the copper pot, the caramelized scent that infused the house as the onion sizzled.

That lone onion could be a base for savory stews like Monir Khanom's *ghormeh sabzi* herb *khoresh* or the yellow split pea and beef *khoresh* my mother said had been my father's favorite (she never made it again after his death, claiming the memories were too difficult). I was shown how fried onion could garnish *aush* soup when mixed with dried mint or act as filling for grape-leaf dolmehs when combined with leftover rice and herbs. Monir Khanom taught Homa and me how to cook pomegranate seeds on the stove slowly and deliberately until they became a molasses that could be used in the walnut and pomegranate *fesenjoon* stew Homa loved so much.

Inevitably, after our frequent playdates, Homa and I descended the smooth cool stone steps that led into the cave-like kitchen. There her mother would be, chador-less in a skirt and flowered blouse, her slippers torn but worn-in to envious comfort. Sara crawled around, babbling and banging pot lids as she pursued her own strange but specific goals. Homa and I stood side by side near the large stove by Monir Khanom, delighting in the shape of an eggplant or the juiciness of a lemon.

And when after many months I worked up the courage to ask how her family could afford this food—this impossible array of color and subsistence—Homa looked at me as if I had asked a most ridiculous question.

"Because of where my father works, silly. Otherwise, we couldn't afford any of it."

"I thought your father was a communist." I had imagined Homa's *baba* demonstrating in the streets or holed up in a basement somewhere, drafting plans to overthrow the Shah.

"Communists work too! He's the headwaiter at the Palace Hotel restaurant. Whatever they don't use and want to throw away at the end of the day, he and a few of the other waiters get to bring home. Aren't we lucky?"

"So, so lucky," I said as Sara nuzzled against my ankles like a little cat.

Lucky to have this mother who trusted Homa and me enough to teach us how to feed ourselves and who made us feel competent and in charge with a casual respect I had not experienced from any other adult.

Lucky for the communist father with access to food, a man I had never met but whose income and lack of dying meant Homa's home wasn't tied to the whims of an uncle.

Lucky for the big-eyed, gurgling baby sister who sucked her thumb and smiled up at me with pure joy.

Lucky for all of it.

I loved Homa's house, and when I walked home from any of our playdates and cooking lessons to go back into the coldness of the space where my mother's grief reigned, Homa's comforts created in me that particular and palpable ache of which I was continuously ashamed.

"You're late," my mother would say no matter what time I returned.

"*Bebakhsheed,*" I would respond. *Forgive me.*

SIX

May 1953

"Elaheh and Homa," the other girls called us as if we were one unit. "Ellie-o-Homa" was our shortened moniker. We were inseparable.

Together we navigated squares of an invisible hopscotch grid containing those early school years. We tossed an imaginary pebble and sailed into landing for second grade. Within months, we were moved up to third grade as we both excelled in academics. Our friendship carried us through that quick transition and the skipping of a grade.

The shifting alliances and dramatic dynamics of the other girls spun like the whirling globe our teacher liked to spin in front of our faces. We learned the names of so many countries—places like Kenya and Uganda and Australia—and memorized the shape and form of them. India and China and Korea and Japan. Across the sea into Europe were places named Germany and France and England. Italy and Spain. Portugal: *por-te-gal* is how we pronounced it in Persian, which also meant the fruit "orange," so we always associated Portugal with oranges. We ran our fingers across the outline of countries called *Russiyeh* and *Amrica*. It felt surreal to know there was a world beyond our borders.

By fourth grade, few in our class read and wrote at the much higher level Homa and I had mastered at ten years old. She and I competed for the coveted *Shagerd Aval* slot of First-in-Class. But what most made me love Homa was her good-natured ability to put aside the competition and make things fun.

One morning in the last days of fourth grade, when the summer holiday felt right around the corner, I entered the school courtyard and heard a loud "psssst" from behind me. Even before I turned around, I answered, "What is it, Homa?"

She came to face me and rested both hands on my shoulders. "What if"—she looked me in the eye—"we take the day off?"

"Very funny. We can't."

"Come on. The school year's pretty much over. We deserve an adventure."

If we skipped school, we would most definitely be punished. I pulled away from her and set off to line up before the whistle rang out.

"Haven't you ever wanted to do something you weren't supposed to do, Ellie?" she called after me.

I stopped and considered her question. Each year, I wanted to eat every single *gaz* candy in the box Uncle Massoud brought over for Nowruz, the first day of spring and our New Year. But I held back because Mother didn't want me to be too fat. I wanted to use the stove in our own kitchen to cook, but I didn't because Mother said the house might turn to ashes. I wanted to be friends with Homa. That was something I wasn't supposed to be doing. And I had done it. But I couldn't very well tell Homa that my being friends with her was my loud act of rebellion.

"Let's just do it, Ellie."

"I can't fall behind."

"Ellie, you're already 'advanced in your studies,' according to Khanom Tabatabayi. You can afford to miss one day. We both can. She told me my reading and writing are *immaculate*."

Had our teacher told her that? I felt a small sting. Was it a coincidence that Homa and I both excelled in school or did we each drive the other to push a little further? But Homa was right—neither one of us was in jeopardy of falling behind.

"And where would we even go?" I asked.

"I am going to show you more food than you've ever seen, *Sheekamoo*!"

Sheekamoo means a person who loves to eat, whose priority is their stomach, and that's what Homa affectionately, jokingly called me. I didn't mind when she called me that because it was, from her, clearly a term of endearment, as though it was a wonderful thing to be so invested in food. And I liked the way it erased "Princess," her first name for me, brought on by the shallow way I'd mimicked Mother and brought up my royal ancestry that fateful morning we ran to school together.

Anyway, it was true that everything about food brought me joy: the gathering of ingredients, their transformation and unification, the presentation and sharing of meals. The only part that didn't bring me joy was my mother bemoaning my weight. I had gotten chubby; some might even say fat. But I loved that Homa accepted my chubbiness as a fact and not as a vice.

"Where?" I asked with doubt.

"You know where. The Grand Bazaar."

Though I had gone there with my parents when I was too young to remember (Mother had told me so), the Grand Bazaar was now a forbidden place. My mother insisted the people there were smelly and the women pushed and the men groped. But the real reason Mother would never take me to the Grand Bazaar was fear. She claimed it would bring back memories of going there with my father. Her heart couldn't take it, she said.

I was torn between my own fear of ditching school and the intense desire to go on a forbidden adventure.

Before I could say another word, Homa grabbed my hand and we took off.

I followed Homa and trusted that she knew where to go. We walked and eventually ran down street after street until narrow alleys opened onto wider avenues lined with big houses and shops and office buildings. I kept thinking our plan might get found out by our school principal, or worse, Mother. That police would be sent to arrest us. But none of that happened.

Finally, we arrived at the Grand Bazaar near the Shah Mosque. I couldn't remember ever seeing so many people in one place.

As we stood in front of the main entrance of the large indoor-outdoor shopping center that had been a mainstay of our city for hundreds of years, a familiar feeling descended over me. I studied the arched entryway with its detailed ornamental mosaics. Had my father stood on this spot and balanced me on his shoulders? Maybe he and my mother had grasped each of my hands and swung me up in between them.

Homa took my hand now, and together we entered a maze of lanes lined with busy stalls and kiosks brimming with goods and crafts. Men hawking their wares chanted and yelled. People bartered and bantered, chatted and cajoled. The air smelled of cantaloupes and mint, of strange perfumes from foreign lands and soaps and potpourri. The sound of metal rods banging against tin and copper drummed in my ears as coppersmiths and craftsmen etched out intricate designs on trays and plates. Carpenters sanded smooth planes of wood. We swerved and bumped into wooden tables heaped with women's underwear and nightgowns. Brassieres hung by clothespins on a line. Some were lacy and red; others were huge white bras like Mother's. Men unpacked sacks of goods from donkeys' backs and women sipped on cold fruit juice as they coyly looked out from under their chadors.

The combination of scents and cacophony of noise was overpowering. I wanted to stop. To touch the lacy underwear, inhale the mounded potpourri. I wanted to graze my fingers against the pyramid-shaped piles of candies in wrappers and feel the silky carpets piled high in corner stalls.

But Homa pulled me through. We finally stepped out from a small passageway past the zigzag lanes of the interior into an outdoor courtyard lined with kiosks but open in the middle. At the far end of the yard stood a single stall with a red-and-white awning.

"My mother gave me money for my birthday last week," Homa whispered. I was grateful she had the sense to quiet her usual loud exclamatory voice. Students ditching school—runaways practically—did best to keep a low profile. Homa reached into her satchel and held up her birthday money with pride. The coins glistened in the courtyard sun.

"You planned this?" I whispered.

"Was I going to bring you to the bazaar without any money to spend? Come on. I told you we deserve this."

She walked up to the stall with the red-and-white awning. I followed. The edges of the awning flapped in the breeze.

"*Agha, dota bastani lotfan.*" Homa asked for two ice creams.

Her confidence astonished me.

A man with a huge belly in a tight-fitting shirt, baggy pants, and cracked sandals on his feet examined the coins she gave him, a lispy sound emitting from his mouth as he counted them out. Then he opened his crate. Inside it I saw huge rectangular blocks of ice on which rested containers of ice cream. We had been studying liquids, solids, and gas in science class, but I had never seen ice like that before.

The man's hair was white and looked like sheep fur. He scooped out ice cream, stuffed it between two thin wafer disks he retrieved from a nearby box, and handed the first ice cream sandwich to Homa. She politely passed it to me as if we were grown-ups who could buy what we wanted and do as we pleased in a distant courtyard in the Grand Bazaar on a Tuesday morning. The man gave Homa the second ice cream sandwich, then turned his attention to his next customers, a group of women in chadors. Could no one see our school uniforms and satchels? How was it this easy to be a low-level, school-skipping criminal?

We found a ledge in the courtyard on which to sit. We took turns, each one holding both ice creams as the other hoisted herself up. Once settled, we cocked our heads and bit in.

The flavor of vanilla infused with rose water and saffron burst into my mouth. The chewiness of the wafer contrasted with the smoothness of the ice cream. To my delight, there were also chunks of frozen heavy cream tucked in—the richness a surprise.

"You like it?" Homa asked.

"So much. Thank you. I'll pay you back."

"It's my treat." She grinned. "Worth getting detention, right?"

"Don't say that." I took another bite. "Okay, maybe it is."

"Imagine, Ellie, being able to have ice cream any day of the week. But I guess you have to be rich to do that."

I didn't remind her that I used to be rich. Or at least not poor.

"My *baba* says the only society worth living in is one where everyone has access to food, shelter, clean water, and health services."

By then I had met Homa's father a few times. He was a short man with spectacles and a balding head—soft-spoken and intellectual. As Homa repeated his words, I remembered them as the same he'd told me on the first day we'd been introduced.

"Baba says we have to contribute to the country. Men and women both." She swiveled her head so she could bore her eyes into mine in that insistent way she had. "How will you contribute, Ellie?"

I looked up, my mouth on the edge of the ice cream sandwich. "What?"

"What job do you want to have?"

"Job?"

"Yes. Do you want to be a teacher? A nurse? A lawyer? Maybe a doctor. You're so good at science."

I just wanted to eat my ice cream. "Not sure," I mumbled.

"Tell me."

"A mother," I said, my mouth full.

"Yes, yes. But women can work too, you know. In a just society. Did you know we could be the first generation of women fully working in Iran?"

"There are women working in Iran now."

"Not that many. And not in more high-up jobs. We'll do that. Won't we?"

A few drops of melted ice cream ran down my fingers. I wanted to get my handkerchief from my bag, but if I rummaged through my satchel, my ice-creamy hands would get it sticky and possibly my notebooks sticky too.

Mother worried about her hands. She wanted them to remain unblemished and unswollen, unlike the hands of working women. She said that true ladies didn't touch a thing to sully their hands. That work for pay was beneath her. She was proud that despite everything, she hadn't sunk to being a "desperate" working woman, even if it meant we were dependent on Uncle Massoud's allowance.

"Well, I'll tell you what I want to be. I want to be a *ghazi*, a judge!" Homa said.

"Women can't be judges."

"Don't believe that nonsense. I have to go to a university program where you learn all about laws first. But then I can decide who's right and who's wrong when people have a disagreement. Doesn't that sound spectacular?"

It sounded awful to me. A school where you just learned laws? I couldn't think of anything more boring. I also wasn't sure we were allowed to go to law school, let alone decide who was right and who was wrong. "Are you sure women can attend?"

"It is 1953. We have a democratically elected prime minister! This country is modernizing, Ellie. Where have you been?" She took another bite of her ice cream sandwich. "I'm going to check it all out with Khanom Tabatabayi. And *if* we're not allowed, that's another reason I should become a lawyer. To change the laws." She winked.

"That makes absolutely no sense."

"*Yek kareesh meekoneem*, we'll do something about it." Then she took a deep breath and looked straight into my eyes. "You know what we'll both become when we grow up?"

"I do not," I said.

"*Shir zan*. Lionesses. Us. Can't you just see it, Ellie? Someday, you and me—we'll do great things. We'll live life for ourselves. And we will help others. We are cubs now, maybe. But we will grow to be lionesses. Strong women who make things happen."

Her face had gotten rosy with excitement. She was on a roll, I could tell. I had heard of the concept of *shir zan*—powerful Iranian women who did not back down—but I did not in any way feel like a lioness. I was the most timid of cubs, if anything. I envied Homa's confidence. Could she be right? Could we one day become the kind of powerful women she was always going on about? Homa could, I knew that. But I wasn't sure I should be included in her "*shir ẓan.*" Even though I excelled in school, Mother planned on my marrying (rich) and having lots of children to avoid her fate as the parent of an only child (implying, hurtfully as ever, that I wasn't enough for her).

"If you want to be this successful working woman," I told Homa, "we need to not skip school. If we leave now, we can at least get there for the afternoon session." I slid off the ledge and jumped to the ground, my satchel bouncing against my hip. I rubbed my sticky hands. "And what are we going to say about not being in class this morning?"

"Oh, Ellie, you're bringing me down now! Come on, let's skip the whole day and tomorrow tell them we weren't feeling well today."

"I'm bringing you back to reality! Someone has to. Some judge you're going to be! You're already breaking the rules."

Homa finished the last of her ice cream, licked her fingers, and jumped off the ledge. "Sometimes you have to break the law, Ellie. Some laws are stupid and unfair and absurd."

I was sure Homa would tap into her parents' enlightened views to educate me about terrible laws I had been blissfully unaware of, but I knew the clock was ticking. "We can't not show up at home for lunch."

She sighed. "Fine. At least let's see more of the bazaar on the way back."

Once we were back inside the heart of the bazaar and I was surrounded by the sounds and blend of smells, once I could see pyramid-shaped heaps of mulberries and walnuts and almonds, once Homa flashed a few more coins she'd retrieved from her satchel and led me to the stall of nuts, I was a goner. This was where I wanted to be. In this messy, delightful, overwhelming, astounding space. It was all I could do to remind Homa again that we had to go back. But first, we wound our way in line for walnuts and dried mulberries. One last indulgence before we went home.

===

We managed to time our return to the regular lunch hour. I was full from the ice cream and the snacks, but would play the part and eat with Mother.

I walked into our house with my heart beating loudly. I would pretend it had been like any other school morning, hide the leftover dried mulberries and walnuts wrapped in paper at the bottom of my satchel. I would take off my shoes and wash my hands and set the plates on the *sofreh* cloth and help clean the rice and we would eat. Then I'd roll out the mattress and plump it up for Mother's afternoon nap.

As I bent down to take off my shoes, I felt a presence behind me. I froze. A second later, Mother was right next to me.

"I see you're back from school."

"*Salaam, Madar,*" I said.

"How was school, Elaheh?"

I couldn't look her in the eye. I focused on the floor. "It was good."

"Was it? What lessons did you have today?"

"Oh, you know. The usual for Tuesdays. Mathematics. Calligraphy."

"I know you love calligraphy."

"Mm-hmm."

"How is your calligraphy progressing, Elaheh? Are you perfecting your strokes?"

I nodded, still focused on the floor.

"Did you draw out your capital letters this morning?"

Nausea rose in my stomach.

"Funny you should say you were doing calligraphy in school. Because what Shaba Khanom told me—what she told me a little while ago—was that she saw someone who looked just like you sucking on an ice cream sandwich in the courtyard outside the Grand Bazaar. Was she mistaken?"

I wanted to disappear. I wanted to vanish into the floor, to leave my shoes there and have my mother stand talking only to my shoes. I didn't say anything.

"Answer me."

"Yes. She was mistaken. She made a mistake," I said weakly. Shaba Khanom lived across the alley with her elderly mother and husband and sons. Her husband was a street cleaner and there were rumors that one of her sons was a thief. I knew Shaba Khanom only barely. Sometimes she chatted with me outside. A few times we found ourselves walking together to the *noonvayi* to buy bread. She always asked about my mother. I always asked about hers.

"Don't ever lie to me again, Elaheh," my mother said coolly.

She didn't grab me by the ear. She didn't slap me. She simply placed her hand on my chin and forced my face up so I couldn't avoid looking into her eyes. When I did, I saw that her eyes were filled with tears.

"You went with her, didn't you?"

There was no need to define who. My mother often referred to Homa by the pronoun "*oon*" or as "that *dahati* girl" or "that friend of yours." She made the word "friend" sound like a curse word. She hardly ever said her actual name. In fact, I wasn't sure if she had ever said it. With my mother's hand still on my chin, anger grew in me and I tried to shake her off. Her grip was firm.

"She has a name," I said. "Her name is Homa. She is my friend and she has a name."

My mother let go of my chin as though her hand had been burned.

"And you're right. I went with Homa. Homa and I went together. We went to the Grand Bazaar. She bought me ice cream. She bought me walnuts and mulberries. They were delicious. It was all delicious. It was amazing."

Mother studied me. "You're proud of this? Of skipping school—this school you claim to love. Miss *Shagerd Aval*, First-in-Class? What do you think will happen to your status now?"

I didn't say anything.

"Do you know what a fool I looked like in front of Shaba Khanom? In front of that dumb peasant who will now lord this over me? Why do you feel the need to be led around by a *dahati* girl? Why are you so obsessed with her? This is not normal, Elaheh. You are not normal."

"Homa is not a *dahati* peasant," I said, my voice shaking. "And even if she were, it wouldn't matter. I'd still be her friend."

"What is she, then? An aristocrat who rides an elephant? Should I bow down to her? Tell me, Elaheh, what do you really have in common with that girl?"

"We are best friends."

My mother smirked. "She is in your school and you play together. It's convenient—nothing more. These friendships don't mean anything. They don't last, Elaheh. They come. They go. *Hameen*. That's it."

That wasn't it. Did she know that Homa and I had a running joke of Mrs. Tabatabayi's innocent slips of the tongue and that we'd written a prank poem out of all the silly sayings? Did she know that I could say something— the dumbest thing—and Homa could respond with the perfect comeback, a quip, a saying, a line of old poetry we'd been forced to memorize in school, and before long, we'd both be laughing until our faces were soaked in tears?

Mother claimed to have had dozens of friends uptown, but where were they now? I didn't see any visiting us. They had abandoned her the minute her fortunes changed. As though my father's death was, like the disease that had killed him, contagious. As if our move to the south side of town deemed us untouchable. Maybe the reason they had all deserted us was because my mother actually was a difficult person to be around most of the time. Or was there more to it than that?

Had my mother ever had a friend to provide her some relief from daily darkness, a friend who made her feel as though this world—the one Mother declared was filled with so many cruelties and people out to *cheshm* us with their evil eye—was also beautiful and filled with joy and adventure?

"Not because we're in the same school," I struggled to say, my words coming out choppy due to my growing anger. "We just . . . understand one another. We're like sisters. We will always understand each other."

"*Velam kon*. Just leave me alone with this nonsense. Her father waits on people all day like a servant. Her mother is illiterate. They are vermin in the alley, my dear. They are nobodies who come from nobodies."

My breath came out in sharp gasps. "They are not vermin. They are generous and kind. They have more dignity than you could imagine. They are hardworking and smart and quite frankly, their house is much nicer than this place. And bigger. I know that wealth matters to you. And pedigree. 'Descended from royalty.' What does that even mean, Mother? We learned in school about Naser al-Din Shah. He had harems. Lots of them. So the fact that you are his 'descendant' basically makes you the great-granddaughter of a whore."

The words came out in a rush. My voice was high and thin.

One did not speak to one's mother the way I had. If she raised her hand and struck me, I would have deserved it.

I expected her to scream. I braced myself for an attack. She had only hit me twice that I could remember, once for stating a preference for downtown over our old neighborhood and another time for forgetting to lock the door at night. Now I had broken the unwritten law of respect.

But she just stood with one hand on her hip, her face pale. "Is that so?" She looked past me at an invisible extra person in the room whom she often seemed to consult. "It's worse than I thought, then," she said to the unseen force. "It's up to me." She covered her face with both her hands. "Nader!" she whispered.

I backed out of the room as she continued to repeat the name of my father as if in an argument with him.

For a few minutes, I stood in the small corridor leading to the kitchen and took deep breaths. No matter what, I had to apologize to my mother. I went back into the main room.

She sat on the floor now, her head against the wall. She was quiet. She had a look of steeliness, a strange decisiveness. She didn't cry. She had stopped repeating my father's first name. When she saw me, she smiled. "Hello, Elaheh." Her voice was gentle but icy.

I would have preferred a lashing to that cold greeting. I knew I had to set things right again. I'd been way out of line. "I am so sorry and ashamed for what I said, Madar. I was wrong. Can you see that I know I was wrong?"

"Of course, I can see," she said in the same frigid manner.

"I'll set the plates," I said.

"You do that."

Her calm alarmed me. "What I said to you was rude and inaccurate and I apologize. But Homa had not one thing to do with it. It was me who said it and I am so sorry. I'll tell the school. I'll tell them I skipped classes this morning. I'll go to detention."

She looked at me dreamily. "Look how you defend her! It's astounding really. You adore her and her whole family, don't you?"

I didn't say anything.

"Go wash yourself."

"What?"

"Go wash yourself because you smell."

"The bazaar was crowded . . ."

"No, you smell like her. You smell like *gedayi*. Like poverty. It's making me want to throw up."

I backed out of the room.

"Oh, and by the way, Elaheh?"

"Yes?"

"Out of desperation is why you're friends. Nothing more. Pure desperation."

I turned around, willing my tears not to fall.

"That girl will be the death of you, you know," she called out. "The sooner you get rid of her, the better."

I walked to the kitchen. I could not drown out her voice.

SEVEN

May and June 1953

Once we'd confessed to skipping school, Khanom Tabatabayi arranged for us to attend detention. She calmly said we left her no choice. For a whole week, as the other girls played during recess, Homa and I spent the hours in a stuffy room. We were assigned to copy word for word thirty-nine pages from the history textbook into our own notebooks. I liked writing and my hand was well versed in holding a calligraphy pen. But copy work pained and bored Homa. As her fingers cramped, I reminded her under my breath that if she ever wanted to go to law school she would have to do much more rote copying. She murmured back that perhaps she should reassess her goals then and become something that didn't require so much writing, such as a washer of hair at the public *hammam* baths. For the rest of that detention period, we exchanged mutterings about random jobs that involved no writing. Sweeper of the streets. Washer of clothes. We landed on threader of eyebrows.

In those final days of fourth grade, Mrs. Tabatabayi posted the class ranks. I garnered the top position of *Shagerd Aval,* First-in-Class, with Homa's grade average earning her a close second.

At home, I proudly told my mother that our school would hold an end-of-year lunchtime crowning ceremony for all First-in-Class students from each grade. Teachers would provide nuts and feta cheese and fresh bread and *sabzi* greens for the occasion.

"*Afarin*," my mother congratulated me. "Look at you. Top of your class. I had no doubt about it, my dear. And on what day did you say they will hold this function?"

"Thursday of next week," I said. "I can ask if parents can attend."

"I wasn't planning on attending." Mother smoothed out her hair.

"Oh. I see. You don't have to."

"You won't be coming home for lunch that day then, I take it?"

"No, they're holding a feast!"

Mother smiled wanly. "*Sabzi* greens and nuts and cheese? Is that what you consider a feast?" She looked at me with great pity.

I fidgeted with my blouse. "Well, it will be fun anyway," I said, wanting suddenly to change the subject before she found more things wrong with the ceremony for which I had been so excited. "Can you believe I'll be a rising fifth grader soon, Mother?"

"Time is not in our hands," she said in a dreamy voice. "You will be altogether different after this school year." She patted my hair. "Little Elaheh. First in her class with a crown on her head."

She left the room.

While I swept the kitchen floor, I replayed her words in my mind. Since the day Mother had caught me skipping school, she'd been cold but agreeable. She had congratulated me and seemed somewhat proud that I had achieved the honor of *Shagerd Aval*, hadn't she?

When Homa had found out I was First-in-Class, she had beamed with excitement, squeezed me hard, and even lifted me off the ground by a few centimeters. And I, burdened with my own stupid personality traits, was jealous of her ability not to be jealous!

The morning of the ceremony, Miss Tabatabayi perched herself on her desk and asked us about our hopes for the summer holiday. The conversation turned to favorite summer fruits. Most girls said cantaloupe, and a few said cherries. Homa raised her hand and described how nothing beat the tart taste of the season's first sour green plums. A murmur rose, and some girls said they'd forgotten about *gojeh sabz* and now wanted to change their votes. A few arguments ensued as to the fairness of changing a vote after it had already been cast and whether sour green plums were actually even summer fruits or more related to springtime.

Mrs. Tabatabayi tried to reel us back in and declared that if we were lucky enough to have a taste of summer's bounty, we should try to preserve some fruit as jams so we could be reminded—when the cold winter wind hissed—that we once had the consolation of strawberries and the benefit of peaches.

Homa gave me a side eye at her dramatic language. "The benefit of peaches," she said in a mock-serious voice as we spilled into the yard for the lunchtime crowning ceremony. "The consolation of strawberries," I said, mimicking Mrs. Tabatabayi's didactic tone. We burst out laughing and repeated the phrases until we melted in unstoppable giggles.

Once we were all lined up, the lower-grade *Shagerd Avals* were called one by one to be crowned. When my name was announced for the fourth grade, my heart beat so fast, I was sure I would trip and fall as I went up to the row of adults standing in the front of the yard.

I bowed before our principal, Mrs. Dashti. Her soft hands grazed my forehead when she placed a blue-and-white paper crown on my head. She smelled like fenugreek and lemons. "*Afarin*, good job," she whispered, and motioned for me to face the schoolyard and take a bow as the other *Shagerd Avals* had done. I did a little curtsy and a few students yelled, "Hoorah!" and when I walked back to Homa and the group of girls I'd been standing with, blood throbbed in my ears. I had rarely felt so proud. Homa hugged me and laughed with pride as she straightened my crown.

For the rest of the ceremony, we listened and cheered as first-place students from higher grades had their turn. The mood was festive and fun. At the end, Mrs. Tabatabayi, Mrs. Dashti, and two other teachers made speeches about the necessity of studying hard over the summer so as not to forget everything we had learned that year. Mrs. Dashti said that memorizing ancient poetry—preferably verses from Saadi and Hafez—could keep our brains sharp in the oncoming heat. Would we promise her that we would memorize at least a few *ghazals* a week? We chanted yes and tried to look serious about our poetry summer projects. Then the platters of fresh naan and feta cheese and greens were brought out and set on tables in the courtyard. Mrs. Dashti stood in front of a giant container of iced cherry *sharbat* and poured out the cool, sweet drink for each girl.

"Does it get any better than this?" Homa said, stuffing her mouth with feta cheese placed in between lavash bread.

"Only memorizing *ghazals* from Hafez over the summer is better than this!" I joked.

"I'm actually going to do it," Homa said, her mouth full. "I want to learn his verses. My father is always saying his poems are perfection. They are tellers of fortune. They can determine your future."

I was familiar with the practice of asking the universe a question, opening up Hafez's book of poetry to a random page, and having whatever verse showed up become the oracle for guidance.

"Fine, I'll do it too," I said a little reluctantly.

Mrs. Dashti held up a megaphone then and announced that once we had put our plates and glasses on the main table outside, we were free to go home.

"But I thought we were still meeting for the afternoon session." I looked at Homa.

"No, weren't you paying attention? We come back Saturday for three more days and then clean out our desks and the room and that's that!" Homa ate the last of her bread and cheese and drained her cherry *sharbat* drink. "I have to go. Promised my mother I'd help with Ali Reza."

Homa's mother had given birth to a boy the previous year. Sweet Sara was now four, and Ali Reza was one year old and quite impossible. Homa's role as eldest sister meant she had a lot of babysitting duties, but I enjoyed pitching in and being part of their bustling family.

I put my plate and glass on the table and helped Homa tidy up. "Do you want me to come? My mother thinks we have a full day of school. She isn't expecting me this afternoon."

"Normally yes, but Baba has some time off, so we're all going to go to my aunt Parvin's house. I'll be making sure my sister and brother don't cause too much trouble at her place."

I was part of their family *at times*. I couldn't always be a tagalong on their big fun family outings. I knew this as a fact, and yet I felt suddenly empty. I shook it off. "*Khosh begzareh*. Have a great time."

Homa picked up her satchel. "I'll see you the day after tomorrow at school?"

"Of course. See you then. Have a good Friday holy day."

We went out the school gate and walked in opposite directions, each turning around for one last wave.

If I tell you I walked home with the crown on my head, would you believe me? I wanted to show it off. I had earned it. And I was sure I wasn't the only *Shagerd Aval* who did so. Our community lauded and celebrated being First-in-Class. I received a few "*Afarins*" from adults as I walked home and only one eye roll from a grumpy older boy.

What would my mother say? I couldn't wait to show her. I took off my shoes, went to the kitchen basin, washed my hands, and even splashed my face, careful to make sure the crown stayed straight and secure.

Over the sound of the water, I heard a slow mewling. Often alley cats looked for any scrap of food. Had a stray kitten gotten in? I walked in my socked feet to the living room, trying to see where the sound originated.

More mewling. And then a small moan.

It was coming from the bedroom. It was Mother.

This was her sound. Her voice.

The moaning grew louder. My body buzzed with worry. Who was hurting Mother? I looked around our living room for a makeshift weapon to attack the intruder who had her in his clutches. I picked up, finally, a small vase. It was one of the few things my mother had brought from our old life. A blue-and-white vase painted with intricate Persian miniatures.

The moaning morphed into cries.

There was a beggar man who shuffled through the alleys at nighttime and as I tiptoed toward the bedroom door, I imagined him with a knife to Mother's throat, threatening to kill her if she didn't give him all our money (stuffed in a valise in the bedroom—it wasn't much, but we counted it regularly).

I had to take action. I placed my hand on the doorknob, turned it, and kicked the door open.

At first, all I could see on the mattress my mother and I shared was a blur of beige, a slab of butter gone bad, a moving ledge. It took me a minute to register that what I saw was a back—a man's back. I made out the legs—long and hairy— attached to the body and a head with hair the color of night. As the ledge of beige moved up and down, forward and backward, I saw what lay underneath. It was my mother completely naked, her arms outstretched, her face an expression of ecstasy. Her cries rang out in the room and increased in frequency and volume and then crescendoed into one final *Khoda!*— a shout to God. Then she shuddered and lay still. The man on top of her trembled, gave out a deep animal-like grunt, and collapsed on top of her.

Next to the mattress lay a hat, velvet and embroidered much like the one of my long-gone father. I realized with horror that this was the hat that belonged to my father's brother—who now rolled off my mother and lay facedown on the mattress. As he rolled, I saw below his stomach an unfamiliar lump like a bee sting gone horribly wrong.

The room smelled of sweat and something feral. It was completely clear that I had intruded upon a glistening, mysterious alternate universe. The sense of leisure and contentment in Mother's limbs, her face turning to Uncle Massoud's as she kissed him on the lips when he lifted his head and then nestled into him, were all actions I couldn't understand. The combination of confusing movements and sounds and smells had me frozen. Thankfully, Uncle Massoud's back was to the door.

My mother shifted to lie on her side with a full view of the doorway where I stood. I tightened my grip on the vase and walked quietly backward. And then came the moment that would haunt me—carve itself into my psyche and make me question everything I thought I knew about Mother. One second. One second to shape a lifetime of torment.

After that I left.

I did not close the door. I worried it would make a sound.

I went back into the living room and sat on the seat cushion. The muezzin sounded out his call to prayer—a long and sensuous moan that seemed to commemorate whatever it was I had just seen transpire. Or perhaps I imagined the muezzin's call. It was the wrong time—the *namaz* should have happened at noon—it was too late to pray now. I stared at the walls. The silence in the living room stacked up onto itself until I felt I might drown under it, my head sinking in an invisible ocean. Our small, comfortable house. The school I loved close by. My friend, Homa. Her mother's stone kitchen. That deep, cavernous space. As I fought to breathe under the silence, I could feel it all flutter away.

I needed to sleep. I could not imagine doing anything else. I needed to lay my head on my pillow and close my eyes and sleep. But on the mattress where I would have lain, my mother was naked with my long-legged uncle.

What I could not fathom, as I sat trying to organize time and rearrange it and change its course and breathe instead of drowning completely, was why, as I was about to leave the room, Mother had caught my eye, brought a finger to her lips, smiled at me, and winked.

EIGHT

July 1953

My remaining days in the neighborhood were close to nil. Mother made lists of what we would take and what we'd leave behind. Of course, it would be unseemly to live with Uncle Massoud under the roof of the big house where Mother had been my father's bride, she said as she rambled about the new plans. So Uncle Massoud had purchased a new modern home in an up-and-coming neighborhood uptown—it was a beauty, she assured me. She promised that she would make sure I had a room of my own.

I did not want a room of my own. I did not want to move. I did not want to leave the neighborhood I loved, the only school I'd ever known. Above all, I did not want to leave my friend.

Uncle Massoud visited almost every day now. He was brighter and lighter than I had ever seen him, and Mother was coy and agreeable. He asked for my mother's hand in marriage two weeks after the unfortunate bedroom incident I'd witnessed. I suspected their naked adventures started that day but did not end then. The ring he placed on my mother's finger was rhombus-shaped and the color of pomegranate seeds. She liked to recite the value of this ruby.

I couldn't believe she had accepted his marriage proposal given how much she had told me she couldn't stand him. One night when Mother and I were on our shared mattress about to sleep, I mustered up the courage to ask, in as polite a way as possible, what had led to her change of heart. It still spooked me to think that Uncle Massoud had climbed on top of my mother on the very bedding she and I lay on each night. "Madar?" I whispered in the dark.

"Yes, Ellie?"

"You said yes to him."

"To whom?"

"Uncle Massoud. His proposal."

"I know," she said sleepily.

"But I thought you didn't like him," I dared to say. "You used to say he had no morals or decency."

"Who? Who did I say that about?" She sounded suddenly worried. She sat up.

"Uncle Massoud! Who else?"

"Oh!" Her voice was relieved. She sank back into the mattress.

"You always said you didn't like him."

Mother's body shifted. In the moonlight streaming in from the window, I saw that she had turned on her side and propped herself up on her elbow to face me. "Ellie," she said. "One day you will understand there are things we sacrifice for the sake of others. So that they can have a better life." She let out a big sigh, then turned her back to me.

I wanted to ask more questions. Had she accepted Uncle Massoud's proposal because of me? But I already had a good life. Right in that neighborhood!

A soft breeze wafted in from the crack we kept open in the window. It cooled my cheeks and moved through my hair. Every night I begged Mother to keep the window open a bit so air could come in and every night Mother worried that the smallest crack would mean thieves intruding, men invading, strangers abducting us. If we moved back to a section of town where beggars didn't roam the alleys, would her heart be less troubled?

I grew to think it must have been my mother's plan from the day she discovered I'd skipped school and gone to the bazaar with Homa. Not long after that fateful day came Mother's arms outstretched on the mattress, her engagement to Uncle Massoud, the pomegranate-colored ring. It all made sense now. Her inscrutable calm after my rude outburst when she confronted me about the bazaar outing. Her lack of punishment. Mother secured our ticket out of that part of town by agreeing to marry my uncle. Had she made the first advance? I would never know. Their afternoon in bed didn't seem like it had occurred against her will. I remembered her winking at me from the mattress as I backed out of the room. As if we were in on this plan together. As if it were our shared scheme to have her give in to Uncle Massoud so we could leave the neighborhood I so cherished.

I walked past the *joob* ditches filled with murky water that lined the streets, past the beet-seller's cry for people to buy from his cart. Summer had sunk in; the air was hot and so dry it felt my bones would crack under the weight of Mother's words. *These friendships come and go, Elaheh. These things don't last.*

I arrived in the courtyard of her home holding my goodbye gift: a dark pink notebook in which I had pressed some flowers and written my new address. The flowers had dried and flattened and were matted to the pages. I would tell Homa she could use the pages to write letters to me or take law school lecture notes one day. Even for our goodbye, for this last meeting in person (for how long? I hated not knowing), Mother would not allow Homa to come to our house.

It was afternoon teatime when I came through the gate. Seated by the *hoz* pond was Homa's father, cross-legged on a kilim rug. His pants were black and he had on a white shirt. His glasses shone in the sparkling sun of the courtyard. In his hand was an hour-shaped glass filled with tea that was perfectly amber in the sun's rays. Next to him sat Homa's mother, Monir Khanom, her hair in the characteristic long braid, her face rosy, Ali Reza in a basket by her. Sara stood perched on the ledge of the *hoz* pond, feeding the fish. She wore a ruffled pink skirt. She had on her father's slippers, and they looked ridiculously large on her bare feet. I wondered what it felt like to have your feet swimming in your father's shoes. To know you stood in the well-worn soles of a figure whose largeness grounded you. When I was Sara's age, had I slid into my father's slippers and staggered around, feeling at once silly and perfectly protected by his shoes on my feet?

Homa walked out of the house holding a plate. She ran over when she saw me.

"You'll spill the dates and cookies!" her mother shouted. But Homa balanced the plate precariously in the air and hugged me.

I looked past her shoulder at her family on the rug. Monir Khanom lifted the white teapot etched with the familiar pink roses. I had first seen that teapot in Homa's kitchen the day we played our inaugural hopscotch game. The baby, Ali Reza, babbled in a language all his own. Sara continued to feed the fish. Homa's father got up and greeted me politely, saying I should take his place and sit down and join the family for tea.

I wanted to preserve that moment. I wanted to slip onto the rug and nestle in between them all. I wanted their safety, their kindness, to engulf me. Perhaps my mother could go with Uncle Massoud to the new place about which they were both so excited and I could stay here. I would clean the floor of Homa's house and I would help cook every day in the stone kitchen and I would sleep on a mat rolled in the corner of the seven steps and I would not be a bother. I wanted to stay. I did not want to say goodbye.

I stuffed away those fantasies and insisted that Homa's father keep his seat on the kilim rug and that I was happy to stand and would soon be on my way, and of course he engaged in *tarof* right back and said no, please sit, have tea, stay for dinner even, and eventually after our requisite back-and-forth I walked to the rug. But even as I did, as Homa chatted next to me and her father guided me gently, as I sat down and took from Homa's mother an *estekan* of tea, I was memorizing the scene.

In my new life uptown, this moment would sustain me. I already missed this family even though I was right here with them. But how could I miss what was never truly mine? I knew that soon, sitting uptown with my mother and Uncle Massoud, in an alien neighborhood filled with wealth and glamour and people of means and education who enjoyed cafés and cinemas and dances, there would be a part of me (all of me) that would want nothing more than to be here, in this courtyard, with this family with the baby in a basket and Sara hopping around and Homa talking nonstop.

"Before you have your tea, I want to show you something," Homa said. "I was going to give it to you when we . . . you know . . . at the end. But you have to see it."

"Let the poor girl eat and drink first," Monir Khanom said. "You're always rushing."

"Elaheh hasn't even had her dates or chickpea cookies yet," her father said.

I had indeed not yet bitten into any of the fat dates on the plate Homa had brought out. I had not touched the chickpea cookies.

But Homa bent down, put the plate on the rug, then fished into her pocket and brought out a tiny red pouch. "Here," she said. "I got this for you." She placed it in the palm of my hand.

The pouch was light and thin, almost transparent. The breeze from the trees in the courtyard lifted Homa's curls. I had envisioned giving my friend her notebook at the very end of the visit when we said goodbye alone outside the gate. I hadn't expected this.

"Open it!" Homa jumped a little as she said it.

I stuck my finger in and felt something metallic. I turned the pouch upside down onto my palm. Out spilled a gold chain. Attached to the chain was a gold-colored charm of a bird in profile. Its beak was curved with a sharp end point. Its wing was wide and painted turquoise blue. The charm was tiny and delicate, but the expression of the bird was etched out in fine detail. It looked fierce.

"Homa," I whispered, my throat tight.

"That's what it is!" she said. "I figured if you couldn't have me, you could have my namesake."

I looked up. She grinned, though her eyes were filled with a new sadness.

I moved my braids slightly as I put on the necklace and clasped it behind my neck. The bird charm nestled perfectly in the dip between my clavicles.

"The chain isn't real gold," Monir Khanom said apologetically. "None of it is."

"It's beautiful," I said. "I will miss you so much." I looked around at the family. "All of you."

"We're not dying. We'll still be in the same city! Come on, let's eat." Homa sat down next to me. "*Sheekamoo.*" She poked me, using my nickname to lighten the mood. I hugged her. Her mother moved over so we'd all fit and handed Homa an *estekan* of tea. Ali Reza babbled. Sara walked over, squeezed herself next to me on the rug, and nuzzled her face into my shoulder. Homa's father went to the edge of the *hoz* pond and looked into it.

When I gave Homa the notebook, she said she loved it. Said the pressed flowers were genius. Told me she would definitely use it to take notes about all the laws—she stopped and looked at her father—that she wanted to change. Her father shook his head, but not in disgust or dismissal. He shook his head as though he could not believe his good fortune to have such a trailblazer for a girl. I gulped my tea. I told Monir Khanom that the dates and chickpea cookies were delicious. I ignored Ali Reza's loud burp and let Sara re-braid a section of my hair. Homa could not stop talking.

When I said goodbye, I said goodbye to all of them.

"We will visit," Homa said.

"Of course," I said. "And we'll write letters. I put my new address in the notebook."

"Good. Don't forget us!" she said.

"I never could."

"Wear the necklace!"

"Always. I promise."

"I love you madly!" she called out.

When I stepped out of their courtyard and closed the gate and walked through the alley, it felt like someone had hollowed my insides and tipped out everything in me. I was weak. Empty. I realized with each step back to my own house that I was leaving home. Their home. My second home. A lump lodged in my throat and my eyes burned with tears. I put my hand on my neck and touched the bird charm. I traced its contour and memorized the rise and shape of it. Until every delicate edge dug into the pads of my fingers and left their mark.

Part Two

NINE

Late Summer 1960

"Stop saying his name!" I said to Niloo and Sousan as the three of us walked to Café Andre for sandwiches. But I couldn't stop laughing.

"Get used to it, Elaheh Joon," Sousan said. "He's in love with you and we all know it."

"May you get married soon and have a half-dozen children who live long lives and stay healthy and strong." Niloo poked me in the side.

"He hasn't said a word about a wedding," I said. I turned my head dramatically, loving the weight of my beehive like a crown on my head.

It was the last week of summer, and I wanted to gorge on every bit of fun before school began and we entered twelfth grade. I could already taste Andre's famous *salad olivier* sandwich: the chopped chicken-potato-egg-carrot-peas-and-pickles in rich lemony mayonnaise. Andre made the best sandwiches in all of Tehran.

We'd have a tough academic year ahead with university entrance exams and all of that. But for now, we could have one delicious day of eating sandwiches in the café where I'd first seen Mehrdad.

"Everyone would kill to have Mehrdad be their beau," Niloo said.

His lanky body made my breath catch. His dark, wavy hair parted down the middle. That sleek, angular nose. The big hazel eyes behind tortoiseshell glasses.

Niloo continued her pronouncement. "You're the luckiest princess, Ela-heh. You even look like Queen Farah."

"Of course she looks like the queen. She's descended from royalty," Sousan said.

"Yes, but she's not related to *this* current royal family," Niloo said.

"She's still royalty!" Sousan said.

Niloo looked at me. "What I would give to be you, Ellie Joon."

Her compliment thrilled me—Mother's views on the evil eye be damned. "Your eyes are beautiful, so they see beauty," I said, reciting one of the old Persian *tarof* sayings. "Did you buy the kohl?"

"Yes, I can make wing-shaped eyes for you, Ellie Joon," Niloo said proudly.

"No offense, but maybe I should draw out her eyes?" Sousan said. "My hand is a bit more steady." Sousan clasped my arm. "And if you borrow your mother's sunglasses, *vay o vay!* You will be the talk of this town."

"As if she isn't already," Niloo sighed.

Sousan looped her arm through mine. Niloo followed suit. I walked the rest of the way to Café Andre flanked by my friends.

The life I had known as a child with a girl named Homa playing hopscotch in the alleys and cooking with her mother felt as though it had happened in a place I could now barely fathom. At seventeen, I was popular. I had suc-cessfully ascended to an enviable status at school. Sousan and Niloo were my closest friends, but just about any girl in all of Reza Shah Kabir High School would have wanted to be part of my social circle. I had become a mini queen.

When we first moved away from the neighborhood downtown and I walked through the vast, echo-filled new mansion with its white walls and glistening chandeliers, the lump that had lodged in my throat the day I said goodbye to Homa lingered. The lump remained as I helped my mother decorate the rooms. It was still there as our country jolted through the coup d'état on August 19, 1953, that ousted our democratically elected prime minister and solidified the power of the Shah.

In the weeks leading up to the coup, when I had gone shopping with Mother for new house items, we frequently had to scurry away to escape loud, potentially dangerous demonstrations.

Uncle Massoud knew my mother was the descendant of the Qajar kings and that the Shah's Pahlavi family had dethroned her Qajar family. Mother was not a fan of this Shah. But we were nothing if not practical in that huge new mansion of ours. Mother had too much to lose by being overtly political or sentimental.

Mother said the country had become divided into three political factions: monarchist, communist, and pro–Prime Minister Mossadegh. She taught me to not say anything that would rock the boat. She told me those who risked their lives in the streets because of allegiance to the prime minister were taking foolhardy risks. She recommended that I look out for myself and not get caught up in ideology. She did not want politics to dirty our future.

One August day, after waking up from our afternoon siesta, Uncle Massoud turned on the radio and there came a crackling sound and then blaring music, followed by the announcement that Prime Minister Mossadegh had been toppled.

It felt like more than just coincidence that a coup creating chaotic upheaval in the fortunes of our nation happened so shortly after my parting with Homa. I saw it as a sign that our separation had rendered cataclysmic change. And I worried for her family. Many communists had been arrested or killed during the coup. I prayed that Homa's father had not gotten mixed up with the demonstrations. I scanned Uncle Massoud's newspaper searching for her father's name—hoping not to see him in a list of the dead.

"My dear girl, they wouldn't list the ones they themselves killed," Uncle Massoud said when I told him I was worried for my old friend's father. "The newspapers are mostly entirely pro-Shah these days. Of course, many people are saying the British and Americans are behind this coup." He sighed. "But you, my dear girl. You need to keep your mouth tightly zipped and to be careful. Never say anything that isn't praiseworthy of the Shah. There are spies everywhere."

Mother added, "This world is filled with liars and scoundrels who will do anything to take advantage of you. Don't let them. Don't let people take what is yours. Put yourself first. Promise me."

I promised so that she'd stop lecturing more than anything else. But like the embers of a fire, her words nestled into the crevices of my body. I internalized them and grew to believe that I needed to protect what was rightfully mine. Why shouldn't I have it all? I deserved the best.

I was ten when I had clasped Homa's gift of the bird charm necklace around my neck. On that very day, Mother told me to remove the necklace. She didn't like it. It's not even real gold, she said. *My God, it's a cheap chain; how could they not be ashamed to give you this piece of junk?*

I didn't take off the necklace. It came with me when we moved and it was still around my neck when we decorated our new house with ornate furniture. As our country collapsed under the coup, the charm remained on my throat right near the lump lodged there. I wore the necklace as I fought nausea on the first day in a new school with strange girls who were all gussied up and knew one another. The necklace was there as I longed for my friend during those initial homesick weeks when I would have given anything for a poke or jab or delightful rant from Homa. I missed her terribly and cried at night, wishing I were back where I belonged with my old teachers and Mrs. Tabatabayi and the girls from downtown and the life I had known.

But slowly, my new reality transfixed me. The fancy school: the prestigious teachers, glamorous girls, the constant flow of exciting frontiers. Mother's words. I couldn't be homesick forever. I had to survive. After mourning the loss of my old school and Homa for quite some time, I observed and adapted and worked hard to become a girl who fit in. And who soared to the top of the social circles.

Puberty helped, surprisingly. It changed me from the chubby, somewhat plain child I had been into a new girl who attracted glances. I became what was known as *khoshgel*, pretty. I realized people were shallow and easy to sway—they treated me so differently based on how I looked. It did not seem fair. But I could feel my stock rise.

And I got sucked in. By the time I was in high school, "pretty" wasn't even the word used—they called me *ziba*, beautiful. I carried my head high and allowed the adoration of my friends—Niloo, Sousan, all the rest of them—to inflate my ego. The boys in town would not stop pestering me. I had a grasp of their desire—how could I ignore it? I could sense a few girls stuck on me too. I became an expert at using what I had to get what I wanted. I was coy, subtly flirtatious without dishonoring Mother or Uncle Massoud. The admiration created confidence and the confidence allowed me to do almost as I pleased in my rarefied bourgeois world.

The necklace came off somewhere around seventh grade, three years after I'd first received it. I felt a flash of guilt at dishonoring my promise to Homa to always wear it. But we had been children when we made that promise. She had probably long forgotten about me. I convinced myself it was silly to be beholden to a childish pact. I placed the necklace back in its pouch and tucked it away in a jewelry box next to actual gold bangles and chains and shiny gems on rings that Uncle Massoud and Mother had given me.

After the fall of our prime minister during the coup d'état, my uncle simply swallowed the new reality and used his skills to further his career as an administrative official working for an oil company. Uncle Massoud's practicality and savvy meant he did not cave in to principles or anguish, but instead continued to build wealth in a methodical, steady way.

I had thought Mother's life with him was a business arrangement. I thought she had agreed to marry him solely so she could take me away from that neighborhood and from Homa.

But when Mother stroked Uncle Massoud's cheek after breakfast as the sun streamed into our large, bright kitchen, when she put his lamb's-wool hat on his head with a chuckle and he playfully patted her bottom, when I heard them whisper to one another in that intimate way adults had during moments where they thought children weren't around, I began to wonder. Maybe they actually liked or even loved one another.

I loathed to think about it. But I did think about Homa. I missed her so much.

We did write. At first. Letters from Homa arrived by mail on the pages of the notebook I had given her: the pressed flowers stuck to the dried ink of her familiar script. I wrote back on onionskin paper I snatched from Uncle Massoud's study. In those early months after the move, Homa's letters drove me to tears.

Did we see each other? In the beginning. Twice. Painstakingly arranged by her parents. But how does a ten-year-old travel downtown on her own? I had trouble making it happen. And of course it was with shame that I had to talk to Homa and her parents outside the high stone walls of our mansion, because my mother barely permitted the visit and certainly didn't invite them in. We spoke and hugged and giggled like old times. And on Homa's second visit, we spoke and hugged awkwardly and did not giggle during the stilted pauses.

And then. We lost touch.

Our bond should have been impossible to fray and then disintegrate. But as time took us each in a different direction, it was astonishingly simple for our connection to dissolve.

The girls in my high school hosted parties at their parents' homes where food was abundant, songs played on gramophones, and futures were planned with boldness. At those gatherings, we traded photo cards of American movie stars. We discussed skirts that were mini and how we would wear them. All around me, girls wore the latest fashions from Europe. Their hair was coiffed and piled high—not covered in hijab. The families in my new neighborhood and school were not—for the most part—very religious. Some of our grandmothers may have been. But we were girls on the forefront of a new Iran. The Shah wanted to modernize the country, which some complained meant to westernize it. In our circles, religion was shed. And I came from a secular family to begin with; we didn't practice.

I found it impossible to resist the glossy glamour available to me. What could I do but give in to Mother's world?

I was no longer the girl who had come uptown with a bird charm balanced over the lump in her throat. I was Elaheh Ziba, Ellie the Beauty, Ellie the Queen.

I was someone entirely new and exhausting.

Friends come and go, don't they? Life goes on.

TEN

Spring 1960

A strange longing now consumed my days: an ever-present anticipation, an unremitting, newfangled desire.

For I had fallen for a boy.

I first noticed him during a lunch break back in eleventh grade at Café Andre. Girls and boys from nearby high schools had poured into the famed eatery to grab sandwiches and drinks. It was a few days before the Nowruz spring holidays and the café hummed with excitement for the upcoming school vacation. I'd already ordered and gotten my *salad olivier* sandwich, my favorite. I waited near the wall to the right side of the queue for Niloo to get her food.

That's when I saw him.

He was in line to order. He looked to be about my age and wore a short-sleeved white shirt and dark pants. His thick, wavy hair was parted down the middle. This intrigued me because most boys I knew parted their hair to the side. On his angular nose rested round tortoiseshell glasses. Nothing about him was all that remarkable. Nothing at all, you could say. And yet, there was something about the way he stood: feet apart, head tilted back so he could study the sign above the café counter, hands casually on his hips. His stance was wholly unfussed and unbothered. As though he did not feel rushed or ruffled by the jostling and the hustling around him.

What strange ease this boy had! Slightly audacious, really.

Then, as if he knew I'd been staring, he turned and looked me straight in the eye. And smiled.

He didn't have the big tobacco-stained teeth of Sousan's beau, the Colonel. Nor did he have the gleaming white grin of American movie stars. His smile wasn't flashy at all. But in that moment, amid the chaos and hubbub of everyone else around us in the café, I sensed in his face a world of kindness.

I should have looked down, embarrassed to have been caught staring. Or looked away, all haughty and proud. After all, didn't I have boys from different schools buzzing around me whenever they could?

But I didn't look down. And I didn't look away. I stared right back at him and found my mouth breaking into a goofy, silly smile. Warmth spread across my chest, up my neck, and throughout my face. When he ran a hand through his hair and looked down shyly, my every molecule melted.

"Come on, Ellie!" Niloo grabbed my arm and led me out of the sandwich shop. "Let's eat!"

For days I replayed in my mind that moment in Café Andre. Why had he smiled at me like that? Why did I care? He was just another boy. And not even the most handsome one at that! For all I knew, I'd never see him again.

It was spring that did it. Spring and the country's celebration of it. At the exact moment of the vernal equinox, when the sun is above the equator and winter officially turns to spring, the New Year begins. For the moment of Sal Tahvil, the official arrival of Nowruz, our Iranian new year, Mother, Uncle Massoud, and I stood around a Haft Seen table laden with objects beginning with the letter "S" that symbolized rebirth, renewal, and good fortune. We had cleaned our homes for weeks leading up to spring and wore all-new clothes for the first day. We jumped up and down around the Haft Seen table at the moment it became spring, kissed one another, and read verses from ancient poetry and the Koran. One of the "S" items on our table was the *sabzeh* I had prepared. I'd soaked lentils on a plate about two weeks before Nowruz and watered the lentil seeds each day until they grew tiny sprouts. I'd watched with wonder as the sprouts extended over days into stalks of green. By Nowruz, the lentils had transformed into a lush round batch of grass-like blades. Renewal. Rebirth.

For the following thirteen days after the New Year, we visited relatives and friends in the tradition of *deed o bazdeed*—to see and see again our loved ones. On the thirteenth day, we went on a huge picnic for Sizdah Bedar, to get out of the house for the unlucky thirteen. Mother made sure I brought the plate of *sabzeh* with us.

A little over two weeks after I had first seen Mehrdad in Café Andre, Mother, Uncle Massoud, and I packed our car with a picnic basket filled with fresh *sabzi kuku,* fried *kotelet* meat patties, bread, radishes, New Year pastries, and a huge thermos of hot tea for our Sizdah Bedar picnic. Uncle Massoud also piled the trunk with small rugs we used to sit on and his favorite backgammon set. The drive out of the city was scenic and bumpy. Tons of other cars made the same exodus. Buses practically spilled with people headed to parks and nature.

Once we finally arrived at our favorite green spot under a cluster of trees near the Karaj River, we set up camp. We laid out the rugs, brought out the food, chatted and ate. All around us, other families did the same. Some men grilled meat on charcoal braziers. Women balanced teapots on samovars they had set up. Children kicked balls around and ran and screeched with delight. The fragrant country air mixed in with the smoke from the grills. Lobed leaves on the sycamore trees stirred in the breeze. I had worn my new blush-colored knee-length skirt. It wasn't practical for sitting on a rug, but it was a gift from Mother and I was too enamored with its soft cotton to pass it up for the occasion.

After lunch, some people lay their heads on the rugs or blankets they had brought and dozed off for an afternoon nap. Others walked off in groups to enjoy the nearby groves. Children continued to play and run.

Mother encouraged me to take the *sabzeh* I had grown, knot the blades, wish for a husband, and throw it into the river so my wish would come true—as tradition dictated. When she got up to walk me to the river, I begged her not to accompany me. I would do it alone, I said, muttering under my breath about her obsession with superstition. Luckily, she didn't hear me muttering and agreed. She lay down to nap on the rug under the trees.

I willed myself and my full belly to get up.

I followed the sound of the babbling river. I didn't feel the need for a husband *just yet*, but I also didn't want to jinx myself by dismissing a good-luck tradition. When I reached the riverbank and could see the small stones at the bottom of the clear water, I knelt down and dutifully knotted a few of the blades of *sabzeh* grass together. I was about to let the whole collection of green blades slide off the plate and fall into the water when a voice said, "I wouldn't have predicted you to be superstitious."

I turned around.

A few feet from where I knelt, a boy's lanky body leaned against a large sycamore tree. He wore a white shirt and dark gray pants. His arms were folded across his chest.

I squinted.

It was the boy from Café Andre. All my senses heightened and my stomach did a somersault. His voice was certainly deeper than I'd imagined it to be.

"I'm not," I said, trying to sound sure of myself. "Superstitious."

"*Velesh kon.* Drop it."

I looked up at him, surprised. Was he doubting the truth of what I said?

He must have noticed my confusion because he quickly followed up with, "I mean the *sabzeh*. Let it go. Into the river. Nature back to nature. It is Sizdah Bedar, after all."

He left his position against the tree trunk and came over and knelt next to me. We were eye-level with one another. He smelled like citrus. His eyes behind the glasses were a light hazel.

I held my breath even as my pulse raced.

"Go ahead," he said.

I carefully lifted the *sabzeh* plate and tossed the green blades into the river. Then I put the plate down next to me with a shaky hand. I had never been this physically close to a boy. If I knelt next to him for a moment longer, I might jump out of my skin. I felt so nervous, I thought I might topple over into the water and be washed away downstream the way my *sabzeh* blades were now floating down the river.

I stood up.

He looked at me, still kneeling. "I'm Mehrdad Tavakoli," he said. "I'm fortunate to meet you."

"Elaheh Soltani," I said.

A sweet wind blew. The air by the river smelled of wildflowers and fresh soil. My skirt billowed out in the breeze for a few seconds and then fluttered against my legs. Droplets from the river hung for a brief moment in the air.

He got up and faced me. We were no longer in a crowded café with fellow students jostling all around us. There was no hubbub and commotion. There was only the burbling of the water in the river and the call of birds in the branches.

"You love the *salad olivier* sandwich, don't you?" His voice caught as he spoke.

I must have looked puzzled, because he reddened and said, "I just saw you order one at Café Andre the other day, that's all. I'm not a spy or a fortune teller!"

I couldn't help but giggle. "What school do you go to?"

"Alborz High School."

"I go to Reza Shah Kabir."

"What grade?"

"Eleventh. You?"

"Me too."

We might have continued like that on the riverbank, an arm's length away from each other, careful yet eager in our conversation. The earthy scent all around us carried the promise of renewal and rebirth. I wanted to keep talking. I wanted to know more. Even though my heart beat far too fast, I did not want to leave.

Suddenly there was a loud swoosh of water.

We both turned in its direction.

Emerging from the stone-bedded river rose a female figure. She marched out of the water and came up to us. Short and stout, in a navy-blue bathing suit with a large crocheted daisy on her chest, the woman walked right up to Mehrdad. "Oh, hello, dear!" she said. Rivulets of water trickled down her body from her wet hair.

Mehrdad's face was beet red.

I stood transfixed and bewildered.

"Maman, you shouldn't swim alone. It could be dangerous," Mehrdad said.

"Oh, I can assure you a dip in this refreshing river is nothing to worry about." She swiveled to face me. "And who do we have here?"

"Um . . ." Mehrdad cleared his throat. "Maman Joon, this is Elaheh Soltani and she . . . she attends Reza Shah Kabir High School."

"It's lovely to meet you," Mehrdad's mother said. She squeezed water out of her hair with both hands as she looked at me. She had the same hazel-colored eyes as Mehrdad. In the shimmering sun, strands of gray glittered in her hair. They reminded me of the strong silver threads that ran through the best embroidered *termeh* wall hangings.

"It's beautiful here, isn't it?" she asked.

I nodded yes. I didn't know what to say. This middle-aged woman emerging from the water like a happy mermaid. Just casually enjoying the cool river. My mother would have worried about bacteria, drowning, about her body being carried away by sudden currents and thrown against jagged rocks. Not to mention that Mother wouldn't want to be seen by strangers in a bathing suit.

Mehrdad's mother continued to squeeze her hair. "You should take a swim," she said.

"Oh, that's alright," I mumbled. "I . . . I didn't bring a bathing suit."

She looked at me, then at Mehrdad, then at the sky. "It is beautiful here," she said softly. "I should go dry off. You two continue your conversation."

"We were just throwing the *sabzeh* in the river," I said as she walked away.

She waved a hand above her head as if to stave off any explanation I might feel obliged to make. Then she disappeared into the thicket of trees.

Mehrdad took a deep breath. "So, you met my mother," he said.

"I did! She's a swimmer!" was all I could think to say.

He shrugged and smiled. That smile that carried all the kindness.

"She's right about one thing," he said as he looked straight into my eyes. "It is beautiful here, and of that there is no doubt."

ELEVEN

September 1960

On the corner of Hafez Avenue and France Street, not far from the prestigious Alborz High School for boys, was Reza Shah Kabir High School for girls, grades seven to twelve. It was a building replete with pillars, wide staircases, and an entrance adorned with stunning tile work.

Those of us who had the privilege of attending this competitive and coveted school did not take lightly the expectation placed on us to excel. While some of us may have been consumed by fashion and romance (I was one of the worst offenders), we were also constantly reminded of our exceptional educational resources and why we could never take our opportunities for granted.

By the time I started twelfth grade, the prospect of university loomed large. I had been encouraged to dream big—Uncle Massoud proved to be a fair-minded, hardworking stepfather who was progressive and open-minded when it came to a woman's right to education. He wanted me to sit for the university exams. But Mother was of two hearts. Her priority was my ascent to the top of Tehran's elite social circles. Marriage to a man of the best pedigree, not university, might help me leapfrog ahead, she said. Net someone, she encouraged. The sooner the better.

"Net someone?" I asked.

"Yes, like a catcher uses a net to trap a butterfly. This Mehrdad boy you met at the Sizdah Bedar picnic? He seems to be a good sort. Comes from a good family. Don't let him slip away, Ellie. Capture him."

Mehrdad had given me his phone number that day of the picnic. We'd seen one another at Café Andre every now and then since and increasingly at social gatherings at people's homes where both girls and boys were invited. When Mother learned that Mehrdad attended Alborz High School, one of the country's best schools for boys, whose students tended to be confident and studious and most of whom were descendants of "established" families, she advocated for him all the way.

"Mother, I am not going to 'capture' anyone. It is 1960. Women don't need to marry to get ahead."

"Please, Elaheh," she sniffed. "Things haven't changed as much as you think. Wait too long and you'll become sour and pickled—*torshideh*. Already the blush of youth is evaporating from your face. I'm worried you've reached your peak."

When she said things like that, insecurities that I had willfully pushed down over the years bubbled up again. Was my beauty fleeting—the way she believed? Would Sousan and Niloo drop me if I was no longer attractive? Would Mehrdad? I wanted to think he wouldn't. Afarin certainly would.

Afarin Molavi was the true queen bee of our school and I coveted her approval. Even her name meant "Well done!" or "Bravo!" A distant niece of the Shah's, Afarin was judgmental, very rich, preciously pretty, supremely sweet when she wanted to be—and when she didn't, completely ruthless. Afarin's opinion mattered to others. Teachers kowtowed to her. Students looked up to her. Everyone wanted either to be her or to get something from her.

Maneuvering up the social ladder, I had cultivated my own brand of charm, mastered whom to impress and whom to ignore. But I still compared my every move and achievement to Afarin's.

I made a list.

For looks, we were on somewhat similar ground. For wealth, there was no contest—her family was steeped in mounds of money. Grade-wise, we had been toe-to-toe for much of our time at Reza Shah Kabir High School.

It's not that I wanted Afarin's clothes (though some of her frocks were made in Paris and flown into Tehran) or her lipstick (outside the school gates, she'd whip out a gold tube and swivel up creamy crimson, her mouth in the shape of a zero as she applied it expertly), or her hair (everyone said I had the best hair).

What I wanted was Afarin's power.

So it was that on a Tuesday early on in our twelfth-grade year, I hung up my coat on the racks at the back of Mrs. Roshanfekr's literature classroom. Each desk had an attached bench seat for two students, and as luck and the gods of anxiety and mockery would have it, my assigned seat in this class was next to Afarin. I slid onto our shared bench and said hello. She gave me an imperceptible nod—an acknowledgment of my presence without looking in my direction. She smelled expensive (how I longed to know the name of her perfume—or was it some fancy soap?). Her notebook was already out on the desk. She sat straight as a rod, ready for action. I got out my notebook and newly sharpened pencil and prepared myself for our teacher's monotone voice.

Mrs. Roshanfekr loved to surprise us with quizzes or occasionally cold-call on us for interpretation of an ancient poem. Hers was one of the most difficult classes. Afarin shone in it. The week before, Afarin had raised her hand and rattled off verse after verse of an ancient Saadi poem. Her performance had made Mrs. Roshanfekr practically melt with delight and yell, "Afarin!" I didn't know if she was calling out her name or saying, "Bravo!" Just by saying her name, "Afarin," we were also praising her!

When Mrs. Roshanfekr came in from the special teacher's door at the front of the room, we all immediately stood in respect. The green board behind her was blank—ready for chalked-on verses and points of history, theology, and poetry.

I poised my pencil above my notebook, prepared to copy whatever she would write. If called upon, I would share my notes about poetry's role in shaping the conscience of the country. I had painstakingly memorized forty-two verses to impress our teacher and one-up Afarin.

The other students chatted as they got out their notebooks.

"*Saket, saket!* Quiet, quiet! Girls, I have two important announcements," Mrs. Roshanfekr said. Her pleated skirt matched the color of the green board, and her lips, lined in burgundy, made her look like she had just sucked on a cherry Popsicle. "*Avalan*, first of all, we are having our inaugural test next Monday morning."

A communal groan rose. Sousan turned from her seat in the front and gave me a look of despair. I could sense Niloo, who sat next to Sousan in the two-seat bench, vibrate with worry. Niloo hated Mrs. Roshanfekr's class more than anything. Afarin perked up even straighter as if receiving exciting news.

"*Saket, saket!* Please be quiet!" Mrs. Roshanfekr said again. "Those of you who have been working hard and keeping on top of the material should have no problem at all."

Afarin looked around the room with pride, as if she had been singled out. Niloo covered her face with her hands and slouched lower in her seat.

"*Dovoman*, secondly," Mrs. Roshanfekr said, "we have a new student joining us this year." She craned her neck toward the back of the classroom. "Come in, don't be shy!"

Now, *this* was an announcement. The hell with the test! Our school was not easy to get into and we rarely had new students. Bodies shifted in seats and pencils dropped onto the wooden desks as we all turned to follow the teacher's gaze. I scanned the back of the room but only saw the familiar faces of girls I had known since seventh grade.

As though emerging suddenly from the coat racks, a head of dark curly hair appeared. Attached to it was a body long and lean, and a tan face. In the expression of the dark eyes was initial hesitancy but also a fierce defensiveness and strange confidence. I sucked in my breath. Small black dots, like those that appear in one's vision after a fall, flashed in front of me. My stomach fluttered as though I had hit a bump while speeding in a car. The other girls murmured. Someone coughed.

For it was she: Homa from the neighborhood downtown, the girl whom I had first called friend, all grown-up, tall and lanky, inserted into our classroom like a bird who'd flown in by mistake from the wild.

It had been seven years since we'd seen each other. We had discontinued writing after our first few letters and those two initial visits and had had no phone calls since then.

"Girls, I would like you to welcome to our school our new student, Homa Roozbeh."

I tried not to stop breathing.

I'm sure Niloo put on her most welcoming face. The kind ones would make this stranger feel welcome, the snobs would avert their eyes and look bored, and I——I felt immersed in a tank of water cold enough to freeze my organs.

Homa walked right by me as Mrs. Roshanfekr pointed to an empty seat on the bench opposite Niloo and Sousan's. Anybody else would have slipped into the seat quietly and blended in. But Homa made her way straight to the front of the room and up to the teacher's stage. No one went to the front of the class without being asked to do so. Least of all a brand-new student!

"I'm very happy to be here," Homa said loudly. She looked out at all of us as if she were an assistant teacher or even the principal. The audacity! It stunned. "I am so fortunate to be at Reza Shah Kabir High School—it has been a dream of mine to attend, and hey, I made it before graduation, right?"

Her voice was the same. It carried the same timbre of outlandish confidence and clarity. Was she cracking a joke? The girls sat in silence, their mouths practically open.

Afarin's hand flew to her mouth to cover a giggle.

Mrs. Roshanfekr stood like a statue on the stage. The familiar glimmer of impatience on her face hardened into a look of forced tolerance mixed with pity. The school prided itself on being open to students from all socio-economic backgrounds. Homa had clearly—somehow—been accepted to demonstrate commitment to the poorer classes. Mrs. Roshanfekr would feel like a better person for putting up with the uncouth ways of a *dahati* peasant.

I felt a rush of panic. Homa was my past. My two worlds were not supposed to collide.

As Homa continued to talk—rambling on about how sorry she was to be late to class—part of me wanted to calmly take her arm, lead her to her seat, and teach her the ways of this rarefied new world, in which I held all kinds of hope for an ambitious future.

Just as I tuned back in, I caught the end of Homa's little introductory speech: ". . . And that is why I am so happy to be here in this school with my dear and bestest friend in all of the world: Elaheh Soltani!"

Afarin stared at me, her expression one of shock mixed with amusement.

I could not move.

"Elaheh Joon, *salaam!*" Homa waved frantically. "I'm so thrilled to be back with you, *doost-e aziz*, dear friend!" She puffed out her chest as though she'd won the highest accolades in the kingdom.

Afarin's shoulders shook. Her laughter bubbled up and out.

Homa continued to wave at me, her smile wide, her eyes shining.

I raised my hand, but it was made of lead. The wave I produced was perhaps the weakest excuse for a greeting ever attempted.

Afarin's snickers then broke free and rippled through the room. Once Afarin let it out, several of the other girls followed suit. Soon, the class was having a full-on laughing fit.

My protective urges melted into embarrassment.

"My good friend!" Homa declared before finally making her way to the empty chair Mrs. Roshanfekr had pointed out for her ten thousand years ago.

Mrs. Roshanfekr sighed the sigh of an elite who had quickly tired of her charity. "*Kheyle-khob*, fine, let's not waste our entire time on declarations of affection. We welcome our student, but learning awaits." She grabbed a piece of chalk and wrote on the board. Others picked up their pencils as they wiped at their eyes, a few snort-laughs hiccuping throughout the room.

I looked down at my notebook. My face burned. It would take weeks to undo the damage done this morning to my reputation. Why was this happening?

Even with my head bent and my face hot, from the corner of my eye, I saw Homa take a notebook and pencil case out of her bag and place them on top of her desk.

I had to look up to be sure I had seen correctly.

Her notebook had a faded pink cover. It was the one I had given her when we were ten. The pressed flowers inside must have been a hundred times dead now.

Homa turned around, held the notebook up in the air like a trophy, and gave me a huge smile.

More hands flew to mouths and a few girls shook with new chuckles. Mrs. Roshanfekr did not hear or pretended not to—she scrawled rapidly and loudly across the board.

Here was my old friend, my dear friend. I should have been elated and welcoming.

I held my pencil. I proceeded to write. And I ignored Homa.

At lunchtime in the schoolyard, Niloo said she'd been looking forward to the *kalbas* sandwich at Café Andre's all morning. She said the announcement about the upcoming test had made her anxious and extra ravenous. She couldn't wait to bite into the baguette. Sousan rolled her eyes and told Niloo not to overreact; it was just a silly test.

"Let's go. Right now," I said. I was in no mood to hang around the yard. We had two hours for lunch and often ate at home with our families. But because we were high schoolers, we could also stay and eat in the school cafeteria. We could buy food there or eat whatever we'd brought in lunch tins from home. If it was too nice outside to eat in the basement cafeteria, we sat in the school grounds and had lunch under the trees. But every now and then, we indulged ourselves and made the fifteen-minute walk, a special sojourn to Café Andre.

"Niloo's hungry—we should go," I repeated. I needed to get away from the school grounds before Homa appeared.

"Let me check if I have my coin purse." Niloo rummaged in her satchel.

"It's my treat! Let's just go!" I said. I'd happily pay for ten *kalbas* sandwiches. Anything to get out of there. I wouldn't know what to say to Homa if she showed up.

"Oh, good—I have it." Niloo held up a small black purse with a gold kiss-lock closure and snapped it open and closed for good measure.

"Off we go, then," I said.

"Ellie!"

I knew that voice.

Homa ran up to me. She came so close I could see again the mole under her left eye. She smelled of fenugreek. Had her mother made *ghormeh sabzi*? Lord knew I loved *ghormeh sabzi*, but the scent of fenugreek could nestle into your skin and hair. I suddenly remembered how Homa's mother always liked to go heavy on the fenugreek.

I stepped back a bit. Homa stepped closer.

Her curls were stiff, as though she'd been in the ocean and hadn't rinsed off the salt water. Her blouse—long-sleeved, button-front, and in the black color required for our school uniform—was threadbare. She wore the gray *ormak* fabric pleated skirt, but her skirt was extra short—embarrassingly so. She must have gotten everything secondhand. And nothing was ironed. The rest of us had our blouses ironed by servants in our homes. How was Homa going to survive this school?

I inched back again and she inched closer still, as though to reclaim her ground. I noticed her nose was dotted with blackheads. A few times a week, Mother made me cover my head with a towel, then hold my face over a steaming pot of boiled water so my pores would stay pure.

Sousan sidled up next to us and looked at Homa sideways. "How do you two know one another?"

"We were kids together!" Homa said. "You see, we were the best of friends, and it all started when——"

"It was a long time ago," I mumbled.

Homa stopped. She looked puzzled at my tone.

Sousan stiffened. "Is that so?" Sousan's father had picked a middle-aged wealthy army colonel for her to marry—they were already officially engaged. Sousan was ensured lifelong stability and status. Or so we naïvely believed back then. "Where did you meet as kids?" Sousan looked Homa up and down.

Before I could answer Sousan or any other girl listening in on the conversation (girls in the yard had gathered close to hear the drama from the classroom play out), Afarin and a few of her lackeys walked up to us.

Afarin crossed her arms as though she was getting ready to watch—at my expense—the unexpected show. "It's so nice to meet Elaheh's bestest friend!" she snickered.

The dry autumn air made my throat scratch. I suppressed a cough.

"Yes, we met at age seven and became best friends right away, didn't we?" Homa said. "We played hopscotch in the alley near——"

"Niloo's hungry," I said to cut her off. "We need to get some lunch."

Homa paused. I realized she didn't even know which one of the girls was called Niloo. Homa searched my face. "Doesn't it feel like just yesterday, though, Ellie?"

I looked down at the colored leaves on the ground.

Homa made up for my silence. "It took so very long to get the transfer to this school. My mother had to move mountains. But I finally got in! It's hard to commute from downtown—the buses are never on time. But I knew it would all be worth it." She paused. "I have missed you so very much, Ellie."

I looked up at her. Afarin let out a huge snort.

Homa's inability to be anything but her unadulterated good self hadn't changed. I had become something—someone—entirely different. I couldn't endanger my position at the top. I would be civil to Homa but nothing more.

Before I could respond, Niloo extended her hand to Homa. "I'm Niloo Mehran. I'm fortunate to meet you."

Homa clasped Niloo's hand in both of hers. "Homa Roozbeh. I'm happy to meet you."

"We were just about to go to Café Andre. Come with us," Niloo said.

"The famous Café Andre? I've always wanted to try it! And I have money with me!" Homa looked like she might hop in place from excitement.

Afarin tittered, her face pursed with pity and bemusement.

Homa turned to me. "Just show me the way, Ellie Joon!"

I hesitated.

"*Biya*, come on, Ellie Joon!" Homa pulled me close and hugged me.

In the middle of the schoolyard with everyone watching, with the lunch break ticking away and stomachs grumbling, with the leaves on the ground fragile and breakable beneath our feet, my old friend wrapped her arms around me. She hugged me as though seven years had not passed, as though we had not transformed into entirely different people, as though we were back in her mother's stone kitchen getting ready to cook and create and play and gossip.

I melted into her all-familiar, unparalleled embrace. I nestled my head into her shoulder—she was so much taller than me now. But it was she, Homa. The girl who was always her full self without apology, without explanation, without shame.

That lunch hour, Sousan, Niloo, and I set off for the café with Homa. Before long, Homa had Niloo laughing at her jokes and even Sousan smiling and curious.

I walked behind their threesome, trying to make sense of my mixed-up emotions. It was remarkable to see my old friend again. It was stunning and annoying and exciting. She was back in my life. She was brave to come here.

She was impossible to resist.

TWELVE

September 1960

Laughter and chatter filled Café Andre as we jostled to get in line. I recognized students not just from our high school, but also from the other schools in the area.

I scoured the café for Mehrdad, and though I did see a few of his schoolmates, I did not see him.

Niloo bent over and surreptitiously pinched her cheeks and fluffed her hair. She swung back up and raised her eyebrows at me as if to ask if she looked okay. I nodded yes. Sousan stood with her nose in the air—her engagement to the Colonel immunized her from the need to impress any high school boy.

Homa stood as unaffected by the boys' presence as she would have been by the company of dust mites. She focused acutely on the menu offerings, looking as if she had arrived in utopia.

As we had walked down Hafez Avenue and turned right on Shah Reza Street, Niloo had explained in detail for Homa the *salad olivier* sandwiches, the *kalbas* sandwiches, the way the tomatoes at Andre's were so fresh and sweet and how the pickles were just the right level of salty. She had described the baguette-style bread and the drink choices of ginger ale, lemonade, and soda. Homa had seemed enamored by Niloo's words, asking specific questions about bread and mayonnaise and the cost of everything.

Never did I think sandwiches could be such an interesting (or long) topic of conversation. But back in the day, Homa and I had had similarly detailed discussions about food with her mother as we learned about cutting onions and placing the knife just so.

Now as we stood in line, I inhaled the familiar scent of baked bread and cold cuts and savory salads. Thank God Afarin and her friends hadn't come. Not that Afarin would ever deign to spend her lunchtime with us, even if it meant gaining firsthand information on a new student.

When it was finally my turn to order, I shouted out for two *salad olivier* sandwiches. A mustached man I recognized from other times I'd frequented the establishment filled our baguettes with the delicious chicken-potato-egg-carrot-peas-and-pickles in lemony mayonnaise. He stuffed our breads with extra. Amid the din, Homa asked if he was always so generous and I shrugged and said, "Well, he knows me" (with more than a little pride, not adding that I got "extra" in many places just because of the way I looked). Homa ordered a bottle of *limonade* and I asked for "Kah-Na-Da," which was short for what we called "Ka-Na-Da-De-Rye." It wasn't until after a girl from the United States moved to our school that I heard our beloved drink pronounced "Canada Dry" in an American accent. She told us the drink was American. All that time, I had naïvely thought the drink belonged to us.

We paid, got our food, and all walked to a nearby park.

I sat with Homa on one bench and Niloo and Sousan diplomatically went to a bench several feet away. I overheard snatches of their conversation: Sousan worried her bridal *sofreh* would not be elaborate enough to please the Colonel's fastidious family and Niloo assured her that Sousan and the Colonel's wedding would stun the city.

Homa and I carefully unwrapped the wax paper casing of our sandwiches.

"Will I wake up and realize none of this happened? I feel like I'm in my best dream right now," she said.

"You're in your best dream because you're about to eat Andre's *salad olivier* sandwich." It came out of my mouth in the exact same tone I would have used when we were friends. We might as well have been sitting on the ledge near the red-and-white awning of the Grand Bazaar ice cream seller when we were ten, picking up a conversation only recently interrupted. Even if it had been seven years since we had last seen one another.

Homa shrugged and grinned.

And that was that.

I had meant to make sure she knew I was no longer *Sheekamoo*, the Ellie of downtown, but Queen Elaheh: a refined young lady at Reza Shah Kabir High School. But I dropped the act. How could I keep it up with someone who, even after all these years apart, probably knew me best?

"I am so proud of you, Ellie. You're in the best high school. Sitting for the year-end university exam, no doubt. It's clear the other girls respect you."

Her words were kind and I consciously pushed away worries about the evil eye. Mother's response to compliments was to burn incense to keep the powers of the jealous at bay. I could always do that when I got home, just to be safe.

"I don't know if I'll sit for the university exam," I said. Truth was, I was still torn. Maybe Mehrdad would ask me to marry him first.

"I'm not going to tell you what to do, but you should definitely take the *concours* and see which university you get into," Homa said.

"You just told me what to do."

She took a huge bite out of her sandwich. "I guess I did."

"There's so much to catch up on," I said. "Let's just say there's someone. I could be married right after graduation."

"*Tabrik!*" she congratulated me, and then chewed as calmly as though I had told her I had gotten over a headache or found a coin on the ground.

"It's kind of a big deal," I said.

"When's the wedding?"

"There is no wedding. Yet."

"Ah. But there is a groom?"

"Yes, potentially. Anyway, Homa, why are we talking about this?"

"You are. I was just asking about the university exam. I'm hoping to take it. I can't tell you how many times I had to apply to get into your high school. There were never enough spots. But I made it, right?" She raised her *salad olivier* sandwich in the air with one hand. With her other, she reached for the bottle of *limonade* and took a swig. "I still can't believe it!"

"Your family must all be so proud," I said.

I pictured them in her courtyard by the koi pond. Her father with his spectacles seated on the kilim rug. Her mother pouring tea from the white ceramic pot with the pink roses. Sara in her ruffled skirt and Ali Reza sleeping blissfully in the basket. It still calmed me just to think of that scene.

"My father's in prison."

I almost choked. "What?"

"Thought you knew," she said. "One of the many arrests of *beest-o-hashte Mordad*."

The twenty-eighth of Mordad. The day of the coup d'état. August 19, 1953.

"Your father . . . was there? I looked for his name in the papers . . ."

"He was in the streets during the coup. He didn't come home that night and we had no idea where he was for a week. Then we learned he was in prison. So many communists were arrested."

"But he . . . ?"

"Is still in prison," she said matter-of-factly.

I did not need to ask more. I had heard of those arrests, many of which were followed by long, unimaginable bouts of torture.

"I am so sorry, Homa."

She looked straight into my eyes. "It was seven years ago. The summer after you left."

A cold wave ran through my body. I had left. And she had stayed. I had entered the dominion of parties and presents and possibilities. Her father had gone to prison. "But we got together twice that summer, remember?" I ventured. As though reminding her would absolve me of the guilt I was suddenly feeling for years of no contact.

"Yes, the second time we met up would have been just a few weeks before Baba was arrested," she said quietly. She sighed. "How could we have known how everything would turn out then? We knew so little, right, Ellie?"

I could certainly agree with that. That perfect family. How I had envied their closeness, their joy! I had been so jealous of the fact that Homa had a father constantly present in her life and I didn't. "I am so sorry," I said again.

She shrugged and took another swig from her drink. "I wish we had stayed in touch. There were months when I wanted nothing more than to be able to talk to you."

I remembered the lump in my throat after I moved. How for several years I wouldn't take off the bird necklace. "I missed you too," I said.

"I should have stayed in touch. I'm sorry," Homa said.

"Don't be silly. I could have tried harder . . . It's just so easy to lose contact."

"Anyway, we're here now, right?" Homa's voice changed, audibly more cheery. "And that is why I feel like I am in a dream."

We sat in silence for a bit. Then I asked, "How do you . . . with your father gone. I mean, do you have . . ."

"Income? Oh, my mother started to work. So did I. Sara too. Even Ali Reza makes some pocket change! We get by. Mother sews dresses and skirts and outfits for the rich women. Best tailoring you ever did see. Probably some of the outfits she's sewn have made their way uptown to be worn by the mothers of your friends here. Maybe even by your mother! How is she, by the way?"

I remembered how Mother would not work even after my father died. How she felt jobs were for the lowly. "She is fine," I said. "Where do you work?"

"After my father was arrested, the restaurant where he was headwaiter helped us out for a while. And then took me in. I work in the kitchen. In the evenings. I help with the dishes. I clean. Sometimes I even cook!"

I stared at the sandwich on my lap, absorbing all this information. How could I have forgotten Homa? Her family?

"Do you know what Sara does?" she asked, excited.

"What?"

"She comes uptown to help clean houses. She's so resourceful, Ellie. She makes more than I do some weeks."

I thought of our own house and the help we had—a live-in *kolfat* housekeeper named Batul—a woman whose every waking moment was spent taking care of our home, our belongings, our stomachs, even our woes. "I'm so glad Sara is well," I said.

"Do you still have the necklace?" Homa asked.

"In my jewelry box."

"O-ho! You have a jewelry *box*? Look at you, Lady!"

It was the way she said it. The inflection of her "O-ho!" The way her eyes widened and her face lit up. She started it. She snort-laughed at her own loud "O-ho," and then I giggled, and soon we were both laughing for no reason. No reason at all.

Blame the sugar in the *limonade* and the Ka-Na-Da for getting to our heads.

Blame the need to not talk about her father.

Blame the relief that comes when someone who's disappeared from your life reappears and conjures up the same magic and re-creates a longed-for connection.

With our half-eaten sandwiches on our laps and our drink bottles to our sides, we laughed till our faces were soaked with tears. Homa occasionally looked over at me and repeated, "O-ho!" and then we burst into a new round of completely unwarranted giggles.

Our giddiness pierced through the lost years and the shattering news she'd just delivered and made it seem, against all evidence, that the world still lay before us for the taking.

THIRTEEN

October 1960

Homa couldn't join in the parties and get-togethers. She lived too far away and had an after-school job that set her apart from the rest of us. Students and teachers alike referred to Homa as "the girl from downtown." A more literal translation of the Persian would be "the girl from the bottom of the city." She popped up from that other side, attended classes, and then dutifully disappeared back to where she'd come from.

But within weeks, she had won the hearts of most of the girls in our grade and definitely those of the teachers. How could they resist her charisma? Homa was still a strong idealist. Her father's imprisonment had intensified her legal ambition. Her most ardent wish was to become a judge and to expand the rights of all Iranians, especially women, so that fewer would struggle like her mother did to make ends meet. It was impossible to not admire Homa's courage and her fervor, even if she sometimes went on rants that made my head hurt.

Homa told me she had seen what the Shah had done since his power solidified after the coup d'état of 1953 ousted Prime Minister Mossadegh. It shocked me to hear the way she talked about the monarchy. Mother and Uncle Massoud were rightful royalists—at least outwardly—and too afraid to speak up against the king. "The Shah is solidifying a secret police," Homa said. "They will be everywhere soon, spying. We have to be careful but courageous. We have to resist autocratization of this country."

I'd mumble about the Shah's plans for reforms and how they could benefit women.

"Fine, but we need more than just reforms," she said. "Don't be fooled by window-dressing changes, Ellie."

How could I tell my old friend that I was happy to sit back and do nothing? I was now firmly back in the world of the Haves. And Mother made it seem like at any moment, our fortunes could be reversed and we could lose it all like before. Being politically active meant rocking the boat. I didn't dare lose everything again.

Unlike the childhood days when we both worked equally hard in school, now Homa worked much harder. And it wasn't just because she wanted (and needed) a career more than I did. My crush on Mehrdad increasingly consumed me. My daydreams consisted not of university halls but of kissing Mehrdad at a wedding ceremony followed by feasting and dancing. As Homa lectured about how only the highest possible score on the university entrance exam would get us into the best programs, all I could think of was the rain of bridal sweetness, whether my mother would rub the traditional sugar cones above our heads at the ceremony with grace or glee or a good measure of both, how my dress would taper at the waist and puff at the shoulders and the exact number of pearly beads that would run down the seams of my sleeves. I pictured the moment Mehrdad would insert his honey-dipped pinky finger into my mouth while cheers erupted for the bride and groom.

"Do you know what happens to a woman's children if she's divorced, Ellie?" Homa asked. "They automatically go to the husband. Do you know how the laws are stacked up against women? Do you know just how much inheritance laws skew in favor of men, Ellie? Do you see how things have to change?" She threw questions at me day after day during lunch.

"It is awful," I'd mumble.

"There's no way we can move forward if we just sit on our bottoms, Ellie. For you to think of not attending university is unbelievable. Education is the only way we can create change. Did you know that fifty years ago, three hundred women entered the parliament with guns hidden under their chadors?"

"I did not."

The difference between Homa and me was that once she recognized a law needed to be changed, she fixated on it and studied every angle and became determined to get to a place where she could bring about the reform. Whereas once I knew a law needed to change—well, I hoped someone would one day get to it. Someone like Homa.

I was living in a part of town now surrounded by Iranians who were "modernized" and westernized. Like Afarin's parents. They traveled to Europe regularly and allowed Afarin to throw massive parties. Mother and Uncle Massoud feared that our hosting a big, mixed-gender gathering might reflect badly on me: make me look too loose, too free, too wild. But Mother let me attend Afarin's parties as a guest because I'd be hobnobbing with the rich elite there.

Before meeting Mehrdad, I had simply wanted every drop of indulgence at these parties. I'd wanted the *fun*. To have the pleasures of the world be mine.

Homa wanted the world to be hers too, I suppose, but only so she could mold and shape it and make it better for the less fortunate. Now, it was as if she had come in and turned off the music as I danced in the middle of the room and became frozen mid-step, my twirling hands fixed above my head, my hips stuck, suddenly aware of everything ugly I'd been trying to ignore.

Three weeks after Homa's arrival back into my life, Afarin threw a huge party on a Thursday night. So grateful to have been invited, I carefully planned my outfit: a crimson velvet blouse and a gold-threaded short skirt. I piled my hair up high into a dazzling beehive the size of a cantaloupe. Before leaving, I examined my eyeliner in the bathroom mirror and applied more of the black ink, touching up the wing-tip at the outer corners.

Magazines of international film stars covered my bed. I had carefully studied the photographs of Doris Day and Shirley Jones and Elizabeth Taylor. I didn't necessarily want to be them, but I did want the romance they had on-screen. I wanted to be kissed. I wanted to be held. I wanted to be twirled around the room at Afarin's ball. And I wanted all of it to happen with Mehrdad, Mehrdad, Mehrdad.

Truly the best thing about Afarin's parties was that Mehrdad was part of the Alborz High School crowd who got invited too. Just the thought of him made me feel like there was a life for me outside of the one that involved my curated and sheltered role with Mother and Uncle Massoud and my striving status at our competitive high school. When I thought of Mehrdad, everything else seemed somehow less difficult, more manageable.

In Afarin's living room that night, there was a table of drinks. I picked up a glass of cherry *sharbat* and sipped, looking around the room for Mehrdad. At another of her parties, I had made the mistake of tasting alcohol for the first time. I didn't care much for the taste of that wine, so didn't partake again. Afarin sipped some wine now quite audaciously as she played the role of the perfect hostess. I tried to ignore the boys who buzzed around me. I only wanted to see Mehrdad. I made my way across the room to look for him.

"Hello, beautiful lady!"

I turned amid the scent of tobacco. Behind me stood the Colonel, Sousan's fiancé. He wore his military uniform with its colorful honorific tabs on the shoulders. Why the Colonel insisted on attending the parties we kids went to, I did not know. He was closer to our parents' age. Though I supposed being engaged to Sousan gave him license to attend. But I always felt uncomfortable around him. There was something just a bit intimidating and creepy about the Colonel. What Sousan saw in him, I failed to understand. He was wealthy—wealthier than most colonels or military men. He had his own source of old family money, apparently. I hated to think Sousan was with him for money. She had her own family money, that much I knew. Maybe it was love. But what was it that made her love this unnerving man?

"Hello, Colonel," I said.

"Elaheh Khanom." He leaned close to me. His breath reeked of tobacco. "Is the evening proceeding according to your favor?" He smiled widely. His teeth were huge. And yellow-brown from smoking.

"It is, yes," I mumbled.

"Wonderful to know!"

Before the Colonel could go on, Sousan trotted over, kissed me on the cheek, said hello, then gently slid her arm into the Colonel's and led her fiancé to the drinks table and away from me. I was relieved.

From a record player on a side stand, a romantic song by an American musician, whom I knew from my magazines was named Neil Sedaka, filled the room. And then Mehrdad came in and the rest of the party did not matter.

The geometric patterns on Afarin's expensive rugs, the fancy paintings on the walls that she claimed were museum-worthy, the sound of her affected voice showing off about the clothes her mother had brought back from Europe all faded away. The Colonel and Sousan evaporated from my mind.

Mehrdad glanced at me from near the doorway. He was wearing a pistachio-colored shirt and dark pants. His wavy hair was parted in the middle, as always, and for some reason his tortoiseshell glasses had fogged up. His lanky frame made my pulse race. When he caught my eye, my legs felt like they were made of melted ice cream. Mehrdad strode toward me, bent slightly, and took my hand.

He smelled of citrus soap and his glasses were still foggy as we danced. I was practically pressed against his chest. His pistachio shirt was so crisp and tight, I wanted to rest my cheek against it, but I knew that would be considered far too forward by the rest of the guests. Trickles of sweat slid down my back as we danced. I was nervous but also strangely at peace. Because in all the world, there was no one like this man whom I had first seen at Café Andre, first spoken to at the Sizdah Bedar picnic, and gotten to know at gatherings and parties like this one, where girls from high schools like mine and boys from high schools like his got to mingle. If there was one word to describe how I felt when I was with Mehrdad, it was this: hopeful. He made me hopeful.

As the notes floated in the air from the record player, as the others around us danced and twirled, as Afarin's laughter thickened the air, I knew somehow at the very bottom of my soul that if I could continue in the arms of this man, if I could simply just be with him, then there was hope. The atrocities of the world would not end. But there was hope for me. He always made me feel like I could just be.

I studied the top button of his shirt. I inhaled that citrusy scent and dared and dared and dared to dream of one day being wedded to him.

The only other person in my life who made me feel hopeful like this was Homa. She and I had shared so much joy in our childhood. Homa had made me feel like the world could be ours. But she always wanted to change the world and improve it, tweak it, fix it, make it just. With her, I felt competitive despite myself. I loved being with Homa but often felt less-than around her and as though I had to match her smarts, her strength, her ambitions.

Yet as I danced with Mehrdad, I realized that with Mehrdad I felt like I was enough.

When the dance finished, he let me go and smiled shyly.

I practically stumbled back to the table laden with drinks. I could see stars float in the air, tiny little stars. My limbs felt weightless.

FOURTEEN

October 1960

About a month after Homa joined our school, the two of us sat cross-legged on the grass in the Reza Shah Kabir grounds underneath a huge tree, our tiffin lunch tins on our laps.

The smell of fried potatoes wafted from Homa's tin as she opened the stacked tiers. I saw lavash bread in her bottom tier and potato *kuku* in the middle and a few wilted radishes in the top section. I wasn't sure what my own lunch tin contained as Batul, our housekeeper, normally filled mine. To my delight, fluffy saffron rice filled the bottom tier, plump beef and chicken kebobs filled the next level, and round fresh radishes and *sabzi* leaves were stuffed at the top.

Homa scooped some of her potato *kuku* with a piece of the bread. "So," she said. "When do I get to really know him?"

"Who?"

"This Mehrdad person."

Surprised, I hesitated for a moment. Then I said, "I introduced you! When we were at Café Andre the second time."

"Saying hello to a boy in a crowded café while he's surrounded by class-mates and then quickly rushes off is not really meeting someone. Shouldn't I get to know him? I need to know who he is deep down. Is he to be trusted? I am your best friend, after all."

She had only been back in my life for one month. Her boldness continued to astound me. "Of course he is to be trusted," I said. "Don't you believe in my judgment?" As if on autopilot, I mentioned the traits that mattered to Mother. "He's well educated. From an established family."

"*Established!*" she snorted. "That tells me nothing."

"His family is . . ."

"What's his soul like?" She looked up.

"It's just fine, thank you."

"I need to look into his eyes—really look into them—to know for sure," she said. "I can judge a person's entire soul by looking into their eyes."

"Well then, you should have looked into them when you met him at Café André!"

"It's always rushed and noisy there. For a good, deep look, I need quiet and time." She sighed. "All I'm saying is, I could save you years of heartbreak, Ellie. What if you've been hoodwinked by his charms and good looks and he's actually the wrong person for you?"

I remembered my dance with Mehrdad at Afarin's recent party. Afterward, he had lingered by the doorway as if he couldn't bear the evening to end. *Thank you so much*, he'd said to Afarin's parents. *Thank you for this wonderful evening*. He'd smiled looking my way. Homa had no idea how sweet and genuine Mehrdad truly was. I was in love with him. This wasn't a passing phase.

"Unless you're ashamed of me," Homa went on. "And that's why you don't want me to get to know him."

"That's absolutely ridiculous," I said a bit too quickly. "It's just that . . . you're not at the parties."

Homa spoke slowly. "I see."

"Come on, Homa, you don't like any of those 'dumb superficial get-togethers' as you call them anyway, right? You hate the materialism and phoniness."

"*Be darde man nemeekhoran*. They don't do me any good," she said. She ate in silence for a few minutes. Then she said, "Never mind. I'll meet him at your wedding. If I'm invited, that is."

"Of course you will be. First he has to ask me . . ."

"If your mother allows it." She smiled wanly.

"To marry him? She adores him. It's so weird, she's so proud of his family's—"

"No, silly. If she allows *me* at your wedding. She still thinks I'm bad for you, after all this time. Am I right?"

The truth was, Mother's distaste for my old friend had only ballooned since she found out Homa was back in my orbit. Her disbelief at Homa's entry into my school soured into distrust. *It's almost as if,* she said, *that girl is in love with you.* She looked ridiculously horrified as she said it, as only Mother could. I knew several girls in our school who had crushes on other girls or on our female teachers. A *barooni* was what we called girl crushes. *Baroonis* became fast friends and much more. But Mother was wrong. Homa's devotion and affection had never felt like they lay outside of friendship.

"Do you have a crush on anyone?" I asked gingerly now.

Homa took a bite of her *kuku* and chewed thoughtfully. She swallowed. "Not a soul."

"No boy from Alborz High School? No person back in the neighborhood?"

"No one. It's a relief, to be honest." She looked down. "Frees me up to study and work!" she then said with forced lightness.

"More time to study for your beloved *concours* entrance exam!" I went along with her joking.

"You know what?" She looked straight into my eyes then. "I just don't feel it, Elaheh. I just . . . don't get it. This attraction/distraction you all feel. I don't . . . have it."

Wasn't Homa lucky in a way to not have been bitten by this bug? Homa was far less shallow than the rest of us high school girls, wasn't the type even to mention the looks of boys.

I wanted to ask her why she was so against romance. I assumed it was her ambition: her intense desire to study and make something of herself. Every day in school we were told about the edge on which we sat. The edge of a cultural shift. Girls in a high school created so we could succeed. Girls in a generation with educational resources unprecedented in our country. Girls who would become the pioneering generation of professional women.

I thought of how Sousan stayed up at nights worrying about her future life with the Colonel: her many plans and concerns for that first bedroom experience and how she would handle herself during it. I thought of Niloo, telling me how this boy she'd met at synagogue, Hooman, had written her a love note and handed it to her slipped in between the pages of a book. Niloo's family was Jewish and she couldn't believe she had found a boy at temple, no less. I thought of Mehrdad, how when he showed up with his friends at Café Andre or at a weekend party or in our new favorite stationery shop, my body temperature rose and I felt lightheaded.

But the look on my friend's face at that moment was one of indifference. She bent her head and focused on her lunch tin.

"Don't worry. Once we're done with senior year and we take your beloved *concours* exam . . ."

Her entire face lit up. "You're going to take it?"

"How could I not? You keep singing in my ear that I must attend university. And besides, Uncle Massoud and Mother aren't against it." I couldn't tell her that Mother wasn't "against it" because she'd become convinced it was my ticket to securing the relationship with Mehrdad. Mehrdad had made it clear that he shared the views of his enlightened crowd who insisted on marrying women who had degrees and credentials. It seemed both Mehrdad and Homa wanted me to go to university.

"That is so fantastic! I hope you've been studying. The higher our scores, the better chance we have at getting into Tehran University. Just think, Ellie. In less than a year from now, we could be students there!" Her entire demeanor had shifted. Her face beamed. "I really want to study law there!" She looked up at the sky as if making a behest of God.

"Well, at the rate you're preparing for the exam, the law program at the best university will have no choice but to take you. I bet you'll get the highest scores."

"You are kind to say that. I'm so glad you finally came around, Ellie! You'll get in, I know. I'll help you!"

I felt within me a small excitement about a future I hadn't dared to truly imagine. "Mehrdad's dream is to study in the science program there," I said. "What if all three of us actually got accepted to Tehran University? We could go hiking at Alborz Mountain on Friday mornings with classmates. Mehrdad and his friends hike every Friday in the mountains even now. When we're in university, we can go all together."

"Wait, the reason you want to go to Tehran University is because Mehrdad might get in there?" Homa looked suddenly crestfallen.

"Of course. I mean, of course not."

She shook her head. "I don't care what the motivation is; I'm just glad you've come to your senses. We'll all three get accepted. *Inshallah*."

"*Inshallah*," I said.

She started to pack up her lunch things. Without looking up, she quietly asked, "Why do you want to get married?"

"That's a silly question. Why wouldn't I want to?"

"I'm not getting married. Ever."

Homa and her radical agenda. Homa constantly questioning every aspect of our society. "You're being absurd, Homa."

"You wait and see. I don't need a spouse. And my reason for going to university isn't so I can go hiking with boys."

"That's not what I meant."

"Or to meet them. Or to be with them."

"You said you wanted to get to know Mehrdad," I reminded her.

She studied me for a moment. "Because I want to make sure he's right for you."

Mehrdad had passed the discriminating and excruciating standards of Mother. Of Uncle Massoud. They both liked him. Everyone liked him. But here was Homa insisting on having her say.

"You say he goes hiking every Friday with his friends?" she asked. She snapped her fingers suddenly. "Let's go, then! This Friday. You could arrange it so we meet them up there."

"Homa, how on earth . . ." She always had outlandish plans. "We can't."

"Why not?"

"Mother wouldn't allow me to just go hiking in the hills with—" I stopped myself. "Don't you work on Fridays?"

"I can get a cover. Did you know, Ellie, that I've always wanted to hike there?"

I did not.

"Yes, but I can't just say I'm off to go hiking with . . ."

"Me?"

"That's not what I meant," I said a little too guiltily.

"Tell her you're going with Sousan. Or Niloo. Or both of them!"

I flashed back to Homa convincing me to skip school to go to the Grand Bazaar.

"Fresh air!" Homa said, practically giddy. "I'll take the first morning bus. We'll get an early start. I have money saved up. I'll happily blow it on breakfast in those teahouses up in Darband on the slope of Alborz Mountain. I've heard so much about them." She stood up. She had a new energy to her, an excitement. It mattered to her. It mattered to her to meet Mehrdad, to be part of my life, to hike the hill, to give her opinion.

She always had plans, Homa. She always seemed to be thinking of the next big thing. It was astounding, really. Her father was in prison. They had nothing. But she was always hopeful.

Her joy was infectious. She was the most convincing person I knew.

"Sure, Homa," I said. "We'll go hiking. You can meet Mehrdad there. You could even get to know some of his friends."

"I'm telling you I'm not interested in meeting boys."

"Fine," I said, though I still found it somewhat hard to believe. "But you just never know what can happen up in those hills."

I even winked.

FIFTEEN

October 1960

Not often was the weather as perfect as it was the Friday morning when we met for the hike. Homa arrived on time at the foot of Alborz Mountain in the north of the city. As we hugged and greeted each other, groups of hikers all around us bent to tighten shoelaces, stretch out and pump their arms, and take in deep breaths of the fresh morning air.

I had gone hiking for picnics in Darband only a few times before, with Mother and Uncle Massoud. Mother had a suspect view of too much exercise for young women and felt it could loosen places that didn't need to be loosened. For this reason, she also worried about my ever riding a bicycle or doing too many calisthenics or, God forbid, a split. But I had her permission today because I had lied. I had told her I was going hiking with Sousan and Niloo. Had I hinted that I would "run into" Mehrdad up the mountain, I doubt Mother would have really minded, believing as she did that each encounter would bring me closer to securing a proposal.

My guilt was diluted to a degree by the crisp air and the vast landscape. Thanks to Homa's boldness, we were about to begin our adventure.

Homa gulped a breath. "Drink it in, Ellie. This is what life is about. This air. Can you feel it? Inhale it so it fills your lungs. When we get up higher and higher, all will only get better and better."

"How do you know?"

"Because." She paused. "It just has to."

I inhaled as deeply as I could.

"You told him, right? He's coming?" she asked as though confirming a bank heist.

"Yes, he's meeting us at the teahouse. It wouldn't look right to hike all the way up with him and his friend group. There's four of them."

"Uggh."

"They're all really nice."

"I don't care about his friend group. I just want to meet him."

"Well, he hikes with them and it's less suspect than meeting him alone."

She grinned. "Of course. We're not those kinds of girls, heaven forbid, Ellie, right? But sneaking off with him to a park bench near Café Andre and dancing with him at Afarin's lascivious parties is just fine?"

I realized the hypocrisy of my own "rules" for my courtship. Or maybe they were Mother's rules.

"Don't push any of his friends on me," Homa said.

I shrugged.

"At least the teahouse will be private," Homa said. "You know, *Tudeh* communist party members often meet up there to talk. It's safer. More secluded. Away from the eyes of spies and the Secret Police."

"Homa, no politics today, please. We'll hike, meet Mehrdad at the teahouse. You can take your time and look into his eyes to assure he's not the actual devil, and then we'll come back down. Alright?"

"Yes, Sergeant." She saluted. Homa swung her arms and marched in place for a moment. "What are we waiting for? Let's go!"

We took off in sync.

Her cheeks were pink from the morning chill. She had pulled her hair into a high ponytail tied with a turquoise scarf with black polka dots. It was the kind of scarf that could have looked gauche or cheap on anyone else. But on Homa, it looked chic and funky. Her coat was belted tightly in the middle, making her waist look positively tiny. We wore blouses and skirts to school and in most of our day-to-day lives, but today we both wore slacks and carried light handbags with shoulder straps. As we strode up the hill, I felt again the ease of movement that trousers afforded. I understood why the village women who worked in fields wore trousers under their tunics.

At first, the trail was mostly flat and covered with leaves in orange, yellow, and bright red. The colors at our feet were intoxicating. But before long, the trail became suddenly steep. My heart beat fast not just from the climb, but at the prospect of seeing Mehrdad. *Meet me there at eight thirty*, I had told him as we sat on a park bench unwrapping sandwiches from Andre's during a rushed lunch before he dashed off with his friends. *I'm bringing my friend, Homa. She wants to meet you.*

I looked at my friend. The breeze lifted the edges of the scarf with which she'd tied her ponytail, her long legs took big strides up the hill, and she breathed deeply. She never seemed to worry about consequences. I envied that.

"Why don't we do this every day, Ellie? It feels so good to be out here. Do folks just get up early and inhale this air and feel their heart beat and just have . . ." She paused and took in the trees, leaves the color of flames on the ground, the incline of the hill. "This?"

"Well, they do on Fridays. Those who can," I said. "It's not so easy during the week when there's work and school."

"When we are in university, promise me we'll do this every week, Ellie. Promise we won't rot indoors with books and homework. We need to do this as much as possible."

"You're the one who made fun of me for suggesting hiking was a good side benefit of being a university student! You're the one obsessed with books and assignments these days, Homa. Not me."

She stopped walking. She tipped her head back and closed her eyes. She inhaled deeply. I waited for her to breathe out. Finally, she let out a slow, long, deep exhale. "Never let me get so caught up in my plans again, Ellie. I love it here! I want to be in the mountains."

I laughed. "Yes, Khanom Lawyer Judge who will change all the bad laws single-handedly! Who will change this country."

"I'm glad we're here now is all I'm saying."

We resumed hiking.

"I know you work on Fridays. Glad you could get away," I said.

She was quiet for a moment. Then she said, "Not all Fridays. Sometimes I go to the mosque."

"You? Go to the *masjed*?"

"I love to go to the big one downtown, near the Grand Bazaar. Whenever I'm feeling down or need to get away from it all, I go to the courtyard in the bazaar and sit on that ledge."

"Where we had the ice cream sandwiches when we were kids?"

"That's the one."

"Your . . . father . . ." I started to say. "Homa, you never talk about it. You can talk about him with me."

"My father doesn't really believe in God. He is a true communist. But since his arrest . . . I don't know. I guess you could say my mother has found religion again."

"Your mother prays?"

"Five times a day."

"Do you?"

She looked down at her hands. "No. I'm a communist, remember?"

We were Muslim, yes, and not Jewish like Niloo's family or Christian like some of the Armenian girls in our school. But my family was secular and did not practice. All along, I had assumed Homa's family was secular too.

"I didn't know your mother is religious." I remembered seeing her mother in a light house chador, but that garment wasn't a sign of being fully observant.

"Now you know," she said.

In this fraction of time, my friend, the one I thought I knew inside-out, was a complete stranger to me. We had picked up our friendship where we left off, yes. But there were changes that had happened through our years of separation that kept cropping up.

Before I could ask more questions, a chorus of birds squawked over-
head. Homa cried, "*Saket, saket!* Everybody quiet, quiet!" Her spot-on
impression of Mrs. Roshanfekr bent me over in laughter.

As we ascended the slope, we lost ground to hikers who were fitter and
faster. The men touched their caps and nodded as they passed us on the trail;
the women gave us quick smiles.

Finally, we arrived at a large, flat clearing. We stood in silence, catching
our breath. From this expansive vista, we took in the view of Tehran's clus-
tered rooftops, grand avenues, zigzag alleys, and block buildings. It felt liber-
ating to see a city splayed in all its mess and glory and confusion and potential.

Homa leaned into me and put her arm around my shoulders. "Did you
know?" she said. "*Donya maleh mast.* The world is ours."

We stood there, our heads touching. What she said was absurd. The
world was vast and broken and filled with strife. The world was chaotic and
owned by men. Not by us.

Homa's polka-dot turquoise scarf blew in the breeze and fluttered
against my hair. "*Donya maleh mast,*" she repeated.

Perhaps the effort of climbing had the chemicals flowing in my brain,
but as we stood there at a vista where we felt we could touch the sky, the
street lines looking drawn into the ground by a child with a coloring pencil,
the buildings that normally towered above us reduced to small blocks, it
felt—if only in that moment—that perhaps Homa was right.

"*Shayad,*" I said. Maybe.

An older man holding a newfangled camera motioned to us. "Would
you like a photograph?" he asked.

Homa looked confused.

"These are called Polaroid cameras," I explained. "They're all the rage.
They spit out your photo right away."

"If that's so, then yes, thank you!" Homa said to the man.

We posed and smiled, and then watched in wonder as the blank square
sheet that ejected from his camera got saturated with our image.

"Thank you," I said. I took the photograph and nestled it carefully between the folds of the freshly ironed handkerchief in my handbag. The man nodded and walked on.

"Look." Homa turned and motioned behind us.

I turned around.

Tucked into the side of the mountain, as if carved into rocky crevices, was a structure of wood and stone. The sign above it said "Alborz Mountain Teahouse."

I glanced at my watch. We were ten minutes late.

For a few seconds more we took in the view. We drank in the city scene below, not wanting to give up that perspective—the gratifying position that was hard-won. And fleeting.

At last, we walked arm in arm to the entryway of the teahouse.

My heart resumed the same furious beat it struck during the uphill climb.

Mehrdad and his friends waited inside.

SIXTEEN

October 1960

We stepped inside, giggling and giddy. At the thought of seeing the boys, I worried that my nose ran, my hair looked mussed by the mountain wind, and my face had become unflatteringly blotched from exertion. I glanced at Homa. She retained the calm stature of someone who would own the world.

Inside the teahouse, low wooden benches covered with Persian rugs were arranged next to tables cloaked in patterned paisley cloth. The air smelled like bergamot and hookah smoke and sauteed onions. A big open window at the front maximized the view.

A waiter in a black vest over a white tunic and baggy white pants greeted us and pointed to a table in the back.

"Ellie!"

I spun at the sound of his voice calling my name. In a corner by the entrance—how had we missed him?—Mehrdad waved from his carpeted seat. He was with another boy—one I did not recognize.

When I waved back, Mehrdad jumped up. He wore a navy shirt and khaki pants. He waved again, encouragingly.

The chubby boy with him struggled to stand, looking ill at ease in too-tight clothes. With black hair covering the tops of his eyes, he resembled a lost sheepdog. When he finally stood upright to acknowledge our presence, he studied his feet.

Homa matter-of-factly told the waiter that we would sit with the "boys in the corner." My cheeks burned. The waiter looked at us indifferently. "As you wish," he said and walked away.

Mehrdad's smile grew wide when Homa and I approached the table. Just seeing Mehrdad made me feel warm and dizzy, and I couldn't help breaking out into what was probably my own foolish smile again in return.

"Please sit," I said, since Mehrdad and his friend were still standing.

We all sat. Mehrdad took charge, talking fast. He was nervous too. I could tell by the way he was smiling and nodding his head. He introduced his friend as Abdol, a classmate at Alborz High School.

Homa and I said we were pleased to meet Abdol and then Homa answered Mehrdad's questions about our hike, describing birds we'd seen and the kaleidoscopic patterns of the leaves; turns in the trail and that air, that air, that air.

Why had Mehrdad brought only one friend? He usually hiked with a group of four. Who was this shy boy, whom I'd never heard of nor met, who sat sullenly silent while Mehrdad politely conversed? Was this Mehrdad's idea of setting Homa up?

The waiter returned to our table and asked for our orders. Mehrdad named a few favorites and looked at the rest of us for reinforcement. I nodded eagerly while Abdol concentrated on the paisley pattern of the tablecloth.

"All sound good to you, Abdol Jan?" Mehrdad prompted him.

Abdol's head shot up, shifting slightly to indicate a yes. Then he looked in Homa's direction and reddened, fiddled with his fingers, and proceeded to study the tablecloth again. Homa mostly ignored him. It was hard not to feel sorry for him.

Homa didn't spend time reading film magazines and sighing over foreign movie stars the way I did, but were we to speak in code, I would lean over and say: it's not that I expected Cary Grant, but I didn't exactly expect this guy. And she would, in her very Homa-like way, look me in the eye and ask me who Cary Grant was.

"Abdol is a dear friend," Mehrdad said, as if responding to my imagined conversation. "He's new to Alborz. The high school, not the mountain!"

At his pun, I laughed a bit too forcefully, trying to make Mehrdad feel at ease not just with his play on words but with his choice of companion.

Homa stared at Mehrdad, not even looking at Abdol.

Abdol did not laugh.

Mehrdad cleared his throat. "As I was saying, Abdol is new to our school. Just as I believe, Homa Jan, from what Ellie has told me . . . you are new as well? To Reza Shah Kabir? Well, you both hail from . . . downtown." Mehrdad coughed.

I cringed when he said "downtown." Had Mehrdad found a fellow "poor" student to bring for the meeting with Homa, thinking it was beneath his elite friends to make this outing today? I must have looked disappointed in Mehrdad because Homa leaned toward me and said, "*Khoobi?* You okay?"

"Yes, I'm fine, thanks, Homa."

Then I said extra loudly, "I was wondering, have you had time to look into Mehrdad's eyes?" There, I said it. What did I care.

Mehrdad looked at me, puzzled, but before Homa or anyone else could respond, the waiter arrived with a large, round zinc tray.

On the tray were small hourglass-shaped glasses of dark tea, a bowl of sugar cubes, a plate of dates and walnuts, and skillets of hot omelet: eggs cooked into a rich sauce of sautéed tomatoes and onions. In an instant, our group was transformed by excitement.

The waiter placed the food on the table and before I even knew he had left, he returned with another tray on which lay fresh hot *sangak* bread, small ramekins of feta cheese, sour cherry jam and quince jam, and a plate of cut-up cucumbers.

"I do believe I'm in heaven," Homa said.

I agreed wholeheartedly.

Abdol looked positively revived after he ate his cheese wrapped in the fresh bread, sucked on a sugar cube, and swallowed some tea. He even smiled and joked a little with Mehrdad and chimed in when we spoke about school and the year-end *concours* exam. Abdol said he'd be taking the exam too and that he wanted to study the law. His voice was raspy but steady.

"Is that so?" I asked. The tea and the breakfast continued to drastically improve my mood. Maybe this boy wasn't so bad. He was certainly earnest. And he had to be hardworking to be at Alborz. "That's so wonderful. Because Homa wants to study the law as well!" I declared it as if I deserved some credit for my friend's ambitions.

Homa looked up with her mouth full. She swallowed. She looked at me, then at Abdol, then at Mehrdad. As if experiencing a revelation, she slowly picked up the ramekin of quince jam and sniffed it closely. Her nose practically touched the jam. "I can tell this jam was made from the freshest, most ripe quince. I can just tell. Smell it, Ellie." She pushed the jam under my nose.

I recoiled and tried to avoid touching my nostrils to it. I pushed her hand away as I laughed nervously and agreed with her.

Homa proceeded to sniff the sour cherry jam. She said her mother's sour cherry preserves were the best in the world. As she spoke, she stuffed her mouth with *sangak* bread and broke off pieces of cheese with her fingers—not using the yellow-handled knife the waiter had placed on the tray. She proceeded to stick her fingers in her mouth, licking each one loudly. She picked up her tea glass and slurped in a most uncouth manner, then declared that the bergamot in it was just right. When she picked a sugar cube from the bowl, it was with the same sticky fingers she had just sucked. She rummaged in the bowl for the perfect square of sugar.

I saw Mehrdad flinch. Abdol followed her every motion.

Homa continued to talk about her mother's kitchen and the preserve making. Flecks of food from her mouth landed on our paisley tablecloth and the rest of the dishes. She ended the monologue by saying that when we were little, her nickname for me was "*Sheekamoo*," and then she poked my belly—hard—with her finger and laughed so that a few more bread pieces showered our table.

Mehrdad stared at Homa with his eyes wide. I took in a breath and said yes, yes, her nickname for me was *Sheekamoo* because I loved to eat. I wished I could telepathically tell Homa to please tone it down.

Homa laughed with her mouth wide open so we could all see the food in it.

I was so mortified for her.

But then I saw Abdol. He couldn't take his eyes off her. To every word, to every joke she made—he listened, rapt. He was red in the face but looked happier than when we'd first arrived. He seemed struck by lightning.

After we said goodbye to Mehrdad and Abdol and made our descent down the mountain, our stomachs full and my waistband tight, I asked Homa why she'd done it.

"Done what?" She looked at me so innocently and with such a straight face that I couldn't form words.

I wasn't sure what to say. Oh, I don't know: talked with your mouth full, been disgusting with the food, stuck your freshly licked fingers into the sugar cubes, maybe that. But I didn't want to sound like a snobby elitist bringing up table manners. "Nothing," I said.

We walked downhill in silence.

"Did you like him?" I finally said. "He was clearly shy, but did you think he was sweet?"

"Mehrdad? Oh, I don't know if I would classify him as shy. He had a nice take-charge attitude . . ."

"No, dummy, not Mehrdad. His friend! Abdol. Did you"—my voice sounded strained—"like him?"

"Oh! Him. He was nice enough, I suppose. Quiet guy."

"But did you like him?"

"Sure. Why wouldn't I like him?"

"No, I mean . . ."

She suddenly stopped in her tracks. "Ellie?"

"Yes?" I said encouragingly. "You can tell me."

"I looked!" she said as if announcing breaking news. "I really looked. Into Mehrdad's eyes."

I stopped too and searched her face. I had been so distracted by Homa's behavior at the table that I had almost forgotten the reason we had gone in the first place.

Homa smiled. "I saw a perfect gentleman. I saw kindness. Goodness. Through and through."

My heart fluttered at her words.

"Though he was wearing glasses. I did the best I could. I examined his soul the best way I knew how even though he had on those tortoiseshell spectacles."

Her ponytail had loosened, but not the bright distinction of the turquoise-and-black polka-dot scarf.

"He is a man of good character," she said. "I see happiness."

I wanted to thank her. I wanted to laugh about it all. I still couldn't believe she was back in my life. She and Mehrdad would now both be part of my life forever more.

We stood still on the trail.

She hugged me until she let me go and stood back a bit. "For you," she said.

"What?"

"For you. I see the happiness."

"Hopefully for you too, *inshallah*."

We resumed walking.

Before I could bring up Abdol again, she blurted out, "If you think for one minute that I would be matched with Mehrdad's friend, you are mistaken. No offense to him; he was a nice, obviously serious and studious fellow. But don't try to set me up, Ellie. I have my studies. I have my *maman*. I have Sara. And Ali Reza. I don't need a boy. I am on a course, Ellie. I have plans. I certainly hope my rude eating turned him off for good. I don't have time for this nonsense."

If any young woman in all of Iran could break the barriers and become a successful judge, it was Homa. She had strength. She had nerve. With the support of Reza Shah Kabir High School, she would study and get into university and she would save us all. That was what I thought as I walked down the mountain with my friend that autumn day.

SEVENTEEN

1961–1963

On examination day, we sat behind wooden desks in the large test hall and took the *concours*. My blouse stuck to my armpits as I perspired through each minute, certain that our test scores would decide nothing less than our place in the world.

Homa's persuasion had been far too effective to ignore. Because of her persistence and with her guidance and companionship, I had studied quite diligently.

She phoned me, screaming, when she first learned the results.

I jumped up and down so hard that Mother rushed into the living room, waving a slipper, ready to kill whatever cockroach she assumed I'd seen.

Our jubilation lasted weeks. We felt so grown-up, so empowered.

The autumn of our eighteenth year found us entering Tehran University. Homa was accepted in the field of law and I was accepted for languages and literature. I would study English and become a teacher or translator. Mehrdad was thankfully accepted into the chemistry department.

It was not customary for local students to live in dormitories. I lived at home and commuted to the university for my entire four years. We referred to our fellow students as "*bacheha*," kids. We truly believed we were the ones who could alter the future. Ready to take on anything that fate sent us.

Within weeks, Homa and I mastered that campus: the best study rooms, the quietest corners of the library, the shadiest trees under which to read and chat and argue. And in the cafeteria, we popped open bags of potato chips as Homa lectured me about the latest doings of the *Tudehi* communist party.

Homa's distaste for the Shah had grown into pure outrage. She said the Shah's attempts at modernization took us away from our own culture, that his policies were not fair, that he stifled his critics by ordering his secret police, the SAVAK, to imprison people.

By the beginning of our second year at university, Homa had emerged as a leader of the student communist movement that organized marches and demonstrations and met to discuss their ideology and actions. I had learned not to argue our political differences. Homa wanted to pour her life into politics. I wanted to enjoy a life devoid of it.

Even though I knew that was an impossibility in Iran.

On a Friday holiday in the second semester of our sophomore year at university, my life changed when Mehrdad asked me out to a *chelo kabab* lunch.

I was so grateful to Mother for allowing this twosome lunch for Mehrdad and me that I let it go while she fussed over my hair and lamented that my nails were too short and stubby. "Why didn't you have them done, Ellie?" I shot her a confused look. "Why would I have them done to go to lunch at a *chelo kababi*?" Mother shook her head.

From the moment Mehrdad picked me up in his car (one that Mother was supremely happy to know he actually owned), I practically held my breath the whole ride to the famed Nayeb restaurant, which had a location right in the Grand Bazaar.

Perhaps Mother had had a premonition that this Friday lunch was to be none too ordinary. For no sooner had we settled inside Nayeb (Mehrdad had ceremoniously pulled the red velvet–backed chair out for me to sit and then gently pushed it in before seating himself on the other side of the white-clothed table) than he looked at me and said, "Ellie, I was hoping we could discuss our future."

Our future.

My head spun and I felt a strange warmth radiate throughout my body.

Before I could ask him what he meant by *our future*, a young waiter came to our table and asked for our orders.

Somehow the spell was broken.

After the waiter left, we spoke only of the restaurant, how toasty it was and how the air smelled of fragrant saffron rice and delicious kabab.

I didn't want to seem too eager, too desperate for a proposal, too forward, so I chimed in casually as Mehrdad turned the topic to exams and classwork, and how his studies in chemistry were going and how my proficiency in English was increasing, and how the cost of goods might go up in the coming year.

We spoke of the weather. Of Homa and of the Shah. We spoke of every darn thing on this planet but our future. Mehrdad fumbled with his napkin, moved the cutlery back and forth on the tablecloth, even mentioned elements in the periodic table.

Then the food arrived.

The waiter placed on our table two skewer platters—grilled beef *kabab barg* for Mehrdad; saffron-and-lemon-marinated chicken drumsticks *jujeh kabab* for me—with pyramid-shaped saffron-sprinkled rice topped with a slab of butter and a grilled tomato. In each of two small bowls sat one half-open eggshell filled only with egg yolk. He also set down a pitcher of the salty, fizzy yogurt drink *doogh*.

The steam of the rice cleared my sinuses and my head. As I mixed the egg yolk into my hot white rice and forked my grilled tomato, as I sprinkled dark crimson sumac over my kabab, as Mehrdad poured into my glass the *doogh*, it was with pure joy that I took my first taste of the national dish before us. We both delighted in our food and talked about the tenderness of the kabab and the perfect juiciness of the tomato, and as if by muscle memory we ate our *chelo kabab*. Around us in the clatter and the chatter of the restaurant, other diners talked and laughed, utensils clinked on dishes, and waiters floated as if dance-stepping back and forth throughout the large room.

I had a spoon of perfectly buttered rice and chicken and tomato raised to my mouth when Mehrdad dropped his fork onto his plate.

"Ellie," he asked, "will you marry me?"

So forthright was his tone, so absolutely earnest.

I froze, my spoon midair, my mouth slightly open, until I caught Mehrdad's eyes. Those eyes behind the tortoiseshell glasses for whom Homa had climbed a mountain. When she'd looked into them, she'd seen genuine goodness. She had predicted happiness for me.

I put down my spoon. My body was as floaty and bubbly as the fizzy *doogh*. Mehrdad leaned over the table and took my hand.

"Ellie," he said. "Since I first saw you that day at Café Andre when the lunch crowd was pushing and jostling in line, since we then spoke at Sizdah Bedar by the river, I've had one simple want. To be with you. I don't know how else to say it. Will you marry me? Will you be my wife? I know I need to ask permission from your uncle and your mother, but I thought . . . I just thought . . ." He cleared his throat. "That we could have this moment first. I wanted to tell you—privately and face to face—that I adore you. I love you."

My heart did a somersault. I could feel the blood in my arms flow; I could feel a drumming in my chest that led to a pounding in my ears.

I could *feel* a future with Mehrdad. And I knew then that it was what I wanted more than anything.

"Yes," I said. I was so deeply immersed in emotion that my voice sounded as if it came from underwater. A fraction of possibility was opening up into a lifetime expanse.

He let go of my hand, rose, and walked to my side of the table. He leaned down, held my face in both of his hands, and, ever so tenderly, kissed me.

That delicious buss might have lasted two seconds; it might have lasted two hours. For me, it was the world.

We savored the rest of our meal. We discussed plans. We'd wait till after graduation, even though it was a little over two years away. "I know it's a long time to wait," Mehrdad said. "But by graduation, hopefully I'll have secured a good lab position. And gotten accepted into a PhD program. I can get a stipend while I do the graduate work. That way we start our lives in a place of our own."

My heart beat wildly at the prospect of having our own space. If we married now, we'd have to live with one of our families, and much as I enjoyed Mehrdad's mother (whom I had met a few more times since that day she emerged from the river like a mermaid) and liked his sweet father, I did not want to live with them. Tradition dictated new brides live with their in-laws.

"Yes, let's definitely wait until we can get a place of our own," I said.

Mehrdad looked down at the tablecloth. "I can't . . . can't describe this feeling. I can't wait to tell my parents! We'll set up a time to come over and speak to your mother and uncle and officially ask for permission, of course. But"—he ran his hand through his hair—"I just wanted us to have this private moment. To ask you first."

"I'm glad you did. And don't worry, my mother is your biggest fan. She will start making a to-do list the minute you come over for the official asking of permission. I think she'll appreciate the long lead time so she can plan everything to her desire. Get the right dress, the best clergyman to officiate . . ."

"Hopefully not a conservative clergyman?" Mehrdad asked gingerly.

"Probably a moderate clergyman. Let's face it," I said to Mehrdad. "Neither one of us is exactly devout."

"It's such a relief," Mehrdad said, "to know we agree on that."

I nodded.

"And by the way, Ellie," he said. "Since we're talking about all the big things. Are we on the same page when it comes to . . . the rest?"

"What rest?"

He looked serious. "Ellie, I know you are studying hard. I respect your academic prowess, your ambition. But . . . are you . . . you want kids, right?"

"Do I? I want five!"

Mehrdad's face broke into a relieved smile. "Phew! Because I want six!"

"We'd better start right after the wedding, then!" I said boldly.

Mehrdad blushed at my allusion. His entire face went red in a way that made me want to jump over the table and bite into him.

"We'll make it work, Ellie. Maybe my mother or your mother, if she agrees, can help take care of our kids if you want to work full-time. You know I'll support you in that. We will figure it all out." Then he looked around the restaurant beaming, as though he might burst with the news of all we'd discussed. When the waiter came to clear our plates, Mehrdad grabbed his arm and said, "Agha, I asked her to marry me! And she accepted! She accepted, accepted, accepted!"

The waiter gave us many *mobaraks* and said he wished for us a life of good health and joy. Then he picked up our yolky plates and balanced them atop several others on his arm, looking like a circus performer mastering an impossible trick.

The following Friday, Mehrdad and his parents came to our home for the official sojourn of asking permission from my family for my hand. Mother fussed all morning. She asked me to button up her best turquoise frock, help arrange her hair in a chignon, and make sure her face had just the right amount of color. She forced Uncle Massoud to wear a three-piece beige suit (he sighed and did her bidding) and shouted order after order to our housemaid, Batul. Batul had already shopped for the biggest oranges, apples, cucumbers, and grapes and arranged them on a huge platter. She poured mixtures of nuts and seeds, *ajeel*, into scoped glass bowls per Mother's directions. She brewed tea to perfection. The furniture sparkled from Batul's polishing.

I hoped Mother would behave in front of Mehrdad's family and not act too overeager at the idea of our marriage. Mother had longed so much for this day. I did not want her to embarrass me with effusive expressions of approval.

Mehrdad and Mr. and Mrs. Tavakoli arrived carrying a huge bouquet of flowers and a light cardboard box wrapped in twine. I could tell from the label on it that it contained the best pastries. I was glad to see Mrs. Tavakoli in a simple navy skirt and beige blouse—it made me feel better that I had stuck to my instincts and worn a nice but unadorned blouse and skirt set despite Mother's suggestions that I dress up more. Mehrdad had shaved closely; his hair was carefully combed, but he also wore his usual combination of light shirt and dark pants.

We all went to the living room, where Mehrdad sat on one sofa in between his parents. I sat on the sofa facing them in between Mother and Uncle Massoud. Mehrdad and I exchanged a glance. I felt like we were little children, expected to be seen and not heard. Mehrdad winked at me as if to signal that we were both going to get through this formality and be fine.

Batul came in then with a tray of tea, dates, sugar cubes, and baklava, and everyone took an *estekan* of the amber brew and their sweetener of choice. Mr. Tavakoli thanked us for hosting them and commented politely about the weather. Mrs. Tavakoli chimed in with a stanza of ancient Persian poetry describing the shape of clouds. Uncle Massoud immediately responded with another poem about the rays of the sun.

Mrs. Tavakoli laughed pleasantly at the escalating poetry exchange. I studied her. Here was a woman in her fifties, so comfortable with herself. Not striving, not trying to cover up her age, but simply elegant. She seemed to have an innate dignity, an unpretentious good nature. I sighed and wondered, not for the first time, how it might have been to have a mother like that. One who did not fuss over herself interminably. One who did not see the world as a place filled with vice and viciousness to be conquered.

Would Mother have been different if my father had lived? If it were he who sat next to me on this sofa and not his brother, would Mother have been another person? I would never know. I looked at my uncle, who was now busy dabbing his forehead with a pressed handkerchief. He was trying. God bless him for always trying. I could not fault my uncle. He did his best. He seemed to truly love my mother; I was realizing this more and more with each passing year.

"You must eat the fruit! My goodness, don't have me peel and cut each one up and force-feed you!" Mother grabbed a few of the small plates Batul had laid on the coffee table, loaded each with fruit, and passed them around to the guests. Mrs. Tavakoli graciously took her plate and proceeded to peel an orange as though it was her favorite activity in all the world. Mr. Tavakoli and Mehrdad accepted their offerings too and ate a few grapes immediately. I knew Mother's relentless *tarof*—her begging us to eat—came from good intentions. Still, I couldn't help but be embarrassed. When Mother picked out a cucumber for herself and bit into it audibly, I cringed. Mrs. Tavakoli cut her own cucumber carefully. Was it just me or did Mother always chew so loudly?

Suddenly Mehrdad spoke up. "Mr. and Mrs. Soltani, if you would give me permission . . ." He swallowed hard. "I would like to . . . I would very much wish to . . . marry your daughter, Elaheh. I promise you that I will do everything in my power to make sure that our lives together are worthy of the attention, care, and happiness she deserves."

I looked down, burning with love and pride for him. I heard Uncle Massoud clear his throat. He was probably getting ready to officially respond and give his permission.

"I don't . . . I just don't . . ." Mother's voice was croaky.

My head whipped up. I had imagined Mother clapping her hands with glee at the prospect of our marriage. I had imagined her crying out, "It will be the festival of the decade! A jubilee!"

Instead, she held her cucumber limply. She looked pale.

"Are you alright?" Uncle Massoud asked.

Mother stared at the coffee table. "I imagined it. Imagined this moment perhaps fifty-five times. I anticipated the joy with which my soul would be flooded. You"—she looked at Mehrdad—"are a fine young man." She nodded at Mrs. Tavakoli and Mr. Tavakoli. "You've raised a fine person. It's just that . . ." She turned to me. She held my gaze and seemed unable to go on.

I held my breath. My scalp tingled. I tried to give off a sense of composure, even though my heart banged.

"You are my only child," Mother finally choked out. "You are mine."

I felt completely ambushed by my mother's behavior. Hadn't she approved of this match a hundred times over? She was Mehrdad's biggest fan. She wanted the proposal, wanted me to *net* him, as she'd put it. Why was my mother doing this?

"She is mine," Mother whispered, her chignon looking like it might unravel against her perspiring face and neck. "She is my baby."

I did not know what to do or say. I widened my eyes at Mehrdad. To my surprise, he had teared up.

Uncle Massoud leaned into Mother. He put his arm around her.

Mrs. Tavakoli got up then. She walked to our sofa, hunched down, and took my mother's hands in hers. "She always will be your child, won't she?" she said softly. "That won't change."

Mother inhaled deeply. She was quiet for a few minutes. "Thank you," she whispered finally. "For understanding a mother's heart."

Mother wiped her eyes with her palms and then pushed and patted her chignon back into place as much as possible. She straightened herself up. "We will," she said in an extra loud voice, "have the wedding of a century! Won't we? Lord knows we have enough time to plan it!"

The others laughed. I looked at each one of them in turn and then at my mother. Though I had just turned twenty, I still struggled to understand this mother of mine.

She was exhausting, confounding, and at times suffocating. Why did she make everything about her?

Would I understand her more when I, *inshallah*, became a mother myself?

"Batul!" Mother sang out. "Come on in here with more tea. Our guests are parched, *vay Khoda*, dear God, they need more tea!"

As the others began to chat again, Mother leaned into me and whispered,

"Forgive me. I want you to be happy. I want it so badly. It's just that things will change once you marry, that's all. And I will miss having you all to myself. But I accept it! I accept." She sucked on her teeth and let out a barely audible whistle. "Sometimes I worry that I, too, could *cheshm* you. I don't want to have an evil eye. I want everything to be perfect for you. No one can ruin your path to happiness. Not one soul. Please, Ellie. Be careful."

I sank further into the sofa. Wishing I could erase from the world the concept of an evil eye. Wishing I didn't have to constantly worry about others jinxing me.

"Even those who love you most can ruin your life, you know, Ellie," Mother said. "Even the ones you trust the most."

EIGHTEEN

March 1963

Homa sat in the cafeteria with a *salad olivier* sandwich, a bag of Pofak Namaki cheese puffs, and a bottle of *limonade*. In between bites and sips, she went on a particularly blistering tirade about our government's ills. To her fervent accusations, I responded with a half-baked argument about "looking at the other side." Though in the months right after the coup d'état of 1953 that overthrew Prime Minister Mossadegh, Mother and Uncle Massoud had worried about our king's expanding role, after a decade they looked around and decided the king had done right by them. They were wealthy, healthy, and loving the direction of the country.

I desperately wanted to change the subject when suddenly the world went dark. Someone had covered my eyes.

I heard Homa laugh.

A familiar scent of citrusy soap came from the hands that blocked my vision. I reached up, yanked them off my face, and wheeled around. Behind me stood Mehrdad next to Abdol.

For it wasn't just Homa, Mehrdad, and I who had studied hard and gotten lucky and made it into that university; Abdol had gotten in too. His scores didn't land him in the law program as he'd desired, but he was able to start his studies in the geography field.

After removing Mehrdad's hands from my eyes, I jumped out of my seat. He hugged me.

Homa groaned, and I shifted away from Mehrdad and our public show of affection.

Homa put down her *limonade*. "By the way, I can't make it to the Chahar Shanbeh Suri festival of fire celebration. There's a meeting."

Every time Homa said *there's a meeting*, I knew she meant the *Tudeh* Communist Party. I never attended, though every now and then she still invited me to join her. I imagined a bunch of enlightened uber-intellectual students huddled in a circle discussing how the British needed to keep their hands off Iran, how the Shah was overstepping his powers, and how a utopian socialist society would be the savior of our culture.

"Don't go," I said. "And don't say your business so loudly." I looked around the cafeteria nervously. Then I said through gritted teeth, "Aren't you the one who's always saying the Shah has spies?"

"Fine," she said. "I have a very important meeting," she added in a whisper.

"You can't miss Chahar Shanbeh Suri. We have a huge night planned," Mehrdad chimed in.

"Homa Khanom, you must come," Abdol said quietly.

In our first year of university, Abdol had asked for Homa's hand in marriage. His father had died when he was a baby, he said, but his mother could stand in, go with him to ask for the official permission from her family.

Homa said no.

A few months later, Abdol proposed marriage a second time. By then, his own mother had sadly passed away from heart failure, but Homa's answer was no different. She wanted them to be classmates. Friends. She didn't want to be his wife. She told me that she explained to him that she did not wish to marry. Ever. Abdol came away from that second rejection wrecked. For weeks he looked blurry-eyed and fatigued. But he respected Homa too much to ask again. He had accepted his fate to be "just friends."

Now Abdol rocked back and forth on his heels in the cafeteria. "All the *bacheha* will be there for Chahar Shanbeh Suri. The fresh air will do you good."

Homa sighed. "I have bigger things to worry about, don't you see? This is a pivotal time for our country."

"When isn't it a pivotal time for this country?" Mehrdad asked. He pulled me closer to him and affectionately kissed the top of my head.

From my peripheral vision, I saw Abdol's face redden.

Abdol came from a traditional, conservative background. He was religious and the women in his family all wore strict hijab. Homa's not wearing hijab didn't seem to stop him from falling in love with her and wanting to marry her, but there was no doubt in my mind that even if Homa had said yes to Abdol's proposal, he wouldn't have so much as touched her before being permitted by a marriage certificate.

I forced myself to relax into Mehrdad's affections. It was 1963. We were a new Iran. And we were engaged, for goodness' sake.

"There'll always be another meeting, another demonstration," I said, trying to change Homa's mind. "Chahar Shanbeh Suri happens only once a year. You need a break from those meetings. Come and have some fun."

"This meeting is important. I can't ignore the needs of the vulnerable. Sorry."

Abdol gazed at Homa with unabashed awe.

Mehrdad repeated his invitation to Homa, then said he and Abdol had to get going. He kissed me goodbye—this time just a quick peck on the cheek.

After the boys had left, I sat on the cafeteria bench next to Homa.

"Why can't you skip this meeting?" I asked in a low voice. "Why is it being held on such an important holiday?"

"Look, we have marches coming up. Protests. We have a whole plan. And I need to get some things translated." She looked down at her lap and mumbled, "Don't be mad, but Afarin is helping me."

"Who?" I asked in disbelief.

"Afarin Molavi."

"From high school? Stuck-up Afarin?"

"Yes, from high school. And she's not stuck-up, Ellie. She's changed. I know you never liked her, but she never speaks of you. She barely remembered me. She wants to help. She's one of us now."

I thought of the lavish parties at Afarin's home. The food, the alcohol, her parents who gallivanted around Europe. "Afarin is helping the communist cause?" I said with deep sarcasm. "That's rich!"

"She's seen the light, Ellie. She's sick of our Westoxification. Ever since she started Bazargani University and met this handsome leftist, she's so much more aware. So she's helping translate, yes." Homa leaned close to me and whispered, "There's a Trotskyite journal in England. They've released a few pamphlets. They outline some key theories and also specific steps for what's needed next in Iran. For revolution."

Homa, forever the idealist. I'd heard it all before.

"You're never going to get a revolution," I whispered back.

"No, these pamphlets lay it all out apparently. It's supposed to help catalyze everything, Ellie. But we need it all in Persian so the word can spread in Iran. And Afarin's English is excellent. Top-notch. Her translation will serve as a blueprint for a set of protests that will set into action irreversible change."

Here was Homa, at it again, raising the stakes with a mention of my old nemesis. I remembered Afarin's smug face. The way she crossed her arms and smirked as though I was a clown for her entertainment. Why was Homa even speaking to her?

"What do you mean Afarin's English is excellent? You know very well I am studying English. Why didn't you ask me?"

"You would never translate a political pamphlet! And Afarin has been attending our meetings. With her new . . . friend. To be honest, Ellie, I've been so impressed with her. She really has quite a brilliant mind."

My body grew hot. I wanted to slap Afarin. "Really? A brilliant mind?"

"And her English is superb. She's perfect. For this translating task, I mean."

"I'll do it!" I said.

"What?"

"I'll translate it for you." Then in a lower grumble, I said, "I can't believe you wouldn't even ask me."

"You always say you don't want to get involved."

"Give me the material and I will translate it. Afarin Molavi can go back to her bourgeois parties and nonsense. She has fooled even you, Homa."

"Look, I never brought up that she's joined our organization because I know you have this thing against her. Apparently, she won an award for English essay writing . . ."

"I said give me the material and I'll do it for you!"

Homa studied me quizzically. "You could get into deep trouble."

"I want to help you. I'll give you the English translation tomorrow. Can Afarin do that? Turn it around in one day?"

"Fine, fine," Homa said. She slipped her arm into her satchel and retrieved three small rectangular blue booklets. "Just keep it quiet. Remember, this is contraband material in the government's eyes. Don't show anyone."

NINETEEN

March 1963

The moon hung like a carcanet in the purple sky and the air smelled of woodsmoke and roasted nuts. Parents, siblings, aunts, uncles, cousins, and neighbors all gathered in the streets. Some of us ate sweet beets we'd bought from the beet-seller's cart. Others tossed sugared almonds into their mouths.

On the last Tuesday night before the spring equinox brought in the Persian New Year, we lit bonfires. It was tradition to run toward the flames and jump over them to release bad energy and bring in goodness and vitality for the new year.

Now this avenue—this part of the night—belonged to us. Students from Tehran University, Polytechnic University, and Bazargani University stood around in groups. Most of us girls wore trousers. I hopped in place, trying to stay warm in my navy peacoat, scarf, and deep crimson leather gloves.

Next to me, Mehrdad panted, bent over with his hands on his knees. "Making the leap is really not that hard, Ellie," he said in between gulps of breath. "Anticipating it is scarier than when you're actually doing it."

I had jumped over a few smaller bonfires that night but was intimidated by the tall flames of the largest one. Only a few brave girls dared try "the mother of bonfires," and the ones who did were athletes who had mastery over their limbs, confidence in their physical prowess, and a need for adrenaline.

"It looks impossible," I said.

Mehrdad straightened and touched my cheek. "I wouldn't lie to you. You'll be fine. Go line up. I'll be cheering you on."

If he thought I could do it, then maybe I could. He wouldn't put me in danger, would he? He gave my hand a reassuring squeeze and let go.

I walked to the group waiting their turn to jump over the largest fire and lined up behind a girl I recognized from high school. She nodded hello. I smiled nervously.

In the chilly night air, I rubbed my gloved hands together. Smoke caught in my throat and filled my lungs. I both craved the warmth of the fire and dreaded it. What if my shoe grazed the tip of a flame and my entire body lit ablaze? And why wasn't Homa here? Why did she care more about her Marxist meetings than about our own Persian traditions?

The line moved up. Soon it would be my turn. I felt I'd made a big mistake. I looked at the sidelines to find Mehrdad. But beyond a few feet, it was too hazy to see. A layer of smoky film made the world indefinite.

The sound of laughter—youthful merriment from the belief that the world is set up for your amusement, your pleasure, your plans—carried into a new year on a wind so dry it almost crackled.

I was suddenly barreled into and almost knocked over. "Have you tried it already, Ellie?"

She wore black pants and her usual no-frills black coat. Her hair circled her face in a wild, curly mane. Her voice was excited and filled with joy.

I hugged her. She smelled like hookah smoke. "What happened—your communist meeting got too boring?"

"The meeting was fine." Homa nudged her hip against mine. "But I didn't want to miss out on this with you."

She wore no gloves. I thought she should have put her hair up; I worried that it would catch on fire when she jumped. "Mehrdad says thinking about how difficult it could be is worse than actually doing it."

Homa grabbed my gloved hand in her bare one. "We'll both do it!"

"You want to go first?"

"We'll jump together."

"There's no way. We'll collide. It'll block our momentum."

We had moved up in line as we spoke.

The girl in front of us jogged in place, prepping for her sprint. I envied her confidence. Cheers emanated from onlookers as she dashed to the fire and sailed over it like an Olympic high-jumper.

Then we were next. Homa tightened her hold on my hand and took off. I had no choice but to run with her. Together we rushed toward the flames until the wind changed from chilly to scorching and heat spread across my face. It felt like we would dive into the blaze and run right through the fire.

Out of habit, out of tradition, out of the memory in my genes from my ancestors, I shouted at the top of my lungs the traditional chant of "*Sorkhiyeh to az man, Zardiyeh man az to!*" Asking the flames to give me their energy and vibrancy and to take away my weariness and dullness. My voice was not alone—Homa's was in sync with mine. We were almost up against the fire now. We had to rush into it headlong or jump.

We jumped.

Time slowed down. My body buzzed itself calm. The blood running through me was charged.

Floating suspended in the air, all the rest of it blacked out—it was just us up there, flying, flames practically licking at our shoes, the air hazy and dreamy, smoke swirling into our hair, flecks of fire landing on our ankles softly as fireflies. We rid ourselves of the toxic and shed burdens from the past year to enter our new year cleansed. Cleansed by the smoke of the fire. Cleansed by the rush of adrenaline that coursed through our limbs. Cleansed by the soaring leap. Hovering above everything like that, the world felt completely ours.

And then we thudded onto our knees. My wrist turned backward; Homa's body was splayed. With effort, she staggered onto all fours and helped me up. Together we stood upright and stumbled out of the way so the next person could land behind us.

We walked until we located the shape of Mehrdad on the sidelines. Homa swung my arm up in victory.

I inhaled the night air, amazed and slaphappy at our unaccountable flight.

Unaware that it would be our last.

TWENTY

November 1963

In our first semester of our third year at university, the big event we all looked forward to was Niloo's engagement party. Her wedding to her fiancé, Hooman, was planned for after graduation, just like mine and Mehrdad's. But to celebrate Niloo's engagement, Sousan had insisted on hosting a huge party for them at her mansion.

Sousan already had a toddler and a new infant. She had gotten married to the Colonel right after high school in a wedding that was grandiose, glamorous, and gaudy. Sousan didn't attend university at all. Hers was a world Niloo and I could not yet comprehend: one of mothering and hosting parties for the Colonel and his large network of family and friends.

I was surprised when Niloo agreed to have Sousan host her engagement party.

"What can I say, Ellie? We're graduating next year and it's all my parents can do to manage the cost of everything plus my upcoming wedding. Sousan so enjoys party planning and setup and is excited to make a special evening for me. It'll be fun."

Even Homa acquiesced to coming to Niloo's party, solely because it meant so much to Niloo. Homa would be well dressed, thanks to me. She'd confided that she had nothing appropriate to wear to Niloo's celebration— her mother's sewn dresses and fabrics were all reserved for the rich ladies uptown. So I brought to campus a brown dress Uncle Massoud had bought for me in London. Simple. Nothing fancy. Perfect for Homa.

"Oh, your uncle is clueless when it comes to fashion," Mother had said. "Doesn't think to get the right size. It's far too long for you, Ellie, and it's rather plain—definitely not worth getting hemmed. Let's give it to Batul; she can take it home to relatives in her village."

I told Mother I knew someone at school who could use it.

"That Homa who you still insist on befriending? Of course, that's who you want to give it to. Always trying to help her out, aren't you, Ellie? Still, after all these years. Don't you know charity never goes unpunished?" Then her face brightened. "Well, it is an ugly garment. Fine, give it to that friend of yours so she has something to wear to Niloo's engagement festivities, poor thing. That way she can blend into the walls and not upstage you."

"Mother, what are you even talking about?"

"Oh, my darling." Mother shook her head. "You still have so much to learn. She would upstage you for a very simple reason." Mother opened both arms wide to indicate all that was around us: the fancy sofa, the marble side tables, the finely engraved vases. "She is jealous of you! Why wouldn't she be? You with that handsome Mehrdad on your arm! You with all this wealth. You with the beauty. Did it ever occur to you that she wants what you have?"

The week before Niloo's big engagement party, Homa and I sat in an empty classroom on campus, books spread out across our study table. We were both prepping for exams. Mehrdad had been busy with lab work and his own studies; I hadn't seen him for days. I was exhausted from trying to keep up with my assignments: sleep deprived and drowning in verb tenses and English grammar. Sometimes it felt like I was carrying out Homa's plan, not my own. Wasn't she the one who wanted me to be at university to make a change? It was her ambition, not mine, that had brought us here. I often felt like an imposter who'd somehow gotten accepted by mistake. I didn't have passion for my field of languages the way Homa did for law.

Homa looked up from her textbook. "The hypocrisy is what gets me."

Had she somehow read my mind? Did she know how little I cared about the subjunctive tense of English verbs that I had to study for my languages exam?

"What?" I mumbled.

"The Shah's White Revolution."

In January of that Western year of 1963, the Shah had enacted a series of nationwide reforms called "the White Revolution." The reforms were given that name to symbolize enacting change without blood being spilled.

"And why is the White Revolution hypocritical, pray tell?"

"Oh, come on! It is hypocrisy at work!" Homa said in a haughty voice I hated.

"For the love of God, Homa. What about reforms on land ownership, profit sharing, women getting the right to vote, and nationalization of water resources is hypocritical? Isn't that what you and your organization wanted? None of it is good enough?"

"Elaheh." She said my full name with a tone that sounded a lot like pity. "Of course, I'm glad women got the right to vote. We should have gotten that long ago, to be honest. But don't be fooled. None of the reforms address— not one bit—rampant human rights violations or corruption or . . ."

I sighed as she recited—again—examples of *party-bazi* and nepotism and pay-for-play rewards of officials beholden to a Shah who employs a secret police and harangues dissidents. Why was Homa so ideological, so impossible?

"My group and I have organized a major university-wide protest for next Wednesday. I'm telling you because I trust you. And your translating of the pamphlet helped so much—thank you again for that, Ellie. Our plan is to initiate a sit-in, and if the authorities resist and don't listen to our demands, we're ready for a full-on strike. Hopefully it won't get to that. But the protest is definitely going ahead. To skirt the problem of arrest, because lord knows we don't have free speech in this country, we're going to start by saying it's a protest against elitist university policies and potential academic cutbacks. But the idea is that we'll be voicing our disgust with the Shah and his pretending that he's passed true reforms when what he's doing behind the scenes is just unconscionable."

I was alarmed that they were actually going ahead with their plans, especially after what had happened just a few short months ago.

Five months earlier, in June, riots had broken out across Iran and people had poured into the streets in support of a religious cleric, Ayatollah Khomeini, who had spoken up against these reforms. Afterward, there had been a strong crackdown by the Shah's secret police, SAVAK. They had combed the campus to root out dissidents.

Homa had assured me—much to my relief—that she and her communist student group had not been involved with those June riots, but now I wondered if she had any fear or common sense.

"It's too dangerous, Homa. Please don't do this."

"Why? So I can sit back and relax and let our rights be continuously eroded and erased? I wish you would take time to understand, Ellie," she continued. "There are more important things to worry about than what you're going to wear to Niloo's engagement party next Friday. All you care about is that *gherti* partying nonsense."

The condescension in her voice grated on me. "You have a whole lot of nerve. When you needed that Trotskyite pamphlet translated, who did it? I did. How can you say I don't care when I did that for you?"

"Because you don't care. You translated it only to one-up Afarin! Not that I don't appreciate it. But be honest. You didn't care about one word of it. You have no passion for the actual cause."

She was right. I did not care the way Homa did. I'd translated the pamphlet because I was hurt that she had asked Afarin over me and wanted to show off, not because I truly cared about its contents. In my daily life, I tried to stay as apolitical as humanly possible, but of course it was impossible to live a life devoid of politics. Even my ability to consider being apolitical was a sign of what Homa considered my privilege in life: my luck, fortune, family money. But I was tired of constantly having to hear how wrong everything was with our country. Homa seemed determined to fault the Shah no matter what happened.

"Sometimes I feel like nothing will make you satisfied, Homa," I said. "Nothing. And the White Revolution reforms? It's what you and your communist group wanted. No? But you're always complaining."

"I'm the complainer? You constantly complain about how hard everything is, Ellie. You complain that we have to take exams!"

"Fine. I complain about school. But you complain about this country night and day. Finding fault with the king, the parliament members, the rich, the company owners. You claim you want to help the 'normal people,' but deep down you think you know better. Do you even respect the people of this country?"

Homa's face crumpled in disappointment. Then one side of her mouth went up.

I hated that sneer, that know-it-all smirk.

"We can't just pretend it's all wonderful, Ellie." She paused. "Or at least when it isn't wonderful for so many. I know it is for you. The Shah's policies benefit *you*. Your family. The people in your neighborhood. You're turning into a rightful royalist right before my eyes. Or perhaps you always were one."

My neck and shoulders tensed. The way she looked at me with disappointment filled me with both shame and indignation. At that moment, it felt like nothing I did would ever be enough for her. She would always see me as too privileged, too shallow, too rich. Her accusation of my being a royalist rang in my ears. And what if I was one? Was that a crime?

"These new policies will benefit everyone eventually, you will see," I said. "That's the whole point of the reforms. You've always cared so much about women's rights. You can't deny how much headway the country is making in that realm. We have to give credit where credit is due. The Shah is helping women."

"We have such a long, long way to go, Ellie. I'm not going to be placated. What about freedom to criticize the Shah? We don't have that. What about minority rights? Do you even care, Ellie, about the rights of Kurds in this country or the rights of . . ."

My head began to throb as she listed all the injustices. I didn't want to hear the litany of wrongs again. I shoved my notebooks and textbooks into my satchel. My voice shook. "It's pointless to study with you. You don't focus. You want to constantly *discuss*. You and your communist activist group do nothing but create problems. You're never grateful for what we *do* have in this country. Go ahead. Plan your sit-ins and your strikes. Plan your 'major protest.' It's all a waste of time."

"It is absolutely not a waste of time," Homa said. "It's the best thing we could do with our time."

"Really? You say you want to become a lawyer? A judge? How are you going to do that if you're on strike?"

"We need the authorities to know that—"

"I don't know what you want, Homa. Utopia is not possible. I know your father is a communist, but look at where that's gotten him. He's in jail, no use to anyone . . ."

Homa sat straight as a rod in her chair. "What are you saying about my father?"

I sucked in my breath. I regretted mentioning her father as soon as I said those words. "Nothing. Look, I am sorry. But what you're doing is futile. Organizing a protest. And then a strike. For what? I'm not like you; you're right about that. I don't even like this university. I want to marry Mehrdad. I want to have children. I want to have five of them. Maybe six. And I will stay home with them. And I will raise them. And I won't worry about women's rights, or the decrees, or even the right to vote. How about that? I will be pretty for my husband and I will serve him dinner and I will make his bed and I will give myself over to him. It's sounding better by the minute!"

"Give yourself over to your husband?"

"Yes, my husband! You don't even have a partner, Homa. You're just not . . . normal." In a clumsy series of movements, I snapped my satchel shut, got up, turned around, and marched to the door.

"Where are you going?" she called out. "We haven't finished studying!"

"Aren't you going on strike? What is there to study?"

I swung the door as I left, hoping it would make a loud slam. But it just swayed. I turned back once. She was still seated, her upper body swiveled toward the door, her face an expression of complete confusion.

I regretted our argument within hours. I should not have brought up Homa's father in such a careless way. I knew she missed him deeply. And Homa had a right to want to fix our country's wrongs. Of course she did.

The next day and during the ones following, Homa avoided me on campus. She was hurt; I knew. We'd had arguments before, but this one felt different. I thought back to right before our friendship began when she called me Donkey and I reminded her that I was the descendant of royalty. Those two girls running to school in downtown seemed like other creatures now. How could I have been so naïve as to believe that our friendship would just sail along despite our new differences in wealth and politics? While I danced at soirees, Homa worked in a restaurant kitchen. And my mother wouldn't even let her into our home after all this time. Maybe it had been simple when we were children to just focus on our delight, our fun, our jokes, what we had in common. But now our lived reality was diverging more and more each day.

I did not like her secret Marxist life. I worried that she'd become too entrenched in the communist movement. Even though she'd told me about the upcoming protest, she rarely shared what went on at planning meetings. I didn't even know where they met! In teahouses in Darband? In secret rooms away from the eyes of the Shah's secret police? When we'd been younger, Homa's view of me had helped bring out my best traits. She had believed in me and seen in me more good and smarts than I had dared to believe I had.

But now? As third-year university students, her view of my lifestyle made me ashamed. I hated to think of the vanity and materialism she saw in my circles. I hated it because it burst the bubble of the world I had so carefully nurtured in my new life uptown.

And yet. Ours was a friendship worth saving. Worth keeping. Worth protecting. For I knew Homa's heart was pure. I admired her inability to ever be fake. She was the most authentic person I knew. And I valued our friendship too much to let this recent argument stymie us.

The protest she'd planned went ahead that Wednesday. As I walked to campus, I saw a crowd of students gathered by the main entrance. Coward that I was, I scurried away, far from the prying eyes of potential secret police, but I could hear the students' demands. They shouted that a university education should always remain free of cost. They asked that the administration make changes to become even more egalitarian. Their chants were targeted, specific. They protested university policies and didn't say anything directly against the Shah. But it was clear that the underlying current was deeply anti-Shah.

Homa stood in the crowd, next to Abdol of all people. So, she had convinced him to join. Of course, Abdol could never say no to Homa. In return, I found out later from Mehrdad, she'd even agreed to go on a walk with him. Abdol told Mehrdad that Homa had been the happiest he'd ever seen her—filled with adrenaline and an infectious electric energy.

We couldn't avoid one another forever.

I decided that when I saw her at Niloo's engagement party that Friday, I would be the bigger person and apologize first. I couldn't go on with this tense *ghaar*—this avoidance of one another due to hurt feelings. We'd have to face one another again. We had to achieve some sort of a truce.

She knew the best in me, but she also knew the worst.

Homa knew me too well—that was the problem.

TWENTY-ONE

November 1963

On the evening of the party, I pinned my beehive as high as it could go, applied my makeup, and rehearsed in my mind what I would say to Homa when I saw her. The dress Mother had ordered from the tailor for me was a rich, deep green silk with a tapered waist and a skirt of tulle designed to display my slender figure and toned arms. I worried that the cut of the dress looked rather childish, but Mother assured me it most certainly did not.

As I opened the dress box, I decided on three points: I would apologize to Homa for unintentionally bringing her father's name into our argument, assure her that she could do as she pleased with her political plans, and let her know that my first concern was always her safety and security.

She would accept my apology—I was sure she would. Homa wasn't one to hold a grudge, a trait that I admired, even envied. By the end of the night, she and I would be eating Sousan's signature cream puffs and giggling about how absurd the Colonel looked in his military uniform, which he would probably wear to the party.

A little after 8 p.m., I rang the doorbell of Sousan's huge home. Like most Iranian hosts, Sousan served dinner on the late side. Party guests often spent their first hours making small talk and eating appetizers. Finding the door open, I entered the large foyer. Inside, the floor, tiled in an octagonal black-and-white pattern, gleamed beneath my feet. A servant with a slight limp came and took my camel-hair overcoat. I looked up at the lustrous chandelier hanging from the high ceiling, at the curved staircase leading to the second floor. Were Sousan's two children sleeping safely up there? I had hoped to catch sight of her son, to see her baby daughter. But of course, they were probably ensconced upstairs with their nanny—leaving the revelry and merriment to the adults.

The servant ushered me down a corridor that led into the large parlor. In that room filled with guests, the air smelled of expensive perfumes and colognes. A huge Persian carpet woven in cream, dark navy, and light blue covered the expanse of the floor in detailed and delicate geometric patterns. Everyone was dressed to the nines: the women in dresses the color of rubies, emeralds, and sapphires with sparkling jewelry to match their frocks, the men in suits and some even in tuxedos. Groups stood and chatted and ate from small plates of hors d'oeuvres. Some guests held flutes of what I assumed must have been champagne.

Sousan's parties may not have been as decadent as Afarin Molavi's, but they were legendary in their own right as rarefied and definitely glamorous. The Colonel was more than happy to fund his wife's every whim, including the makeshift bar at the end of the parlor stocked with bottles of whiskey and champagne, drinks I had first learned about at Afarin's parties. I had only tasted alcohol once at Afarin's—a few sips of red wine that tasted like cherry *sharbat* gone bad. I had a torn feeling about alcohol: plenty of people in our "Muslim-majority" country certainly did drink, but that one time I'd had wine hadn't been anything special. I looked around the parlor. This crowd was exactly what Homa would have called "the westernized bourgeoisie."

Where was Homa? I was ready to finally face her and apologize.

A tuxedoed waiter holding a round tray walked by and handed me a flute before I could say no.

"I don't drink," I said quietly to no one, but I'd taken the flute in my hand. I mustered up the courage, told myself to grow up, took a sip, and burped immediately. I hadn't expected it to be so bubbly. Kind of like my favorite Ka-Na-Da but less sweet, more crisp.

I took another sip, thinking of Mehrdad. I wanted to see him so badly. Thank God we were both done with exams for a while. Tonight we could finally catch up properly—be together again. Earlier, he'd driven to the airport to pick up a cousin of his returning from studies in London. To save him the crosstown drive to my house, we'd arranged to meet at the party. Where was he?

Out of the corner of my eye, I saw Niloo.

She came up to me giggling and beaming, her smile wide. She hugged me right away.

I inhaled Niloo's familiar rosewater scent as we hugged. Then I held her at arm's length. "Look at you!" I said, aware that I sounded exactly like my mother. "All gorgeous and smiley. Congratulations, Niloo Joon!"

"Thank you, thank you!" Niloo said. "I'm so glad you're here. Sousan has gone and completely outdone herself. It's all so over the top." She burped and giggled.

"Have you been having champagne too?" I asked.

"Just a little. Let me show you the food . . . just the appetizers. There's more to come!"

She took my hand and led me to a long table on the other side of the room laid out with silver platters, china plates, and tiered dishes of every size. Wedges of *kuku sabzi*, potato *kuku*, and eggplant frittata slices, dolmehs heaped in a pyramid shape, roasted peppers, eggplant and tomato in whey, slices of cold cuts and mounds and mounds of *salad olivier*, and caviar on toast overwhelmed my senses. Niloo handed me a small plate and arranged on it two triangular slices of toast covered with caviar. "From the Caspian Sea," she said. "Our own Iranian caviar is the best." I bit in and savored the salty sea flavor of the caviar. I could taste lemon juice on top. I took another sip of my champagne.

"Have you seen Homa, Niloo Joon?"

"Yes, she arrived early! I've been here since 3 p.m. to help Sousan with all the preparations, though of course Sousan's army of servants didn't let me do much. Homa was the first guest to arrive and insisted on going into the kitchen to help the cooks. Sousan told her she didn't need to, but you know how Homa is—she wouldn't take no for an answer! By the way, she looks gorgeous in that dress. She said you gave it to her?"

"She does?" I asked.

"Oh, she looks stunning. The cut really flatters her."

"Oh." I was happy the dress looked good on Homa, of course I was. I gulped more of the champagne.

Niloo must have registered some level of insecurity in me because she immediately said, "And you look beautiful in that green, my dear! It suits you so!"

I thanked her. I replaced my worries that the cut of my own dress was juvenile with the sober thought that although Homa might look stunning, I still owed her an apology.

"So she's in the kitchen? She's probably bossing the cooks around!"

Niloo laughed. "I'm guessing so! I haven't seen her out in the parlor. You know how Homa hates these party things. I'm honored she even showed up, to be honest."

"She adores you. For you she's made the big sacrifice of attending a bourgeois party with caviar and champagne!" I laughed uneasily and lifted my flute in the air. I hadn't told Niloo about the argument and from Niloo's easy manner, neither had Homa. "I'm going to find Homa, okay? Enjoy, enjoy! By the way, where's that handsome fiancé of yours?"

"He's with the Colonel and some other men in the side room off the parlor. Smoking the Colonel's imported cigars. Hooman always stinks like the Colonel after he smokes them."

"So does Mehrdad!"

Ever since Sousan had gotten engaged in high school, Niloo and I had a running joke about the Colonel's love of cigars and his inescapable tobacco smell.

"Well, we'll have to tell them to air out their clothes, that's for sure," Niloo said.

I put my empty champagne flute down on a table, exited the parlor, and made my way down a corridor to the white swinging double doors of Sousan's large kitchen. Sousan kept one live-in cook but hired additional chefs for her big parties. I pressed my hand to the door and its hinge gave a small squeak. I stopped, then, and for good luck, patted my beehive. I pushed the door open and stepped into the steamy and fragrant kitchen, the tart scent of pomegranate molasses overwhelming me. So, there was *fesenjoon* on the menu tonight. I felt a childish delight at the thought of it. I would say how sorry I was and Homa would forgive me. Then I'd drag her out of that kitchen. Maybe I would even convince Homa to dance.

At first, I barely even saw her. But there she was, alone at the stove, bent over a large pot with a big spoon in her hand. She dipped it into the pot, brought up a spoonful, and blew on it.

From the back corner of the kitchen, he came and walked right up to her. He stood close and leaned in. She lifted the spoon to his mouth. He closed his eyes and tasted what she offered. When he opened his eyes wide, he looked enchanted and smiled.

He smiled the way he only smiled at me.

My arms began to tingle, and the feeling spread until every single fiber of my being buzzed with what I could only say was fury. For right there next to Homa was Mehrdad. He was dressed in the shirt I had bought him. In the kitchen steam, his hair was extra wavy. He kept smiling at Homa.

She laughed.

My body was tense with anger. As I stood there, holding one of the double doors open with my arm, I had a strong sense of déjà vu. Suddenly I was ten years old again, coming home from school with a paper crown on my head to find my mother and Uncle Massoud entwined with one another on the mattress. This wasn't the same—part of my brain could register that truth even in my fury. And yet. Blood rushed to my ears; the back of my neck and scalp felt as if they were injected with sharp needles. He shouldn't have been so close to her. She shouldn't have been giving him a taste of whatever it was, lifting that spoon to his mouth as he bent over and leaned into her. Where were the staff? It wasn't right. It wasn't fair.

Did it ever occur to you, Ellie Joon, that she wants what you have?

I heard Mother's voice in my spinning head. I shouldn't have had the champagne. The salty sea taste of the caviar returned to my mouth with a nauseating metallic flavor.

I needed to leave that kitchen. Had the words I spoke in anger and frustration during our argument in the empty classroom bothered Homa that much? Was this some kind of sad revenge?

I turned to leave. The door swung and the hinge squeaked again. This time she must have heard it. "Hey!" Homa called out. "Oh, is that you, Ellie? Hello!"

I turned around.

"Ellie Jan!" Mehrdad looked surprised but jolly.

I ran.

In the large parlor, a live band was performing, their music strangely alluring. Jazz. I knew it from American movies. Sousan and her stupid parties. Always imitating foreigners. And then I realized I was sounding like Homa and it made me angrier still. She was always in my head, always entwined with me. Even when she had just betrayed me.

For it did feel like a betrayal—their closeness in that kitchen. I didn't know if I was angrier at him or at her. Homa insisting she didn't feel anything for any boy! Wanting to "look into Mehrdad's eyes"! She had a thing for him and it was crystal clear to me now. What a fool I had been not to see it before!

I pushed past the bodies in the parlor and walked to the first corridor and then to the foyer. The octagonal black-and-white tiles dizzied me. I needed to get some air. I opened the front door and hurried down the few steps. The front garden was lit up with lanterns in the trees. The night air was cooling, refreshing. My breath was jagged. My body still trembled.

"Ellie! Ellie, wait up!"

Homa had followed me outside. She came and stood near me in the brown dress I had given her. The ugly dress that had been too long for me fit her perfectly. Even in the dim light of the lanterns, I could tell Niloo was right. Homa looked elegant and quite beautiful—and I hated that she did.

"Please, don't talk to me," I said.

"Ellie! I've been wanting to apologize to you."

I noticed then that she had a carpeted bag hanging from her shoulder. It was rectangular and large and hung from a braided strap of different colored pieces of wool. The bag clashed terribly with her dress. Who would think to carry such a bag to a fancy party? I had a rude thought: you can take the girl out of the bottom of the city, but you can't take the bottom of the city out of the girl. Now she wanted to apologize to me? She had no shame!

"Look, Ellie," Homa said. "That argument we had last week—it was silly. We were both overwhelmed with exams ahead. I didn't mean to hurt you with my avoidance since."

I shook with disbelief. "That's what you want to apologize about?"

"Yes. Look, I don't want us to be *ghaar*—to give one another the silent treatment. Let's make up, please. Sousan has gone crazy with this party, don't you think? And Niloo looks so happy . . ."

Did she think I was stupid? How naïve did she think I was? "Don't talk to me," I repeated.

"Ellie! I said I was sorry—come on . . ."

"I saw you in the kitchen with Mehrdad."

"I know," she said.

Again, the anger ran through me. "It's not enough that you came to my high school, stole my friends, competed with me every step of the way? That you are a maniac at our university, obsessed with politics and grades? Now you have to flirt with my fiancé too?"

From the light of the lanterns, I could see the expression on Homa's face change. She looked purely puzzled. "No one was flirting."

I wanted to turn my back on her and walk home, leave the party behind: the music in the parlor, the caviar on toast, the pots in the kitchen, and my feckless fiancé and two-faced friend.

I started down the path toward the gigantic gates of Sousan's front garden. Homa followed me, grabbed my shoulder, and made me face her. "You are so wrong. Perhaps you've been drinking alcohol? Are you okay?"

I shook her off me.

"Here's what's going to happen," Homa said calmly. "*I'm* going to go home. And you're going to go to Mehrdad and enjoy the rest of this party. I will forget we ever had this conversation." She turned, walked to the gate, and exchanged a few words with one of the Colonel's security staff. The guard unlocked the gate, whistled with his fingers, and within a minute, a taxi drove up from the line Sousan and the Colonel arranged for their big parties.

The security guard helped Homa into the cab.

"Wait!" I called out. My brain was in a fog and I could feel a headache coming on. I staggered down the pathway.

Homa leaned out of the back of the taxi as I got closer. "Go back to the party, Ellie. Go back to Mehrdad. Go back to Niloo and Hooman and let Sousan know you're okay. I can tell you're not yourself. Look, there's a reason I don't come to these parties. I don't belong here. I never did. I came for Niloo. That is the only reason. Well, maybe for you as well. I was hoping we could talk. I wanted to explain to you about the other day when we argued about the protest . . ."

Before she could finish, before I could say anything, the taxi drove off.

I stood alone for a few moments and took in deep gulps of the night air.

Mehrdad was in the foyer when I went back inside. "Are you alright? I've been looking everywhere for you!"

"I needed some air," I said coldly.

"Why did you run out like that? I wanted to come after you, but Homa told me not to. She told me the two of you had had a political argument and you were upset? She said she wanted to talk to you alone. To apologize."

A resentful snort exited my nose. "Did she now? '*Homa told me not to!*'" I imitated him in a childish way.

"Ellie, what has gotten into you?"

"I saw you in the kitchen. Cozying up to her. Smiling like a damn fool, all of it!"

He stared at me with the same confused expression I had seen minutes ago on Homa's face. "What on earth?"

"I don't want to talk to you right now, Mehrdad." I didn't want to look at him. My head pounded.

He put his hand on my arm, but I shook it off. "I really don't feel well. I need to be alone."

Sousan came by then with the servant who had first taken my coat, chanting out what felt like orders. Mehrdad must have given Sousan a desperate look, because she immediately asked, "What's wrong?"

"Nothing." The nausea hit me again. I grabbed my stomach. "Can I just lie down somewhere for a few minutes?" I looked at Mehrdad and then back at Sousan. "Alone."

"Of course," Sousan said with the look one woman gives another. "You look pale. Don't you worry. Come with me."

She took my hand, gave Mehrdad and the servant a reassuring nod that signified she knew how to take care of female troubles, and then led me down the corridor to a dark room off the parlor.

Sousan turned on a lamp and I realized we were in the Colonel's tobacco-scented study. Bookshelves lined the walls from floor to ceiling, filled with books with burgundy, hunter green, brown, and black covers. On the shelves closest to me, I could see lettering printed on the spines in Persian, English, French, and other languages unknown to me.

Sousan took me to a leather sofa set a few feet away from a giant mahogany desk. "You just lie down here, Ellie Joon," she said. "Do you want me to bring you some *chai nabat*?"

"Oh, no, no need for that." I declined her offer for the rock candy in tea that was supposed to heal every ailment, including menstrual cramps. "You go back to your party, Sousan Jan. Niloo will be looking for you. Apologize to her on my behalf. I just need to lie down for a few minutes." I continued the "female troubles" charade and held my stomach. "You know how it is." I certainly didn't want to tell Sousan about my impulsive and jealous rage over what I'd seen transpire in the kitchen.

"Alright," Sousan said. "You lie down and I'll have the servant check in on you in a bit? Take as long as you need." She lowered me to the sofa, kissed me gently on the cheek, and then whispered, "The good news is that when you become pregnant after your marriage, *inshallah*, you'll have a break from these god-awful cramps. You have a lot to look forward to, Queen!"

TWENTY-TWO

November 1963

Sousan turned off the lamp as she left. The leather of the sofa felt buttery and surprisingly soft. Of course, the Colonel would have nothing but the best in his study. The air still reeked of tobacco, though—I supposed not even the scrubbing of his servants could make that stink go away. I lay there and closed my eyes. My jealousy quickly morphed into shame. As if a switch had suddenly gone off, I saw quite clearly what a fool I had been. I had allowed my worst impulses to get the better of me. I had been childish and literally driven Homa away. In front of Mehrdad, I'd behaved like a dolt. And for what? I hadn't seen them kiss or touch in an inappropriate way, had I? I had seen Mehrdad smile at Homa. In a kitchen. What if they were just happy to be at a party filled with friends and good food? They too were now friends because of me. I knew they genuinely enjoyed one another's company. When oh when oh *when* would I outgrow my worst trait: this insane jealousy? I was twenty years old, for the love of God. I was a third-year student at university. I wished I had better judgment in general. I wished the green-eyed monster didn't so often get the better of me.

As I lay in the dark room, I couldn't hear even the faintest trace of music or laughter or voices. Nice setup the Colonel had for himself. He could always retreat here: escape the chaos of the household, his children's needs, his wife's ups and downs, even the servants and their possible dramas. I pictured the Colonel at his desk writing important documents. What kinds of documents did military men write? War plans? I sighed. How little I knew of the world! How much I wanted to change and grow up and become mature and whole! My own tantrums exhausted me.

I'm not sure how long I lay with my eyes closed. My tulle skirt puffed up ridiculously above my knees—a veritable symbol of my childishness. One day I'd grow up. I had to. One day I would be calm and not so beholden to my insecurities. I'd be a good wife to Mehrdad and the best of friends to Homa. One day I'd have children and be the kind of understanding and compassionate mother I'd never had. I'd not make my children feel as though everyone was out to get them, out to *cheshm* them with their evil eye, out to ruin their happiness. I would teach my own children differently. I would teach them that the world is filled with people who care deeply about them and want to see them thrive. Imagine that. Imagine if I could not just outgrow my own toxic vices but also transmit to my children the best of traits. Yes, I would raise secure, confident people. I would break the cycle of suspicion and superiority and paranoia that seemed to run in my family line. Perhaps my father had not been this way. Why did I know so little about him? Why had I lost him? My original grief bubbled up. Perhaps my mother would not have become so distrustful and overly suspicious of others if her husband and sister hadn't died so young. If life hadn't dealt her those blows. Perhaps. Perhaps not.

I missed my father. I wanted a father who still lived.

The door opened then. I imagined it was the servant returning with a tray of *chai nabat* and dates—until I heard a phlegmy cough and caught the pungent scent of fresh tobacco. The light snapped on. I blinked at dark spots swimming in front of my eyes.

"Eh! My dear, I didn't see you there."

It was the Colonel.

I quickly sat up, bowing my head modestly and covering my legs with my fluffy skirt. "*Sarhang*, hello," I said. "I'm so sorry—I was just resting in here." Sousan and the Colonel had been together for years, but the age difference still made me feel like a nervous student talking to a parent or teacher. He always made me wary.

He came closer to the sofa, towering over me with shoulders that loomed impossibly wide. To my surprise, he wasn't wearing his military uniform. The Colonel's elevated military rank was a source of great pride to Sousan. I took in his elegant light suit, white shirt, and the whimsical touch of a lavender bow tie.

He put his hand on his chest and bowed slightly. "*Eradatmandam.*" He greeted me formally yet with a hint of amusement.

When I got up to leave, he cleared his throat and spoke again. "Elaheh Khanom, please. *Rahat bash*. Relax. Please, stay, be comfortable. I won't eat you." He laughed so deeply after this last declaration that it sounded almost like a cough. He backed away from me and went to sit behind his desk.

I stayed frozen by the sofa. I had never been alone with him before. His words left me uneasy.

Why couldn't I just be brave for once? See the best in people and not the worst. For once.

I settled into the sofa, determined to be mature.

"I saw your beau out there in the side room. Shared a smoke with him," the Colonel said. He lifted a fountain pen from his desk and unscrewed the cap. He removed the barrel housing from the body of the pen. "He's a lovely fellow, that fiancé of yours. What's he studying?"

"Chemistry," I said.

"A scientist!" he sighed with deep admiration. He opened a bottle of ink and dipped the nib of the fountain pen into it. "And you . . . Sousan tells me you are studying foreign languages?"

"Yes, *Sarhang*." I addressed him by his title. The Colonel may have been married to my high school classmate, but he was still my elder and a high-ranking military officer. I showed my respect and stayed seated. "I'm studying English," I said.

He looked surprised. "English, you say? Not French?"

"No, English."

"Most of us studied French as a second language. At least I did. Do you like it? English?" He proceeded to pump the cartridge of the pen with his huge fingers. "I suppose you're quite well versed in it. Do your studies of English allow you to translate the works of the greats, my dear?"

"I'm making my way," I said. "Learning a lot."

"Some say English will be the future language of business and commerce," the Colonel said, emphasizing his last words with derision, as if *business* and *commerce* were fields for the less sophisticated. "And, lord knows, plenty of political drivel."

He finished filling the pen with ink, replaced its barrel and cap, and laid it down on the desk. Then he dragged toward him a large, circular crystal ashtray. From his breast pocket, he took out a thick cigar and matchbox. He struck the matchstick, his face in shadow as he lit the cigar.

After he'd taken a suck on the tobacco, he asked, "It won't bother you?"

I returned his vague courtesy with an equally vague assurance.

"I am in awe"—he exhaled the smoke—"just in awe, of your generation. You young women are to be applauded. We are a patriarchal society in Iran. I don't need to tell you that!" He laughed his phlegmy laugh again. "But the way you young women are educating yourselves and progressing and making a mark—it will make our country an even bigger star on the world stage! I believe in women's education. I believe in progress. I believe in the march toward the future. I keep telling Sousan that once the kids are a little older, she too should go and get her university degree. I keep telling her it's not too late."

Maybe he was more progressive than I'd given him credit for, though in all the times I'd visited Sousan after she was married, not once had she told me of the Colonel encouraging her to get her university degree.

"And Niloo . . . she's the one studying, what?" he suddenly asked.

"Business administration," I said. "She's not at Tehran University with me and Mehrdad. She's at Bazargani University."

"Well, that field too, in the scheme of things, I suppose has its place."

He tapped cigar ash into the ashtray. "Brava to all you accomplished young women! And that other friend of yours . . . the very bright one who Sousan tells me hails from downtown? Studying the law, I believe. What is her name?"

"Homa?" I asked. I saw in my mind's eye the image of Homa leaning out of the departing taxi's window. My poor dear friend. My heart sank with shame at my jealous outburst. I looked up at the Colonel. "You are right, Homa is brilliant. She will be a judge one day."

The Colonel leaned back in his chair and sucked the cigar again. "Imagine that!" he said with wonder. "I dream of the day when women judges rule our halls of justice. Honestly, I think we'd be better off! I'm not the old-fashioned curmudgeon you think I am, dear Elaheh!" He laughed again at his own words.

I smiled politely. I didn't even know how my father would have felt about these issues; how it would have been to share with him the ambitions of my good friends. Would he proudly encourage me and Niloo and Homa and Sousan? I stared at the Colonel. Would my father's sideburns have grayed in middle age? Would he have sat behind a big important desk?

"The shallow think I married Sousan because she's young and beautiful. Which she is, she is." He smiled and looked off in the distance. "But the truth is I so prefer the bravery of your generation of women. That's what I admire. You're not afraid. You're fierce. You and your friends are *shir ʒan*!"

Shir ʒan. The Persian phrase that translates to "lion women." Homa had always loved to tell me that we would grow up to become lionesses. The first time she'd said it we were sitting on the ledge in the courtyard of the bazaar, eating our ice cream sandwiches and discussing our futures. I sat up a little straighter on the sofa. I held my chin a bit higher with pride. The Colonel was right. We were now *shir ʒan*, weren't we? On the cusp of a brand-new frontier in our country. "That is kind of you to say. And true!" I dared to say.

"I am a proponent of the rights of women," he said. "And I admire the activists. You are all so politically aware. Awake. Not afraid."

"Some of us more than others," I mumbled.

He looked up. "Is that so? Who's the bravest? It's you! I bet it's you, Elaheh Khanom!"

"The bravest? Oh, there's no question who's the bravest." I thought again of my friend disappearing into the night after I erased her from the party. "The bravest is Homa Roozbeh."

He grinned and nodded. "Your lawyer! Your future judge! Or should I say *our* judge! The country's judge!" He lifted his cigar in tribute. "And why is she the bravest exactly?"

"Well, the girl has no fear. She is truly concerned with the rights of the people. The rest of us . . . I'll speak for myself . . . we can be a bit selfish and insular. But Homa truly cares about the future of this country."

"How admirable. She sounds like the kind of lionhearted woman not afraid to organize?"

"Absolutely! She is nobody's fool. She is filled with courage."

The Colonel sucked on his cigar thoughtfully. "We need that in this country. I find the most valorous young women out there are those who are involved with the Tudehi communist movement. Aren't they the bravest? I don't agree with their politics—I am, mind you, a proud capitalist. But I am also a scholar of sorts who strives not to live in an echo chamber. I've read my Marx. I like to read all kinds of opinions. And, well, the young communist women of this country—I do admire their *shojaat*. Their courage. They certainly have been spreading their views through writing and whatnot. Look, Elaheh Khanom, between friends, let me tell you that my own younger sister is no stranger to communist beliefs."

"Really?"

"Sure! And again, I may disagree with her politics, but I cannot deny my sister's lion heart. She is a communist through and through and quite active in the youth movement." He whispered the last part. "Kind of like your Homa?"

"Yes!" I said. "I don't agree with their politics myself. But she is so courageous. She even helped organize the university protest last week."

He looked at me in wonder. "Did she now?" His eyes lingered on me.

If he did want to "eat me up," he now gave the distinct impression that he'd already had his fill.

They didn't do it in the restaurant kitchen.

They didn't follow her into Café Andre or to a teahouse in Darband.

They didn't—thank God—do it in the alley outside her home, where her mother and sister and brother might have witnessed it. They grabbed her outside the university grounds. The very next day.

I was going to campus to study. Ahead of me I saw Homa's back. She walked with her usual confident gait, her satchel by her side. I ran to catch up to her, to say I had acted like a fool to be jealous of her and Mehrdad in the kitchen.

She was about to cross the street. One foot had already descended from the curb. I called her name. Suddenly, a car drove perilously close to me and for a minute I thought it would hit me. Then the car whooshed past my side and zoomed right up to Homa. Two men in black suits and dark sunglasses jumped out, grabbed her, and pushed her into the back seat.

I screamed, but it was too late.

I wanted to run after the car, to chase it down the road. Within seconds, she was driven out of sight.

I stood limp and silent.

Later, I called her mother and begged for information. The charges against Homa were an attempt to bring down "crown and throne," she said. Homa was arrested and checked into Evin Prison.

"How did this happen?" I asked with a shaky voice. "Why now?"

Her mother said she didn't know. She said she had to go.

After I put down the receiver, I sat by the phone, wrapped in fear and worry. How long would they keep Homa? What would they do to her?

As time ticked on, what I wanted to deny above all else became impossible to ignore: *What if I had something to do with it?*

TWENTY-THREE

November 1963

Couples in the park walked hand in hand in the cool November air. I shifted on the slatted wooden bench. It would be evening soon. The air had the kind of chill that precedes the year's first snow. At any moment, I expected the first fat flake to float down and then another until all of Tehran was blanketed in softness. I wanted the city to be shrouded in white. I wanted something to distract me from constantly looking at my watch. Two boys shared a packet of roasted nuts on a bench not far from me. They chatted continuously and occasionally laughed. I looked away. I had tried to set up this meeting for weeks. Where was she? We had agreed to meet in this park on this bench and I had arrived half an hour early, eager to see her and get things out in the open. But now she was certifiably late.

"Ellie, hello."

I looked up and there she was. Sousan. Her face was surrounded by a black fur Cossack hat and she wore a long black fur coat. In her manicured hand, she held a snakeskin purse with a gold chain. She looked like she'd stepped out of a photograph of the Russian aristocracy. Her makeup was impeccable, but there was a grayness under her eyes that no amount of concealer could hide. She sat down next to me.

"Thank you for coming," I said.

162 •ı• Marjan Kamali

"I can't stay long."

"I won't take too much of your time," I said. It felt awkward to speak so curtly to my old friend.

We stared out ahead instead of looking at one another. Sousan was uncomfortable, I could tell. The park filled with the squeals of three young children running fast in the pathway. Their beleaguered mother trudged after them.

"How could you, Ellie?" Sousan whispered finally. "How could you tell him?"

"I didn't mean to. I didn't want to. I promise on my mother's life!"

"You gave Homa away, Ellie. You told my husband about her communist activities. How could you be so stupid?"

My words spilled out in a rush. "Sousan, he chatted with me as though he was a caring father. He asked all these questions about what everyone was studying, not just about Homa. About Mehrdad. And Niloo. And me. What was I supposed to do? Ignore him? You know I couldn't do that. I was being polite!"

The sun was fully setting now. The air seemed to drop in temperature with every ticking minute.

"You should have been more careful."

"It was . . . it *seemed* like a harmless conversation! He said his own sister was a communist. He told me he admired this bravery in young women. He made it sound like he applauded all of this. Did the Colonel . . . did he talk to SAVAK agents? Tell me. Was he the one who told the secret police about Homa? Because of me? I need to know the truth."

Sousan sighed deeply. It was the sigh of a long-suffering woman who had to bear the company of fools. "He doesn't need to talk to them."

I sat very still on the bench. My entire body flashed hot, then went cold and clammy, as perspiration pooled in the curve of my lower back. "He doesn't need to talk to the agents because he is one? Is that what you're saying?" My voice was raspy.

Sousan looked down at her hands and said quietly, "I thought you knew."

"You married a spy? How long have you known?"

Sousan was silent.

"How could you live with him? How could you live with yourself?"

Sousan thrust her chin up and looked at me with revulsion. "Oh please, Ellie. Spare me your self-righteousness. As if you and your family have not benefited greatly from everything our government does. I don't need a lecture from you."

I turned toward her to protest but found I couldn't say anything.

Sousan clutched her coat tightly around her. The cost of her purse alone could have probably fed a family in the slums for weeks. But as I faced her, I saw deep within the fur in which she was encased a trace of the friend I had known in high school. The same Sousan who had gossiped with me in class, shared sandwiches with me at Café Andre, and lined my eyes with kohl as we joked and giggled.

"Your family has their own money. You don't need to put up with him," I said in a softer tone.

Sousan inhaled deeply and looked around the park. "It's not for the money," she said, "that I stay."

"How many people has he tricked? How many has he helped put into prison?"

Her eyes welled with tears. "You don't have children yet, Ellie. One day you'll understand. Do you know what would happen if I left him? The children would go to him. Plain and simple. Women may have gotten the right to vote as of last year, but try looking at the divorce laws. The child custody laws. I wouldn't have a chance."

"You sound like Homa now," I said, a lump lodging in my throat. "You sound like her. That's the kind of stuff she always says."

Sousan looked down. One tear slid down her cheek and then another until her face was soaked. "I was careful," she said. "All this time. Never once did I share with him Homa's activism in the Communist Party. He tried asking me. I pretended I barely knew Homa."

My heart sank as I remembered how I had not kept my own mouth shut. "Can you talk to him now? The Colonel must have connections. He's in the SAVAK, for God's sake."

Sousan shot a look at me as if to tell me to not speak so loudly.

"Can he help get her out? Surely, he could pull some strings?"

"Ellie, he doesn't know I know. I can't let on that I know about his secret life."

"But why not? He's your husband! And Homa was your friend in high school too!"

"That's not how it works. I can't let on that I know anything."

"You have to," I said. "Please. See if there's something he can do. I'm begging you, Sousan. Maybe he could undo the wrong I caused. Get her released."

Sousan looked at her lap for a long minute. The frigid wind rippled the tiny hairs on her fur hat. I wondered what animal it had been before. A rabbit? Fox? Muskrat? How had the animal been transformed into this object on Sousan's head? It made me sick to think about it.

"I should get back now." Sousan stood up. "The kids are waiting for me." The wind whistled through the tree branches.

"Take care of yourself, Ellie." She looked at me with a sad smile. "You are a lot more *sadeh* and naïve than even I thought. Be careful." She walked away from the bench. Then she turned and said, "He doesn't even have a sister."

I watched her figure in black recede into the park.

That was the last time I spoke to or saw Sousan, my old high school friend.

I did not tell Mother and Uncle Massoud about Homa's arrest. It would only have led them to worry about my own safety—and theirs. As they talked over dinner later that evening about a ridiculous radio comedy, I was so restless, anxious, and racked with guilt that I had to excuse myself, telling them I needed to help Niloo, as I sometimes did, light her house for the Sabbath.

When I got to Niloo's home, she commiserated with me and told me how devastated she was to hear of Homa's arrest. Niloo said over and over again that there was nothing any of us could have done to prevent it: the actions of the police were out of our hands. Clearly, Sousan hadn't told her about my conversation with the Colonel or our conversation in the park. She probably never would. I didn't have the heart or courage to divulge my role.

I asked if I could use her phone. I called Mother and said I would stay longer at Niloo's.

But I didn't stay at Niloo's. I told Niloo I was going home and said goodbye.

Outside, I walked aimlessly in the streets for one hour, then two, in the cold air whipped by a bitter wind. I had never been out alone at night for this long. I had always been with Mother or Uncle Massoud or both, or with Homa or Mehrdad or other friends. A girl did not walk the streets at night on her own. In certain parts of the city, a girl did not go out alone even in the day.

Strangely, the night was filled with life. There were groups of people here and there: parents walking with children, couples strolling hand in hand, teenagers fooling around. The chatter around me should have been a comfort, but I felt completely removed from the rest of the city. I could hear the sound of water running in the *joob* ditches, the call of diligent street vendors still hawking their wares. I could register—barely—the names of alleys down which I wandered endlessly. Even if I walked the streets until dawn, I could never tame the worry in my heart. The suffocating guilt and shame.

Now my friend was all alone in a cell.

She had been arrested.

Because of me.

Part Three

TWENTY-FOUR

November 1963

HOMA

Those louts want me to beg for their damn mercy. They think I'll reveal the information they want from me. They expect dread to make me divulge it. Well, they're dead wrong.

Quite frankly, the overwhelming force that fuels me is anger. I want to scream and explode, to stab them. To have my voice carry through the windows of the car and over the rooftops of Tehran.

From the moment the two men grab me and shove me into the vehicle and later lead me into a dank building with a dark lobby and then a narrow corridor into a waiting area to be "registered"—as if I'm signing up for school, for God's sake—and even as I'm thrown into a tiny cell where a gate of bars clangs shut, what I feel more than anything is not fear but a powerful, boiling fury.

My rage is enormous.

No one tells you how physical anger feels. Each follicle on my scalp stings; a hot liquid runs through my arms. My face burns; my teeth throb. My legs do not give out or feel weak—they are tense and ready for combat. We learned about the fight-or-flight instinct in school. Now I know that when push comes to shove—when I am literally shoved—every fiber of my being wants to fight.

The injustice of it feeds my anger. For trying to better a country, for fighting for our rights, for demanding equality and a fair chance for all, a woman should not be arrested, imprisoned, shut up, enclosed, forsaken.

The first morning after my arrest, a guard leads me from my cell down a corridor and through turns and mazes into a small questioning room that smells of sweat. Under a lone bulb hanging from the ceiling sits a bald, middle-aged man in uniform. The guard pushes me into the room and sits me down at a chair across from the man, then goes and stands in the doorway. The middle-aged man looks me over with a mixture of boredom and weariness and says, "*Khosh omadi.* Welcome."

I do not need his patronizing greeting. I look him directly in the eye. He proceeds to question me about our communist organization, activities, leaders, and those who'd helped spread the word of protests through what he calls "propaganda."

Over and over again, I think: *shir ʒan, shir ʒan, shir ʒan.* I will be the lioness, I will be lionhearted. From me they will not mine one bit of information. Had I known when we drew up the plans for our protests that I would be fueled by so much anger when arrested, I would have done more, not less. Because my rage is a shield. It increases my confidence. I do not give the questioner one inch, one name, one tidbit of information.

The questioner grows more impatient. He raises his voice. The guard at the door clears his throat as if to remind me of his own vacuous presence.

But I refuse. I refuse to give anything away.

The questioner stops and sighs. He is quiet for a few moments as he studies my face. He breaks out into a smile. Three badly chipped teeth make him look maniacal, almost comical. "What we do, girl," he says, "for the likes of you, is that we pretty quickly hand them over to our Aghaye Mohandess. Did you know that?"

I continue to stare at him calmly, cursing him and all his ancestors in my heart. He needs to know he doesn't scare me. He cannot break me.

His ugly smile grows wider. "Aghaye Mohandess will know *exactly* what to do with you," he says.

He waves his hand at the guard.

The guard comes in, yanks me up by the armpit, and leads me out of the room. As we leave, I hear the questioner say, "Too bad she's so stubborn."

That night, I lie in the cell that smells of iron bars and urine and think of all the people I love. I think of my mother and father, my sister and brother. Is my father in this very prison? Have they brought me closer to him? Could he be in a men's section of this place? I think of Ellie and her kindness—the friend who I have known since we were seven. The memory of the faces of my loved ones calms me. When the anger makes me want to combust and scream until my lungs burst, their faces force me to remember grace.

Early the following morning, I'm taken again to the interrogation room and asked the same questions by the same middle-aged bald man, only this time he loses his patience faster, gets up, and tells me he's given me a second chance and I've blown it. He says women like me are idiots who don't understand their place. Then he leaves the room.

I sit there waiting for the guard to come from his post at the doorway and take me back to my cell. But instead of entering the room, the guard simply stares at me, then closes and locks the door. The thump of his bootsteps recedes into the hallway.

I sit there alone.

A new man comes in, whistling. As if he's entering a greenhouse to water plants or a park to watch pigeons peck at bread crumbs. He is tall and unremarkable, dressed in a military uniform and wearing a hat with a captain's peak. He smells of cologne, the kind that is sold in expensive shops in bottles of heavy glass. Is this the Aghaye Mohandess I've been warned about? He acts as though I'm invisible to him as he saunters over and lowers himself into the chair where the questioner sat. Then he rests his right ankle on his left knee, leans back, and finally says, "You're a nuisance, you know that?"

My body burns at his insult.

"You're crazy," he continues. "Anyone who would be so stupid is crazy. All you have to do is give us the information we seek. That is it. And then you will be free. Simple as that. We will release you tomorrow if you just say it."

I look into his face. Under the light of the bulb, I can tell he's recently shaven. A tiny piece of tissue sticks to a bloody clot on his chin.

"I refuse," I say.

He snorts. He shakes his head. "*Moteasefam*. I'm sorry for you."

I have heard stories of horrors that happen in these chambers. Seen pictures from this very prison with a sign inscribed "Torture Room" above a door. But how can I tell him what he wants? I could never do that. I won't. My compatriots have said that in prison, young communist women are spared the worst of the atrocities. I hope that is true.

"I'm sorry that vile people like you get so easily brainwashed by the Russians," he continues. "I'm sorry that you think communism is the answer. I'm sorry that you don't appreciate what we have in this country. I'm sorry that you are so stupid and so young as to believe the lies they've fed you."

Fueled again by anger, my words spill out of me. "Don't feel sorry for me. You are the one who's been lied to. Yours is a sycophantic cult of which my generation is ashamed. We want a better country. We want equality in all aspects. We want freedom. We want to live with dignity."

That I would say this to a man with so much power over me in a moment like this is beyond unwise. But I can't help it. I am speaking the truth as I know it.

I expect him to become furious at my audacity. To yell. Send me to the torture room. But he stares at me with a look that can only be described as genuine surprise. He looks me over, first studying my face, then my whole body, slowly. "Who are you?" he asks. His voice has thickened. Under the lamp, I can see his pupils have enlarged.

I have seen this look before in men. It is a look of lurid hunger. I want with all my being to negate it, cut it off, nullify it.

He seems to be battling something within himself. He clears his throat. "Just give us the information we are asking for. Last chance."

"I refuse."

He inches his chair closer to me. He looks me over again as if trying to understand me. Inhale me. "As a rule," he says, "we do not harm the young women." He takes in a deep breath. "As a rule. But you are different. Did you know that? Where do you get your courage from?"

He gets up, goes to the door, and makes sure it is locked. He groans. "I don't know why you are doing this to me. Why are you doing this to me?"

My entire body suddenly freezes. In small shards, all my anger slides off, and instead I taste in my mouth the unmistakable metallic taste of fear.

I hear him say, "*Kesafat!*" He calls me garbage.

He turns off the light.

TWENTY-FIVE

December 1964

For one year—since she had been grabbed by the men and shoved in the car—I had not seen Homa. For one year, we had not spoken. For one year, I had occasionally worried that she'd died, that her mother and sister lied when they said she was fine every time I called.

Now, finally, I would see her.

I pressed the button on the intercom outside a yellow brick building. A soft breeze made the chador around my body billow. The chador belonged to our housekeeper, Batul, and she had fretted when I asked to borrow it— worried her religious covering was too shabby for me, too unfashionable. I didn't tell Batul chadors weren't exactly meant to be fashionable. I needed a decent covering to go downtown. On this day I wanted to be sheathed from head to toe. I didn't need eyes on me as I walked in Homa's new neighborhood. I just wanted to see my friend without trouble.

I pressed the intercom button again.

A staticky voice asked *keeyeh*, who is it?

My heart jumped. Was it her? I couldn't tell with all the interference. I said my name.

"Second floor. On the left." This time I knew it was Homa's voice, even with the words muffled through walls and wires. My stomach did a somersault.

An ear-splitting buzz followed. I almost didn't open the door. Maybe it was a mistake to try to make amends. What would she say to me?

I had walked until about 2 a.m. after leaving Niloo's house that night, wishing I could erase myself from the world, delete what I'd said to the Colonel, change the trajectory of what happened to my friend. When I finally went home, Mother's screams crescendoed. She knew I'd lied about being at Niloo's, she said. She knew I wasn't to be trusted. She couldn't believe I'd been out alone. She insisted I'd caused her a heart attack (though she was fine and had had no such attack). Uncle Massoud's fury and worry at my having been out so late and lying about being at Niloo's led him to banish me to my room for two weeks.

I welcomed this punishment. I deserved to be shut up in my room. Shut off from the world. To have my only human interaction be with Batul when she brought up a tray of food and entreated me to eat before quickly leaving. To have even Mehrdad forbidden to see or call me.

When my two weeks of punishment were up, I was told by Mother and Uncle Massoud that I could rejoin society if I promised to never, ever, ever again walk the streets alone at night. Did I even know what I had put them through—my God, who knows what people would have said about my being out there like a loose woman.

I was allowed to speak to Mehrdad again, and on the phone he asked if I was fine, healthy, and if I had heard anything from Homa. "Nothing happened the night of the party in the kitchen, Ellie. I feel silly even saying it. You know that, right?"

I said I did.

"I can't believe they arrested her. How did they find her out?"

If I was going to marry this man, we couldn't have a secret like this between us. "I said far too much to the Colonel that night, Mehrdad. The Colonel's a SAVAK agent. I didn't know. I gave her away."

There was silence on the other end of the line. Then Mehrdad sighed deeply. "It's not your fault."

"It is absolutely my fault."

"You can't think like that. It will destroy you."

"My blabbing destroyed her."

"Does she . . . know it was you who gave her away?"

"I'm not sure."

I hung up in shame.

Each time I called Homa's house, her mother, Monir Khanom, was polite but firm about Homa's desire to not see or speak with me.

"Do you know when she'll be released?" I asked.

"God willing, before . . ." She stopped.

"Before what?"

She said they were moving because their house was being given away. She didn't say "sold," but I assumed they could no longer afford to live there. They must have had no choice but to sell. It was hard to think that Homa would no longer be in the house with the stone kitchen, the *hoz* pond in the garden, the small courtyard containing the sounds of our childhood. But it was no surprise their money had run out. It was a miracle her family had stayed in the house as long as they had after her father's arrest.

Monir Khanom promised she'd call me when they had a new phone number. And to her credit, that following summer, she did call and give me the new number. Homa was out now, she said. She was safe.

I was overjoyed to hear it. I asked if I could visit now.

She told me absolutely not.

The university to which Homa had applied with such fervor and great hope proceeded without her. We attended classes, took exams, learned facts and figures—without her. We advanced in our studies, congratulated ourselves on our grades, went out to celebrate—without her. But nothing tasted the same nor felt as crucial without her. Mehrdad and I studied hard. Abdol transferred to a different college. He said he needed to be closer to home because he had to help his family. Despite efforts from Mehrdad and me, Abdol lost touch with us pretty quickly. I wondered if Homa's arrest and absence from university led him to leave. He had been so in love with her.

Not one day passed when I did not miss her. Once again, I was the ten-year-old longing for the friend from whom I'd been separated. Only now my guilt was compounded. I didn't feel guilty for moving to a wealthy new neighborhood like I had back then. This time I felt guilty for so much more.

I couldn't understand why Homa wouldn't reenroll in her classes. Was it too dangerous? Maybe she was too traumatized. I begged her mother over and over on the phone to be able to see her. I asked so many times, her mother finally relented and gave me a new address.

"Is this where you all live now?"

"She doesn't live with us anymore," Monir Khanom said quietly. "Look, you need to catch up. I told her how relentless you've been about seeing her. She gave in, finally, and said you could visit. Go this Friday afternoon. After the lunchtime nap. She said you could go around 4 p.m."

I wrote the new street name and number in my small black address book under the "H" tab. Never had I written down an address for Homa. I'd always known her information by heart.

After the buzzer sounded, I pushed open the door and walked into the yellow brick building. The entryway smelled like fried onions and mop water. Peeling paint curled on the walls. I clutched my chador tight and climbed the steps to the second floor, remembering the way to Homa's old stone kitchen, down the seven steps with a dip in their middle. The warmth of that magical space, the ceramic sink, the piroshkis under the white cloth on the plate danced in my mind.

When I reached the second floor, I saw a scarred door with the number 15. That was the apartment number her mother had given me. Before I lost my nerve, I forced myself to walk to it and knock.

The door swung open, as though someone had been waiting for me.

She held a house chador loosely around her. Under it I could see part of her blouse. It was white with small blue flowers—reminiscent of her mother's when we'd been kids. Maybe it was the very same one, handed down. Though we had not seen one another for only a year, Homa had aged ten. Her face was sallow and she had dark circles under her eyes. Her mouth turned down at the corners in a way I had never seen before.

"*Salaam*, Homa Joon," I said.

"*Salaam*, Ellie." Her voice was the same, but the tone was formal. She looked past me, anxiously, up and down the hallway.

She ushered me in. I took off the chador and hung it over a hook near the door. The main room of the apartment had no tables, sofas, or chairs. A rug lay in the middle and cushions lined the walls. A *sofreh* floor cloth was laid out to the right. Next to the *sofreh* was a pink blanket. On the blanket lay a sleeping baby. For a minute my vision blurred. The baby breathed deeply and rhythmically. I remembered another time I had seen a baby on the floor—when I first visited Homa at her home in the old neighborhood— how her baby sister, Sara, had cried, how her mother came in and swooped her up.

"Bahar," Homa said. "We named her Bahar."

In all the times I had spoken to Homa's mother and sister, begging them to tell me how Homa was doing, they had told me she was fine, just not ready to come back to school yet after prison. They had not told me about Bahar.

I wanted to say she was a beautiful baby, because she was. I wanted to say congratulations, but I couldn't.

"She's a good baby," Homa said firmly, as though drawing a line in the sand. As though not allowing me to judge that child in any other framework.

I peeled my eyes off the small sleeping body and looked at her. "Yes," was all I could muster.

She motioned to a cushion against the wall. "Sit."

I sat cross-legged with the cushion behind my back. This was how we used to sit when we were kids in the neighborhood where everyone sat on the floor. Homa lowered herself across from me. The baby continued her peaceful breathing.

"The tea is coming," she said.

"I don't need tea."

"It's brewing anyway. We're just a little late with it because I had to feed Bahar."

We? Did she mean she and the baby? I needed to put together the pieces and yet, part of me did not wish to know. Part of me wanted Homa back in school, in her classes, climbing the ladder, on her way to being the Lady Lawyer. On her way to being a judge. To owning the world.

A door at the back of the room opened then, and in he walked on socked feet.

At first, when I saw him, my breath caught and there was a moment of complete and utter disconnection.

"Abdol!" I whispered.

"Please, Elaheh Khanom, stay seated, don't get up."

His socks were black. His pants were brown. He wore a baggy stained beige shirt over the pants and his beard was stubbly. He looked exhausted. He nodded at me. "Welcome. I am so glad you came."

I sank into the cushion. Tension knotted the small of my back. My friend, the mother. The baby on the blanket: asleep. Abdol in Homa's home.

Homa insisted she should get the tea, but it was Abdol who disappeared behind the door at the back of the room into what I assumed was the kitchen.

Homa said, "Our wedding was simple. Quick. Just us. And my mother. Sara. Ali Reza. Sorry I didn't invite you. Abdol's father died when he was little and his mother, as you know, has passed away. He has no siblings. His extended family is from the city of Abadan. They didn't come."

I remembered news of Abdol's mother dying of a heart attack when we were all at university together. "I . . . I didn't know you got married," was all I could say.

"I accepted his offer of marriage as soon as I was released."

"Were you . . . did you . . . have the baby when you . . ."

"I was in prison for six months. I was about six months pregnant when I got out."

My head swam.

"I was lucky to have the baby outside. My mother and Sara have helped."

The door at the back of the room opened again and Abdol came in, carrying a tray with tea *estekans* and a bowl of sugar. He laid the tray on the *sofreh* cloth in the corner. We shuffled over to it on our knees. He apologized for there being no cake and I said I didn't need cake. He explained how they had run out of dates and I said I was perfectly fine without dates. He said he wasn't sure if his brew was all that good, that the baby had been hungry and Homa wasn't able to oversee the tea-brewing the way she normally would have. I took a sip of the tea he handed me and insisted it was perfect.

"Again, my apologies," he said, "if it's not to your standards."

"Please, it's excellent," I repeated.

For a while we did the Persian *tarof* dance where he was self-deprecating and apologetic for his tea and I insisted it was the best I'd ever had. We did our polite formalities, no matter what. We were raised to be that way. We were raised to keep up appearances.

"Isn't she a *topoli*?" Abdol motioned in the direction of the sleeping baby. "Isn't she just to die for?"

"Yes, she is," I said. "She is wonderfully chubby, a *topoli*." I sipped on the tea. "She is to die for."

Abdol apologized for having been out of touch over the past year. Then he looked directly at me and said, "We cannot control what happens to us. We have to accept the destiny God carves out for us."

Homa stared at the rug.

"She is a wonder," Abdol said. "God's child."

I knew Abdol was devoted to his religion. But safeguarding this pregnant woman who had been violated in prison was something else. Women who were raped were often thought of as "ruined" and were frequently shunned.

Abdol took a sip of his tea. "Homa has struggled with her *rouhieh*, her spirits. Thank you for coming. It helps her to see a friend."

She'd been arrested in the first place because of me. Guilt ran through my body like a tangible force.

"I had to leave Tehran University," Abdol continued. "It was too far, too much. I was able to transfer to a trade school close to here. I go part-time. At nights. After working at the garage where I'm training to be a mechanic. We're lucky Homa's mother and sister can help us. With time Homa will, *inshallah* . . ." He stopped.

I stared at him. Will what? Go back to university? Resume her dream?

"She will, *inshallah*, be her old self again as she recovers," Abdol said.

Homa's chador had slipped down from her head. Her curls were pulled into a tight bun at the nape of her neck. Her ears were bright red. She was eerily still. Then, as if to snap herself out of a trance, she jerked her head up. "Would you like to see our place? There's not much to it. This is our main room. But we have a bedroom. And a small kitchen. Would you like a tour while the baby sleeps?"

She got up, and I followed as she guided me through the space of the new home in which she was a wife and a mother. The bedroom was tidy and smelled of soap. Near the mattress on the floor lay a tiny plastic doll. I assumed it had been a misguided gift or a purchase for the future. The baby at this age could not pick it up and even once she could, she might easily choke on it. Homa said, "We'll eventually buy a good stove."

I remembered the large stove in her mother's old stone kitchen. "Why did your mother and siblings move from the house?" I asked.

I felt awkward standing in the bedroom she shared with her husband, attempting to get basic information about her life. Once, we would have shared the details of our days. Now there was so much unsaid between us.

Homa stiffened. "Maman moved to a small apartment with Sara and Ali Reza. They're fine."

"Listen, Homa." I touched her arm. "If you ever need any help at all, I can lend you money, give you as much as you need . . ."

Before I could go on, she tightened her chador around her torso and left the room, leaving me feeling like an intruder.

I followed the sound of the clatter of dishes and running water. Abdol was in the kitchen. I stepped back into the main room. The baby still slept. Homa was by the front door, holding it open.

I wanted to apologize for what I had done. I wanted her to know how much I regretted it. Did she know I was responsible?

I walked to her and stopped short of the threshold. "I just wanted to say that I—"

"You shouldn't have come," she interrupted me.

"We all care about you. Mehrdad really wanted to know why Abdol lost touch . . ."

"Abdol's been busy," she snapped. "Sorry if we can't keep up correspondence with old school friends."

"That's not what I meant."

"Never really friends." She looked down at her feet.

"What?"

She looked up. "They were never really friends," she said. "Your Mehrdad and Abdol. Mehrdad befriended Abdol because it made him feel good to help a lesser-than. It made him feel virtuous to show Abdol around town and take him hiking in the mountains and act benevolent and kind to one less fortunate. It wasn't a deep bond. Too many differences."

"I thought they were quite fond of one another."

She looked out into the hallway and then back at me. "I would like it if you didn't come here again," she whispered.

"Homa, if you just give me a chance. I want to explain. I want to get to know Bahar. Next time, I'll bring a gift. I just didn't know—"

She shook her head quickly. "I don't want presents. Or money. Or your *pity*." She looked back out into the hallway.

"You've gone through a trauma—"

"*Saket bash!* Be quiet!" she cut me off. "I want you to leave me alone. I don't want to see you again. Ever."

I had never seen her look so infuriated and helpless at the same time. I took my chador off the hook near the door and stepped over the threshold and into the hallway to show her I wasn't going to linger against her will.

From inside the flat, a loud howl rang out.

Homa turned and called into the room, "I'm coming!"

She faced me again. "If you care about me, you won't come back. I cannot do this. I have"—she ran her hand across her forehead—"too much to handle right now. Please. Just leave me alone. From now on. Promise me."

The crying from the baby grew louder. Homa made a clucking in her direction, then gave me one last pleading look. "Promise not to come here again. And don't ever call my mother or sister or brother."

I stood very still. My ears buzzed and my face grew hot. Tears pricked at my eyes.

"*Ghol bedeh*. Promise me. It's the least you can do," she whispered quickly.

I didn't deserve to be forgiven, to have our friendship go on as if nothing had happened. I didn't deserve her. "I promise," I said.

She shut the door in my face.

TWENTY-SIX

1964

HOMA

When you're drowning and the world feels as though it was not meant for you, when the lack of sleep and appetite make you want to curl up and give up, when the demands of a baby are overwhelming and absolutely crushing—how do you fake the persona of a woman who is alright?

For Abdol, I am grateful—who wouldn't be? Abdol's kindness is a miracle, a gift from God, an absolute aberration from the way most men would have behaved. Abdol does what few men would ever do. He asks me, for a third time, to marry him. He asks me despite knowing what happened in that prison cell, for I emerge from prison six months pregnant.

I say yes. My mother has so little; my father is still incarcerated for his own political activities. Here is Abdol, willing to provide me with shelter and protection after I am considered soiled and spoiled. For that is exactly how I would be seen by anyone—to be pregnant and alone after prison. My poor mother would try to protect me, but living with her would never strip me of the mark of shame. Living with a husband gives me a chance at redemption and release from forever being stigmatized by the community as a damaged "whore."

Even after I marry him, people talk. They can do the math. Some can see the baby was conceived before our marriage. But we hope—with time—they'll look the other way. We hope they'll forget my saga and focus on their own lives. If only they could.

True, in the very early hours and days of prison what fuels me is anger. But after what happens in that closed room with the door locked and the light out, after what happens as my screams fall against cement walls and my clothes are torn and my flesh bruised, I am made of grief. I now scratch the surface of my anger and peer beneath the skin of it and find only a well of sadness so deep there seems no way out.

Each day, I sink and spiral.

I feel there is no path back to my confidence, no space for my old energy.

All of it evaporates by the one act in that room.

Ellie, when she visits us in our new apartment, alludes to the traumatic episode in the prison cell, but I'm not ready. Not ready to talk, not ready to think about it, not ready to heal. The edges of my self blur and fade. I struggle to remain in this world.

I want very much to give up.

The only thing that keeps me tethered to continuing the farce of life is a tiny human who depends on me.

I remain for her. My child has no fault in how she was brought into being; the crime is not hers.

I hate what fate has doled out. I struggle to stay above water. But I know I cannot afford to sink entirely.

For despite all the grief that drowns my soul or maybe because of it, I love her.

I love her madly.

TWENTY-SEVEN

June 1965

In a wedding dress of my dreams that tapered at the waist and puffed at the shoulders with pearly beads running down the sleeves, I sat next to Mehrdad on a low bench under a canopy of silk. The silky white cloth above our heads was held by Mehrdad's mother on one end and his aunt on the other. My mother ground gauze-wrapped cones of sugar onto the cloth so the grains rained sweetness for the bride and groom. A clergyman in an *aba* cloak and turban stood nearby and spoke about honor, marital bliss, and purity.

Laid out on a *sofreh aghd* cloth on the floor, Mother had placed the traditional Iranian wedding objects symbolizing important elements for a marriage. In a mirror lit by candelabra I could see only Mehrdad's reflection, and from his seat he could see only mine. Among the many items, my favorites were a bowl of decorated eggs to symbolize fertility, bowls of sugar-coated almonds for a life of sweetness, and a tray of *esfand* Persian incense to ward off the evil eye.

After our vows were exchanged, Mehrdad called a meeting in the corner of our living room with the main stakeholders in my deflowering theater: the closest female relatives. Mastering the confidence and authority of a man on the threshold of a prestigious career in a patriarchal society and being practically worshipped by all for it, Mehrdad calmly explained that he would not be partaking in the handkerchief tradition. He did not want to receive a white handkerchief so he could hand it back bloodstained later that night to female relatives excited for proof that he'd consummated marriage to a virgin.

Mehrdad's mom, gracious and calm as ever, agreed that we should be left alone and forgo the old-fashioned handkerchief hoopla surrounding the marriage night. With the mother of the groom decreeing it, the rest of the close female relatives—even my social-climbing mother—gave in. I breathed a sigh of relief that I wouldn't be forced to prove that Mehrdad was my first in every way. He was, of course, but the entire "proof" theater felt so demeaning. I was happy to skip it.

After the ceremony, the guests were invited into the garden. It looked magical with fairy lights strewn in the branches of the trees, dinner tables laden with flowers and clay jugs of wine, and a band set up on a make-shift stage. Mother had envisioned the idyllic setting and hired an army of servants to organize it. Uncle Massoud played the role of proud uncle/father.

I remember a bite of the traditional wedding jeweled rice with its rich, tart barberries tucked in, the bitterness of the slivered orange rind a great complement to the plump raisins. This medley of sweet and sour and bitter— perhaps a symbol for married life. And I had a morsel of a baby chicken drumstick marinated in yogurt and saffron for so long that the meat practically slipped off the bone. But barely any of the other dozen dishes brought in for my wedding can I recall. I do remember biting into a tiny toast spread with Iranian caviar and squeezed over with lemon.

The hired band played as guests danced in a blur.

At the age of twenty-two, I was the perfect bride, happy, standing next to her intelligent, accomplished, and handsome groom, the man I loved most of all because he was kind.

Cheers rose as I twirled in my wedding dress in front of Mehrdad. My new husband spun me in the air in his strong arms and I was grateful. I was grateful for the transitory gifts of youth and good health, for the privilege of the pomp and circumstance, for the abundance of food and ambrosial drinks and effusive good wishes, for the cicadas accompanying the live band, and for every tiny light in the branches of the trees.

It was a perfect summer night, the kind where in the quiet of the dark, buds release their most tender scent into the garden, where peals of laughter ring out and travel above the walls, the kind of night where relatives pinch the cheeks of kids weaving among the tables in a spontaneous game of tag, begging for more ice cream laden with saffron and rose water and small frozen chunks of heavy cream tucked inside the mounds of vanilla. The kind of summer night where glasses of wine—and glasses of *sharbat* for those too religious or too young or too disinterested to drink alcohol—are raised.

Cheers all around. Cheers to us.

When Mehrdad fed me a piece of the towering cake, icing almost oozed onto my dress. His deft hand caught the sugary bit just in time so as not to create a spot of demarcation on that pure white silk.

The relatives who had lost touch when we'd lived downtown now stood around dressed up—ready to celebrate my new union, then no doubt go home and gossip. I heard one guest at the dessert table say that the rice had been a tad too sticky and Mehrdad was good-looking and apparently studious but, well, "a little like yogurt"—as she reached for another plate of *zoolbiah bahmieh*, her chin already glistening from the syrup of the last few fried dough pastries she'd consumed.

As I hugged each guest, including many I barely recognized, I bowed my head in thanks for their compliments and their presence. But I could not help but harbor heartbreak over those who were not there. My father. More and more a ghost to me with each passing year. Lost to me at age seven, and yet. How would it have felt were he there in the garden? To have lain my head on his shoulder, heard his advice in my ear? I conjured up a phantom of the man I wished I'd known. How I longed for him as the anchor to the evening and my life!

And Sousan was also not there. She and I stopped talking after we met in the park shortly after Homa's arrest. I couldn't forgive her for staying with a spy, whose deception had led to Homa's arrest. And she couldn't forgive me for being stupid enough to out Homa to her beloved Colonel.

I didn't taste the ice cream that summer night. I didn't have the heart to partake in the saffron and rosewater flavor, the taste unforgettable since the day I had sat with my friend in a courtyard at the end of the bazaar, our legs swinging as we bit into the ice cream sandwiches and exchanged plans for the future. A friend whose absence was the real presence that night. Whose laughter would have echoed off the high stone walls of our garden, whose joy for life would have dwarfed the dancing moves of the swaying, rocking relatives, whose happiness for me—I knew—would have rung through the rooftops of the city.

That was the person I missed most, far more than the father I never knew. But she was not invited that night. Too much time had passed, and I had kept my promise. And how could she have come with her baby in tow, her husband no one knew about, her dreams interrupted, her university attendance truncated, her future altered, her ambitions thwarted, all because of a night when I shared too much and made her suffer in ways I never intended, never wanted, never imagined?

As we stood together in the garden, a look of concern crossed my husband's face. He leaned in and took my face in both his hands. In a whisper that only I could hear, he said, "I know you miss her. *Jaash khaleeyeh.* Her place is empty. She would have danced the most for us, Ellie Joon. She would have brought the house down with her antics."

Amid the music and madness, I studied him. This was why I loved this man. He had the decency and compassion to acknowledge the friend I missed. He knew what I had done and still loved me. He knew the fate I had created for Homa with my mistake and still he forgave me. He understood that I missed her, missed her, missed her.

"She would have made fun of every single bit of this wedding," I said, practically sobbing. "She would have said the caviar was ridiculous and the lights in the trees . . ."

"Can you imagine what she would have said about this band?" Mehrdad held me close and nuzzled into me. "I can just hear her calling them 'absurd'!" He kissed the top of my head, right where the veil was held in place by a tiara Mother had ordered. "You know what?" Mehrdad whispered into my hair. "I miss her too."

And in that sweet moment, I knew that he loved Homa in his own way, that over the years she had become his friend as well.

It was then that Mother shouted at the top of her lungs, "Stare up at the heavens!"

For Mother had even organized fireworks. A small amount that burst into the air a little anticlimactically. Still the guests clapped and insisted it was the best show they'd ever seen.

I stood there, my face tilted to the sky, Mehrdad by my side, tears streaming down my face.

"Look at her," all the guests said. "Look at the bride; she is so overcome with emotion. May they live a long and healthy life together. May they grow old together. May they have many, many children together. May their children be raised under the long shadow of protection and guidance of both their parents. May they never see blackened days."

Those wishes of the wedding guests proved as effective as the lackluster fireworks. They traveled into the night sky with alacrity and speed, only to burst into shreds and then into nothingness. For only a fraction of them could come true.

But not in the way the guests intended.

Not at all.

TWENTY-EIGHT

1965–1970

The gift Mother knitted for me was pink, triangular, and soft. At each corner, two strings ended in poufy pom-poms. What I first thought was a blanket for the baby, she explained was a shawl for me to wear when the baby was born. She had envisioned me in the birthing bed, cradling the newborn, smiling for a Polaroid shot.

Mehrdad and I were both college graduates, but while he continued his education in chemistry, I did not work.

Every day, he came home from the graduate-school chemistry lab filled with ideas and hope.

Twice a week, I came home from the beauty parlor with the hair on my head styled sky-high and my face made up. Monthly, I had my face freshly threaded of peach hairs and my body hair waxed off by the roots.

Tara Khanom's beauty parlor became my entertainment, a place to make new friends and gossip with the ladies while the owner smothered my under-eye circles with makeup and curled my lashes. She rubbed rouge onto my cheeks and applied smoky eye shadow across my lids.

My beauty parlor cohorts cared about how a table was set and how to carve a radish so that it looked like a rose. They squealed over news of our country's royal family's adventures and planned bonnets to be knitted for their own unborn children.

They eventually had children.

One by unequivocal one.

Niloo had had a baby by the time I got married. I heard Sousan had three children by then. She didn't leave the Colonel. She stayed with him and looked the other way.

Once my children arrived, I could at least justify my desire to stay home.

I had graduated with good enough grades despite the hollowness and guilt that followed Homa's arrest. I had gotten the degree. What the world had given me, it had denied many who preceded me—women who may have wished to be educated, who may have wanted a profession, but were expected to stay home and raise the children.

Go forth and be brilliant, a hungry country seemed to say. Girls of my class, my generation, so privileged to have the option, could break new ground. Just like Homa had wanted.

But without Homa to push and encourage me, I felt wholly dispirited to pursue a professional path. Without her, it wasn't right. I took that under-graduate degree, folded it, and placed it in a box.

We can't control what fate plans for us. Can't foresee it, can't prevent it, cannot mold and alter it no matter how much we may wish. Mehrdad and I were in love. Mehrdad and I had it all: a good education, solid home, secure finances, our health, friends, family, our country's best prospects.

What Mehrdad and I could not have was a child.

One year goes by and the smiles of others are still polite. Two years go by and the whispers get louder at social gatherings. Several years go by and the pity that is cast upon a childless couple is hurtful and offensive.

My role became that of "Auntie." I bought gifts: wooden ducks on wheels to be pulled by a string, dolls with blond hair and blue eyes that opened and shut, stuffed owls and teddy bears and a cute cloth hedgehog with a braided short tail. I listened to my friends vent about bad nannies and marveled with them at their children's milestones.

Niloo pushed the stroller down Lalehzar Street and cooed and sang in between her rushed updates about Hooman's new job at the passport office and how her baby daughter loved to sing and could probably become an opera singer.

"She sings?" I asked.

"Oh, you should hear her, Ellie!"

"She's an infant, though."

"I know! Isn't it remarkable? She just makes these little sounds as she sucks and nurses. It's like magical music."

I had grown accustomed to my friends bragging about the talents of their offspring, gushing at real and imagined skills. What could I do but be happy for them?

I walked home thinking of how Niloo and Hooman, and everyone else in our circles—including the ladies at the beauty parlor—clucked in concern over my four years of barrenness. I knew they talked behind my back about the babies I could not make. Fretted over the embryos that did not form for me. But did they know about those that did?

Three times. Hence the knitted shawl from Mother. The small, private celebration with Mehrdad. His grabbing me by the waist and twirling me around the living room. The joyful fantasies of baby names. The crib picked out. We could envision it all. What we couldn't envision was the bleeding and the loss. The violent hemorrhaging that led us to the hospital. Each and every time.

Mehrdad's tears came in a rush. As soon as we left the hospital, his grief got contained. He retreated into himself. My days felt irretrievably blackened. A depression took over unlike any other.

Mother made potions of saffron dissolved in bone broth for me to drink. She took to praying five times a day to somehow entreat God to change my fate. Too little, too late was her transformation into someone devout. Her prayers didn't work. Her potions didn't materialize what we most wanted.

Mother claimed it was the evil eye at work. "All those people," she said, "jealous of our health and wealth. All those envious souls casting a hex on us."

"But I never announced I was pregnant," I countered. "We listened to you and didn't share the news with anyone but you and Uncle Massoud and Mehrdad's parents. How did others cast the evil eye on us if they didn't even know?"

"Oh, they have their ways," Mother retorted. "You don't know how powerful jealousy can be, Elaheh. It can destroy lives and friendships."

One night during dinner, the smell of fenugreek almost made me vomit. Mehrdad had added too much to the *ghormeh sabzi*. Grateful that he'd helped cook, I didn't express fault.

"Maybe it's not our fate," I said from my place across the table.

Mehrdad looked up from his plate. In those eyes for whom a friend had once climbed a mountain so she could determine the purity of his soul, I saw the mirror of my loss.

He chewed quietly.

We had briefly discussed adoption. But had never quite agreed on the how of it.

Mehrdad picked up his glass of water and said he didn't mind at all. He said he didn't mind one bit if he never became a father.

"Maybe it's God's plan," I said.

"You've never been religious," he said.

"Well, maybe it's just not our destiny."

"'Destiny' is another way of saying 'God's plan,' no? Anyway, we have so much to be grateful for."

"So much," I said.

"I mean if you really think about it, children are a burden."

"Truly."

We ate the rest of the meal in silence.

Part of me wanted to simply leave that city. Run away to another land where no one knew us.

TWENTY-NINE

1977

"It would be for two years. A temporary assignment. But an opportunity of a lifetime," Mehrdad said at breakfast. "If I do this research in New York, afterward I could qualify for a much better position here in Iran."

In the twelve years since our wedding, Mehrdad and I had managed to craft a tender and sweet life together. We gathered regularly with friends and family and rejoiced as their kids grew up. We attended birthday parties, weddings, and a few funerals of distant relatives. When Mehrdad had said he wanted to apply to research positions in the U.S. and Europe, I encouraged him.

It was 1977 and in the streets of Tehran, unrest and dissatisfaction with the Shah was intensifying into an increasingly frequent cycle of demonstrations, protests, and crackdowns. Activists were routinely jailed. The acute pain I had felt at Homa's arrest was now commonplace for many.

"I would start in the new academic year," Mehrdad said. "This particular laboratory in Manhattan is headed by a legend in biochemical genetics. An absolute superstar. They would even pay for our lodging right across the street from The Rockefeller University."

I read and reread every line of Mehrdad's acceptance letter from The Rockefeller University, grateful I had studied English at Tehran University.

"I know it's a lot to consider. But you already speak their language,

Ellie!" Mehrdad said. "You'd have to help me on that front. It's only for two years. And then we'd come back."

Later, when Mehrdad was at work, I went to the largest bookstore in Tehran. I had a vague knowledge of New York City but needed to do some research, get a more visceral sense. In the travel section, I found three memoirs by Iranian authors who'd visited or lived in New York, two photography books, and a few small guides.

I flipped through pages of photographs and recognized the United Nations building among images of skyscrapers and a library flanked by two stone lions. The energy pulsing from the pictures of yellow taxis caught in traffic jams and people waiting under "Don't Walk" signs for their chance to cross busy streets was one I knew from my own crowded, bustling city.

A strange wave of excitement washed over me. I returned the large book to the shelf and picked up one of the travel guides made to fit easily into a pocket. At the back were Persian phrases translated into English: "How are you?" "I am fine, thank you." "Excuse me, can you please tell me where I can find a restroom?" Photos of New York "delicacies"—a hot dog with squiggly yellow sauce; a huge pretzel flecked with what had to be salt; hamburgers and french fries; a shapely glass filled with Coca-Cola; a slice of "New York cheesecake"—looked more familiar than I realized.

During my teenage years, American products and habits had made their way into Iran through movies and television shows, as well as the growing population of Americans living and working in Tehran for American companies invested in our country. Afarin knew a lot of the American expats. She'd never married and instead had gone back to throwing massive parties that now included Americans and British living in Iran. Her stint as a communist was apparently short-lived. She had reconnected with me in our mid-twenties after we'd run into one another at a restaurant. The Americans I had met at her get-togethers complimented my English. They seemed nice enough!

"My dear, your husband has a career opportunity," Mother said. "The fact that he even pretends to consult you is adorable—he's such an enlight-ened modern man! Wives follow their husbands—it's as simple as that. And why on earth would you deny him this advancement? It's not like you have to worry about . . ." She paused and sighed. "Disruption . . . to . . . any chil-dren. This may be just what the doctor ordered, Ellie Jan. I know you and Mehrdad don't like the Shah all that much. Don't know why since despite his flaws, our king has done this country a whole lot of good, if you ask me. But Ellie Jan, I think it would be good for you."

It had been only a few days since the letter from The Rockefeller Uni-versity had arrived. I was sitting with Mother on her green velvet couch.

Mother looked at me and said, "I will miss you. So very much."

My head felt fizzy. A lump rose in my throat. Despite all her overbear-ing behavior, I did not want to leave my mother. "But it is so far . . ."

"You can guarantee that I will visit, my dear! I've always longed to go to New York City."

"There's a ton of paperwork if we say yes. They provide lodging across the street from the university, but we have to fill out these forms . . ."

Mother got up and paced the room. "I need to get a map. And you have to buy good outfits to wear. It's no joke in New York. You can't look like a *dahati*. What do they think of us, I wonder. I hope they've read about the glories of the Persian Empire!"

Mother continued pacing and rattling off things I had to get done to prepare for the move. She mentioned a trousseau and how I should fill it with gifts for Mehrdad's future coworkers and boss. She said I had to buy the best Iranian handicrafts and souvenirs. Handmade tablecloths. *Khatam* mosaic boxes. Artisan-etched decorative plates. And our delicacies! Fresh pistachios. Delicious *gaz* nougat candy. Would they like those in America? Take saffron! Yes, Ellie, take them Iranian caviar too. The Grand Bazaar was crowded and stinky, but for a big trip like this, she said, it would be the best place to get everything all at once. And for a good price. As long as I wasn't too shy to haggle.

Mother turned to the paisley-patterned wallpaper. "You see?" she shouted to an invisible audience. "My daughter's a big lady! I have to get a map!"

I didn't know whether to laugh or cry. But she was right: my fate was sealed. As a wife, it was expected that I would follow my husband. I couldn't sully a huge career opportunity for Mehrdad. And who wouldn't want to live in the world's most exciting city? Rather than be petrified out of my mind at leaving home, family, and friends, I told myself, I needed to see this as a positive spin of the wheel of fortune.

I watched my mother pace the room and make her plans. My face burned and I felt a strange *deltangi*, a tightening of my heart for how I would miss this mother of mine. She was the most infuriating person I knew, and yet. And yet. Her love was the one constant in my entire life. Even if it came with her often confounding conduct. My eyes teared up at thinking of a life far from her. How would I even do it?

Two weeks before our departure, I stood in the middle of the crowded lanes of the Grand Bazaar holding the list Mother had written on paper torn from the pad she kept by her telephone.

It had been years since I'd last been in this part of town. Moons ago, Mehrdad had proposed to me over our shared meal of *chelo kabab* at Nayeb restaurant. And of course, seared in my memory was the day Homa and I, age ten, had skipped school and first traversed the zigzag lanes here, together.

As if no time had passed, flowery potpourri mingled with the scent of rotting melons. Carrying my bags, I walked past piles of thick rugs, stalls filled with gold bangles on mannequin arms and silver chains on velvet trays. I stopped to check the list Mother had made, clumsily crossing off the gifts and Iranian goodies I had already bought. I could hear in my head Mother's voice: "Never accept the first price they tell you, Ellie. Don't be a fool. Speak up! Push back. That's how it works."

Shopkeepers chanted about their wares, the sound drumming in my ears as craftsmen banged rods on metal. I had already purchased a beautiful, hammered-metal plate with the most graceful bird etched onto it by the hands of a quiet middle-aged craftsman. When I'd asked how much, he suggested what to me seemed like a fair price and I surprised him by paying right away. I didn't have the heart to haggle, but he had the generosity to look up at me, serenely grateful. Maybe the craftsman's metal bird would be the gift we'd give to Mehrdad's boss at The Rockefeller University.

Now, I approached a stall jam-packed with burlap sacks and barrels filled with colorful spices, dried fruits, and nuts. I was carefully examining a pyramid of *esfand* seeds, wondering whether it made sense to take this Iranian incense to America to ward off the evil eye, when I heard her.

"Just wait a minute, Bahar Joon. *Sabr dashteh bash.* Be patient."

For a moment, I felt I might be imagining it. But her voice was unmistakable.

Her tone was tender, reassuring, but firm.

Out of fear or shame or nervousness, I shuffled behind a nearby barrel. But even the tallest barrel filled with walnuts wasn't tall enough to make me invisible. My legs were hidden, but my head and body were still exposed.

The voice came closer. "I'll help you pick out the best ones."

Now certain that the voice I'd heard belonged to Homa, my heart began to beat so loudly, I was worried she would hear it and look up.

Near the barrel of walnuts was a burlap sack filled with a pyramid of pistachios. She came right up to the pistachios, only a meter or two away. She wore navy slacks, a cream-colored blouse, and brown walking shoes. In one hand she held a basket brimming with bunches of parsley and scallions. In the other, she held the hand of a girl.

The girl, like her, had thick, dark curly hair, and she looked to be about twelve or thirteen. She wore bell-bottom jeans, a yellow T-shirt with an iron-on decal of Snoopy, and denim clogs. Homa stayed by the pistachios, but the girl walked toward the barrel of walnuts. She was now so close that I could see she had a mole under her left eye, just like Homa.

I froze.

"Baba said we already have pomegranate molasses at home," the girl said.

At the sound of her voice, so much like her mother's at that age, I couldn't help but whimper slightly.

"Okay, you get the walnuts, then," Homa called out absently as she studied the pistachios.

With my heart in my mouth, I stood stock-still.

Bahar had now reached the walnut barrel where I stood, gloriously half-exposed. When she saw me, a stranger, she smiled politely, then lifted the small copper shovel from the barrel to measure out nuts.

"Let me help you, Bahar Joon." Homa approached her daughter.

And there we were, face to face, eye to eye. Thirteen years had passed since my ill-fated visit to her apartment, when Bahar had been an infant lying on a pink blanket on the floor.

My body grew cold; my limbs seemed not mine; I felt an acute pain in my chest. I wanted to melt, to flee, to throw my arms around this stranger who had once been my friend. Gone from her was that lost, haggard look. She was dressed smartly and even had on—to my shock—a little makeup. I had never seen Homa with makeup before.

"*Salaam*," I said, my voice coming thin and creaky out of depths within.

"*Khodeti?* Is it you?" She sounded as though she had seen a djinn.

"It's me," I said.

"Maman?" Bahar looked at her mother and then at me.

Homa turned to her daughter vacantly, as if she had forgotten she was there. "Oh. Bahar Joon. This . . ." She motioned toward me. "Is . . . an old friend." She pulled Bahar protectively toward her. "And this is Bahar."

Homa hadn't said my name, but she had called me a friend. For that I was grateful. I came out from behind the barrel and lowered my head to Bahar. "*Khoshbakhtam*. Pleased to meet you," I said.

The girl looked at me with huge dark eyes and gave a polite nod. Then she tugged at her mother's sleeve.

"I know, I know. You want to get the walnuts." Homa studied me with the same vacant look she'd had from the moment she first recognized me. "Excuse us," she said. "We are in a bit of a rush. Getting ingredients for—"

"For *fesenjoon*, no doubt," I said.

The girl looked up with widened eyes. "How'd you know?"

I didn't say because it was always your mother's favorite. I simply said with forced levity, "Well, you're at the barrel of walnuts, aren't you? I figured if you were buying walnuts, it was time for *fesenjoon*."

The girl grinned.

"How old are you?" I asked because I did not know what else to say.

"Thirteen." Bahar shifted on her feet.

"We were just getting going, weren't we, Bahar?" Homa asked.

"But we haven't bought the—"

Homa interrupted her. "Never mind. You know, Abbas Agha, a few stalls down, has the best walnuts."

"But you said to come to this stall."

"Well, I made a mistake. Come on, Bahar," Homa said. She took her daughter's hand, rebalanced the basket on her arm, and began to walk away.

"Wait!"

Homa and Bahar turned around.

I wanted to say I was sorry. I wanted to fall to my knees right there by the barrels of nuts and spices and ask for forgiveness. My face was hot, my arms exhausted from the bags I carried. I felt as though I might faint. But the shoppers around us continued their movement and haggling and Bahar's huge eyes bored into mine.

"Homa," I said. "I'm leaving. In two weeks. I'm moving. We're moving. Mehrdad and me. To America."

Homa's face went blank. "America?"

"Yes, New York."

"Why?"

"Mehrdad. He got a position. As a post-doc in a lab. A very good one. Prestigious."

The Homa I had known would have rolled her eyes and said, *Ellie, stop showing off.* But this new one, this stranger, simply said, "*Movafagh basheen.* May you be successful. Goodbye."

I couldn't believe I was losing her again. I couldn't just let her go. "If you ever need anything. Anything at all," I said desperately. "Please write to me."

"And how would I do that? Address it to my old friend in New York?" she asked sardonically. There was the old Homa back.

She clutched Bahar's hand tight and turned back around. They began to make their way out of the nuts and spices stall. They were almost at the exit, about to rejoin the massive hallway that led to other stalls, when I cried out. "My mother! She'll know how to reach me. Ask my mother!"

When she turned around one last time, Homa's expression was at once frustrated, sad, affectionate, and yearning.

I stood there unable to move.

Bahar waved to me as they left.

The date printed on the carbon copy of the tickets was August 19, 1977, according to the Western calendar. We regarded flying a luxurious experience and had dressed to the nines for the Pan Am flight. I was in a tight skirt and matching blazer, in nylons and heels. Mehrdad had on his best tie and had polished his shoes.

On the day of our departure, Mother burned *esfand* incense to ward off the evil eye and waved its smoke over us. She held a Koran above our heads and we walked under it three times. Mother and Batul splashed water on the ground behind Uncle Massoud's car as we drove off.

I had insisted that Mother not accompany us to the airport. Despite her bravado and blessings, I knew she would likely take to her bed for days after I left.

On board the plane, flight attendants who looked like fashion models strolled down the aisle and smiled benevolently. I could not stop crying. We were off on an adventure—the opportunity of a lifetime. We were more than lucky. And yet. I would miss them all: Mother, Uncle Massoud, Batul. My friends. My home.

Mehrdad reached out and took my hand. He smelled like citrus soap and fresh cologne.

We ascended into the sky and surrendered our fate to the hands of the pilot and his ability to navigate that metal container.

It was to be a temporary assignment.

Part Four

THIRTY

1965–1974

HOMA

We have a secret pact—Abdol and I. We will forge a family together. But we will never, ever bring *that* up. What happened to me in that prison interrogation room.

I'm sure SAVAK has files on me, is watching me. I see only my immediate family, and only because we need one another. My mother tells me with her eyes that she is worried sick about what happened to me in prison, but even she cannot bear to ever approach the subject. Sara and my brother are the same. They all care. But they do not want to discuss it. Nor do I.

My father remains incarcerated. I used to visit him during sporadic allotted times with Maman. Now I can't bear to go to the prison to see him. I drop out of politics entirely. I resign officially and in my heart from the communist organization.

Whereas I had once fought for human rights, I now fight to stay afloat.

My life revolves around my child. I nurse Bahar. I change her diapers. I take her to the park.

Abdol—bless his soul—treats me with kindness. He loves Bahar like his own. Abdol's assigned shifts at the garage change from late nights to full day ones. He is an industrious worker. His income keeps the three of us sheltered, fed, and clothed.

God, how I miss Ellie.

When Bahar is an infant, I very reluctantly, finally accept Ellie's visit. Only because she's Ellie. And even then, I'm worried sick she'll get into trouble for being seen with me. And even then, I am so hurt by her offer to give me money. By her pity. Ellie feels *sorry for me*. And I can't stand it.

I focus on surviving not one day at a time, but often one hour or even one moment at a time. It is the only way I can keep from drowning in sorrow.

This tiny baby delights me and, yes, can infuriate me. But her laughter. Her face when she first tastes a lemon—priceless. She grabs my chin with her chubby, tiny hands and tries to suck it. Her absolute fascination with life is enchanting. A bowl. A falling leaf. The sound of the wind. All have the power to enthrall her.

Maman helps. I am supremely sleep deprived and tired, so she brings her tailoring projects, comes over and watches Bahar while Abdol is at work. When Bahar turns six months old, Maman encourages me, then insists, to go on morning walks. "*Rah-to boro*. Go on your walk," she says.

I go reluctantly. I come back home quickly.

The next day, Maman tells me to walk again. This time I go a little farther than the day before.

I walk that city I knew so well, where as a child I played and as an adolescent fought for rights.

In the ensuing weeks and months, I walk kilometers and kilometers in the morning hours.

One day, I walk past Tehran University, where before I dropped out of my studies in law, I dreamed of one day becoming a judge. Another time, I walk through the neighborhood where Ellie and I played hopscotch as kids. Later in the month, I walk through the mazes of the bazaar she and I traversed when we skipped school that day.

And as I walk, a voice whispers in my head. Not every day. And not necessarily in the first kilometer or the second. But it is a voice that speaks truths I cannot access until I am deep in motion.

The voice reveals to me:

He cannot make me into nothing.

He cannot evaporate me.

He cannot render me invisible.

He cannot make me lose myself.

I won't let him.

He destroyed my soul. But the voice tells me to reclaim myself. No one else will do it for me.

At nights, in bits and spurts, I try again to regain the passion for reading I'd lost as a tired, fearful new mother. I borrow from the library; I go to the stationery shop that sells books. When I am surrounded by books, I feel most at peace. The politics—the activism—I don't have the heart nor the time for them. But maybe, just maybe, with time I might return to that as well.

The voice whispers more truths as I walk:

What happened in that room will not define me.

I am who I've always been. I am Homa. I love to move, run, hike. I love *fesenjoon*. I love to cook. My mother's recipes are still in me. He cannot take all of that away from me.

With other mothers in the neighborhood, I eventually chat. They pretend Bahar is Abdol's kid. Or maybe some of them—who didn't know me when I emerged from prison or that I'd been there at all—actually believe it.

Abdol gets promoted to manager at the garage. Bahar grows from a sweet infant into a mischievous toddler into a chatty preschooler. Abdol and Maman help me care for her. Sara and Ali Reza do too.

And then one day, it is time to enroll Bahar in school. She starts her first year at our local elementary. As I wave goodbye and walk away, I am overwhelmed with tears. I walk in circles round and round her school building, feeling at once bereft and liberated.

The anger that filled me when I was first arrested no longer dominates. And I am no longer entirely made of grief. Through the walking, tons of reading, the presence of loved ones, even praying and the passage of years, I have slowly climbed back into myself.

He cannot erase my power.

I resolve to contribute not just to my family but to my community.

I do not return to Tehran University. My study of law remains unfinished. But when Bahar is six years old, I enroll in a small teacher's college. Abdol does not protest; he is perhaps relieved to see again a glimmer of the ambitious student he first met.

It takes a while, as I can only attend classes part-time. But with the help of Abdol, Maman, Sara, and Ali Reza, I achieve my certificate in teaching when Bahar is ten years old and I am thirty-one. I am supremely proud of this achievement. When I visit my father in prison (for by now I have regained the heart to visit him there), he tells me to go to the Office of *Amoozesh and Parvaresh* Education Ministry and fill out the necessary forms to apply for a teaching position.

I do just that.

And I get my first teaching assignment.

THIRTY-ONE

1974–1978

HOMA

They stand up to show respect when I enter the room.

I am shaking with nerves.

When I ask them to sit, thirty pairs of eyes bore into me.

I introduce myself and talk about the lessons ahead. I am so nervous, trickles of sweat run under my arms. Soon my underarms are soaked. I have worn a form-fitting white blouse. Bad idea. I don't have to look down to know the perspiration stains are visible and expanding.

I wait for titters and giggles to ensue. None come. These girls listen to me with full attention.

They are seniors in a high school in an impoverished neighborhood much like the one I come from. I know they are desperate to get ahead, to graduate, and to somehow break the cycle of poverty.

I steady my voice and tell them we will work hard together so they can apply for college later that year.

An arm shoots up.

It belongs to a birdlike girl with messy hair. Her face is pale, her eyes black and intense. "*Khanom, ejazeh,*" she says, asking for permission to speak.

"Yes," I say.

"We want to know, Khanom, if we get to read and write a little bit." She looks around at the other students as if asking for encouragement. "About what is happening with the protests. What is happening in this country. With everything that's been going on. We want to be able to discuss it. With you." She quickly lowers her hand.

Do they know? Do they know about my past? My former involvement with the communist organization?

It's an unwritten rule among teachers: Don't say or teach anything that disparages the Shah. The girls know this. But they might also know that I am one of them, that I come from the same kind of neighborhood, the same background. Maybe they do know I used to be very active politically.

"*Bebeeneem*. Let's see," I can't help but say to my own surprise. I continue to perspire. There is so much to teach these girls. Much to learn from them. I've been thrown into the ocean and asked to somehow swim and keep others moving.

The girls shift in their seats and exchange looks of relief.

And I remember. I remember being that young and believing the world could one day change for the better. That I could help make it so.

Two girls who share a bench in the back lean into one another.

For the first time in years, my heart fills at the thought of how I can help.

I look out at their hopeful young faces. I'm not sure how I will do it, but I know I cannot let these girls down.

I read more and more. My students keep me alive, engaged, unable to forget what is happening in my country. And Bahar grows into a vibrant, sensitive, and compassionate young person. By the time she is thirteen, she follows with great interest the demonstrations against the Shah that are building in the streets. I forbid her to attend any. I cannot afford to let my daughter get caught up in the same cycle of protests and arrest that I was.

When we run into Ellie at the bazaar, I feel a part of my soul simply soar.

To see her again! My old friend. And yet. I don't want to get her embroiled in my web again. And she tells me she is leaving. To America. I can see her there, in the streets of New York. She will be fine, I know. She was always westernized—she'll fit right in. When I see her in that nuts and spices stall, a thousand different emotions tug at me. But I've learned to button myself up. To not be as impulsive and transparent as I used to be. And I don't want to get into it all with Bahar there. Later, I replay the scene in my head countless times and wonder how I could have behaved differently. What I could have said. What I could have let Ellie know.

Does Ellie worry about our country the way I do?

It is impossible to ignore the shouts on the streets. It is impossible to look away from the increasing demonstrations. On December 31, 1977, we watch on the evening news the visit of the American president, Jimmy Carter. He is in Tehran and raises a glass of champagne with our Shah. The American president calls Iran "an island of stability."

Bahar, with all the self-assuredness of a thirteen-year-old, snorts. "He doesn't seem to know what's coming. We're no longer in a protest stage. My friends say this could become a *revolution*."

Abdol is surprised to see our leader drink alcohol so publicly with an American president. We are a Muslim country, after all. No one has embraced the ways of the West the way this Shah has.

The next day in the holy city of Qom, clergy revolt and march. The police shoot at the crowd.

In the ensuing days of 1978, the protests increase in size and scope in several cities around Iran. People want the Shah out. An end to his rule. They want democracy.

The fervor and anger seem sudden, but in fact this has been building up for months. Years. One could say the seed was planted on August 19, 1953, when Prime Minister Mossadegh was overthrown in a coup abetted by the U.S. and the U.K.

For years, students like the one I used to be protested. We were arrested.

Then released. Some were tortured or fined. Many were killed. We wanted freedom. Freedom of speech, of assembly.

I forbid Bahar to attend any protests. I don't attend any myself. Not anymore. I've learned my lesson. I will not get arrested again. My child needs her mother.

One night, when Abdol is working late, Bahar and I sit in our small living room together. I grade student papers while Bahar does homework.

"Maman, you work too much," she says.

I look up and see she has pushed away her spiral notebook with all the carefully penciled algebra equations inscribed on its graph paper pages.

I quote a popular Persian idiom about the value of hard work. "*Boro kar kon va nagoo cheest kar, ke sarmayeyeh zendegi ast kar.*" Go and work and don't question it, for work is an investment in your life. I tell Bahar how important it is to engage and be productive and industrious. I remind her that a woman, especially, should have her own source of income.

She looks at me with an expression that says she's heard me say it all before. Then she grins mischievously. "Do you think a woman should have her own *gher?*"

I put down my red biro pen and take off the reading glasses that I now need prematurely in my mid-thirties. My excessive reading is probably the culprit of my failing eyesight. "Excuse me?" I say. Did I hear her correctly? Did she just ask me if a woman can have her own *gher*, her own swagger? Her own way of swaying her hips?

Bahar drops her rectangular pink eraser into her Snoopy stationery case. She hops up, goes to the cassette player Abdol bought for her birthday, and pops in a cassette tape. The familiar notes of Googoosh's song "*Man Amadeh-Am*" fill the room.

"Get up, Maman!" Bahar bops toward me. "You can't not dance to Googoosh! Always working, working. Your grading can wait. Dance with me!"

She pulls me into the middle of the room. Her eyes twinkle as she hams up singing the lyrics along with Googoosh's emotive voice. She lifts up her arms, twirls her hands above her head, and sways her hips from side to side. She raises first one eyebrow, then the other at me. We both burst out laughing. My daughter definitely has *gher*. She has the groove, the flow. As I stumble about and do my best to keep up with her, to move my hips in a rhythm that mirrors hers, Googoosh's voice washes over us.

Our living room is our dance floor; the melody is our anthem. Together we move our bodies. Together we make up new moves and pay homage to old ones. Our arms reach higher in the air, our feet toe-step on the rug, our voices rise louder and louder in chorus with our Persian pop diva. "*Man Amadeh-Am*," we sing. "*Vay Vay Man Amadeh Am*." "I have arrived. My, my, I have arrived."

Bahar's face lights up across from me. She swirls in the middle of the room, then grabs my hands and whirls me around and around. We are like dervishes who have discovered the secret to bliss. In that moment, we are removed from the drum of protests in the streets, the shouts that want a new regime, the problems we face. We forget all that is wrong. *What if*, I think to myself as I hold tight to my daughter's hands and spin, *What if it all goes right?* We are mother and daughter, kindred spirits. We are a thirty-five-year-old woman and a fourteen-year-old girl dancing for our lives, with all of our hearts, melting into laughter, ensconced in unadulterated joy.

THIRTY-TWO

August 1978

HOMA

When Abdol tells me his first cousin is getting married, I encourage him to attend the wedding. We do the math. It is too expensive for all three of us to go. "But you should go," I say. "It will be good for you to take some time off. The garage will give you a few days for a family wedding. Go and see your cousin."

With much excitement, Abdol agrees to make the trip to the southwestern part of our country. His cousin's wedding takes place on a Friday in the city of Abadan in the Khuzestan Province.

The morning after the wedding, Abdol calls and tells us it was all so beautiful. "I wish you could have been here," he says to me and Bahar on the phone. His voice is so exuberant that I hold the receiver away from my ear so Bahar can hear everything. "You would have loved the food, you two," he says. "The bride's family made a veritable feast!" He says he is going to the cinema. He tells us he can't wait to see us soon.

The first thing I notice when I walk into class is how my students are visibly shaken. Their chatter is constant, and it's all I can do to stand there and ask them to please be quiet. But the cacophony of voices continues.

A girl with a ton of confidence named Sanam finally shouts and shuts everyone up. She turns to me. "Khanom, you do not know?"

Know what?

They look at one another with pale faces.

Sanam takes a deep breath. She looks haggard and sad. "Khanom, there's been a fire. Hundreds of people are dead."

"A fire? Where?"

"In Abadan. In a cinema. No one could get out."

I force myself to go and sit behind my desk. "What?"

Everyone begins to talk all at once again. A skinny girl in the back yells out that it had to be the Shah's forces who did it. Killing his own people, she says with deep contempt.

The news of this tragedy has clearly further lifted any caution around political speak.

"*Saket, saket!*" I demand quiet, realizing how much I sound like my own teachers growing up. I need air. I need something to assuage this growing dread in me. All I can think of is Abdol. He is in Abadan this week. He told Bahar and me just the day before yesterday how he was going to the movies with his cousin.

"If it was anyone that did it, it would be the Islamic extremists fighting the Shah," Sanam says.

Voices rise in protest. "And why would they do that?" the skinny girl shouts out. "To make everyone hate them?"

"No!" Sanam says. "To make everyone think the Shah did it and come out into the streets even more against him! They're framing him!"

For this one moment, I am disinterested in the politics of it. I cannot even wrap my head around how it happened. All I need to know is whether any of this is even true. It can't be. But if it is, I need to know if Abdol was in that movie theater.

The girls continue to argue. Let them.

They continue to throw about theories. Let them.

During lunchtime in the teacher's lounge, our principal turns on the radio and the news is confirmed. Cinema Rex is the name of the theater. Burned to the ground with everyone inside.

I tell myself there must be several cinemas in Abadan. There must be.

On the way home, I join a crowd at the newspaper kiosk to get a look at the latest headlines. Everyone around me is shocked. Furious. Sickened. Saddened.

"It's the Shah's secret police, SAVAK, who did it," a man next to me says.

"Oh please. It's the opposition and Ayatollah's Khomeini's growing coalition who is responsible. The date, August nineteenth, exactly twenty-five years after the coup d'état of 1953, can't be an accident, can it?" an older woman behind him says.

I rush home. I call the number of Abdol's cousin's house. A young woman answers.

She confirms my worst nightmare.

Abdol and his newlywed cousin were in Cinema Rex when it was consumed by flames.

Bahar cries, when she finds out the truth of it, like someone made of sorrow. I stare at her face.

The only father she has ever known is gone.

I feel numb.

Then the familiar rage that consumed me when I was first arrested.

But also grief. Grief that overwhelms. And disbelief. This time it is all combined.

I cannot rest. In the rare fractions of time when I am able to catch a fitful few minutes of sleep, I dream of Abdol.

In my dreams, I don't see the calm man kind enough to yoke his life to mine when I was a woman raped and pregnant, discarded and abused. I don't see the considerate father who helped raise Bahar. The Abdol in my dreams is not the sheepish, shy young boy I first met at a teahouse in

Darband in another life with Ellie. Nor is he the lovesick, devoted student who proposed when we both attended—for a short time—the best university in the country. The man who lay by my side night after night after life served me a fate I had not expected but one I'd learned to accept, the hardworking man who came home after a long day with hands blackened with motor grease and overalls stained, who knew I could never love him back—not in the same way he loved me—is not the man I see in my dreams.

I see the man in Cinema Rex.

He is seated next to his cousin. They watch the film, delighting maybe in its twists, partaking in this rare recreational time.

The fundamentalist opposition forces rising in the country have called even the act of going to the cinema one that is based on Western values, Western traditions. I know Abdol doesn't see it that way. We have discussed these issues and I know he believes the art of making films belongs to all in the world, not just to Westerners. The need to tell a story and listen to one is universal and timeless, no matter its form or whichever new technology brings the story to us.

Did he fidget in his seat, bopping his right knee up and down in that habit he so often had? Did he laugh when the film inspired a chuckle, was he engrossed in the details?

Who sensed the danger first? Who smelled the smoke? Saw the first lick of a flame? Was the screen suddenly imbued in an orange hue?

Smoke slowly permeating the air. People shifting in their seats. Abdol turning to his cousin.

Flames curl around the edges of the room. It feels like a tease at first. A possible trick of vision. It can't possibly be fire—until suddenly it is everywhere, and with alacrity and speed the flames climb the walls and burst across the rows of seats, and then what becomes more overwhelming than the smell of smoke is the sound of screams.

People rise, push through the rows, make an exodus for the double doors that lead to outside, to freedom. The flames expand their territory—they are audacious, crackling throughout the theater as bodies shove, as some fall to the ground and the softest velvet of a woman's handbag is crushed in a stampede. It is a surge like none Abdol has ever seen.

Abdol. My Abdol. He is not the kind to trample on fallen bodies. If anything, and I know this in my soul, he is one to extend a hand to others. To anyone in need.

Above the clamor of shouts and screams, Abdol and his cousin make their way to the doors. If anyone can corral the mayhem, if anyone can create a path with calm and resolve, it is Abdol. He will lead the others to the coveted smooth texture of the doors, inch along and take them to air, sweet air. He will open the doors and let the air in and the people out. Have folks pour onto the streets gasping and grateful, keeling over with hands on their knees, free at last to breathe.

But the doors do not open. The flames burst and grow, the air gets thicker and denser, and the doors, though Abdol has by now reached them, do not open. No matter how much he moves the handle, no matter how much he throws his body against them, they do not budge.

The doors are locked from the outside.

This imprisonment and suffocation are intentional.

Smoke snuffs out people all around him. Coughs deafen. Abdol pushes and pulls; the entirety of his mass heaves against the doors over and over again. There is a loud crash as a section of the theater collapses. It drops as if made of matchsticks. The movie screen that seemed impenetrable singes and scorches into nothing.

The world outside does not hear their screams. Or maybe they hear them but are too afraid of the vigilantes who set this fire. Of the arsonists who would commit such a crime.

No one can get out. Not when murderers have sealed the people in. Ensured their demise. Guaranteed their hearts will never again know the bliss of a free night.

Grasping, wheezing, ever-enterprising, Abdol tries.

To no avail.

No person can beat the force of those locked doors.

The cinema burns that night. All the hopes, triumphs, petty grievances, wild laments, joyous memories, and plans for life of all within it turn to ashes.

There is no applause at the end of the film that night. No conversation, no quiet walk home by the light of the moon. No argument about whether the director did a fine job or which actor was best. There is no discussion of the story.

There are only screams that muffle into silence. Flames that bring the house down. Dreams that turn to dust.

And there on the floor of that cinema is my Abdol.

Fallen from the fire not one of us could stop.

Maman comes over wearing black. She carries a plate of homemade halva. We sit in our small apartment on the floor and in chairs as visitors pour in to pay their respects and share in our mourning. Abdol's coworkers from the garage, their hands callused and bloated from use, sit on our living room floor with lowered heads. The mothers with whom I had become friends in Bahar's early childhood days come in muttering prayers for salvation under their breath. Bahar's school friends sit and hold hands as tears continuously stream down Bahar's face. My students show up. Current students, old students, my first students from that time when I sweated through my white blouse.

They mourn with us.

But underneath, there is a deep anger. For Abdol's death is different from one that happens from an accident. The death of all those who were in that cinema is the result of a premeditated, calculated, planned action aimed to cause maximum pain.

And so the offerings of comfort barely mask the subcurrent of rage.

The fire at Cinema Rex only strengthens people's resolve to get rid of the Shah, even though we will later learn it was the Shah's opponents who set the fire.

But right now the fury in general is beyond containment.

The protests continue.

Anything but the Shah!

I walk in a city now littered with burning cars and trash cans ablaze, a city boiling in fury, a country desperate for change and freedom. My heart is heavy.

I am once again cloaked in grief.

As I walk, the voice in my head whispers again. And I cannot help but be chilled from head to toe:

If the revolution succeeds, what if what follows is worse?

THIRTY-THREE

1979

HOMA

January 17, 1979. I stand in a jubilant, cheering crowd.

Yesterday the Shah left Iran. He carried with him a batch of Iranian soil.

All around me, people dance and sing. Motorists honk their horns and flash their headlights. Pastry shop owners pass around free treats. Someone throws hard candies into passing cars. A woman sings. I have never seen the Tehran streets filled with so much hope.

This is what you wanted, I say to myself. *This is what you fought for when you were young. You wanted the Shah gone. Now he has left.*

And yet. I cannot feel the hope the others feel. I am filled with nothing but dread.

As I start to walk in the opposite direction from the masses, everywhere I see portraits of Ayatollah Khomeini, the religious leader whose followers have finally succeeded in forcing out the Shah. Though Khomeini is exiled in Paris, even from his perch in the West, his influence grows and his popularity spreads.

February 1, 1979. Ayatollah Khomeini descends the stairs of an Air France plane and steps onto Iranian soil for the first time in fourteen years. When a journalist asks him what emotion he feels today at landing in his country, he answers, "Nothing."

I see the writing on the walls. The streets of Tehran are spray-painted, in the color of blood, "*Enghelab! Azadi! Jomhouriye Eslami!*" Revolution! Freedom! An Islamic Republic!

An Islamic Republic? I worry about the fervor for a religious fundamentalist whose adherence to a stringent version of Islam is alien to me. Though I left the communist movement a long time ago, every fiber in my body shudders at the thought of religion as the new (old) elixir.

The Shah has gone overseas, but the army is still loyal to him. For now.

When every night at 9 p.m. people stand on their rooftops and shout "*Allaho Akbar*" into the darkness, tanks roll into the streets of Tehran to quell their celebrations. Everyone assumes my reticence to join my compatriots in shouting "God is great!" is because I am a mourning wife.

Early February. We are a nation in limbo. Different factions fight for power. Political prisoners from the Shah's time are freed.

Finally, finally, my father is freed. His reunion with Maman, Sara, Ali Reza, and me is filled with tears. He holds Bahar at arm's length and weeps at the sight of a granddaughter who is now fourteen.

While we are grateful to have my father back, the turmoil on the streets is worrisome. National curfew and martial law are declared. People rise up and revolt.

On February 11, the military declares neutrality. The old regime is now officially gone. The revolution has succeeded in installing a new hard-line government.

And we enter a strange new world.

THIRTY-FOUR

1979

HOMA

The sentence Ayatollah Khomeini utters on March 7 is one I cannot get out of my head. "Women can go to offices, but they must be veiled."

Must be veiled.

Must.

My mother covers her hair. She wears a chador and has for my entire life. No matter that my father has been a communist for decades, no matter that her own daughter was one too. It is my mother's choice to be veiled.

And I respect that choice.

As she does mine. Not once has Maman asked me or Sara to cover our hair or bodies. It was always up to us to choose hijab or not.

But now. Our new leader, Ayatollah Khomeini, is making a decree.

That's how losses of rights build. They start small. And then soon, the rights are stripped in droves.

Suddenly, women who have finished their studies in law might no longer be able to take the oath to become judges.

Rumors circulate that the hijab will soon become mandatory. First, they'll say it's required only in government offices or shops. Then schools. Eventually, we worry, we will lose the freedom of choice altogether.

My students tell me about a march to celebrate International Women's Day.

On March 8, 1979, my students and I do not show up to school. I arrive at Tehran University with Bahar by my side. She will turn fifteen in a few months and she, too, is worried about women losing their rights.

We meet a group of my students at a designated spot. More and more women join us. Women wearing raincoats, women with their hair up and hair down. Tehranian women of all ages and walks of life: little girls, schoolgirls, college students, women like me, grandmothers. Women who are worried that if we do not remain careful and vigilant, our rights will erode in front of our eyes. In our collective presence, we find solace and strength.

I am awed by the turnout. We are, I will later read, a crowd of tens of thousands.

Together, we will take to the streets to protest against the encroachment of mandatory hijab, to fight for bodily autonomy. We will speak up. We will make our voices heard.

"*Azadi bayad nabayad nadare*" is the chant we say louder and louder. "Freedom has no musts."

The air is cool against my skin as we begin our march west from Tehran University in the direction of Azadi Square. Several of my students soon move on in the crowd, though two stay with Bahar and me: a small young woman named Yassi and her friend, Rudabeh, who is famous for her dimples and the tinkly laugh she now shares with our companions.

"I give this new regime six months tops," an older woman with graying hair shouts into the crowd. "Look at us. Look at our power!"

"They're too incompetent to last!" another woman shouts.

"Well, I feel we can work with this regime, I really do. As long as they don't take away our freedom to choose what we wear and how we worship," a young mother holding her daughter's hand says.

Bahar's hand is in mine too. She is my star.

It's the jeering that I hear first. I look up. On a bridge above the street where we march, a mob of men shout what, from the timbre and tone of their voices, are clearly obscenities. As we get closer, I can see that some of them hold clubs. They yell: "Prostitutes, prostitutes, prostitutes!"

Bahar gives me a worried look. I tell her to ignore them.

We continue to march. They cannot intimidate us.

We move down the large avenue. The obscenities from the men continue. Suddenly, I hear screams. And then I see that those men have come into our midst, their faces incensed. They have broken our march.

A young man approaches my section of the crowd, pulling women apart like he is making his way through stalks of wheat in a field. He is up close to us now. I smell garlic on his breath. He sees Bahar and leers at her, screaming in her face, "Whore, whore, whore!" *Kesafat*, he calls her. Garbage. He screams in my daughter's face. "What is so wrong with covering your hair? Why do you insist on being Western and naked? Why do you prostitutes resist modesty and chastity?"

Kesafat. The word makes my heart hurt. It is the word I was called in that interrogation room. The man continues to scream in my daughter's face. He holds in his hand a club. He raises it.

Perhaps it was dormant during the years I was an exhausted mother trying simply to make it through the day. Perhaps like the gathering of energy that powers an ocean wave, my rage was existent far away and never left. But when that man gets close to my daughter, every fiber of my soul activates. I grab him by his hair and pull him back. I hit him and hit him and hit him until screams of others beg me to stop. I hit him until my arm is weak and limp. I hit him for calling my daughter *kesafat*, for daring to come near her, for lifting his club and shouting in her face.

He backs away and staggers into the group of men, blood running down the side of his mouth. Chaos has ensued. Other men are attacking other women; screams and shouts fill the air. For our audacity to march, to question their dear leader, we are being punished and beaten.

I look at Bahar amid the increasing violence.

228 ·ı· Marjan Kamali

"Are you okay, are you okay, are you okay?" is all I can ask.

She nods, startled.

She has never seen me hit a man before, hit anyone before, and once again I am surprised by the force of my own fury, shocked at how the rage inside me, when activated, can cause great harm and also protect me. Protect my daughter.

The women scream, fight back, stand strong.

Again, I am surprised that my body is fueled for fighting. Surprised that I have the fight left in me. After all this time, my anger at injustice remains sky-high and forceful.

I am ready to protect Bahar and every woman in this march. And then. Before I can move, we are surrounded. Another group of men have made their way across the street and into the chaotic crowd.

These men do not jeer. They do not shout obscenities. They push past the thugs attacking us, come close to us, and hold hands with one another.

They form a human chain around us.

"Maman, what are they doing?" Bahar whispers.

Tears prick at my eyes. I hold Bahar tight, close to me.

"They are standing with us," I say to her. "These are men standing with us."

We didn't march just that one day. Many of us continued to go out into the streets for six days straight. "We didn't have a revolution to go backward!" we yelled.

The misogynistic thugs continued to harass and attack us. And some male allies also continued to show up in solidarity.

Later, I read a newspaper report that quoted Kate Millett, an American author and feminist who came to Iran for International Women's Day to offer support.

"It was a brilliant sight, a stirring demonstration," she says. "I am here because it's inevitable. This is the eye of the storm right now. Women all over the world are looking here."

THIRTY-FIVE

1979–1981

HOMA

The world looks away as we are being bombed. The bombs fall relentlessly, randomly, with little warning.

From the heady days of the women's march in March 1979 we go into headier, unimaginable days. In November, extremist students take American Embassy personnel hostage, saying the American Embassy is a den of spies. The only good thing in December is that we have some snow. I dare to think that the Americans held in captivity by our brainwashed radicals can at least see snow for their Christmas.

With each passing month, people leave Iran in droves. Niloo and Hooman, like so many Iranian Jews, want to leave Iran for Israel. But they are waiting, hoping for now that things get better here. Niloo tells me Sousan and her children have landed in Los Angeles. They are lucky to get out. The Colonel never makes it. When the new Islamic regime takes power, he is among the many military officers from the Shah's forces who is executed.

In July of the following year, 1980, the Shah dies of cancer while in exile in Egypt.

And the marches we had, the tens of thousands who showed up, the screams we made heard, are all in vain. Hijab becomes mandatory. Improper hijab is punishable by fines, beatings, even imprisonment. We have a new morality police. They patrol the streets looking for visible strands of hair.

And I look around me at a country that is unrecognizable.

Like a phoenix rising from the ashes, I am back at it. The minute that thug touched Bahar and yelled in her face, I knew. My daughter's future depends on my fighting.

I think of my old friend, Ellie, in that other country. I wonder how she is. I hope she is happy. Does she see what is happening here?

With the help of one of my former students who is now very active in the feminist movement against this new regime—as I will forever think of it—I take action. I start an organization for women's rights.

The regime is absolutely deaf to our demands, but soon we grow in numbers and in reach. We have meetings in basements and we draft mission statements. We also begin to write and distribute articles and pamphlets. Several of our members were lawyers who have been demoted since the new government changed everything. But I watch these young women write articles and fight for the rights of clients represented by men they used to work with, who consult them in secret and with admiration.

We will not take this lying down. We are making a difference. I feel like we can only see things improve.

Then in September 1980, Saddam Hussein invades Iran and a full-fledged war with Iraq begins. The age of the draft gets lowered. Ever younger men are conscripted to serve. Child soldiers. We cover our windows with aluminum foil so Saddam Hussein cannot see our cities at nighttime. In several cities, buildings lie in rubble from the war.

In the middle of the night, when the "red alert" siren goes off, the sound is deafening, triggering, frightening. I wake Bahar from her deep sleep and together with the other building residents, we make our way down the steps to the basement. There we stay huddled in the dark.

One night as we sit, waiting for the bombs to stop falling, Bahar slumps into me, rests her head into my shoulder, and silently weeps.

We are tired.

Tired of the many ways we are continually told to shut up and obey.

Tired of being worried about constant arrest because a strand or two of our hair might peek out. Because a patch of our skin might show.

Tired above all—above all in God's almighty planet—of being bombed. Night after night after night.

Bahar continues to weep. I stroke her hair, kiss her cheeks. I tell her I am doing everything I can to make our country better. To fix things.

She nods, snuggles into me, and eventually falls asleep.

And it's true that I am trying. My organization is making more and more of a name for itself.

I am fighting every single day to fix this country. So my daughter can be free again. So we can have a real country.

So we can reverse this send-back to the Iranian Middle Ages.

We are making strides. We are making progress.

My organization is growing.

And yet. I know now that I am a threat again. They are watching me. Only this time it's the new government. I am at risk again.

I look at my daughter in the dim light of the kerosene lamp in the basement. She is sleeping now, her long eyelashes still wet against her cheeks. My beautiful daughter. The constant worry of harm that could come to my child is overwhelming.

The ground above us shakes. I can hear distant thunder.

Bombs.

Again.

How much longer can I put my daughter in jeopardy?

How much longer can she be exposed to war, to oppression, to this heartbreak?

And what if I get arrested again? What will happen to Bahar?

We had big dreams, didn't we? We were going to own the world. I was going to be a lawyer, one of Iran's first female judges. Now I'm still fighting.

But my daughter.

She deserves better.

If there is a way out for her, I have to find it.

Another blast. I can feel the vibrations in the ceiling above.

I close my eyes.

If I ever make it back out of this basement, if we are not bombed to death tonight, if I survive this one more attack, I promise.

I promise that when I can get back to our apartment, I will contact El-lie's mother.

I will ask for Ellie's address.

And I will see if I can find an escape route for my daughter.

Just for a little while.

Just until things get right again.

It can be a temporary assignment.

Part Five

THIRTY-SIX

1977

Together, Mehrdad and I crossed York Avenue at 66th Street and went through the main gate of The Rockefeller University.

Mehrdad talked with pride about the campus. "The laboratories are connected by a labyrinth of underground tunnels, for when the snow is heavy, Ellie! For transfer of the chemicals. They've thought of everything!"

It had been three weeks since we moved into our apartment across the street from campus and it was the first day Mehrdad was taking me to meet his coworkers and boss.

In the elevator up to his lab, I attempted to calm my nerves with a vain, insecure mental review of how I looked. Gone were the beehives of my university days.

Determined that I should grace the streets of America looking like our Queen Farah Pahlavi or international star Farrah Fawcett, Mother had given me a set of pink, bristly rollers, and I had used them for this auspicious day. My hair turned out successfully bouncy with big waves. I wore a sapphire-blue dress with a band neckline, full skirt, long sleeves, and one-button cuffs. In the days of skinny eyebrows and super-shiny lip gloss, I was on point with both.

The elevator dinged, and Mehrdad led me into a dimly lit corridor lined with open and closed doors. Through one of the open doors, I saw men and a few women in white coats standing at rows and rows of long tables with benches. I felt I was watching an American movie where brave scientists work around the clock to save the world from a virus gone wrong.

Mehrdad led me into the second room on the left. The air inside was sour, but large windows and a view of the East River made the space surprisingly bright. Mehrdad pointed out his bench with pride. Tiny syringes were lined up on the table. "Pipettes," Mehrdad said.

One by one, he introduced me to his colleagues: the world's best and brightest, recruited to work together on experiments. There was a petite woman named Ling Fei. A redheaded man named Thomas. A smiling woman with flipped black hair named Gabriela. They were from China, Germany, and Brazil respectively, experts, Mehrdad had explained over dinner, in "chemical reaction efficiency," "particle aggregation," and "solid-phase peptide synthesis." I still didn't fully understand what they did.

As we left the lab, a young woman in the corner inserting the small syringes—pipettes—into trays filled with holes waved at me with her blue-gloved hand.

We moved down the hall until Mehrdad stood in front of a frosted glass door. He opened it. Inside the small, cramped room, a coffee machine balanced on a filing cabinet. A window in the back was half blocked by a teetering pile of papers. And in front of us, a young, brown-haired woman who couldn't have been more than twenty-two sat at a cluttered desk. Her messy ponytail made her look busy and slightly sad.

When Mehrdad asked if he could briefly introduce "the boss" to his wife, the young woman sighed. "Dr. Kohler prefers appointments."

She mumbled into a receiver, then motioned to a door on her right as she looked up and down at my sapphire-blue dress, my bouncy hair, and super shiny lip gloss. I should not have come to this laboratory looking like a knockoff of a Persian queen. I cursed my mother. Following her absurd advice to avoid looking like a *dahati* left me feeling like an overdressed immigrant. I cursed myself for being so wrong in this country.

Dr. David Kohler's office was enormous and clean, with an even better view of the East River than from Mehrdad's lab. Rising from his desk, Dr. Kohler was tall, unbelievably so. Between his white hair and salt-and-pepper mustache, his blue eyes drooped with weariness and the burden of what I assumed was too much knowledge. He motioned to two leather chairs across from his desk and asked us to sit.

"How do you like New York?" Dr. Kohler asked, loudly and slowly. "How is the apartment?"

"The apartment is wonderful," I said. "Thank you so much."

After I spoke, Mehrdad sat a little taller at the sound of his wife's good English.

Dr. Kohler, with a small raise of his eyebrows, registered surprise.

"We are delighted to have Mehrdad with us," he said, no longer speaking too loudly or slowly. "His research is incredibly promising. His background is stellar. He has already settled in. Nicely."

Now it was my turn to puff with pride. Dr. Kohler had pronounced Mehrdad's name in a comical way, making it all blurry "r"s for no reason, but no matter. My husband was a rising star.

"And how about you, if I may ask?" Dr. Kohler said. "Have you found ways to spend your days?"

I had cried every single morning after Mehrdad left for the lab—not because my new city wasn't exciting or energetic or filled with possibilities for adventure. It was all those things. I had cried simply because in this new city I was very much alone.

Once I'd dried my tears, I got to work. I cleaned our two-bedroom apartment (really, a one-bedroom plus a tiny room for Mehrdad's study) furnished with an orange floral-patterned sofa. I had shopped at the closest supermarket, puzzling over the abundant variety of boxed, prepackaged food and neon-yellow mustards and cheeses. In our avocado-green kitchen, I learned to prepare avocados and how to use the coiled-wire electric stove to cook.

I had walked, between 59th and 79th streets, up and down York Avenue.

First Avenue. Second Avenue. Even Third Avenue. The array of stores and restaurants, kiosks and newsstands, reminded me of Tehran sometimes. I had bought the *New York Times* three times. I had bought the *Daily News* five times. The *New York Post* twice.

When Mehrdad came home, sometimes I couldn't help but burst into tears again. I felt blind in this new country. And as though the people in it were blind to me. I was invisible. I could never have existed and it would make zero difference in the thrum and rhythm of the vast, great city. I wasn't ungrateful for this opportunity to be in a new country with the wonderful amenities Mehrdad's post-doc position afforded us. But I knew no one. I understood the language, yes, but I didn't understand much else. I missed the familiar routines of home, even missed the ladies at the beauty parlor with their small-minded gossip and petty competition over who best carved a radish into the shape of a rose. I telephoned Tehran every few days just to hear Mother's voice. I walked the streets like a ghost.

Sometimes I thought of my old friend, Homa. Imagined walking these streets with her. What would she think of these tall buildings? Would she like New York? I would think of Homa and again feel blanketed with guilt. If I could ever see her again, how would I word my apology? Make my confession?

But I did not need to worry about how to apologize to her because she was not with me. In those New York streets I walked alone. Friendless, just another immigrant face among the masses.

Were it not for the way I felt when Mehrdad was home, I might have fled. But once he walked through the door and we had dinner, once he shared with me a few details of his day, he would hold me and kiss me and take me to bed, and there in his arms with his body intertwined with mine, my every woe was lifted and momentarily I floated, I was in bliss. With Mehrdad's voice in my ear, I was whole again, myself again. Until the next morning when seven forty-five rolled around and I faced a day of nothing.

"I keep busy," I said in my best American accent. "New York is a lovely city."

Dr. Kohler studied me with his droopy eyes. "That it is," he said. "But I tell you what. Might you be interested in joining other spouses of post-docs and our doctors and fellows from all over the world for a get-to-know-you? There is happy hour every Friday afternoon at Caspary Auditorium."

It sounded adorable for the Americans to have designated a specific hour as a happy one. And I was in no position to refuse my husband's boss's suggestion. He was the reason we had traveled across the world to be in this strange and fascinating laboratory. I tried to muster a look of excitement at the prospect of happy hour.

Dr. Kohler proceeded to speak to Mehrdad about amino acids and reagents. As they discussed the science, I looked at Dr. Kohler's desk. Among the objects on display were three snow globes, a few amethyst rocks, and a large cowbell with a Swiss flag. In a framed family portrait, a much younger, brown-haired version of Dr. Kohler and a woman with a huge-toothed smile posed standing behind two little boys wearing bowl haircuts, orange shirts, and brown vests. And there, in the corner of his desk, was a familiar decorative plate. I had chosen the elegant design of the hand-etched bird the day I ran into Homa and Bahar in the bazaar. On Mehrdad's very first day at The Rockefeller University, I had told him to give it to Dr. Kohler as a gift from our country.

After the meeting, Mehrdad walked me to the main gate and said, "You'll meet people soon. That Delightful Hour sounds promising."

He kissed me. And in that kiss, I felt the salty familiarity of his scent, the comforting landing, the buzz that his proximity still elicited in me after all this time.

I walked back to our apartment, well aware of the reason I was in this country. I was in it for him. I chuckled at how he said "Delightful Hour." Dear, dear Mehrdad.

The buffet table in the corner of the Caspary Auditorium held a tray of cubed, bright yellow cheese.

A blond woman about my age wearing wide-legged red pants and a white button-down shirt walked over and took a plate. She looked at me. "This cheese is the pits," she said. "Here, try the chips." She dipped her hand into a big bowl of potato chips and plopped some onto my plate. As if she knew me, as if we were already on familiar terms. The chips were ridged and large and all the exact same shape.

I bit into one and it shattered into tiny pieces. I must have made a face, because she laughed.

"I'm Angela." She held out her hand. "I moved here from California last year."

"I'm Ellie." I took her hand and shook it. I'd learned to use the shortened version of my name in this country. "Ellie" was a lot easier for Americans to pronounce than "Elaheh."

She picked up a chip and bit into it and smiled.

It was Angela who took me shopping for a pair of high-waisted, wide-legged polyester pants in a soft lavender. She wanted me to buy the canary yellow, but I wasn't quite ready for that. It was Angela who showed me how to use the subway and how to avoid being splashed by puddles as cars drove by and how to hail a cab in Midtown.

Angela's husband, Ryan, worked at the Laboratory of Molecular Genetics at The Rockefeller University, and they were our neighbors in the building at 1175 York Avenue. We lived in apartment 17C and they lived in 20D.

Angela loved to cook. She took me to Gristedes and helped pick out linguine and clams and sauce, and then took me to her apartment to show me how to "throw it all together." Sometimes we cooked dinner for four, or our husbands met us at nearby restaurants "for a bite."

It was Angela—age thirty-seven to my thirty-four—who campaigned for me to apply for a part-time job at Bloomingdale's, where she worked at the cosmetics counter.

"What do I know about makeup?"

She stopped and looked me up and down. "Honey, you know plenty!"

I was able to get the job with the visa we had. It helped that the language I had studied for years was the language of this new country.

When people from The Rockefeller University found out I was from Iran, they would often recite a verse of Omar Khayyam or Rumi or talk to me of Persian rugs and kittens. The associations Americans had with Iran were mostly positive at that time. Sometimes there were strange questions. At Angela's Christmas party, I stood next to a bowl of red liquid "punch," when a young man asked if we had electricity in Iran.

"*Yes*," I said, making no effort to hide that he'd offended me. He blushed and walked away. A few minutes later, a professor's wife asked if there were seven days in a week "over there" in Iran. I assured her that we did in fact have seven days in a week, but that we followed a solar calendar.

On December 31, 1977, Angela, Ryan, Mehrdad, and I celebrated New Year's Eve together. We watched the news, transfixed. President Jimmy Carter was in Iran. He had raised a glass with the Shah and said, "Iran, because of the great leadership of the Shah, is an island of stability in one of the more troubled areas of the world."

Our countries were the best of friends. Allies in a dangerous world. We could not have imagined the friendship between our nations ever being severed. We could not imagine that they would ever become adversaries.

The friendship between Iran and America seemed like it would last forever.

But I should have known that some friendships fracture and rupture beyond belief.

THIRTY-SEVEN

Summer 1978

"I am coming, Ellie," Mother said on the phone. "This summer. And it's good I'm coming because this country is roiling in riots like never before. But I can't stay too long. My social engagements here are too many. There's a huge, end-of-summer party the Rezayis are throwing and I cannot miss it. So don't you worry—I won't be like every other Iranian mother who visits their child abroad and stays for months. Me, I only have three weeks to spare. The French have a saying, Ellie Joon. They say, '*on doit profiter.*' Better we make the most of each day I'm there!"

I wrote down the date and time of Mother's arrival. She would come alone, without Uncle Massoud, because he was busy with work, she said. But I knew the flight was expensive, and despite their wealth it was quite a stretch to buy the plane tickets for one person, let alone two.

Before picking Mother up, I patted my hair again in that leftover superstition from my youth where I used to tighten each braid for good luck. I had missed my mother and was excited to see her, of course. But I knew that from the minute she landed at JFK International Airport she would begin her fault-finding and list of grievances. In her presence, I would again become that chubby child afraid to be scolded and criticized. I braced myself for a rocky three weeks.

And true to form, when I hugged Mother, even as her eyes welled up at seeing me again, she did declare that my hair looked far too frizzy.

"Remember: I told you to crack an egg on your skull, Ellie. It's the only thing that works for frizz."

"Yes, Mother," I said.

When she entered our apartment, Mother walked around and sniffed. "My goodness, is this little place where you've been living for the past year? You poor thing! And that green kitchen—it's hideous!"

When Mehrdad came home that evening, she was genuinely happy to see him and gave him a huge hug. But then she patted his belly and said, "You're beginning to look too American. Better watch what you eat!"

Mehrdad and I exchanged a helpless glance, though later as we lay in bed Mehrdad said to me, "Is her commentary really '*passive*-aggressive'? She's purely aggressive!"

I couldn't disagree.

For the first week of Mother's visit, I bit my tongue at her subtle digs. I was grateful to be with her again, to hold again her papery veined hands, to hear her voice exclaim "*Va!*" at every unbelievable thing in America.

On her first morning, I prepared her a glass of orange Tang.

"An orange powder that dissolves into water to turn into orange juice?" Mother asked. Then she followed it with her exclamation of wonder/outrage: "*Va!*"

"Isn't it something?" I said, feeling slightly protective of this strange dissolving powder marvel. "Mehrdad and I love it."

For dinner, I chopped parsley, cilantro, and scallions to make her *ghormeh sabzi* and in the ensuing days, Mother watched me prepare many an Iranian *khoresh*. But on the fifth night of her visit, I showed off smartly by putting in the oven frozen fish sticks and bringing them out hot and crispy.

"Fish in the shape of a stick? And breaded? *Va!*" Mother looked horrified as I squeezed out a dollop of ketchup on her plate.

On her first weekend in New York, Mehrdad and I took her to the Empire State Building on Saturday. We pressed our eyes into the cold, metal circles of the binoculars and zoomed in on other famous landmarks. Mother kept going on and on about a favorite movie of hers where the characters were to meet at the Empire State Building but how fate intervened and did the usual mastery it does. Mehrdad and I listened to her describe the plot of the film at length. On Sunday, we took Mother to Fifth Avenue. She marveled at the Plaza Hotel and F.A.O. Schwarz across from it. Then we went for a walk in Central Park. We frequently had to stop and rest on benches so she could catch her breath. In the one year I had been in America, my mother had seemed to age so much. In the park, she told us about the protests in Iran and the feeling of mounting danger there. She said she worried that a revolution was in the offing.

"But wouldn't that be a good thing?" I dared to say, knowing she had grown into a huge fan of the Shah.

"Only if what follows isn't a nightmare, Ellie! We have these religious fundamentalists gaining ground. You think they would be better than our dear Shah? God help us if they're the ones who take over."

After that second long day of sightseeing, I didn't cook. Mehrdad helped me heat up frozen TV dinner trays. We were both excited to share with Mother this very American invention. As we placed the shiny foil tray in front of her, Mother's eyes widened. The largest compartment held fried chicken. A smaller one held potatoes, the package promised, "whipped with fresh milk and butter." A third compartment contained mixed peas, corn, and carrots. And the fourth held apple and peach slices in juice.

"What in fresh hell is this?" Mother asked.

"It's a frozen TV dinner!" I said.

"What on earth does dinner have to do with TV?"

"You place the tray on your lap and watch television as you eat," Mehrdad explained.

"Why would I want to watch television as I eat my dinner?" Mother asked. Mehrdad and I were both quiet.

Mother just stared at the tray and said, "*Va, va, va!*"

Pretty soon I was scrambling some eggs and Mehrdad was boiling rice, because Mother's expression at the sight of the segmented aluminum tray was that of a scared child.

Mother was less than thrilled when I proposed a visit to Bloomingdale's.

"What happened to your ambition, Ellie?" she asked. "You're a lowly perfume saleswoman."

"I sell all kinds of cosmetics, not just perfume," I countered.

"Still," she said. "Why are you working in that *shop*?"

I knew just the fact that would sway her. When I told her that only two years earlier, in 1976, Queen Elizabeth had visited Bloomingdale's, Mother's face changed. "The Queen?" she said. "Of England? Came to America and saw your shop?"

"Yes," I said. "It's a pretty important shop. It's possibly America's most famous department store."

"Well, I suppose as your mother I should take a tour of the place where you work," Mother said.

On Bloomingdale's shiny first floor, Mother looked carefully at the arrangements of scarves and handbags, racks of pantyhose, and countless display counters of makeup. I led the way as we zigzagged across the busy sales floor, swerving around shoppers.

Mother turned to me and said, "You know what, Ellie? This is just like a bazaar! It's a modernized, cleaner, shiny tile-floored bazaar that smells of cologne instead of potpourri and rotting fruit."

"Well," I said. "As a matter of fact, when this store first opened in 1872, it was called 'The Great East Side Bazaar.'"

I waited patiently as she registered what I had just said. Then it came. "*Va!*"

I took my mother's arm. "Why don't we go down to the cellar and get something to eat. There's a lot of stimulation here and you must be tired."

"I'm not tired!" Mother said.

"Fine, but I want you to taste a dessert that was first introduced to America in this very department store."

"Did Queen Elizabeth have it when she visited? What is it called?"

"I don't know if she did. But it's called frozen yogurt."

"Frozen yogurt?" Mother repeated as though the two words had no business being said in the same breath.

Before she could say it, I said it for her. "I know, right? *Va!*"

The counter at the Forty Carrots restaurant in the basement was high. I helped Mother climb up onto a stool so we could sit perched together behind the long, horseshoe-shaped table. Luckily, we had arrived at the tail end of the lunchtime rush, so we were able to get seats. Farther down, I noticed another mother-daughter pair. The mother was dressed in a pink plaid blazer with a necklace of large white baubles and the daughter had on a light green blouse with a big pussy-bow tie.

"Hey, Ellie, hon', what'll it be?" the waitress, Roseanne, said when she came to me.

On our lunch breaks, Angela and I loved to join the fashion-conscious shoppers at Forty Carrots. Splurging on sandwiches, salads, and muffins made both of us feel extra hip and in the flow of New York society.

Now I felt a surge of pride. Roseanne knowing my name made Mother see how well-entrenched I was in this place.

I ordered two plain frozen yogurts, then explained to Mother how the dessert had been invented right here at this restaurant. She didn't seem impressed. Would she be as critical as she had been of the Tang, fish sticks, and frozen TV dinners?

As I watched Mother nervously eat her first spoonful, then smack her mouth, I hoped the flavor wasn't too tart for her.

Then she said, "*Beenazir!* Amazing!"

Thank the lord above.

When we were halfway through our bowls of yogurt, Mother cleared her throat. "So," she said. "Ellie Joon. Are you happy here?"

"Look, I know you think I could be doing more, but it's a good job. I like it. I like interacting with the customers. And I have fun coworkers."

"I don't mean here in this . . . shop. I mean in this country."

I thought of those first lonely weeks.

"It took time," I said. "To adjust. But it's been a year now. We've made good friends. There's Angela, whom I've told you about. Her husband, Ryan. And Mehrdad has made connections with his colleagues and the many Iranian graduate students and other post-docs. We're increasing our social network."

Mother took all of this in carefully. "Good," she said. "Because I always wanted you to have good friends. Even though you used to have terrible taste in them. But I patiently put up with the riffraff friends of your childhood."

I felt my neck muscles tense. I stared into the swirl of the yogurt in front of me. I remembered all the times she had undermined my friendship with Homa. She had loathed our connection from the very beginning. I harbored so much guilt over what I had said to the Colonel and how that had caused Homa to be arrested. I carried the guilt with me like a constant awful companion. But not once could I confide in my mother about this pain. I had learned as a young child that I simply didn't have the kind of mother I could turn to when in despair. I didn't have the kind of mother who would be understanding about my predicament, who would listen calmly, who would listen at all. Had I told Mother about the arrest, she would only have said that Homa got her comeuppance. Because that's how Mother was. Had she known the full extent of Homa's communist activities—which thankfully I had never shared with her—she would have liked her even less. If that was possible.

Over the years, I had often imagined what it would have been like to have a different kind of person for my mother. In many ways, Mrs. Tavakoli, Mehrdad's mom, had the traits I wished my own mother had. Patience. A nonjudgmental outlook. A simple calmness. Grace. And a filter when she spoke. My mother said whatever came into her head, no matter how hurtful.

And her jabs had been hurtful. They had been hurtful when I was growing up, and they were hurtful now as I sat with her in a restaurant in a Manhattan department store. To hell with it. I was thirty-four years old. Living and working in New York. I might as well have it out with her here and now.

"Do you know how much it hurt me to know that you cared not one whit about my friendship? She was important to me. She mattered to me. Maybe not to you. But I valued her. And all you could do—and all you can still do!—is find fault with her. Why? Why couldn't you just be happy for me? Why couldn't you just celebrate that I had a good friend? Why couldn't you rejoice in what I had? Was it the evil eye, Mother? Is that what worried you? Or were you simply just not happy for me? You did everything you could to break us apart."

"What?" Mother looked genuinely surprised. As if I had accused her of being a fire-eating dragon with wings. As if I had said something frightfully untrue.

"Come on, Mother. You say you want me to be happy, to have friends. But you only wanted me to have the *right* friends. To be with the right strata of society. You never liked Homa. Because she was poor. Because you were always afraid of us staying poor. Isn't that why you . . . accepted Uncle Massoud's proposal? So we could move uptown again?"

I didn't ask if that was why she slept with Uncle Massoud in our little house downtown when she thought I was away at a school celebration. I shivered at the memory.

"Elaheh." My mother pronounced my full name slowly. "Since you want to be so crude as to bring up those dark days, then fine, I'll tell you. Yes, I gave in to your uncle. He pursued me relentlessly. He pursued me even when your father was still alive, I'll have you know. Flirted with me. Made it clear he desired me. Of course, I didn't respond in any way while your father was alive. And even after he died, I resisted. I didn't give in to Massoud's advances, though had I given in right away, it would have meant *not* living in that slum neighborhood. I held strong.

"But then," she sighed, swirling her spoon around the yogurt listlessly. "I was so worried for you in that neighborhood. Homa was the least of it. And yes, I did not like her. That much is true. I did not want you to get in trouble being with the likes of her. And didn't she end up in prison? Don't think I don't know that she was arrested, Ellie. Word gets around. But what did she expect? She was foolhardy. Idealistic. Her head was filled with nonsense from day one. That father of hers was a communist too. I hate communists. Even as we sit here, it's the communists making an alliance with the religious right to topple the Shah. How disloyal they are! I thought they didn't even believe in God. But they are happy to make an alliance with fundamentalists if it gets them what they want. I'm not as stupid as you think, Ellie. I was worried for you. Always. But that Homa girl was the least of it. What would I do if, as you grew up, you were accosted by one of those alley boys? Or fell in love with one? I wanted to protect you. To give you a better life. I finally gave in. Your uncle and I became one."

I stared at her in disbelief. So she had known about Homa's arrest. But she couldn't possibly know about my role in it.

"Don't fault me, Ellie. Don't judge me. Your uncle is a good person. Is he not? Has he harmed you in any way? Has he harmed me? What has he done but given us both a good life ever since I said yes to him? Your uncle is a very good man."

I couldn't argue that Uncle Massoud wasn't a good person. But as I heard Mother speak so highly of him, my face grew hot. "But what about my *baba*? You married his brother, fine. I am not begrudging you that entirely. But you never, ever spoke to me about Baba after he died, not in a real way. You never let me ask you about him, to keep alive his memory. You were so quick to dismiss him, constantly saying it was the work of the evil eye that he died. And that's all you'd say! Did it ever occur to you that I wanted to know my *baba*? Through you? That I wanted to hold on to any memory, any clue? You erased him from our lives."

Mother stared at me as if she were listening to me speak in a foreign tongue. She looked confused and disappointed. But above all, she looked afraid.

"Oh, Ellie." She looked down at her bowl of melting yogurt.

"Well? Mother? Is that all you're going to say? Didn't I deserve to have the memory of my father live on? Why wouldn't you ever speak of him?"

"Because he was a philanderer," she said in a voice so quiet I could barely make out her words. Then she looked up at me and said in a much louder, clearer tone, "He cheated on me, Ellie. Many times. I hid it from you. You were seven when he died. What did you want me to say? That he was never ever a good husband? That he had mistresses left and right? For all I know there could be other children out there. Children who are your half-siblings. I was only trying to protect you."

Still as a rod, I sat on the stool behind the counter. The waitresses scurried back and forth. The murmur of others in the restaurant receded. I felt only a deep and heavy silence. Was there any truth to what my mother was telling me?

I replayed in my mind my few childhood memories of when my father was alive. My father traveling for work. Constantly. My mother alone with me. Constantly. My father and mother arguing behind closed doors. And I remembered Uncle Massoud and his disinclination to ever talk about my father. Had he known? Was he the one who actually loved my mother?

Mother looked at me and shook her head. "I am so sorry. But yes, your father was not a man I wanted to venerate or memorialize. Didn't you ever wonder why you had no other siblings?"

I had wondered that. A lot. And when I had suffered my miscarriages, I wondered if Mother had suffered her own. Or maybe she'd had babies that died of illness in infancy, as babies sometimes did those days in Iran.

"I loathed it when he touched me. I did not want more children with him once I knew about his cheating and dishonesty."

"Why didn't you divorce him?" I asked. Even as I said the words, I knew what a ridiculous question it was.

"Ha! Divorce him? And lose you? You know what child custody laws in Iran were like. It wasn't until 1967 that our divorce and child custody laws were improved. The Shah did that—he gets credit for helping women, whether your generation wants to admit it or not. These angry young people on the streets want the Shah gone. Do they know what will happen if the religious fundamentalists take over? We'll go back decades—centuries! The laws will be awful again for women!"

My mother. My social-climbing, borderline narcissistic, always seemingly selfish mother. Talking to me about child custody laws. About divorce laws. I took in a deep breath and stared down at my lap. So, all these years. All those years the father I had mourned and missed was a jerk. And I had cast a thousand presentiments onto my mother.

"Tell me, then," I said. "If the entire narrative I had about my father is untrue, is it also untrue that you were descended from kings and queens?"

She held her head high with aplomb. "That, my dear, is entirely true. Why do you think I named you Goddess? You are indeed the descendant of kings and queens!"

Then, in a more serious voice, she said, "Perhaps I did take that ancestry a bit too much to heart. I'll give you that. I refused to work, to get a job. I see now that maybe that was too prideful of me, too foolish. I'm not saying I haven't made mistakes, Ellie. But I am saying that with all the mistakes I've made, please do not doubt that I have always, at heart, wanted the best for you. For you to be happy. I may have gone about it the wrong way. Look, perhaps I was too harsh on your friend, Homa. On your friendship. But all I ever wanted was the best for you."

I sucked in my lips. The remaining frozen yogurt in my bowl was now liquid. I stared down at the sugary mess. *All I ever wanted was the best for you.* I thought back to when Mother and I shared a mattress and slept together in that small house in downtown Tehran. At the time, I could not have imagined what it must have been like for a young woman and her seven-year-old daughter to be alone in a new place in an unsafe neighborhood with only one another. I conjured up again the blurry, ever-fading image of my father's face. He was hardly the hero I had made him up to be in my mind. I wanted my father to be good and true. I wanted to believe he was the paragon of duty and kindness and responsibility. I did not want to believe that my father was filled with these flaws. But as I continued to stare at the unfrozen yogurt in my bowl, I knew in my heart that my mother was finally telling me the truth about my father. And about wanting the best for me. For her, keeping me away from Homa was a method of protecting me. I did not doubt she believed what she said. Nor did I doubt her own foibles and flaws and follies. We all had them. My mother maybe more than most. But perhaps she did—in her own warped way—do just about everything she did because she wanted the best for me.

"Why do you think I wanted you to marry Mehrdad?" she asked softly.

I looked up. "Because he comes from a good, *established* family and that's what matters in your eyes," I said.

"Yes, he comes from a good family. But that wasn't the only reason! I could tell he is a good man, an honest man. I did not want you with someone like your father."

I considered what she was saying. It was a struggle to process it all.

"And Ellie? Listen to me. I know you and Mehrdad are here for a two-year assignment. But what I am seeing unfold on the streets in Iran is not good. I have a terrible feeling about it. I'll speak to Mehrdad myself. Believe me. I'll tell him that once his post-doc assignment is over, he should do his very best to get a professorship here."

"What?"

"Do not come back, Ellie. I'll miss you. Terribly. But our country? It's a mess right now. And you would do well to sit right here eating your frozen yogurt and orange-colored powder drinks and sticks of fish. You would do far better settling here and making a life for yourself in this country. Being oceans apart will hurt my heart forevermore. But. Hear me, Ellie. That country is not a safe place. Not if right-wing fundamentalist thugs take over."

She leaned in and stared right into my face. "Ellie Jan. Forgive me if I have wronged you."

"And the evil eye?" I asked quietly. "You blamed all our misfortunes on the evil eye. Baba's death . . ."

"I *still* blame it all on the evil eye!" she said, unbowed. "Because we were happy once, he and I. We started off happy. He then unraveled into a monster of a husband. Unkind and emotionally abusive to me. He even hit me once. I know that's not uncommon in some circles in Iran, but it was not something that my parents or I ever thought would happen to me." She sniffed. She looked at me and shrugged. She was silent for a moment. Then she said, "Blaming the evil eye is easier, isn't it? To say that the reason he cheated was because of a curse cast on him by those around us who were jealous of our love. Easier, isn't it? Than to believe I married an asshole."

I looked into my mother's watery, opaque eyes. We would never quite see eye-to-eye on much. I had so often longed for a mother different from the one I had. And yet.

As I looked at her, my heart swelled with what was nothing less than love. She was imperfect, striving, shallow, and infuriating. And yet. She had suffered in ways she had hidden from me for my entire life so far. She did, in her own way, love me more than anything. That much I knew. That much I sensed in every fiber of my soul.

That much would always be true.

And it would have to be enough.

After Mother returned to Iran, we followed the news of what was happening on the streets there with fear, excitement, anxiety, and hope. We watched from afar as the Shah left, as the revolutionaries took over, as hope expanded, as political factions fought for power, the religious fundamentalists won out, and hope collapsed.

I continued to work at Bloomingdale's and Mehrdad finished his postdoc assignment. Thanks to his hard work and the support of Dr. Kohler, his research was extended and funded by an NIH grant, and he secured an assistant professor position at The Rockefeller University.

Which is why that cold Christmas season, four and a half years after arriving in New York, I remained worried about my motherland but increasingly at home and settled in my new one. I had set aside the striving, competitive parts of my younger self and settled into a routine that served me. Things in our New York circles—if not in Iran—were somewhat at peace.

Until that fateful December day in 1981, when I pulled from the airmail envelope the onionskin paper and read the request made of me by my old friend.

THIRTY-EIGHT

December 1981

I woke up early and brewed Earl Grey leaves in the teapot I had bought from a dusty Middle Eastern store in Rego Park, Queens. The pot looked just like the one Homa's mother had used in her kitchen all those years ago. When I had first seen it in the shop, I worried that if I bought it, it would remind me of my guilt about Homa daily. But then I told myself it could remind me of the best of our friendship, instead of how the friendship ended. And up until Homa's letter arrived, I'd succeeded in building an American life where I (mostly) stuffed my guilt about her arrest far into the depths.

But now, with the arrival of her letter, old emotions and worries came flooding back. When the tea was ready, I poured it into a huge mug printed with "I ♥ NY." If Homa could see me drinking tea from this large vessel instead of a delicate clear *estekan*, she would say I had become Americanized. At least, that's what the old Homa would have said. How would I know what she was like now? So many years had passed since we last spoke.

I took my tea to the living room, calculating that morning in New York would be late afternoon in Tehran. Putting the mug on the coffee table, I stood by the rotary phone, inserted my finger into the hole for the zero, then turned the dial until my finger hit the stopper. A clicking sound emitted, and I then dialed the next zero to make the international call. With each swish of the dial for Homa's ensuing numbers, my heart beat faster.

There was silence, and then the line must have connected across the oceans because I heard a trilling.

"*Allo?*"

My stomach did a somersault. I knew that voice anywhere. "*Allo? Khanom-e Homa?*"

"*Baleh?*"

"Homa Jan, I am . . ."

"Ellie? Elaheh? *Khodeti?*" she asked in the informal tense, just as she had when we had run into one another at the bazaar.

"*Khodam hastam.*" I assured her it was indeed me.

Homa took over. She repeated questions she'd posed in her letter: about our health and Mehrdad's work and New York. I answered breathlessly, my heart racing, as though responding to questions on a quiz. Homa shouted in that way we all used to shout when calling long distance. I shouted back. Homa laughed when I told her I worked at a cosmetics counter and said, "Oh, Ellie. Never would I have imagined that for you."

"How is Abdol?" I asked.

There was no sound save a thick static. For a moment I worried we had been cut off.

"I couldn't write it in the letter. Couldn't bring myself to. But my dear Ellie. He was in the cinema."

"What cinema?"

"The cinema," she said. "Cinema Rex."

My head grew heavy and dizzy. I sat down. I clutched the receiver tight. Abdol was from Abadan. Cinema Rex was in Abadan. Newspaper articles reporting the Abadan fire flashed through my mind. At least 377 people dead. Moviegoers trapped inside the theater burned to a crisp.

"Homa," was all I could say.

I thought of our old university friend, how smitten he was with Homa from the very first day when he saw her at the teahouse in Darband, his looking at her in awe as she stuffed her face with quince jam, his asking her to marry him twice when we were in university, how he had stepped up and taken care of her when she was released from prison six months pregnant. I could see Abdol serving me tea when I went to visit them. The way he talked about Bahar as "God's child." I did not want to think of him in that movie theater. I did not want to think of his life ending in that horrific way. Poor Abdol. And poor, poor Homa.

"Bahar is like him in so many ways. She even loves the same foods he did," Homa said.

"She does?" My head still spun. "Homa, my condolences. I am so sorry. I never should have listened to you and stayed out of touch. Homa, I am so sorry. You need to know that . . ."

"You absolutely should have listened to me. But Bahar needs to leave," Homa said quickly, interrupting me. "She is traumatized by the war. We are being bombed every day. She hates school. The mandatory hijab. All of it. I've told her she just needs to hold out and graduate high school, but Ellie, she is severely depressed. I am so worried for her. I fear she has no future as a young woman in this country."

I thought of Homa and Bahar, alone now without Abdol, hiding in basement shelters as Saddam Hussein bombed Iran. I thought of the nights Mehrdad and I went to the movies in Manhattan, secure in the knowledge that it was nothing more than a fun night out. Not worried about the cinema being engulfed in flames with us trapped inside. My guilt made me want to vomit.

"Look, Ellie. You haven't been here. I don't think you know what this country has become. We thought we got rid of one dictatorship, but we only got another."

"Homa, be careful." Didn't she know our phone call could be bugged by the regime? Mother reminded me of the regime's spying in a roundabout way every time I spoke to her on the phone.

"I don't begrudge you leaving, Ellie."

"No, that's not what I meant." I wanted her to know that when I said "be careful," I meant that the regime could be listening in on our conversation, but how to get that across? I hated that our conversation had this added layer of worries about spies.

"I wouldn't ask you if I wasn't desperate," Homa went on. "But my mother is not well. She has become so frail, Ellie. Sara takes care of her and is deeply depressed herself. And Ali Reza has his hands full with his own family, his own kids; he's just struggling to survive. Look, Iran is not safe for Bahar. I'm still . . . active. I've talked to Niloo. Her husband's high up at the visa office now. He's been helping me to get Bahar's paperwork in order. Please, Ellie. If you can host Bahar, help her finish high school there, she could apply to a university, make something of herself. I will send money. You wouldn't have to pay for—"

"I know nothing about children," I mumbled like a fool. What was she proposing?

"She's seventeen. Very responsible. A hard worker. It would only be temporary. She has no one else here."

"She has you," I said.

"I won't be . . . any good to her. You don't know what we're going through here, Ellie. Someone has to keep fighting for the women. They've taken so many of our basic rights away. We have gone back to the Stone Age. We have lost our right to dress the way we want. More importantly, they've pushed back the marriage age—child brides are absolutely fine for this regime. They've made the marriage age nine years old, Ellie. Nine! And don't even get me started about custody laws and reproductive rights . . ."

"Homa!" I said firmly. If she didn't stop, the authorities listening in could have her arrested for what she was saying in this conversation alone. Didn't she care?

"Don't be so scared, Ellie. I know I'm asking a lot. But I'm worried so deeply for my daughter. This war. This repression. It's all destroying her."

"Come with her. Apply for your visa too. You can stay with us. I'll help you," I whispered, as if that would prevent the authorities listening in from hearing what I just said.

"You don't understand. I need to be here."

"Why?" Why did she insist on fighting in a repressive society that held women down? It was a losing battle.

"People deserve to live in freedom," she said.

"Which is why you should leave and come to the United States."

"We can't all leave. Then there will be no one left to fight."

People, I was learning, fundamentally don't change. Homa would always fight. She would, in a way, always put her country first. Even now. But I knew Homa. I knew her pride. She would not make this heavy request of me unless she was desperate. "Let me talk to Mehrdad and I will . . . I will call you again."

"Thank you, Ellie," she sighed with relief. "Thank you for considering it."

After I hung up, I sat and stared at the sofa. My mug of tea was still on the table. If I picked it up and took a sip, would it be cold? How long had we spoken? The phone bill would explain every minute later when it came. I hadn't even had a chance to bring up her arrest and my role in it. How could I rehash the past with her when her present situation was so urgent and awful?

I looked up. Mehrdad stood in the doorway in his pajamas, his arms crossed.

"How much did you hear?" I asked.

"Oh, everything. Everything you said for sure, and I could pretty much hear Homa as well. You were both shouting."

"It was long distance," I said. "Sorry I woke you."

He came over and touched my cheek. He looked at the mug of tea. "Say yes," he said. "Call her back. Think of that girl in Iran. In a war. How can we sit here in our Manhattan apartment and not help her?"

I felt like sobbing. It had been overwhelming to hear Homa's voice again after all this time. It was as though we were seven again, ten, seventeen, twenty. All those ages wrapped into one. "What she's asking is impossible," I said.

Mehrdad shrugged. "Is it?"

I looked up at my husband. At his calm, scientific, nonchalant, infuriating self. "Yes!" I said loudly. "It is."

"This is Homa we're talking about," Mehrdad said. "Her *daughter*."

THIRTY-NINE

January 15, 1982

Mehrdad wore a black hat we had described in detail for Homa on the phone so she could tell Bahar to look out for it. I craned my neck and searched the face of every young woman who came out of the designated gate at JFK International Airport.

"I think that's her!" Mehrdad suddenly said. He pointed, waved his hat, and jumped up and down.

I looked to where he pointed. Exiting the gate with a blue suitcase in one hand and a gray raincoat in another was a skinny girl with curly dark hair. She wore jeans and a blue turtleneck. A black scarf hung around her neck. No doubt the mandatory headscarf now off. Bahar was taller than when I'd last seen her at the bazaar that afternoon in the nuts and spices stall. She was more developed and mature looking. But I recognized the mass of curls and those dark eyes.

Mehrdad stopped jumping, grabbed my hand, and led me to the girl.

"Bahar Jan," I said when we got up close. Bahar was already about my height. A smattering of acne covered her left cheek.

She stared at Mehrdad, his hat, and then at me. A look of recognition registered on her face. She remembered me from our encounter at the bazaar, I could tell. Nevertheless, she introduced herself in the formal tense and said she was pleased to see us. Her voice was less high and girlish than it had been when I'd heard her speak near the barrel of walnuts.

I touched her arm awkwardly as Mehrdad took the blue suitcase, and we pushed through the crowd and went outside.

"Welcome to America," I mumbled.

On our drive to Manhattan from Queens, Mehrdad pointed out neighborhoods and rattled off street names. He was proud of his hard-earned knowledge of New York. I glanced in the rearview mirror. Bahar looked forlorn and disoriented.

When Mehrdad's steady patter of neighborhood facts was responded to with only a few mechanical *balehs* from Bahar, he wisely stopped his guided tour. We drove for a while in silence. In the mirror, I could see Bahar's forehead pressed against the window.

More than forty-five minutes later, Mehrdad pulled into a parking spot not too far from our building—we had gotten lucky and found a vacancy quickly. Suddenly, Bahar spoke. "It is a great gift," she said.

"What's that?" Mehrdad asked, looking in the rearview mirror.

"What you're doing. Taking me in. Thank you."

Mehrdad and I exchanged a look. Had Homa told her to say that? But it sounded strangely, deeply sincere.

"*Az tahe del,*" Mehrdad said, his voice cracking with emotion. What Mehrdad said translated to: from the bottom of our hearts.

After we entered our building, I unlocked the apartment door, switched on the lights, and ushered Bahar inside. For years, we had used our small second bedroom as an office for Mehrdad. He had a desk and a chair there, loads of science journals, and a lamp. When Mother had visited, we had added a sleeper sofa to the room and she had slept there. For Bahar's arrival, we had also furnished the room with a zip-up plastic closet and a chest of drawers.

I had prepared the sofa bed with fresh sheets and placed a set of towels, a bar of Ivory soap, and a Snoopy toothbrush on top of the comforter. "She's too old for Snoopy, Ellie! She's a *teenager*!" Mehrdad had said when he first saw the toothbrush. We almost always spoke Persian to one another, but Mehrdad said the word "teenager" in English, emphasizing it in an American accent. There was no good equivalent for the word in Persian that I knew of—nor an understanding of the concept of being a teenager the way there was in America. We had simply been young people once. We didn't get the benefit of a phase of life where rebellion and recalcitrance and moodiness were expected or excused. Hopefully, Bahar wouldn't become a rebellious American *teenager*.

Mehrdad welcomed Bahar over and over again, then bid us good night. He had to get to the lab early in the morning.

After he left, I picked up the Snoopy toothbrush encased in clear plastic packaging and handed it to Bahar. "I know it is babyish," I said. "Sorry."

She turned the package over in her hands. Her whole face suddenly lit up. "He's my favorite!" she said with a wide grin. "I love Snoopy!"

In that moment, I glimpsed vestiges of my old friend. The way Bahar's eyes lit up—so different from her forlorn look in the car. And that grin.

I relaxed. "I remember you were wearing a Snoopy T-shirt when we saw one another that time. In the bazaar. Wasn't sure you still were into him." I smiled. "Glad you are!"

Bahar smiled back at me and looked around the small room. "Is this your office?"

I was surprised at her question. "Mehrdad's," I said. "But don't worry, he's at the lab so much, he doesn't need it. It's entirely your room now."

"You've gone to so much trouble," she said. "Thank you again."

"It is absolutely no trouble."

We engaged in *tarof*—the classic thanking and praising of the other and self-deprecation of the self so common in our culture. Homa and Abdol had raised her well—that was clear so far.

"Thank you," Bahar said again.

"You don't need to keep thanking me."

"Well, I do. But also, I want you to know that this is temporary. All of it. It's just until things calm down in Iran. This new regime can't last much longer. They can't."

It was January 1982. The Islamic Revolution had succeeded in February 1979. "They've lasted three years," I said quietly. "Why would you think they wouldn't last much longer? They seem pretty strong."

Bahar looked at me with complete earnestness. "Because of people like my mom. She is fighting them tooth and nail. She won't let them win. They are horrible—*horrible*—to women. And my mother. Well, she won't stop. She won't stop till they are toppled. That's why."

I was surprised at her absolute belief in the powers of her mother. "I see," I said. "But your mother wants you to try to go to university here. We can help you apply." Almost immediately, I regretted saying it. Was I saying too much too soon?

"I don't know," Bahar said. "That's what she wants for me, I guess. But there are good universities in Iran too. One of the ironies of this revolution is that more girls go to university now than even pre-revolution. Isn't that crazy? Enrollment for women is actually up. But my mom's convinced I'm depressed, and she wants me out of there for now."

"Yes," I said. "Because of the war. And the political repression."

Bahar looked at me with her big eyes. "I feel bad leaving her there. I'm so scared she'll be arrested again."

"Excuse me?"

"Prison," Bahar said matter-of-factly. "She could go to prison soon. She and her feminist group. They're working on some big, big stuff. She's a true *shir zan*, my mother."

I stared at the young girl in our room still holding the Snoopy toothbrush. Homa was still fighting. Of course she was. When would Homa ever not fight? *Shir zan*. A woman with the courage of a lion. Homa had introduced me to the phrase when we were kids playing hooky from school, talking about our dreams for ourselves as adults. The Colonel had used it when he'd interrogated me in his office that night of the party.

I shook myself free of the memory of that night. Here was this girl—this young woman—standing in front of me on a New York night. "Well, now," I said. "We can't worry about a potential arrest right now. We have to hope for the best. Your mom always comes through. You'd best get some sleep. I'm sure you're tired."

We stood face to face awkwardly for a moment. Then I gave her the most graceless hug in the world.

Bahar stiffened and politely patted me on the back.

I told her where she could put away her clothes, where the bathroom was located, and that she should get me if she needed anything. "See you in the morning," I said.

She stood there holding the toothbrush as I left.

FORTY

January 1982

The receptionist's eyeliner was a bright green, her hair a blond beehive harkening back to the sixties. Heavy foundation accentuated wrinkles around her eyes.

I held on to Bahar's hand tight. Both our palms were sweaty. I wanted Bahar to feel confident and safe in this new school. I cannot tell a lie—before venturing out to the school with Bahar, I had even patted my feathered hair on each side.

We had frequent phone calls with Homa those first few weeks. We spoke every other day—expense be damned. Bahar assured her mother that she was well, she was fine, yes, she was enjoying this new country. We were constantly told how generous we were by both Bahar and Homa. Each time I heard them say "generous," a part of me felt like an impostor. There was so much Bahar did not know about my friendship with her mother.

Homa thanked me over and over again, and also insisted repeatedly that Bahar be enrolled in high school so she could then get a college education. Just like all the other times, I found myself swept up by Homa's persuasion.

The receptionist took down our names and made us wait on a wooden bench across from her counter-high desk. The bench was slithery and smooth. I thought of students who had sat on it after they had done something wrong, after they had upset the teacher, after they upended the roles of subject and authority and earned a meeting with the principal.

We had done nothing wrong, Bahar and I. We were here to register for school. A public school in New York City. She had entered the U.S. with a valid visa.

I realized only after the fact that Homa had been campaigning and applying for her daughter's visa for years. She, with the guidance of Niloo, had waited her turn. Mehrdad was working hard, an established assistant professor. Our place here was legitimate and now Bahar was under our care.

A radiator hissed. I couldn't wait for spring to come. The collar of my blouse felt tight. On top of the blouse, I wore a blazer, and on top of the blazer I wore my camel coat. I was damp with sweat. I took off my coat.

When the principal finally came out of his office to greet us, bald head shining under the fluorescent light, Bahar and I stood up and she shuffled closer to me. I'd expected him to be dressed in a suit and tie, like principals were in old books I had read in Iran about English boarding schools. But there was no nobility in his frazzled, weathered face and the tweed of his coat was worn.

"So, your daughter is seventeen years old?" he asked.

"She's not actually my—" I started to say.

"I seventeen," Bahar interrupted in her best English. Her accent was heavy. Would it eventually lift? Mine never would.

Her English wasn't good, but it could improve quickly. I'd offered to give Bahar English lessons myself, to help her get up to speed. Every afternoon, I quizzed her as we both sat with workbooks and notebooks at the kitchen table.

"Would you like a peanut butter and jelly sandwich for lunch?" I would ask. "What is that?" Bahar would respond. Bahar called me "Khaleh," which means Aunt in Persian, and Mehrdad "Amoo," which means Uncle. "Do you need new shoes?" "These are fine, thank you, Khaleh."

The principal smiled wanly. His smoker's teeth were yellow.

He motioned for us to join him at the receptionist's desk. The receptionist gave me a ballpoint pen and several paper forms interspersed with thin, crinkly carbon sheets.

I filled out the forms, grateful again that I understood English. I signed the papers where I was told to sign. The impression of the ballpoint pen on the blue carbon paper made a copy on the bottom sheet. The principal took a cursory look at Bahar's birth certificate. I had gone to great care to translate the Persian words into English, but he and the receptionist barely read them. He looked at his watch and said, "You're in Mrs. Falcon's capable hands now. Have a good one, and welcome."

He disappeared into his office.

With a heavy sigh, the green eye-shadowed receptionist named Mrs. Falcon came out from behind the counter and said, "Follow me."

We walked down gray, linoleum-floored hallways, past walls decorated with student artwork and compositions, through a labyrinth of corridors. The air smelled of glue and paint. Every now and then a student walked by and said, "Good morning, Mrs. Falcon," in a singsong, bored voice.

Mrs. Falcon suddenly stopped and addressed Bahar.

"You want Mom to come?" she asked.

Bahar nodded.

"As you wish!" Mrs. Falcon said. Perhaps it struck her as odd to have a "mother" accompany a seventeen-year-old to class.

Outside Room 227, by a door decorated with silhouettes labeled "Ralph Waldo Emerson" and "Louisa May Alcott," was a handwritten sign with an unfamiliar phrase: "Time is Money!"

"Time to let go, Mom," Mrs. Falcon said.

To my surprise, Bahar gave me a tight hug goodbye.

I had taken the day off from work to make sure Bahar was settled and as I walked home, I found myself circling the blocks incessantly. I hoped Bahar would be alright in the new school, but I was filled with worry for her.

How would I handle this new child in my life if the mixture of emotions at having dropped her off were already so overpowering? Was this what it meant to mother someone? The constant worry, the strange hope, the feeling of wanting everything to go well for the child combined with morose anxiety if it didn't?

I checked the time. It was almost noon. If I were to cross the street and walk onto the campus of The Rockefeller University, if I were to take the elevator up to Mehrdad's lab and find him, could I steal him away? I never dared ask him, during his working hours, to take time for the two of us. But after dropping off Bahar, I was a ball of worry. So I did just that.

He got up from the lab bench when he saw me, came outside to the corridor, and I must have looked a wreck because he said, "Why don't I get my coat. Want to get lunch?"

He took me to a newly opened Persian restaurant on Second Avenue and 74th Street, one we had been hearing a lot about and wanting to visit.

We ordered *chelo kabab* and when the platters of saffron rice, grilled meats, and roasted tomatoes were brought to our table, when we drank from pitchers of salty, fizzy yogurt *doogh*, when Mehrdad leaned back in his chair and sighed with satisfaction, I could not help but remember another time I had sat across from him at a restaurant, at Nayeb all those years ago when he proposed.

Now here we were in America, temporary makeshift guardians of a girl whose very presence had roiled up a plethora of emotions in me. I told Mehrdad I was worried about Bahar's first day of school, that I wanted her to fit in but not feel like she had to conform to the extent that she would lose who she was. I told him I worried about her English.

"She'll come up to speed in English. You're helping her."

"Yes, but she's Iranian."

"So?"

"You know how it's been since the hostages were taken. Iranians here are personae non grata. What if she's teased? Bullied? What if people are mean to her? Prejudiced toward her?"

Mehrdad studied me. "It's highly possible they will be. God knows, the hostages being taken by a bunch of nitwit fascist students has made some people think every Iranian the world over is somehow culpable for the heinous acts of a few. But that's something we will help her through, Ellie. She won't face it alone."

It occurred to me then, not for the first time, that had fate had different plans for us, Mehrdad would have been a wonderful father.

"I want her to feel safe here."

"Hopefully, she will."

"I want her to have a different experience than I did growing up."

"Well, in some ways quite sadly, her experience is already so different from yours. She's had to experience war. And the worry of a strand of hair showing landing her in detention. Thanks to this feckless 'revolutionary' regime."

"More than that, though. I want Bahar to live a life devoid of the constant worry about the evil eye."

Mehrdad laughed. "Don't worry, Ellie! I know your mother fed you that nonsense, but I'm pretty sure Homa isn't into these old-fashioned superstitions. And we won't expose her to them either."

"Good," I said. "Phew! That's just great, then, that you agree."

"Oh, come on, Ellie! Do you really think I don't see right through you? You may be worried about Bahar being bullied for being Iranian or you may genuinely want to not bring up evil eye BS with her. But there's something else that's bothering you. Tell me what it is."

He was right. I couldn't hide much from him. I put both my hands on the white tablecloth and let it out. "When we were little. Homa and I. From the very first time I visited her, I wanted what Homa had."

Mehrdad raised his eyebrows. "What? A toy or something?"

"I wanted her family. Her living father, her kind mother. Her cute baby sister. Later her adorable brother. Sometimes . . ." I lowered my head.

"Yes?" Mehrdad prodded me.

"Sometimes I fantasized about something awful happening to my mother so I could become an orphan and be taken in by Homa's family."

"Okay," Mehrdad said. "Not exactly a crime to do so. Considering your father was dead and your mom, God bless her soul, is just a tad of a narcissist. We both know it even though of course we love her. And what were you, seven when you first met Homa? I think we can forgive a seven-year-old? For this fantasy?"

I looked up at him. "Yes, but now. Now look. Bahar is here. With us. I have Homa's daughter. I have," I sighed, "her family! You don't think it's strange? Like I willed this to happen? Especially given . . . given, you know. My betrayal of Homa and all of that. Maybe *I* had an evil eye . . ."

Mehrdad grabbed his hair with both hands. He gave me a crazed look. "Oh, for the love of all that you think is holy, dear Ellie. Please stop with this evil eye nonsense! You don't have an evil eye. Homa didn't have one." He pointed to a man in a suit slurping *aush* at the table next to ours. "That poor guy doesn't. No one does! It's a superstition, Ellie. It's a blasted superstition. Please. Enough with that *khorafat* folklore."

I picked up my fork again. Nothing like being married to a scientist to have a constant refrain in opposition to my mother's own supreme belief in superstition. "You're right, you're right," I said. "It's just hard for me to shake these things off. It was ingrained in me from the get-go."

He nodded and resumed eating with relish.

"Mehrdad?" I asked.

"Hmm?" he said, his face practically burrowed in his plate.

"How is that you are so kind and supportive of hosting Bahar?"

He looked up at me. There was a softening in his eyes. "Ellie," he said. "How could we say no? She needs us."

I studied his face and realized he meant it entirely.

He held my gaze. "It's the least we can do," he said.

FORTY-ONE

February 1982

Of all her classmates, the name Bahar mentioned most was "Madison." Madison was oh-so-pretty and popular. Madison was smart. Soon it became Madison this, Madison that.

Three weeks into her stay, Bahar asked if she could bring Madison over to our apartment so they could study together after school. In came a tall, skinny-legged blonde with stick-straight hair and dazzling blue eyes. Madison was dressed in khaki pants and a black turtleneck and carried no winter coat, her every movement signaling that she came from big money.

For some reason, Iranians have a hard time pronouncing words that begin with "s" and are followed by a consonant. So when I asked the girls if they wanted a snack and pronounced it "es-snack," Madison giggled at my pronunciation.

I didn't like how Bahar fawned over that girl.

But there was something I could show Bahar that Madison could not. After Madison left that day, side by side in the avocado-hued apartment kitchen, I dropped walnuts into the food processor for *fesenjoon* while Bahar opened the bottle of store-bought pomegranate molasses.

"Your mother taught me how to make this dish," I said above the whir of the food processor. "We'd stand together in her old stone kitchen for hours."

"She told me," Bahar said casually.

I stopped the pulse on the machine. Had I heard correctly? "She did?"

"She told me all about you for as long as I can remember. How the two of you hiked up to Darband. How you used to imitate your teachers. Your favorite teacher was a Khanom Tabatabayi, right? She even told me about that day you skipped school and went to the bazaar." Bahar wagged a finger. "Naughty, naughty," she said in English.

In all the years since Homa and I had been estranged, I had never imagined her sharing stories of our childhood with her daughter. I'd assumed she didn't want to even think of me.

I ran my fingers across the buttons on the food processor. "That's surprising," I said.

"Why surprising?"

"Because your mom and I weren't exactly . . . in touch over these past many years." I paused. "But if she'd told you all these stories, why is it when we ran into one another at the bazaar, she acted as if . . ."

"As if you were just some random old friend, right? Not the famous Ellie I'd heard so much about? I know! I didn't realize the woman hiding behind the walnut barrel was *the* Ellie, until Maman told me she wanted me to come to America. I think she was just pretty overwhelmed that day at the bazaar. She was in a stupor afterward for some time."

The question that gnawed at me was something I knew I shouldn't ask. It wouldn't be fair to Bahar. No need to drag her into it. But I couldn't help myself. "Did you ever wonder," I said quickly, "if your mother and I had been so close, why we never saw one another? When you were growing up, I mean?"

Bahar put down the bottle of molasses and stood quite still. Pretty soon she would be taller than me. "I know why." She looked at me steadily.

My heart sank.

She knew about what I had done to her mom. Which meant Homa definitely knew. "I see," I said.

"Because she didn't want you to get into trouble. That's why. Just like she didn't want her other friends to get into trouble. The Shah's regime had files on her. She always believed that. For a long time, she worried she was being watched, monitored. She washed her hands of politics. But then—this current regime came into power. And she couldn't stay on the sidelines." Bahar lowered her voice probably out of habit, even though we were standing in a New York kitchen. "She's active against this current regime now. She says we still haven't gotten it right in Iran."

"That we haven't. Not by a long shot. I wish one day for a democratic Iran," I said, almost mechanically. Mehrdad and I had been saying it for so long, it was almost rote in me now. But Homa not seeing me because she was worried about being monitored? Had she cut contact out of fear for my safety?

I wanted to inhale this new piece of information, register it. I wanted to go to the living room, sink into the sofa, and cry. But here stood this girl who was petrified for her mother. I put aside my own desire. Since the night we picked Bahar up at the airport, I was learning intensely that the needs of this child outweighed my own.

"Wishing is one thing," Bahar continued. "Everyone 'wishes.' But my mom. She doesn't just wish. She doesn't 'dream.' She's a doer. As active now as ever. I'm so worried about her. When she was arrested . . ."

My shoulder muscles tensed. "What do you know about her arrest?"

"I know she was arrested in the Shah's time. But since she's started her new women's organization, well, she's constantly worried about being arrested again. She's on their list. She's being watched. My father said . . ."

Bahar's voice broke off. She swallowed hard. She played with the ends of her shirt. Then she looked up at me. "You know what? I miss my father so much. But missing him, in a way, is easier than missing my mom. With him, there is a finality. He is gone and there is nothing we can do about it. I hate to think of how he died and I try not to think about his last moments anymore, but the truth is he is at peace. It's been four years since he died. For the first two years after his death, I felt like I was going to lose it every single day. It was only in the third year that I learned to manage his being gone. To be somewhat, some days, at peace with it." She fought back tears.

"I know what it's like to lose a father," I whispered.

"But my mom?" Bahar went on as though she hadn't heard me. "There is so much uncertainty. They could take her from me at any time."

"I am so sorry."

Bahar looked out of the window of our tiny kitchen. The trees were still bare on York Avenue, their spindly branches a dead gray. But spring would come. The season of her name: Bahar. Eventually, the trees would bloom with nascent buds that would develop into stunning green everywhere.

"They can't hurt my dad anymore," Bahar said. "That is my one comfort. He was the best father anyone could have. The absolute best in the world." She looked at me, her face trembling. And then she dissolved into tears.

I stepped closer to her. I touched her arm tentatively and then I hugged her. Her face nestled into my neck. Her sobs dampened my blouse, my skin. I held her tighter. She unraveled in my embrace.

They say much of who we are is determined in the womb. That we cannot affect the cocktail of genes that make us. As I held Bahar in the kitchen that February night, I didn't know what geopolitics held in store for the country of our birth, nor could I have imagined the weight and impact of her mother's activism in the coming years. But I knew that I would move heaven and earth for this child.

This child—this teenager—who had been sent into my life for a short time had already lodged herself into my heart. No matter what happened, I would protect her. There was a purity to her that I never wanted marred.

FORTY-TWO

June 1982

"Drugs and alcohol could kill you!" My voice was high and shrill on a day in June when the city felt like it would dissolve from unexpected heat. I sat trying to talk sense into Bahar after a late breakfast on a Saturday morning. "I knew Madison was trouble from day one. She invited you and you said yes? Just like that? Angela has told me what happens at parties after prom. It's horrifying!"

"Khaleh Ellie, you're overreacting." Bahar straightened in her seat at the kitchen table. "It's no big deal. Just a little party. I mean we're graduating soon—there are parties left and right. If you only knew how *little* I am partying. I don't tell you about all the things I say no to. But this one matters."

"You shouldn't be partying at all. Your mother had to beg and plead and wait to get her temporary visitor's visa. She's lucky she can come see you graduate. Her dream is to watch you walk across that stage. Everything she wants is for you to succeed academically, for you to go to college here. That's what matters. She doesn't need to have her daughter gallivanting around Manhattan with drunkards! What will I say to her?"

"Madison is not a drunkard. She is—"

"She is a privileged, snobby Upper East–Sider who thinks she owns the world. And she's got you under her spell, Bahar."

Bahar stared at me, her cheeks turning red. "You could not be more wrong, Khaleh Ellie. Madison is a good person. She is my friend. Didn't you want me to adjust to this American life? Fit in? Well, I'm trying. It's not like you think. This is a small get-together after prom and it won't be about drugs and alcohol. It's just kids having fun. And I have worked hard. I got into college, didn't I? I'm doing all the right things. This is my last chance to be with my high school friends before we all go our separate ways. Madison will look out for me."

"The only person people like Madison look out for is themselves," I muttered. Even as I said it, I was keenly aware that I sounded like my own mother. But I couldn't help it.

Angela told me she lost her virginity at an after-prom party. She made it seem like the goal of losing one's virginity around the time of prom was almost a rite of passage. I had listened aghast. When Bahar had arrived at JFK airport and we had taken her home, I couldn't have imagined that one day we'd be arguing about parties, with me fretting about drugs, alcohol, and sex. But here we were.

"It's one night! Why don't you trust me, Khaleh Ellie?" Bahar sighed. "And I have a feeling my mother won't mind."

"We will see about that," I said tersely.

Five months and three days after Mehrdad and I picked up Bahar at the airport, we were back at JFK with her to get Homa. I felt like a schoolgirl. Butterflies fluttered in my stomach at the thought of seeing my old friend. I hopped from one foot to the other; it was impossible to stay still.

I had sent photographs of Bahar to Homa with my letters, including a few with me and Mehrdad in the frame. But only two photos of Homa had been returned. Revolution, war, and continued separation from her daughter had taken a toll on the thin, worn body pictured seated in an armchair, arms crossed, her face in a forced smile, and in a garden, holding a small shovel, a huge hat on her head.

"Maman!" Bahar suddenly yelled and bolted to the gate.

Then I saw her. She was tall and thin and wore jeans, heavy, military-style boots on her feet, and her hair in a ponytail. Around her neck was the characteristic headscarf now required on Iran Air flights and removed, no doubt, after getting off the Iranian aircraft at the stopover in Europe.

Bahar ran straight to her mom and hugged her, and they both burst into tears.

Homa showered Bahar's face with kisses and simultaneously laughed and cried. The ease with which mother and daughter held one another took me by surprise.

Mehrdad and I stayed a few feet away.

Eventually, Bahar and Homa ambled toward us. Bahar's arm was linked in Homa's—they both smiled as they wiped away tears. When they reached Mehrdad and me, Homa let out a shriek and almost pushed me to the floor as she flung her arms around my neck. I lost my balance. Homa pulled me straight and held me at arm's length. "Ellie! Ellie Joon! *Doost-e man!*"

At hearing her call me "my friend," I almost became undone. I had forgotten how much joy the strong, exuberant Homa could exude. She still had it.

The car ride home was filled with Homa asking questions, Bahar talking nonstop, and Mehrdad and me interjecting with updates and responses. Now our chattering seventeen-year-old would be graduating from high school in ten days. She would be starting Queens College in the fall.

And here she was next to her mother.

I turned around in the car. Homa laid her head on her daughter's shoulder and closed her eyes, soaking her eyelashes in new tears.

FORTY-THREE

June 1982

The next morning at breakfast, Bahar campaigned for not going to school so she could spend the day with her mom. Homa was sleeping off jet lag in the room she now shared with her daughter. "We're practically done anyway," Bahar said. "We're graduating soon. There's nothing new we're learning."

Homa appeared in the kitchen doorway. "You absolutely should go to school," Homa told Bahar.

She wore an orange-and-red plaid blouse with a Peter Pan collar and faded blue jeans. Her hair was down, and I was surprised at how long it was. On her feet were plastic slippers like the ones we used to wear in Iran. I had a flashback to Homa's father's slippers—how her sister, Sara, had slipped her feet into them and staggered about the courtyard of their old house.

"Don't worry." Homa walked to where Bahar sat and kissed her cheek. "My visa is for four weeks. I'll be imposing on Khaleh Ellie and Amoo Mehrdad for some time. Off you go. I'll be here when you come home."

After Bahar and Mehrdad had left the kitchen in a rush, I served Homa some scrambled eggs and sat at the kitchen table across from her. The big round clock on the wall ticked loudly.

"You didn't have to take off from work. You should go on with your life as though I'm not here," Homa said.

"Are you kidding? I don't want to miss this first day with you! Work can wait."

"Remember when we were little? And spoke about what we'd be when we grew up? Life sure had a way of derailing some of those plans, didn't it? Though I think you are happy with your job here, yes?"

"I like it. I enjoy the customers—for the most part—and have great coworkers. I don't know." I paused. "It can seem like I lost my drive or something. And maybe I did. I stopped competing, striving so much. It happened right around when——" I stopped. Should I say the truth? Should I say *right around when you got arrested?* I needed to apologize to her for what I'd done. Maybe we could finally get everything out in the open. Let the chips fall where they may. Homa would probably hate me. But I couldn't keep this awful truth from her anymore. She had to know what I had done.

"Right around when you got married, right?" Homa said almost chirpily. "The dutiful Persian wife is what you became! Look, Ellie, there's nothing wrong with that. In my women's organization and in our activism, one thing we're trying to uphold is that feminism comes in many shapes. We should not shame women who choose to take care of home and family. As long as it's the woman's choice. I don't mean to imply that your job now, or even if you chose in the past or later choose to stay home, is in any way antifeminist. Because all of it has a place in true feminism. A woman has a right to live a life of intense career ambition or one of more mellow ambition or what have you. As I say, whatever *she* chooses."

I hadn't thought my trying to bring up the night of her arrest would result in a lecture on feminism. Though I was grateful for her outlook.

"And this Mehrdad of yours. How wonderful is he? I am so glad it all worked out."

I smiled. "Me too. I keep waiting for him to turn into a monster or something." As I said it, I shuddered at the memory of what my mother had revealed to me about my father in that Bloomingdale's restaurant four years ago.

Homa shook her head. "He won't."

"How can you be so sure? I mean, I'm not saying he's absolutely perfect now. Believe me. You don't want to go into the bathroom after he's been in it, I assure you of that! The guy has bowel issues of huge proportions!"

Homa laughed. "All kidding aside, I knew he'd be good for you. Didn't I tell you? When I looked into his eyes up at that teahouse café in the mountains. I told you I foresaw happiness."

"You did."

"And I'm glad I was right. I mean, the man has agreed for both of you to take in my daughter! These kinds of people—truly good people—are rare and few. We were lucky, you and I."

I straightened in my chair. "Yes. Abdol too. He was a true gem."

His death hung around us in the room. I saw before me again the newspaper articles about the Cinema Rex fire. We both studied the sugar dispenser on the table.

I needed to air things out with Homa more than ever. I tried a different tactic. "You know, Homa Joon," I said, "I was reading an article in a magazine called *The Atlantic* about the phoenix. Your name came up."

"My name?"

"Yes, your name. Homa. The bird from Persian mythology."

"Let's see," Homa said. "Did they get it right? That the Homa bird never lands? We Homas live our whole lives above the ground."

"Yes, it did cover that. And the article also mentioned how the Homa is the most compassionate bird. It casts good fortune on all those it touches. And I just . . ."

"You just what?"

"I think that's true of you."

I was about to launch into my explanation and apology when Homa suddenly waved her arm to the teapot balanced on an unlidded kettle on the stove and said, "Hey! We used to have a teapot just like that." Her face broke into a huge grin.

"I know. When I saw it in a shop here, I had to buy it." I got up. This conversation wasn't going to happen easily. I poured us both mugs of tea.

When I handed Homa her mug, she lifted it, play-acting at how heavy it was. "These gargantuan vessels. So American!" She took a few sips. Then, in a quieter voice, "How can I ever thank you, Ellie?"

I sat back across from her. "It's just tea."

"You know what I mean. For taking care of my daughter."

"You would do the same," I said. "If the roles had been reversed." I mumbled the last part. She couldn't have known how hard Mehrdad and I had tried for kids. There was so much we had missed about one another's lives.

Homa looked out the window. The trees on York Avenue were now in their full green glory. The promise of summer was everywhere.

Bahar couldn't go back now, not in the middle of a bloody war. She had worked so hard. She had gotten into Queens College. Would Homa agree to let us pay for it? There was so much to discuss, to figure out. But I owed Homa an explanation for the damage I'd done to her when we were college kids.

"Homa, I need to apologize to you."

A darkness came over her face. "*Pasho!* Get up!" she said. "Stop with this hand-wringing and rehashing. Are you going to show me around or not? I'm a tourist in New York! Bahar is in school. Let me see this city of yours!"

"But we need to also talk about—"

"*Basseh*, enough! Let's enjoy this day. Show me your city. I am all yours."

I remembered how when we first moved to New York, I had walked the streets alone wishing with all my heart that I could have had my old friend by my side. To share the sights and sounds with her. Now here she was. Almost five years had passed since I was that homesick immigrant. But she was here now. With me. Even if temporarily.

My confession could wait for the right time. We had to make the most of today. *On doit profiter!* I heard my mother quote in French. I had a ready-made list of places to see.

"Where would you like to go first, Homa Joon?"

"Where do you suggest?"

I put the dishes in the sink. Homa helped me. "Well, when my mother visited, we took her to the Empire State Building. Everyone always wants to see that. And the Plaza Hotel. It is so grandiose! There is F.A.O. Schwarz, this huge toy store across from the Plaza on Fifth Avenue. Toys like you've never seen in your life! *Deedani-yeh*. It is worth seeing. And of course we can walk through Central Park. Happy to also take you to Bloomingdale's, where I work. You could have frozen yogurt. There is also Serendipity, near Bloomie's, for the best frozen hot chocolate. And we could go to the museums. See the new exhibit at the Metropolitan . . ."

Homa gave me a sheepish smile. "You know where I'd really like to go, Ellie?"

"Where?"

"The library."

"What?"

"The big one. With the two stone lions outside. I've read a lot about them."

A soft breeze blew as we walked down Fifth Avenue toward 42nd Street. It wasn't officially summer yet, but the weather was warm and signs of summer abounded. Carts selling Italian ice were already out. People bared their skin in tank tops and shorts.

"It's still so strange," Homa said. "To think you all dress like this here. I've gotten so used to being covered up. Can't tell you how long it's been since I've felt the sun on my hair."

I looked again at her orange-and-red plaid blouse and jeans, her hair down. Simple choices forbidden in what Iran had now become. I wore a denim skirt and white T-shirt. For that I could be whipped, even arrested, by the morality police in my old country.

I linked my arm in Homa's. "Come on," I said. We walked fast together and reached the New York Public Library. We looked up at the massive structure with its old-fashioned columns and the tiers of granite steps leading up to the entrance. Flanking each side of the steps were two stone lions on pedestals. They looked stoic and regal.

"Did you know," Homa said, "that earlier in this century, these two lions were called Leo Astor and Leo Lenox, after the library's cofounders?" She pronounced Astor *Astoor* and Lenox *Lenoox*. "Later on, during the Great Depression, the mayor of New York named the lions Patience and Fortitude. To inspire people to have those qualities in tough times. Did you know that?"

I did not know any of that. "You've been in my city for less than a day," I said, "and you are teaching me about it. How do you know so much about this?"

"Because I read about it . . . in a library!" She chuckled. "Get it?"

"I do." I clasped her arm tighter with my own. "Homa, remember when we were going to be Lion Women?"

"*Shir ʒan,*" she said. "Of course."

"You definitely are one."

"You are too, Ellie," she said. "Don't sell yourself short."

I cringed, thinking of what she did not know about my role in her arrest.

"Come on!" she said. "Let's go in!"

Arm in arm, we marched up the steps. When we walked into the building, the large marble hall was cool and hushed. Luckily there weren't too many other visitors. Homa wandered around the hall with a flushed face. Watching her look up at the tall ceiling and study every corner, I realized that for Homa, this was a sacred space. Maybe even more so than a mosque or church or temple could ever be.

She came over to me and whispered, "Did you know, Ellie, that when I first . . . got out, three things saved me?"

This was the first time she had alluded to her time in prison since she'd arrived. I held my breath. I could confess right here, right now, in this hallowed hall. But Homa went on speaking. "Of course, my family saved me. I am so grateful to them. And walking did too. I walked kilometers a day, just moving. It helped me order my thoughts. Come to certain terms. And the other thing that saved me? Do you know what it was?"

"What?" I whispered, not wanting to break the flow of *her* confession.

"It was books. I read and read. Went to the library as much as I could. And to bookstores. Lost myself in books. Did you know that books can heal you? They helped restore me."

"Well then," I said. "There's another library I need to take you to after this one. I bet that's one even you haven't read about!"

We took the bus to Madison Avenue. When we entered the Pierpont Morgan Library, Homa's marvel at the beauty inside was all I needed. She studied the cases of antique books, old manuscripts, and letters in hushed silence. Inside these halls it was cool and enchanting. Something about the scent reminded me of Homa's old kitchen. How we'd descended into the cavernous magic of that place as girls. Now here we were, in a millionaire's library.

"Did you know the person who started this library was J.P. Morgan? A railroad tycoon who had amassed great wealth," I said.

"Good to know capitalist wealth can create some good," she mumbled.

"Homa, you're not a communist anymore, though, right?"

She laughed. "No. Most certainly not. I was a communist when I was in university and that was it. After I . . . got out, well. I gave up my communist activities."

"But you're still super politically active?" I said in a whisper, both because we were in a library but also because I was used to lowering my voice whenever political activism was discussed. Even after almost five years in the United States.

"Yes," she said. "Very. But my focus is not communism. It's not capitalism. What I care about, Ellie, more than anything is democracy. And women's rights. That is the focus of the organization I have started."

An older woman flashed a look of annoyance at our whispering and we both quieted down.

I took Homa to the East Room. She stood still, taking in all the books, the gold leaf–decorated ceiling, and the Persian rugs.

Once we were outside, she turned to me and said, no longer in a whisper, "Isn't it funny, Ellie? No matter where you go or how far you travel, when you are in a place of substance, the floor is covered with the rugs of our country. The artwork of our land. Which means really, in all these places, you are with the labor of Iranian women."

I thought back to the rugs we had seen in the East Room of that gorgeous library. The geometric shapes I knew so well. The trees and flowers and intricate designs that felt as familiar to me as home.

"Doesn't matter who owns the rug workshops," Homa went on. "It's the women who do the knotting. It's women doing the weaving. The art of Iranian women is scattered throughout the world. Their work is everywhere."

I had never thought about it that way. But as ever, my friend was making me see the smallest things in a way that made them not small things. She gave meaning to what would have been mundane.

This is what I missed. I missed her. Her company. Her viewpoint. Just her random thoughts and musings. Her mind.

I linked my arm in hers again, so grateful for her presence. And selfishly not wanting to mar this day with a confession that could make her hate me. I'd have to wait for the right time—we had time. "Where can I take you for lunch?" I asked.

"You know what I really want?" she said. "One of your famous New York hot dogs. I've seen those carts in all the movies and books."

We made our way across the street to a hot dog cart operated by a middle-aged man who looked like he had stepped out of the Grand Bazaar in Tehran. I ordered two hot dogs with sauerkraut and mustard and paid, waving off Homa's entreaties that she should pay.

We settled on a ledge nearby and bit into our hot dogs.

"Now tell me," she said. "What on earth is this prom thing Bahar keeps going on about? She talked my ear off all night explaining evening gowns and corsages. It's an American tradition, no? And this party she insists on going to after? We should let her, I think. Let the girl live!"

FORTY-FOUR

June 1982

BAHAR

Bahar walks into the chic lobby of the Upper East Side apartment building and tells the doorman her name. He's not someone she recognizes from the other times she's been here. He looks her up and down from under his captain's hat and says, "You're going to the Cutlers'?"

"Yes." She tries to sound American and smooth, hoping her accent isn't too strong. "The Cutlers'. Madison Cutler."

In the carpeted bag that used to be her mother's, Bahar carries a present for Madison's mom: a ceramic pomegranate that can be used as décor on a shelf. She hopes Mrs. Cutler, whom she's met a few times, likes it. Mrs. Cutler is very tall and very thin. She wears smoky eyeliner and sounds bored in the coolest way. Madison said her mother works at an auction house. She sells expensive old things to people who like them.

When Bahar gets out of the elevator and walks to Madison's apartment—an apartment she has been to exactly seven times to study, hang out, read *Tiger Beat*, and chat about Brett Robinson and his smile—she can hear loud music from behind the door.

She rings the doorbell. Maybe Madison's mom will answer. Madison's dad lives in Nantucket, where he writes books about ex-presidents.

Her parents are divorced but, according to Madison, "it's amicable." Bahar had had to get out her thick Merriam-Webster dictionary and look up the word "amicable." Bahar met Madison's dad once when he had been in the apartment talking with Madison's mom. He seemed kind, with thick gray hair and a fitted jacket and leather loafers that had—Bahar was surprised to notice—pennies tucked into their tops. She had been fascinated by the pennies.

Tonight, it is Madison herself who swings open the door to the din and flow of music. She's wearing a white tank top and denim cut-off shorts called "Daisy Dukes," another term Bahar had to look up in her Merriam-Webster dictionary, but the words were defined only separately, not together, as a flower and as "a sovereign male ruler of a continental European duchy." Why was it that often when she looked up words, it led her down a rabbit hole where she needed to look up more words? Like "duchy."

Bahar feels her face grow hot. "You changed."

"Of course I changed, silly!" Madison shouts over the music. "Everyone did. When you went home after prom, I thought that's what you were doing as well."

Madison smiles sweetly and leads Bahar into the apartment. There are bodies everywhere—kids dance and sing and move to the blast of The Human League's "Don't You Want Me." The air smells of something yeasty and acrid. There is also a weird skunk-like smell. At least Bahar knows this song; she has played it repeatedly on the Panasonic cassette player Auntie Ellie and Uncle Mehrdad gave her for Persian New Year.

When Madison said she was hosting an after-prom party, Bahar imagined a sophisticated affair with cut-up orange slices and perhaps punch. She knew what punch was, had had it at other American get-togethers. Madison had mentioned there would be a lot of people, but Bahar hadn't imagined there would be this many. Madison is popular, part of the school's inner circle. Why has she invited so many people? It seems like every single person from their high school is at Madison's party, dressed in shorts and tank tops.

T-shirts and jeans. No one has come to Madison's party in their prom outfit. Except Bahar.

"I did go home!" Bahar shouts above the music, though she wants to speak this part quietly. "I went home to freshen up. I thought . . . I thought we were all staying dressed up."

"Oh my God, I think it's adorable that you're still in your dress! You look so cute! Don't worry! You'll have a good time wearing whatever!" Madison takes Bahar's hand in hers. Madison's hand is supremely soft. They push past people in the dining room into the living room, where more kids are dancing and a few—to Bahar's shock—are making out. "What can I get you to drink?" Madison asks. "A Bud?"

Bud of what? But before she can answer, Madison disappears. Bahar wants to disappear too.

She is wearing an ankle-length red taffeta Gunne Sax dress with a big rose bow and puff sleeves. Her mother and Aunt Ellie had oohed and aahed over this prom dress at Bloomingdale's, and Aunt Ellie had used her employee discount to buy it. Even so, her mother had mumbled that the dress cost more than a month's salary of an Iranian office worker. But they had both wanted her to enjoy prom. Aunt Ellie had even eventually, finally, come around and agreed to have Bahar go to the after-prom party at Madison's house, but only because her mom insisted that Bahar should go. Bahar had felt guilty leaving her mom while she was visiting all the way from Iran, but it was one night, right? And her mom understood that this was one last opportunity for the students to celebrate together as a class. In the fall, they'd all be off to college.

Bahar sits down on the mustard-colored velvet couch in Madison's living room. The room looks darker than usual because the main lights are off and only some table lamps are on. A girl in a ponytail and a boy wearing a football jacket kiss on the other end of the sofa. To think she had left the Puck Building, where their prom was held, to go home and, with the help of her mother and Aunt Ellie, freshen up her hair, and look even more fancy.

Such an immigrant fresh-off-the-boat move! Her mom had mumbled the whole time that she didn't like bourgeois parties, but she had also said, with a certain amount of pride, that she wanted her daughter to live, to live, to live.

Because those bastards in charge of our government in Iran want our girls to shrivel into invisibility. No dancing for women. No singing. No fun. You go, Bahar Joon. You go and have a good time!

"Be safe, okay?" Aunt Ellie had said when she and her mom drove Bahar up to Madison's building for this party. A party she had imagined would be fancy and . . . not this.

"Here you go!" Madison is back and hands her a red and blue and white can. "For you!"

Bahar twirls the can in her hand. In the dimly lit room, she makes out the word "Budweiser" in fancy cursive. This is beer; that much she knows. She shouldn't drink it. She's only had beer once, at Madison's birthday party, in front of Madison's mother. Madison's mom had mumbled something about "better in front of me than behind my back."

"Thanks, Madison," Bahar says. "Where is your mom?"

Madison looks confused, but then throws back her head and laughs. "My mom? Oh my God, Bahar, you are just too cute. My mom is away, of course. Why the hell would my mom be here? Drink up. Enjoy. There's more over there." Madison points to the other end of the room, where all kinds of cans and bottles are placed on a table. "And I have the good stuff too and you know you deserve it, so I'll be back for that."

Madison disappears again. The couple at the other end of the couch are now partially lying down and the girl is rubbing herself against the boy's prone body. Bahar hides her carpet bag. It doesn't fit in here. Inside the bag is the ceramic pomegranate she has brought for Madison's mom. She didn't understand. She didn't understand what this party would be like.

The beer is hard to swallow. Bahar forces it down, promising herself it will taste better as she goes along. At some point, someone hands her a second can. (Is it the ponytailed girl from the couch who has now gotten off the boy? It may be.) The third can is something Madison takes great delight in giving her. Rick Springfield's "Don't Talk to Strangers" plays from the stereo. Madison and others shriek. And then another Rick Springfield: "What Kind of Fool Am I." Madison drags Bahar onto the makeshift dance floor in the middle of the room.

Never have her limbs felt like this. It's as if the fizzy liquid is swimming in her arms, her legs. Her head feels strangely light and finally free. She notices details she's never noticed before in Madison's apartment. The intricate carving of a mask from Asia that hangs on the wall. The way the curlicues of the pattern on the velvet mustard-yellow sofa look like her mother's curls. Madison's beautiful arms—how they are long and slender and sway above her head as she dances. And Bahar notices for the very first time that she herself *can* dance American. She can move like these kids. She doesn't have to be limited to her Persian hip-swaying. But when she does sway her hips Persian-style, there is such a loud *whooooop* from Madison that Bahar momentarily stops. "Oh my God, don't stop—it is the absolute most cool thing I've ever seen. Dance, Bahar! Dance!"

She will dance all night. She dances with Madison and other girls and even briefly with Brett Robinson. *The* Brett Robinson. Well, he is in her general vicinity as she dances. Bahar didn't go to prom with a date. But it wasn't a big deal. She had gone "stag"—a lot of girls said they were going "stag."

Bahar had looked that word up in the dictionary and was surprised it meant "an adult red male deer," but *whatever*, as Madison would say. She had gone with friends to the prom and Madison had been so kind. So, so kind. Inviting her to this party. Though truth be told, now that she is here, it's clear the guest list wasn't exactly selective. Still. She is here. Like all the other kids. And she is having beer. She's had three. Maybe four. It is strangely hard to know.

The smell of skunk, apparently, isn't from a skunk. It's from some kind of herb-like substance that Madison calls "weed" and Brett Robinson calls "grass," and they roll it into pieces of paper and smoke it like cigarettes.

Bahar inhales "a joint" when Madison offers her one. It tastes disgusting, but she pretends it doesn't. There is also a white powder that appears on the coffee table in the living room, to a great amount of celebration from the guests.

No one eats cut-up orange slices. In fact, to Bahar's surprise, there is very little food save some puffed cheese balls in a bowl in a corner. When she staggers over to the bowl and pops a cheese puff in her mouth, the taste reminds her of the *pofak namaki* her father used to buy for her from the corner bodega near their yellow-brick building in Tehran. As she stands pressed against sweaty teenage bodies in Madison's living room and remembers the kindness of her father and how he burned in a cinema in an act of violence so unfair, so unjust, so unthinkable, Bahar takes another can (number five? Or six?) from the table and drinks up. Then she picks up a cup filled with amber liquid and forces herself to drink it. It smells like kerosene. She remembers how kerosene was rationed during the war. Is still rationed. The war is still going on in Iran. Will her mother have to go back to that war? Shouldn't Bahar go back with her own mom? She picks up another cup filled with clear liquid. It tastes like rancid sweat mixed with rotten potatoes. She drinks it all.

At some point, they are in the kitchen. Lights fuzzy. Madison and a few other girls get up on the counter. They stand on the stove and dance right there. The ceiling of this kitchen is so high, their heads don't even graze it. Their feet march on the burners. And Bahar thinks of her mother and of the meals she cooked on their stove in their apartment in Iran. She thinks of how they stood side by side near that stove, cooking. She thinks of how her mother read her picture books even though she was fifteen, then sixteen, then seventeen, in the basement as bombs fell on Tehran. She thinks of the war, the never-ending senseless war between Iran and Iraq. And she drinks some more.

Her mother fought, constantly, for women's rights. Her mother marched in the streets for their rights and took Bahar to the march. Her mother cares, she cares so much, she cares so very, very much for women's freedom. Her mother disappeared, she disappeared once for months, to avoid being caged again in Evin Prison. Bahar cooked; she cooked for her father and herself when her father was still alive, and then for just herself while her mother was hiding. And yes, Uncle Ali Reza and his wife checked on her and insisted that she stay with them when her mother was "away." But she didn't want to be with Uncle Ali Reza and his wife. She wanted to be with her mother. Her mother and her own father. Her father, who should not be dead.

She drinks some more. The amber liquid. Then the clear rancid one. One. Then the other.

Someone has brought a tambourine. Someone has handed the tambourine to Madison and she is playing it, tapping it and shaking it. Bahar had thought tambourines only existed in Archie comics. In Archie comics with a girl band called Josie and the Pussycats. Or was that another comic?

Her head hurts. It is no longer light and free. It is as if someone has inserted a metal rod behind her eye and is hammering on it, hammering on it and hammering on it. Her legs feel weak. What will happen in the fall? Madison is going to Yale. She will be in upstate New York. Or, wait, is Yale in another state? She can never get the U.S. state names straight. Yes, Yale is in a state that starts with a "C." It has a complicated name. Bahar can't remember it.

More kids jump up onto the kitchen counter. They are dancing to a Queen song. Queen. Freddie Mercury. Auntie Ellie insists that Freddie Mercury is of Persian descent. She is so proud of anything or anyone remotely Persian. Uncle Mehrdad says the post office was invented by Persians. He keeps a long list of other things that have been invented by Persians. Alcohol. Alcohol was one of them. Some Persian scientist named Razi discovered alcohol by mistake in his laboratory.

She wants to throw up. People are on the counters still. She wants to erase so much of what has happened. Freddie Mercury sings. Queen. Queens College. Her head spins.

"Good for you!" Madison had said when she found out Bahar had gotten in. "Good for you, Bahar!"

Madison never quite says "Bahar" the right way, making it sound like "Babar." Instead of drawing out the first syllable, "Baaa." No one can pronounce her name here.

How long will she be here, in this country where no one can pronounce her name? And what will her mother do once Bahar goes to Queens College? How can her mother get a different visa to stay here? Uncle Mehrdad and Aunt Ellie worked hard to have Bahar's student visa extended. She has no choice but to go to school—it's the only way she can stay legally in this country. And the only reason she had that first visa was because her mother's old high school friend, Aunt Niloo, had a husband who worked at the visa office and used his connections overseas. It is hard as hell for Iranians to get a visa to the United States.

Everyone hates Iranians. Ever since the revolution. Ever since American hostages were taken by Iranian students at the embassy. And now she is here. In the country where they hate people like her. She is here. Where will her mother be?

Her mom is so proud of Bahar having gotten accepted into Queens College. Her mom wants her to study law. To become a woman lawyer, like she herself never got to be. Bahar doesn't want to become a lawyer, but she can't disappoint her mother. She should just go to university in Iran. Be near her mother. But it is not an option to say no. Look at how lucky she is. She got to leave a war-ridden country and come to America to stay with Aunt Ellie. Her own country is no longer safe. She will go to Queens College and study so much. She has to be worthy of all their sacrifices.

Why didn't her mother get to be a lawyer? Her mother said she started college but stopped when she'd had Bahar. But then she went back and got her degree to become a teacher, didn't she? That's the kind of mother she has. A fighter.

She comes from lion women. From a line of women so strong, no one can destroy them.

She sways to the music. She spins around, getting dizzy far faster than

296 •|• Marjan Kamali

she could ever have predicted. She remembers spinning with her mother's hands in hers, dancing in the living room together, whirling around and around.

She's sinking into the ground now. Sinking as if she has no legs. An abrasive carpeting scratches her legs. Her dress must have ridden up because she feels the rough carpet against the skin of her thighs. The Persian rugs in her old apartment in Tehran were silky soft. The hammering behind her eye does not stop. The roiling in her stomach is overwhelming. She is a lion woman. She has to be. But with the force of a wave that is impossible to control, her insides rise up and oceans escape her mouth. She roars with violence. She is soaked now. She is tired. She doesn't know what will happen to her mother. Why is she here? Why is she even here? She should have stayed home. She could have been in Iran. Her father loved to buy her cheese puffs.

She hears Madison scream.

FORTY-FIVE

June 1982

"When can we see her?"

Homa and I stood in front of the nurse's desk. Madison had called our apartment. She said she had ridden with Bahar in the ambulance and checked her in. Mehrdad, Homa, and I got into our Ford Escort as fast as we could. Now, here we were: Mehrdad parking the car and Homa and me under the fluorescent light on the sixth floor of the hospital.

"Which one is the mother?" the nurse asked. She was middle-aged with a red bob. Her eyes had large circles underneath. She was trying to be kind, it was clear.

"I is," Homa said in her halting English.

"Can I see a form of ID? And you'll need to fill out these forms—please include the name of the insured as well as their relationship to the primary sponsor, and you'll have to also sign here as the legal guardian of the child."

Homa looked at me desperately. She hadn't understood a word the nurse said.

"I am the child's legal guardian," I said. I opened my handbag and took out the kiss-lock purse Mother had given me as a child. I kept my ID in there.

After I filled out the forms and assuaged the nurse's confusion, she led us down a corridor that smelled of rubbing alcohol and mop water. Bahar was in Room 7, behind a dividing curtain separating her from an elderly woman with white hair who was fast asleep and snored loudly. When I saw

Bahar—our Bahar—I gasped. She was attached to tubes and wires, with a ventilator tube in her mouth.

"Alcohol poisoning" was the reason she had been admitted to the ER, the nurse explained. After treatment in the ER, she had been brought to the sixth floor for continued monitoring. To my many questions, the nurse gave direct answers. Yes, her system had suffered due to too much alcohol drunk in too short a time. Her situation, when she'd arrived, had been extremely dangerous.

"We were told," the nurse said, "that that friend of hers saved her life by calling 911 and bringing her to the hospital when she did. Your daughter's breathing and blood circulation"—she looked at me and then at Homa for good measure—"have become extremely slow. She has no gag reflexes. No motor responses."

"He can die?" Homa asked, her voice barely a whisper. She had confused the gender pronoun, as many Iranians did when speaking English. In Persian, we don't have gender pronouns—just one neutral one.

"*She*," the nurse emphasized, "luckily received emergency medical attention before it was too late. But she's not out of the woods. She is, in effect, currently in a coma."

Homa turned to me. "*Vay khoda!*" She recognized the word "coma." It was the same word in Persian. "You do something?" Homa asked the nurse.

The nurse now only looked at me when she answered. "She has a breathing tube that has opened her airways. We're giving her oxygen therapy and IV fluids. Her stomach has been pumped and a catheter inserted."

I translated for Homa. She then begged, through my translations, if we could spend the night, or at least if she could, but to that the nurse gave a firm no. "I am so sorry. No more than forty-five minutes," she said, pointing to a chair next to Bahar's bed. "And then out."

"My husband is parking, and then he will—"

"Your husband?" I could tell the nurse was confused, but she didn't ask questions. "He can't come in here," she said. "Two is more than enough."

"Yes, but he's going to come up after he—"

"Everyone has to check in at the nurse's desk and when he does, we will tell him he cannot come in here. He'll have to stay in the waiting room. I am so sorry." With that, the nurse left.

Against the heavy rhythmic breathing of the woman in the other bed and the machines whirring and running on Bahar's side of the room, Homa pulled a chair from the old woman's side to Bahar's, and the two of us sat side by side by her daughter's bed. The room smelled of a cherry cough medicine I had had as a kid in Iran and of sterile chemicals I assumed came from the machines. On a small table with wheels next to the bed were a kidney-shaped pink dish and a blue plastic pitcher with a white lid. There was a Styrofoam cup next to the pitcher. As if Bahar, with the thick tubes in her mouth, could even drink. Her source of hydration was currently a fluid-filled sac on a pole attached to her through thick clear wires.

"I hate it here," Homa said.

"Me too."

"Their rules are absurd. Forty-five minutes."

"But we are lucky," I said. "That she got here in time."

"Lucky for that friend of hers."

"Yes," I had to agree.

We sat in silence again. If worry could be a cloak that could choke, we were both suffocating.

"I never should have let her go to that party. These crazy, stupid, foolish teenage parties."

"You didn't want her to go," Homa said. "I was the one who insisted."

"It's not your fault. We just wanted her to be free."

"Oh, Ellie." Homa took in a deep breath. "Why, why, why?"

"She'll be okay, Homa Joon." I stroked the sleeve of her plaid blouse. A rough thread must have run through the fabric because I could feel it raised against my hand. "Let's talk about other things for a bit. Good things."

Homa frowned and looked bereft.

"Bluebirds and rainbows?" I offered weakly.

"Sure. Or *piroshkis* and *café glacé*," she said.

"Remember how we jumped over that huge bonfire?"

"Oh, you want to go down memory lane? Of course I remember. You were so scared, Ellie."

"But we did it. We came out the other side," I said.

"The sandwiches at Andre's. The *salad olivier*," Homa said.

"And the Ka-Na-Da-De-Ry!" I responded.

We were desperate to hang on to fond memories from our childhood and adolescence, as if they could somehow sail us through this awful waiting. But would Bahar even have much more of an adolescence? I didn't want to think of the question that lay in the deepest parts of my soul. *Would she ever be the same?*

"The look on Mrs. Tabatabayi's face the day after we came back from the bazaar," Homa said in a trance.

"You were always getting me into trouble!" I said. But then I stopped. Bahar's machines whirred. The old lady's heavy breathing filled the room. "Homa," I said. "You need to know."

I had to tell her. I had tried to tell her several times. But now, with Bahar on the brink, I could not go on one moment longer with this wall between us.

Homa said nothing, but simply stared at her daughter in the bed.

"Homa," I said, my voice supremely shaky. I willed it not to falter. "That night. At Sousan's house. At Niloo's engagement party. I spoke to the Colonel. He asked so many questions. About me. Us. Your work. I thought I was chatting with someone safe. Someone who could be my father." My throat tightened and I felt again that painful lump. I looked at Bahar lying there with the white tubes protruding from her mouth. I had to use my voice. I had to clear this up once and for all. We had to talk about the truth. "Your arrest. The next day. It was me. It was because of me. I told him about your activism and your role in the communist opposition. He made it seem like he was proud of young women who were at the forefront of resistance."

My face grew hot and I felt every muscle tighten. "I didn't know it would lead to your arrest. I am so, so sorry."

Homa turned to me. Her eyes were filled with sorrow. Then she said, "Okay."

Just like that. The word "okay" in English.

"You knew?"

"I had an inkling; let's leave it at that. What does it even matter. *Gozasht.* It's past."

I struggled to form words. "It matters. It matters because you were in prison because of me. And everything that . . . followed . . . was because of me."

Homa looked down at her lap and was quiet for a minute. Then she said, "I was in prison because of my own actions."

"I'm the one who gave you away." I remembered walking to campus the morning after the party and seeing Homa up ahead. How that car drove so close to me and then sped up to her. The two men jumping out and shoving her into the vehicle. "I am so, so sorry," I said. "Please, you need to—"

Homa interrupted me. "Just stop."

"If I could take it back, I would. If I could somehow atone for all of it, I would."

"You have."

"Not by a long shot."

"You gave my daughter a home. You gave her your love. You and Mehrdad have been beyond generous."

"We could host Bahar for the rest of our lives and it wouldn't make up for what I did."

Homa turned to me. "Look, when you came to see me when Bahar was just an infant, I couldn't do it. Couldn't talk to you like nothing had happened because I was . . . what would you say in English? 'Traumatized.' That's why I asked you to stay away. I wasn't ready. And when we ran into one another at the bazaar, it wasn't the right time. To get into anything. There were people all around. It was rushed."

I thought of my kitchen conversation with Bahar a few months ago. Bahar had said that Homa had not seen friends because she was always worried about being monitored.

"They were watching you, weren't they?" I asked. "The Shah's secret police?"

"Yes, and after the revolution, the Islamic Republic monitored me. Still does! I am what you would call an equal opportunity pest. Both regimes have hated me."

"You told me to stay away because they were watching you and you didn't want to get me into trouble?"

Homa continued to study my face. Then she patted my hand. "Yes, let's say that."

"What do you mean, 'let's say that'?"

"We are here now. I have worked very hard to heal."

One of the machines made a beeping noise and we both jumped in our seats. Adrenaline rushed through my body. "Should we call the nurse?" I asked.

The machine went back to its whirring, and all the hooked-up tubes and wires seemed to be attached and working.

"I think it's fine. We just have to wait. And to pray," Homa said. The tips of her ears were bright red. Just like all those years ago when Abdol went on about her *rouhieh*, her spirits, during my visit.

I bent my head down and whispered prayers for Bahar to recover. I closed my eyes and kept repeating: *God, find a way. God, let her heal. God, keep her safe.* I wasn't a religious person—at all—but I repeated entreaties to God in my desperation. When I looked up again, Homa's head was also bent and she murmured under her breath.

"I hate that we lost all those years. We could have stayed friends. You didn't have to feel like I couldn't come because you were being monitored . . ."

Homa's head jerked up. "Oh, Ellie. When I tell you let's keep the past in the past, you insist on discussing it all. And here and now, of all places! I was angry for a very long time. And then deeply depressed. I needed to figure things out. Abdol was helpful, but we never talked about what happened. I withdrew inside myself. But my dear, Ellie . . ." She stopped.

"What?"

She took in a deep breath. She looked at Bahar on the bed. She seemed to be fighting something inside herself. Then she whispered, "Ellie, they wanted you. They were after you. They questioned me over and over and over again when I was first arrested. They wanted names."

"But I wasn't part of your communist group," I said. Had she gone mad? Perhaps grief and worry had overwhelmed her to the point of delirium. I regretted bringing up this thorny topic. I should have waited. It was the wrong time to discuss it, clearly. Homa was rightfully too preoccupied with worry about Bahar to remember anything correctly. "Never mind," I said, trying to comfort her. "Let's drop it."

"What they wanted, Ellie," Homa said slowly, "was to know who was behind translating the pamphlets before the protest. They wanted to arrest the translator. They knew the translator couldn't be me."

My body grew ice cold.

"They harangued me for information. They offered me a deal. Reveal who did it and I could be released."

I sat very still. The cough medicine–like smell in the room was overwhelming. I felt nauseous. "What are you saying?"

"They wanted to arrest you. But I wouldn't give you away. So they kept me. And they . . . punished me. And once that violation occurred, they did not release me out of spite . . ." Her voice trailed off for a moment. "But I didn't give in."

The force of what she said settled into the white lid on the blue plastic pitcher next to Bahar's bed, into every strand of white hair on the elderly woman's head in the next bed, into the grooves of the thick white tubes that extended from Bahar's nose and mouth. I wanted to believe beyond a figment of doubt that Homa was mistaken. She had stayed in prison because she protected me? I thought back to my conversation with the Colonel. Was he trying to get information about me? "They were just some pamphlets . . ." I said.

"They felt it started that whole string of protests," she said quietly. "To have the pamphlets translated into Persian."

I wanted to scream, to fold into myself, to run away, to hide. Everything that followed—the rape, her violation—was because she kept her mouth shut about me? "You *should* have told them I did it," I said desperately. "Why didn't you?"

"Because you are my friend."

She said it so simply and directly, as if stating a mere fact, a universal truth that could not be questioned, a principle of physics that was immutable. All the jealousies I had ever harbored of Homa—her kind mother, her intelligent father, her sister, Sara, her brother, that house with the stone kitchen, Homa's activism and bravery, her drive, her good nature, her ability to not give up—came flooding back. My own envy was a living, breathing energy in the room. And then I remembered the visit. The visit I had made to Homa's apartment when she was living with Abdol. Her staring vacantly at the rug as if in a trance. Her distance. The tour she'd given me of her place and then the anger with which she had rejected my touching her arm and her refusal of my offer to help.

"When you finally agreed to see me and I visited you in the apartment . . ."

"Was I furious at you? Yes. Especially when you offered me *money*. I didn't want your money. I didn't want your lifestyle or any of those trappings."

I tried to hold back my tears. "I gave you away, Homa," I said.

"I forgive you."

She said the words I had secretly longed to hear for years. The words I had waited all this time to hold in my cupped hands. I felt a heavy burden simply burst. What mattered was that I was with Homa, what mattered was

I loved my friend and would love her until the end of our days. I was done trying to compete with her, to be her, to forget her, to outdo her, to come to terms with her.

She had given me a gift. It was a gift extended when we were seven years old and she first invited me to play. A gift continued when we had adventures where we explored the city and traversed new paths and pushed against the boundaries drawn out for us. A gift sustained when she came to my high school in a flash of surprise. The gift Homa had always given was simply to be my friend.

Unconditionally.

I reached over and took Homa's hand in mine. Her tears when they came racked her entire body.

"Thank you," I said. "For what you did."

"*Gozasht*. It's past," Homa said. "Do you understand? They took a lot from me. But I won't let them steal my spirit. I refuse. I refuse to give them that power. Even with the threat of arrest now, that is what they want to do. They want to strip us of our dignity. To remove our capacity for delight. But they cannot win. Not this new anti-woman regime. So much has changed since you left, Ellie. Iraqi planes find our cities at night and bomb us. But none of it. None of it"—she took a deep breath as if gathering oxygen to continue—"can destroy me. Do you understand?"

I didn't, but I was beginning to. The swagger as she ambled toward Mehrdad and me in the airport with Bahar on her arm. Her laughter with her daughter after the initial torrent of tears. I had assumed Homa's bravado was masking deep pain and suffering. But as we sat in that hospital room, I realized Homa's bravado wasn't masking her pain. It was because of it. She would fight. Always and forever.

"I think I'm beginning to," I said.

It was then that Bahar opened her eyes.

FORTY-SIX

July 1982

Once Bahar came to in that hospital bed, once we'd both heaved sighs of relief, once we brought Bahar back to our apartment after a few more days of watchful care in the hospital and then nursed her—the two of us—at home, it was clear that this kind of separation could not go on.

Homa wanted to be with Bahar. Bahar wanted to be with her mom. Homa said she was willing to give up the country she loved, the country she had fought for, the one for which she had sacrificed her freedom over and over again, in order to be with her daughter.

As Bahar lay on our sofa getting her strength back, Homa stroked her daughter's hair and promised that as soon as she returned to Iran, she would meet with Niloo and start the official process of applying for a new visa—one that did not expire in four weeks—and do whatever it took to be with her daughter in America. We all knew it was not a good option for Bahar to go back. Not in the middle of a war. Not when she could have a better future going to college in the U.S.

Two days before Homa was due to fly back to Iran, Bahar and Mehrdad sat on the sofa flipping through that week's issue of the *TV Guide*, looking forward to a night of watching their favorite TV lineup, which would, I knew, culminate in *The Love Boat* on ABC at 9 p.m.

Homa came into the kitchen with me. I opened the newspaper and spread the pages on the table. I read out loud the movies playing at the theater nearby. *Poltergeist* sounded too scary. *Star Trek II* wasn't a great option, as neither one of us had seen the first Star Trek movie (much to Mehrdad's dismay). *Rocky III* was a possibility. In the end, we decided on a new film called *E.T.* I read out loud the movie description from the newspaper. It was about an extraterrestrial creature who visited America. Homa chewed on her lip. She looked worried.

"We don't have to go," I said.

"I want to."

"Are you sure you're ready?"

"Only if you come with me," she said.

We walked sideways down the row of seats, apologizing to the moviegoers who had to lift their knees so we could get by. The tubs of popcorn being sold in the lobby had shocked Homa with their size. We didn't have the stomach for soda or popcorn, but I did buy a yellow box of candy named Jujyfruits. We sat down on red velvet chairs. I looked at my friend. Her face was pale.

I took her hand and held it.

The lights went off and the screen came on and we watched a few trailers about a bumbling duo of crime fighters, a bunch of teenagers in a camp house, and a barbarian. I had hoped the trailers wouldn't be frightening, especially since this *E.T.* movie was rated to be fine for children.

I squeezed Homa's hand. She was scared enough as it was.

Our film began, and soon the wrinkled alien with the large head and expressive eyes stole the show. People in the theater laughed when E.T. was dressed up in a wig by the adorable little girl in the family. They gasped over E.T. saying the phrase "home phone" and then "phone home." When the boy in the movie rode his bike into the sky against the backdrop of a full moon with E.T. perched in the basket, a hush fell over the audience, followed by raucous and appreciative applause.

Homa simply rested her head on my shoulder and wept.

Others in the theater that night may have reveled in the cinematic special effects. They might have enjoyed the dialogue or the trajectory of E.T.'s journey.

But Homa and I were not in the theater to follow the little alien's voyage, truth be told.

We were simply there for Homa to break her fear.

So Homa could normalize again this simple condition of being seated in rows with strangers in the dark.

So she could experience no fire and no flames. So she could get up at the end of the film and see the screen still intact. The chairs in place. The building standing. Everybody alive, filing out calmly.

We emerged from the cinema into the sweet air outside. Homa leaned into me and whispered thanks. We walked home. I thought of Abdol and every other person in Cinema Rex on a summer night in Abadan four years ago.

We went back to Bahar, who was now in bed asleep, and Mehrdad, who was watching a late-night comedian on TV. He raised his eyebrows when we walked in, as if to ask whether the mission had been successful.

I said that all was well.

She was safe.

The night before her return to Iran, Homa and I chatted in the kitchen as we cooked. Homa had insisted on helping me—she said it relaxed her to be using her hands in the kitchen like in the old days when we cooked together. "Call Niloo as soon as you get back," I said. "She knows the correct procedure to apply for your *eghamat*, for residency. We can get you refugee status. You are ripe for being a political prisoner—that qualifies you for asylum."

Homa chopped parsley and cilantro for *ghormeh sabzi*. "I promised Bahar I'd apply and I will." She continued to chop. Then she looked up at me with a bitter smile. "But how I wish we could stay in our own country.

All of us. Bahar. Me. You. Mehrdad. Those fundamentalist thugs took over Iran and hijacked it. It's not fair that my daughter has no future there. It's *her* country."

"We'll help you apply," was all I could say.

"It could take years."

"We can hire a good lawyer. We'll make it happen. You'll see."

Homa looked around our kitchen and then at me. "The streets could be paved with gold and everybody in this country could be an angel sent from heaven. It won't change one fact: this place is not my home. And it never will be."

"It could be, one day."

"If we all leave, what will happen to Iran? The brain drain is already astronomical." She looked down at the chopping board. "My students . . ."

"They'll survive."

"My organization. For women. We have members who are new, who are ready . . ."

"Homa," I said. "Let someone else fight for a change. Your place is with your daughter. And your daughter can't be in Iran. Not right now. Not until things change."

She sighed. "Yes, yes, I know."

We continued to prepare the meal in silence.

After we had put everything in the pot on the stove and I had lowered the heat to simmer, Homa washed her hands and said, "I have something for you. Hold on a second."

She left and returned moments later with her hands behind her back. "I had a fantasy," she said. "Of coming to you with a paper bag. A paper bag filled with money. Money that could somehow make a dent in what I owe you."

"Stop with the money talk. I told you a thousand times. It's taken care of."

"You know I would if I could, right, Ellie? It's just that I don't have money. Never did. But one day I will pay you back for all you've spent taking care of Bahar."

"I know," I said. "*Gozasht*. It's past." I used her own words on her.

Homa brought her arm out from behind her back and revealed what she'd been hiding.

I gasped. "You still have it?"

"Don't you have my necklace? You told me on my first day here that you keep it in your jewelry box."

"I do!"

"When you left the old neighborhood and I stayed, I cherished this notebook and hardly ever wrote in it save for a few letters to you back then." She handed the notebook with its faded pink cover to me. I felt again its weight and shape. I had carefully selected it from Mr. Fakhri's stationery shop that early summer of 1953 when I was ten years old and went in with Uncle Massoud. "That first day you came to our high school," I said. "You brought it."

"I wanted to impress you. So you could see I still had it. I even wrote some notes from Mrs. Roshanfekr's class in it." Homa came to my side and opened the notebook as I held it. She showed me her Persian script.

"Those old poems!" I said.

"Eventually I felt silly. Bought myself one of those spiral notebooks every other girl had. *Conformed*." Homa grinned.

"Homa Roozbeh *conforming*. Imagine!"

"Ha! But look," she said. "This holds up pretty darn well. What kind of pulp did they use in paper back then? It's practically cardboard stock! What I did is"—she flipped through more pages—"I wrote all my mother's recipes in here."

On the ensuing pages, I saw recipe after recipe. Her mother's *fesenjoon khoresh*. The pomegranate-filled *ghotab* we had the first time I'd gone to her house. Her mom's chickpea cookie recipe. I looked up at Homa in astonishment. "You should keep them. Save them for Bahar."

"I want you to have them," Homa said. "One day, Ellie, you'll graduate from your job at Beloom . . ."

"Bloomingdale's," I said.

"And maybe, just maybe, you'll open your own restaurant here. How amazing would that be? A café. Show these people our culture. Show them our food. Let them taste our dishes. Let them know who we are. What do you say?"

Me, open up a restaurant? A café? In America? And serve Iranian food? It was a cute fantasy. I looked at my dear friend. She grinned with absolute hope. She was at once the thirty-eight-year-old about to go back to Iran and the friend I had known when we cooked together in her mother's kitchen. "You never know. Maybe one day I'll do just that," I said.

"Use my mom's recipes. Promise."

"Fine, but I'll do it with *you*. Because you're coming back, remember?"

Homa nodded through tears. She moved closer to the counter and gathered up a few dirty dishes and put them in the sink. She squirted detergent onto the sponge and washed. I dried. Together we worked in sync, as we had when we were kids.

"Of course," she said. "Of course, I'll come back. Just as soon as they let me."

FORTY-SEVEN

September 2022

On a September day with air crisp enough for even the grumpy stationer to grunt hello at the high school kids, when leaves on trees are beginning their auburn transformation, at that tender time of twilight during which it is impossible to imagine a world ever robbed of hope, they see her on their screens. Her unexpected emergence pulsates like an echo, a memory unspooled, a wound from the past, a ribbon of hope.

Hours before the moment of her unexpected appearance, Leily and six of her high school friends had marched down Massachusetts Avenue. Past the numerous banks and nail salons of the town center, past the shoe shop founded a hundred years ago and the independently owned pharmacy, Leily led her friends and then stopped right next to the old-timey cinema.

In the window of Miss Ellie's Café hangs a familiar green *termeh* tapestry. Delicate birds sewn with shimmery silver thread onto the cloth sparkle in the afternoon sun. On the glass door, a taped-on piece of paper declares, "Café closed for private party!"

Leily pushes open the door and the bell above it chimes. Inside, the air smells of coffee and cardamom and something yeasty. Seven circular tables with four chairs around each are all the café holds. As her eyes adjust from the brightness outside, Leily notices minuscule gold stars covering every table. Helium balloons festooned with "Happy birthday!" float around the room like ghosts.

Framed photographs and calligraphy verses cover the café's walls. There are photos of the famous polo square in Isfahan, the Si-o-Se bridge and its thirty-three arches lit up at night, the poet Hafez's tomb in Shiraz, and the iconic Azadi Tower in Tehran. In the picture holders of Persian calligraphy, flowy cursive spells out verses from ancient poems. And right behind the counter is a framed faded Polaroid photo of two dark-haired girls at a mountain vista, their arms around one another, both in slacks, one with her hair in a ponytail, the city of Tehran behind them.

Miss Ellie looks up, rushes over, greets the group, and kisses Leily's cheeks. Her silver hair is in its characteristic chignon. She wears a yellow blouse, black pants, and her favorite boiled wool clogs. With each passing year, Miss Ellie grows shorter and rounder. But she is still quick on her feet and never misses a beat.

"Hi, Miss Ellie"; "Thank you for having us, Miss Ellie"; "The place looks great, Miss Ellie!" Leily's friends sing out. Like everyone else in town, Leily calls her grand-*khaleh* "Miss Ellie."

Leily notices now that Miss Ellie holds in her hand a small circular container that looks like a petri dish. In it are countless more gold stars. For a minute, Leily thinks Miss Ellie might raise her arm and sprinkle the kids with a confetti of stars. But she simply puts the container down on a table and touches, out of habit, the bird charm on the necklace she has worn for as long as Leily can remember. The tiny gold bird with the turquoise wing always rests in the hollow between her clavicles. In biology class, Leily learned this part of the body is called "the suprasternal notch." The bird twinkles under the café lights.

"Heyo!" Leily's mom appears from the back kitchen door as she wipes her hands on an apron emblazoned with a sneaker-wearing peanut and the words "I'm a health nut!"

"Hi, Bahar!" the kids call out as they sit down at the tables. Leily's mom hates being called Mrs. Murphy and insists that her daughter's friends call her by her first name.

314 ••• Marjan Kamali

In this historic American town, Leily's family has built a café that serves traditional Persian dishes. Less than half a mile from the Battle Green—where the shot heard around the world in 1775 started a battle that turned into a war that led to a revolution that then created these United States—she serves up delicious plates that comfort both residents and tourists of Lexington, Massachusetts.

Since its opening twenty-seven years ago, the café has expanded not in physical size but in its offerings. No longer does it serve just coffee, tea, and pastries. Boldly and with the help of her husband (who Leily affectionately calls Babu Mehrdad) and Leily's mom, Bahar, Miss Ellie introduced Iranian appetizers as part of a "Weekly Special" when Leily was in preschool.

Word about the new fare spread fast. All it took were a few rave reviews posted on the town-wide email list, and business exploded. Rather than become intimidated by the exposure and increased expectations, Miss Ellie embraced her new responsibilities with energy and drive. Now, tourists exploring the main street through which Paul Revere once galloped on his horse saunter in. Miss Ellie can charm even the most xenophobic terry-cloth-suited wanderers with heartfelt conversation and Iranian food too good to hate.

Leily knows her mom is super excited. She's planned Leily's eighteenth birthday party for weeks, written down what to buy on her Notes app, and cooked herself silly. They'd all worked together to prepare. They'd used the highest-quality olive oil and squeezed extra lemon juice on the *shirazi* salad. Leily's dad (known to her friends as "Mr. Murphy"—he does not like being called "Steve" by high schoolers) had chopped the cucumber, tomatoes, and onions into tiny cubes. For the jeweled rice dish, her mom had sauteed the barberries, careful not to overdo it. Miss Ellie had arranged orange rinds on a tray to dry in the sun. For hours the chicken was marinated in saffron and lime. Leily decorated the platter for the fried *kotlet* meat patties with sliced pickles, sprigs of mint, and radishes shaped like roses.

Miss Ellie made sure the crushed cantaloupe was mixed with just the right amount of honey and vinegar to make Persian smoothie drinks. Everything had to be perfect for Leily's eighteenth birthday party.

And it is perfect. For a fraction of time, Miss Ellie, Babu Mehrdad, Bahar, Steven Murphy, Leily, and all her high school friends revel in the food and the good cheer and celebrate Leily turning eighteen. In those moments, they forget their troubles and enjoy the shared food and drink together. To think that just two years ago, they were all locked down and isolated because of a global pandemic. How glorious to be together again!

And lovely it is.

After the birthday party is over, after Leily's friends leave and the dishes are all taken to the small kitchen in the back, after Babu Mehrdad sweeps the café floor even as Miss Ellie warns that it could hurt his back, after they all help to load the dishwasher in the kitchen and wash the bigger pots by hand, they gather to sit quietly together in the café.

The heaviness in their hearts that was temporarily put on hold during the party returns. For the past week and a half, Leily's entire family has been glued to the screen to see updates from Iran. A young woman named Mahsa Amini—her Kurdish name was Jina Amini—was arrested in Tehran by the morality police for improper hijab and brutally beaten. She went into a coma and died. The photo of this young woman lying in a hospital bed with white tubes protruding from her mouth has spread all over social media. The photo made Bahar shudder as her husband held her.

The death of this young woman has sparked protests that are spreading around the country like wildfire.

Leily has never been to Iran, but she harbors a huge curiosity about the country. When she sits at night and stares at her phone and watches reels of the protests in Iran, Leily is at once entranced, hopeful, heartbroken, fearful, and inspired. She watches on TikTok and YouTube and Twitter and Instagram the video clips of young women taking to the streets. These women bravely defy the mandatory hijab laws. They throw their headscarves into a bonfire and twirl, chanting for freedom and human rights.

Men join them in the protests. To quash dissent, the government shuts off the internet. Arrests protesters. Beats them. Kills some. But still the protests go on. People have had enough. They are tired of being told how to behave, what to say, what to wear, whom to worship. Tired of their rights diminished. Their slogan, born of a Kurdish fighting slogan, is "Women, Life, Freedom." In Kurdish: "*Jin, Jiyan, Azadi.*" In Persian: "*Zan, Zendegi, Azadi.*"

Leily knows she comes from a line of lion women. Miss Ellie and her mom have told her of her grandmother, Homa, and the work she has done for women's rights throughout her life. They have told her all about her grandmother's tireless, decades-long activism. How Leily would love to one day meet this grandmother of hers! To sit across the table from her and ask all the questions she has harbored since she was little. What made her grandmother so brave? What makes the women in Iran fighting on the streets now not afraid? Half of her runs with the blood of those women. Though her father likes to remind her that her Irish side is no less brave and no less accustomed to fighting oppression. Which is probably true.

"What news from Iran?" Bahar asks now at the café after the party.

Leily takes out her phone. She has been offline during her birthday party and she's not sure what has transpired in that time, even though it is now the middle of the night in Iran. She brings up Twitter and scrolls the hashtag #MahsaAmini obsessively, as she has done every day since the protests began. Miss Ellie and her mom lean in to view her screen as Babu Mehrdad and her dad look on, waiting for Leily to relate what she sees.

Endless new photos, videos, and updates have trickled in from Iran despite the government's internet crackdown. Leily scrolls. She can hear the breaths of Miss Ellie and her mom as they nestle in on either side of her. The videos show schoolgirls chasing a regime official out of their schoolyard, a young woman marching in the middle of traffic with her headscarf off and her hands holding the "V" sign being encouraged by people pressing down on their car horns, protesters running from tear gas and falling to the ground bloodied. Photo after photo goes by. Video after video is played as they watch in silence.

"Wait, wait, wait," Miss Ellie says. "Stop right there."

She asks Leily to replay a video. She points to it on the timeline on Leily's screen. Leily goes back and replays it. It is twenty-one seconds long.

An old woman, her hair white, walks at night in a crowd of protesters. She holds her arm up in the air, her fist tight. Her gait has a limp, but she moves to the chants of the crowd. Her voice can be heard quite clearly: "*Zan, Zendegi, Azadi.*" Women, Life, Freedom.

Leily feels a throbbing in her ears; her face is now burning; she is transfixed. For Leily knows what her mother sitting to her right and her grand-*khaleh* Ellie sitting to her left know. This is her grandmother, whom she calls Maman Homa. They are watching, as they sit in the café her family built in the northeastern United States, her seventy-nine-year-old grandmother join the women protesting in the streets.

Tears stream from Miss Ellie's eyes.

Bahar is very still, but there is the slightest quiver in her chin.

"Of course she'd be in the streets," Miss Ellie whispers as she shifts closer to Leily to watch the video again. Leily plays it on repeat over and over again.

"I would expect nothing less," Leily's mom says.

The balloons float around the room. The minuscule gold stars on the tables shine on.

EPILOGUE

Dear Leily,

Most days before I get out of bed, I lie as still as possible. As long as I don't move my left hip, as long as I lie flat on my back, I cannot feel it. The bursitis, the stiffness, the tightness in my right knee.

As I lie in that sweet place where pain is not yet mine, I imagine running. I sail past blocks outside my small apartment in Tehran, past the bazaar, the mazes through which I used to dart as a child. In my mind's eye, my legs move the way they used to, before stiffness lodged into my joints, before the wear and tear of decades set in. The wind whooshes in my ears and my heart beats so fast it's impossible not to feel the rush of adrenaline and liberation—the sense that the world is mine.

When I run like this, in my peripheral vision, I see the friend I once knew. We played and dreamed the world could be ours. She and I—we dared to believe two girls from Iran could have not just a little but actually all. We wanted to study and give back to the world. When we were still children, we couldn't imagine a time where we wouldn't be together.

I came back to Iran that July of 1982, having promised Bahar I'd apply for my papers to reside in America with her. I was arrested the moment I passed customs at the Tehran airport. From prison, I called Ali Reza and asked him to update Ellie and Bahar in New York. I could not have foreseen that I would not be released for four more years.

On March 10, 1986, I was finally released. I went back into my apartment, but they took away my passport. I became *mamnoon khoorooj*—Denied Exit. Forbidden to leave the country.

Bahar sent me letters with photographs from her college graduation, of day trips with her friends, of her college boyfriend whom I was told was named Steve. When they moved to Lexington, Massachusetts, for Mehrdad to start his new position at Northeastern University, Ellie sent photos of the green patch of land where the shot heard around the world started the American Revolution. I was so proud that Bahar finished her Master of Public Health degree at Boston University and started working in hospital administration at Mass General.

Not one day went by when I did not think of her. Miss her. Wish to be with her.

And later, you.

They did not allow me to leave Iran for twenty-one years. Photographs. Letters. Phone calls. That was how we kept in touch throughout the 1980s. In the mid-1990s, we began emails. And when Bahar came to visit with Ellie in 1996, the reunion was so sweet, I felt I might break.

I was finally allowed to leave Iran and go to America in May 1997.

By then Bahar was thirty-three and married. She and Steve both worked and led productive lives, and what was there for me to do in Massachusetts? I had no residency, no green card, no legitimacy in that country. I came back to Iran.

And continued to fight.

Now, with the protests after Mahsa's death and the country re-verberating in grief, I feel the rage continuously. I feel it in every limb of my body, in every milliliter of my blood. Of course I go out with the young women and men protesting night after night. How could I stay home?

Let them beat me with their batons, let them bruise my body to a pulp, let them shoot and kill me. For a lifetime we have fought. We have fought and fought and fought. We want to be free. We want to be equal. We want to be able to live our lives.

I recently read a theory about ocean waves. This theory says that while to our eyes waves appear suddenly on the shore, their abruptness is an illusion. Waves begin their journey thousands of miles out at sea. They accumulated shape and power from winds and undersea currents for ages.

And so when you see the women screaming in Iran for their rights, please remember, dear Leily, that the force and fury of our screams have been gathering power for years.

In all the video calls we have had, in all our online texting and connection, I look at you, my dear granddaughter, and I wish for you not the world, nor the owning of it, nor even success in it.

I wish for you the ability to be free.

And I hope that you experience some moments so tender and dear that they make up for a thousand harsh ones.

Remember above all to always love.

Love madly.

Your Grandmother,

Homa

AUTHOR'S NOTE

In 2019, a few months after my novel *The Stationery Shop* was published, I started writing the story of four mothers from different backgrounds in suburban New England experiencing the fear and excitement of their first-borns going off to college. But a minor character in the story, a certain Miss Ellie who owned a café, kept bubbling to the surface. So compelling was this minor elderly Iranian character to me that I chucked the 125 pages I had already written about the other moms and started over entirely to tell the tale of Ellie and her friend, Homa, an indefatigable Iranian women's rights activist.

Writing about Iranian women has been a central theme of my life. I come from a line of strong, very vocal, and opinionated Iranian women who in some instances broke new ground (my grandmother was one of the first full-time career women in Iran in the 1940s), in other instances saw their lives stymied and constrained by a patriarchal culture, and in all cases experienced a hard-line government eradicate almost overnight rights for which women had fought for decades.

In my first novel, *Together Tea*, I follow the story of a girl whose childhood is upended by revolution and the war that followed and whose mother is fiercely trying to hold on to a life and dignity that oppressive forces are determined to crush. In my second novel, *The Stationery Shop*, I went back further in Iran's history to follow the story of a bookish young woman who falls in love during the time of the 1953 coup d'état in Iran and whose life is forever shaped by that love from which she can never recover. And in this third novel,

I follow the friendship between two girls who come from very different families and stations in life but who forge an indestructible bond when they are seven. Together they share the joys of childhood, the ups and downs of adolescence, the fractures of betrayal when they are young women, and the relief of redemption as their fate takes them across oceans and borders. All along, one of them, Homa, fights tirelessly for Iranian women to be free.

I started writing this book in 2019 and continued through the snowy winter of Boston into 2020. While the world shut down during the pandemic, my heart opened up to these two girls. I continued writing through the following year and the next, and I was more than halfway done with the story of Ellie and Homa when a young woman in Iran named Mahsa Jina Amini was killed by security forces in September 2022 for wearing improper hijab. Like many Iranians in the diaspora, I was filled with hope and heartbreak as women and girls took to the streets after that incident because they had had enough. Enough of being controlled. Enough of being held down. Enough of having what they wore, what they said, and who they loved dictated by those who did not value their vibrancy, talents, skills, or dreams. I watched as the women and men of Iran rose up to fight for freedom and were quashed by security forces. As I finished this book, Iran's long quest for freedom and tragic cycle of protests and crackdowns happened in real time.

I am neither a scholar nor a historian and I do not pretend to have written a book about the entire history of the women's movement in Iran. But I am a novelist and I know the power of story. For as long as they have lived, Iranian women have known that power. It was with story that Scheherazade kept herself alive, and it is through story (both the reading and the writing of it) that so many of us find solace, refuge, hope, and understanding. With my pen I hope to show you, dear reader, the joys and losses and loves and hopes and dreams and worries of two girls from Iran. I made them up, but they are real to me. I hope you enjoy their journey. I hope in their hopes, you see some of yours. I hope from their tale, you sense that all our hearts are one.

ACKNOWLEDGMENTS

The years I spent alone with these characters felt infinite, expansive, difficult, joyous, and transformative. I am grateful for all the people in my life who helped bring this story into the world.

Thank you to Wendy Sherman, agent extraordinaire, for understanding my heart and for always being there with wisdom, guidance, and a much-needed push. Thank you, Wendy, for being an indefatigable advocate for my work. I am grateful to have shared this wild and wonderful road together for the past twelve years.

Thank you to Aimee Bell for embracing my book and leading the way. It means so much to me. Thank you to my talented editor, Hannah Braaten, whose skill and excellent instincts made this story richer and stronger. Your insights were spot-on and I'm so glad we birthed this book together. Thank you to all the Lion Women at Gallery Books: Jennifer Bergstrom, Jennifer Long, Sally Marvin, Carrie Feron, Jessica Roth, Eliza Hanson, Mackenzie Hickey, Sarah Schlick, art director Lisa Litwack, copy editor Lisa Wolff, production editor Alysha Bullock, and Wendy Sheanin and the rest of the amazing team at Simon & Schuster. I appreciate all your hard work and great energy. And a forever thank you to Jackie Cantor for falling in love with *The Stationery Shop* and bringing me to Gallery in the first place.

Jenny Meyer at the Jenny Meyer Literary Agency sent my work out into the world literally. *The Stationery Shop* has now been translated into twenty languages and *Together Tea* has been translated into ten. Thank you, Jenny! And for championing my stories outside the realm of publishing and blazing an exciting new trail, I owe a big thanks to Katrina Escudero of Sugar 23. Here's to all the exciting projects that lie ahead. Thank you also to Callie Deitrick and Heidi Gall for all their hard work on my books.

As I struggled through the early drafts of this book, I was lucky enough to have Denise Roy lend her expert eye to help me strengthen the plot and uncover the truth of what I wanted to say. Thank you, Denise. Thank you, as well, to all my past teachers and to my students at GrubStreet, Brandeis, and beyond who make me proud.

When I received the call from the National Endowment for the Arts letting me know that I had been granted a Fellowship in Creative Writing, decades of struggling and scraping and working into the night felt legitimized and validated. Thank you to the NEA for this honor. I hope to continue to give back to this community of arts which has given me such unexpected empowerment and joy.

A special shout-out goes to Stephanie, David, Abby, Julia, Rachel, and Lily (the Lavs!), Marjorie Travis, Pam and Peter Lawrence, Victoria Fraser, Wendy Czarnecki, Maria Mutch, Michael Wang, Tracey Wright, Lara Wilson, and Kwi Young Choi. Thank you for your friendship. I finally finished the third book. Now, let's get a coffee and go on a walk!

For keeping me grounded with their humor and understanding in tumultuous times, thank you to Naz Deravian, Misha Zadeh Graham, and Omid Roustaie. Your friendship saved me.

I owe the biggest thanks to my family, especially to my mother and father for teaching me so much about the country in which they were born and raised. My time in Iran was short but my curiosity about it is endless. Thank you for sharing the stories of your youth and for all your love and kindness. From you I have learned resilience and the capacity to find joy through all the hardship. Thank you to my sister, Maryam, whose laughter I love and with whom I share so many meaningful memories. We have survived war and moves to several continents together and I know the best is yet to come. And to my sister's children, Darya and Emma, thank you for your love and support. I love you with all my heart. A huge thanks also to the extended family on both my side and Kamran's.

Mona and Rod, I am beyond grateful for all our adventures and quiet moments, for the times we spent reading together at the library and exploring new cities, for the sweet conversations around the dinner table and the jokes you share with me via texts and in person. You are the best buds in the world, and I am so lucky to be your mother. Kamran, you are my love and soul. Thank you for believing in me, being there through thick and thin, and infusing my life with so much goodness. To you and our children I say: Without you none of it would have happened and for you all of it happens. I love you madly.